SOMETHING NEW

SOMETHING NEW:
OR,
ADVENTURES
AT
CAMPBELL-HOUSE.

Anne Plumptre

edited by Deborah McLeod

broadview literary texts

Canadian Cataloguing in Publication Data

Plumptre, Anne, 1760-1818
Something new: or, Adventures at Campbell-House

(Broadview literary texts)
Includes bibliographical references
ISBN 1-55111-079-2

I. McLeod, Deborah, 1954-   . II. Title.
III. Title: Adventures at Campbell-House.   IV. Series.

PR5187.P27S6   1996   823'.7   C96-930154-5

Broadview Press
Post Office Box 1243, Peterborough, Ontario, Canada K9J 7H5

in the United States of America:
3576 California Road, Orchard Park, NY 14127

in the United Kingdom:
B.R.A.D. Book Representation & Distribution Ltd., 244a, London Road, Hadleigh, Essex SS7 2DE

Broadview Press is grateful to Professor Eugene Benson for advice on editorial matters for the Broadview Literary Texts series.

Broadview Press gratefully acknowledges the support of the Canada Council, the Ontario Arts Council, and the Ministry of Canadian Heritage.

Typesetting and assembly: True to Type Inc., Mississauga, Canada.

PRINTED IN CANADA

Contents

Acknowledgements

I am indebted to Isobel Grundy for her help and interest in every phase of this project. I would also like to thank the staff at the Bruce Peel Special Collections Library at the University of Alberta for their assistance; I am particularly grateful for the support of librarians John Charles and Jeannine Green. As well, I am pleased to acknowledge the support of the Killam Trust and the Social Sciences and Humanities Research Council of Canada. Finally, I thank Ted McLeod, Jean Renner, and Linda Sinclair for their generous sacrifice of time and effort on my behalf.

Deborah McLeod
Victoria, British Columbia

Introduction

Anne Plumptre's Life

Anne Plumptre was born into a well-established and respected Norwich family, the Plumptres[1] of Fredville. The family was an old one; it had derived its name from the village of Plumptre near Nottingham and represented the borough in Parliament from the time of the Plantagenets. The family could boast of a number of distinguished scholars and clergymen in its ranks: Anne's great-grandfather, Henry Plumptre, was the president of the Royal College of Physicians from 1740 to 1745; her cousin John was a classical scholar who became the Dean of Gloucester; and her father, the Rev. Dr. Robert Plumptre, served for twenty-eight years as the President of Queen's College, Cambridge, and was Prebendary of Norwich. Anne was named after her mother, the second daughter of Dr. Henry Newcome, her father's former schoolmaster. The third of nine children,[2] Anne was likely born early in February 1760 since records indicate that she was christened at Cathedral Church in Norwich on February 22nd of that year.

Anne Plumptre had three brothers. Joseph, the eldest, became a clergyman; Robert, the second son, a barrister; and James, the youngest of the family, a playwright, critic, editor, and divine. At least two of Anne Plumptre's five sisters married: Diane to her cousin, the Rev. John Plumptre, and Jemima to Frederick Layton, a captain of the Marines. Little is known about Mary or Lydia Plumptre. Annabella, like Anne, remained unmarried and became an author, publishing at least one poem ("On Moderation" in *The Cabinet*, Norwich, 1795), a cookery book (*Domestic Management; or, The Healthful Cookery-Book*, 1810, rpt. 1812), and a number of translations including *The Mountain Cottager* (1798), *Domestic Stories* (for children, 1800), and plays by Iffland and Kotzebue. She also produced three pieces of fiction: *Montgomery; or, Scenes in Wales* (1796), *The Western Mail* (1801), and *Stories for Children* (1804). *Tales of Wonder, of Humour, and of Sentiment*, a collection of stories written with Anne, was published in 1818.

The education of the Plumptre girls was unusually liberal for the time. According to *A Biographical Dictionary of the Living Authors of Great Britain and Ireland* (1816) Robert Plumptre gave his daughters

> an education very different from what generally falls to the lot of even well instructed females. The doctor was himself of a studious turn, and he took a delight in cultivating the inclination of his children to letters, particularly his daughters, who became by his tuition proficients in several modern languages. (277)

Anne, for example, was fluent in French, German, Italian, and Spanish.

By all accounts Anne Plumptre was an enthusiastic supporter of Napoleon, a position that gained her the contempt of a number of her contemporaries. Henry Crabb Robinson, for example, vilifies Plumptre in his memoirs as a woman "revolting in her sentiments," giving as an illustration her assertion at a dinner party in 1810 that she would welcome Napoleon's invasion of England:

> People are talking about an invasion. I am not afraid of an invasion. I believe the country would be all the happier, if Buonparte were to effect a landing and overturn the government. He would destroy the church and the Aristocracy, and his government would be better than what we have.[3]

Plumptre's estrangement from the church—obvious in this fragment of reported conversation—was apparently shared by her mother and one of her sisters and was the source of a family rupture.[4]

Henry Crabb Robinson not only denounces Anne Plumptre's politics in his memoirs, he also questions her moral soundness and judgement. After discounting her politically as one of the "old Jacobins" who refuse to give up their "political prejudices," he mounts an attack on her character in the continuation of his dinner party anecdote:

> After dinner literature was the theme. "Did you ever read *La Guerre des Dieux*?" said she [Plumptre] to Will. Lloyd [the host]. "No, What is it?" "Oh! The cleverest thing that ever was in the World. Pray get it".... "Do you know it?" said Mrs. Lloyd to me .... "Did you ever read it?" "I began it, Mad[ame]: but it is so filthy & obscene, that I was not able to finish it"— "to the pure all things are pure" said Miss Plumptree [*sic*] with a toss of the head. (punctuation added)

Robinson's view of Plumptre as a moral degenerate is balanced by George Dyer's mention of her in a letter to Mary Hays. Dyer writes that although he knows Anne Plumptre "only by letter," he has been informed that she "is an excellent moral character, a practical philosopher."[5]

Robinson, who has earlier in his memoirs referred to Plumptre's "ugly person," concludes his recollection of her by recounting Charles Lamb's reaction to the news of her death:

> It was many years after this when some one said, Anne Plumptree [*sic*] is dead. "Dead" exclaimed Lamb, "What an ugly ghost she will make."

Henry Crabb Robinson's assertion that Anne Plumptre was physically unattractive is particularly interesting given her determination to create an ugly heroine in *Something New*. It is possible, however, that Robinson, whose dislike of Plumptre is obvious, was simply making a clean sweep of her in his memoirs, presenting her as irreclaimable politically, rotten morally, and monstrous physically. Plumptre certainly is not physically repellent in the engraving included in her *Narrative of a Three Years' Residence in France, 1802-5* (1810). This engraving, taken by Henry Meyer from a painting by John Northcote, shows a reasonably attractive woman with strong features and dark hair and eyes.

In *The Sexagenarian; or the Recollections of a Literary Life* (1817) William Beloe makes no comment about Plumptre's looks. He does claim, however, that Plumptre made herself "generally obnoxious" except to fellow-worshippers of Napoleon, those "who considered all as deserving of the burning fiery furnace, who did not fall prostrate before the shrine of Bonaparte, and adore the Briarean Idol of the French Revolution" (363). Beloe's view of Plumptre is more moderate than that of Robinson; to Beloe, Plumptre is a talented but misguided miss, led astray by a sojourn in London and her friendship with the "perverted writer" Helen Maria Williams (359):

> On the death of her parents, and at the accursed crisis of the French Revolution, she [Plumptre] came to the metropolis. Here she immediately, with unreserved confidence, threw herself into the kindred arms of H. M. W.[,] divided her enthusiasm, and partook of all her follies. (365)

This linking of Plumptre's radicalism with London and Helen Maria Williams is still generally accepted. Roger Lonsdale, for example, writes that "[a]fter Dr. Plumptre's death at Norwich in 1788 ... Anne ... went to London and under the influence of Helen Maria Williams, became an ardent enthusiast for the French Revolution."[6] Two points must be kept in mind, however. First, although we know that Anne Plumptre was living with Annabella in London by 1799,[7] it is not certain exactly when she moved there. Because available references tend to place Anne in Norwich rather than London in the early 1790s, it seems likely that she continued in Norfolk during this period. At the very least, she spent a good deal of time there. On January 4th and 6th in 1791, for example, the "Misses Plumptre" took part in a production of *Adelaide*, a play by Anne's "intimate friend" Amelia Alderson [later Opie]. According to Margaret Eliot Macgregor, Alderson received her father's permission to produce the play at the private theatre of his friend, Mr. Plumptre [probably James], and two performances resulted with Alderson and the Plumptre sisters taking the principal parts.[8]

In 1794 Anne Plumptre was again with Amelia Alderson in Norwich, this time supporting her friend while she gave a political speech. According to a letter from Sarah Scott to her sister Elizabeth Montagu dated July 15th, 1794, a "most curious incident" occurred during a political gathering at which the Norfolk Whig MP William Windham was reelected:

a young woman of uncommon talents of about 25 years of age made a long speech in the Town Hall to about 1,500 of the Jacobins assembled against Mr. Wyndham, and two daughters of a late Doctor of Divinity stood one on each side of her to encourage her in her proceeding. The girl herself is Daughter to a phisician [sic] of Scotch creation lately an Apothecary.[9]

Macgregor identifies the "young woman" as Amelia Alderson Opie and the "two daughters" as Anne and Annabella Plumptre.

The fact that such a meeting could attract 1,500 Jacobins is an indication that although Norwich was provincial, it was also extremely politicized. Walter Graham has noted that the existence of the radical periodical *The Cabinet*, published in Norwich "by a Society of Gentlemen" in 1794 and 1795 "brings to light ... the extremely radical atmosphere of Norwich in the day when the names of Godwin and Mary Wollstonecraft were on many tongues."[10] We can assume that Anne Plumptre was familiar with this periodical since Annabella's poem, "Ode to Moderation," appeared in it in 1795.[11] Graham also notes that Susannah Taylor—who we know to be a friend of Plumptre's—"made her home in this provincial city a centre of advanced social and political thought." All this makes it unlikely that Anne Plumptre's political views were developed entirely in London under Helen Maria Williams's tutelage. Instead, we must consider as potentially significant a number of influences: a mother unconventional enough to take the anti-church side in a family of clergymen; a number of radical friends including Susannah Taylor, Ann Jebb,[12] and Eliza Fenwick, as well as Amelia Opie and Helen Maria Williams; the encouragement of the free-thinking Alexander Geddes; and the fact that Plumptre must have known many of the radicals centred in Norfolk in this period.

Anne Plumptre took advantage of the opportunity to travel to France when the Peace of Amiens opened that country to visitors in 1802. She was one of many British citizens who crossed the channel to see the effects of the Revolution and to examine the art treasures Napoleon had seized and placed in the Louvre.[13] According to Cecilia Brightwell in *Memorials of Mrs. Opie* (1854), Plumptre travelled with a party that included Amelia Opie and her husband, John, as well as Norwich friends Mr. and Mrs. Samuel Favell (97). They arrived in Calais on August 14, 1802, and left almost immediately for Paris.[14]

Plumptre, however, makes no mention of either Mr. and Mrs. Opie or Mr. and Mrs. Favell in *A Narrative of a Three Years' Residence in France, 1802-5*, her own account of her visit published in 1810. According to the *Narrative*, Plumptre set out for Paris on February 3rd, 1802, in the company of friends, a French gentleman and lady she refers to as "Monsieur and Madame B——."[15] This couple, detained on a visit to England by events in France, were taking the first opportunity to return home. Plumptre spent eight months in Paris and two years in Provence as well as some time touring the French countryside. She returned to England almost exactly three years from the date of her departure, arriving in London on the 31st of January, 1805 (*Narrative* 3: 239). A letter to a London bookseller, requesting a number of French books, places Plumptre in St. Martin's Stamford in June 1806,[16] but little more is known of her personal life until her visits to Ireland eight years later.

Plumptre made two visits to Ireland in the summers of 1814 and 1815. On her first trip she travelled with "Mr. and Mrs. C ... ," leaving England in early July and returning in early September. She carried with her a letter of introduction to Sir Charles and Lady Morgan in Dublin, as well as a copy of Lady Morgan's novel *O'Donnel*. Plumptre saw the standard sights in Dublin, then travelled to Belfast and Carrickfergus, before retracing her steps and returning to England. For her second trip Plumptre varied her route but engaged in similar sightseeing and visiting. Throughout both journeys, Plumptre stopped at various points to collect botanical and mineralogical specimens.

Plumptre had travelled alone in France, and she continued to travel only with a servant in Ireland, despite warnings about the unsettled state of the country. In her account of her journey, *Narrative of a Residence in Ireland* (1817), she writes:

> I have not unfrequently been asked, "*How did you dare to venture upon travelling over a country in such a disturbed state?*"—Yet my Narrative will show, that it is possible to travel many and many miles over this disturbed country in the most perfect quiet. (342)

The picture of Anne Plumptre which emerges from the narrative is that of a confident and capable woman. When her Irish driver attempts to take advantage of her, for example, Plumptre handles the problem firmly:

> I then summoned the driver, and told him that in consequence of his ill-behaviour I should not pay him or give him any thing for himself, that I should send the money to Mr. Barwis, and desire him to settle with his [the driver's] master for the chaise; and as for what I should otherwise [have] given him, I should desire Mr. Barwis to distribute it in charity in the town in any manner he judged most proper. The driver did, indeed, seem thunderstruck; it was an effort of decision which seemed totally unexpected, for *a lady* ... (320-21)

Even after the driver apologizes and begs forgiveness, Plumptre is resolute:

> I was however inexorable, for he made me completely angry by taking advantage of my servant and myself being both strangers to the road ... and I dismissed him. (321)

There is a marked contrast between Plumptre's support of the revolt of the French in *A Narrative of a Three Years' Residence in France* and her lack of enthusiasm for the rebellion of the Irish in *Narrative of a Residence in Ireland*, a difference that may be rooted in the difference between theory and experience. During her second visit to Ireland Plumptre was badly upset by a near encounter with actual violence when a mail coach was attacked and a British soldier killed by Irish insurgents in quest of weapons. In her account of this experience Plumptre condemns both the exploitation of the Irish, and their use of violence to protest that exploitation:

> That the situation of the lower classes in Ireland, particularly in that part of the country, was very deplorable, could not be doubted; but who could witness without deep regret the mistaken, the perverted notions they had adopted of the means by which it was to be ameliorated? (*Narrative of a Residence* 2: 312)

Violence, Plumptre maintains, will only be repelled by further violence with martial law as the end result.

Plumptre returned to London from her second trip to Ireland in September of 1815. A letter from Richard Hey to James Plumptre dated October 30, 1815, mentions "Mrs. Anne Plumptre"—as she apparently referred to herself—living at No. 17. Percy Street.[17]

Although references in various letters and publications indicate Anne Plumptre maintained a busy social as well as intellectual life, full of trips to the theatre, musical parties, house guests, and balls, little is specifically known about the final years of her life. A letter dated June 14th, 1818, places her in London four months before her death. In it she requests Mr. Colburn to "make out her account, & call on her with it, at Mr. Carlisle's Soho Square" and notes that she wishes to settle her business with him as soon as possible as she is about to leave London.[18]

Anne Plumptre died in Norwich on October 20, 1818, at the age of fifty-eight. In her will, dated September 28, 1818, and witnessed by John and Susannah Taylor of Norwich, Plumptre left everything in her possession to her brother Robert, whom she also named as executor.[19] Her death was marked by a short obituary in the *Gentleman's Magazine* in which she was mentioned as an "author of many ingenious writings" who was "particularly skilled in German literature."[20]

Anne Plumptre's Literary Career

Plumptre is believed to have started her literary career with "some slight performances in periodical publications" but these have never been identified.[21] Her first known work is a two-volume novel, *Antoinette* (1796) (*Antoinette Percival* in the Philadelphia edition of 1800), published anonymously at the Minerva Press but later acknowledged in a second edition. Plumptre sets this two-generational novel in Ireland and France. The main plot centres around Theodore Arlington, a young man who yields to parental pressure to marry even though he has already contracted a secret marriage in France. Haunted by the fear of having committed bigamy and unable to learn the fate of his first wife, he eventually disappears for a fifteen-year adventure that sees him captured by pirates, enslaved by an oriental despot, and imprisoned in the Bastille. Meanwhile his wife in Ireland staunchly raises their son and a mysterious orphan, Antoinette, later discovered to be Theodore's legitimate daughter from his first marriage. There is little indication of Plumptre's radicalism in this novel; *Antoinette* is conventional both stylistically and thematically. Although the narrator calls for women to become men's "rational companions and friends" rather than "the wretched slaves of their husbands' caprices," the narrative effectively negates this stance with its endorsement of the Griselda-like forbearance of Theodore's second wife.

Plumptre's second novel, *The Rector's Son*, published by Lee and Hurst in 1798, has been called "a little-known forerunner of the modern thriller" because of the strong element of intrigue that animates its plot.[22] The novel focuses on the trials of a young man, Charles Meadows, and the woman he has secretly married, Amelia Aubyn. When Charles goes to India to make his fortune, Dawkins, the novel's Machiavellian villain, schemes to bring about the permanent separation of the young couple. Foul play is suspected when Charles disappears in a mysterious manner; he is believed dead for a good portion of the novel but is ultimately discovered alive and reunited with his long-suffering wife. The plot is complex and partially driven by Charles's overly emotional—indeed, almost hysterical—personality; he is successively overwrought, depressed, and suicidal. Charles's excessive sensibility and weakness for meaningless amusements is contrasted with Amelia's strength of character and the importance she places on honour. Here we see an important thread linking all of Plumptre's fiction: her interest in exploring gender roles through a reversal of gender stereotypes and conventions. Plumptre further foregrounds such issues in *The Rector's Son* by contrasting the results of Charles's marital infidelity with an equivalent lapse in a secondary female character. Charles is not only forgiven by Amelia for his illicit affair with a "fair Hindoo," but Amelia adopts the daughter that results. In contrast, Fanny Warren spirals downward from "one false step" in her youth to a life of dishonour and ultimately a miserable death. *The Rector's Son* was not as well received as *Antoinette*, the *Critical Review* for one disapproving of the improbability of its plot.[23]

Something New: or, Adventures at Campbell-House, which will be discussed in more detail below, was published in 1801 after a particularly busy few years for Plumptre. Between 1798 and the publication of *Something New* she offered the public translations of seven plays by the German dramatist Augustus von Kotzebue: *The Count of Burgundy* (1798),

The Natural Son (1798), *The Force of Calumny* (1799), *La-Peyrouse* (1799), *The Virgin of the Sun* (1799), *The Horse and the Widow* (1799), and the very popular *Pizarro* (1799). During this period Plumptre also published translations of Kotzebue's autobiography, *Sketch of the Life and Literary Career of Augustus von Kotzebue* (1800), and his *Miscellaneous Writings* (1801), as well as translations of works by three other authors: *Letters from Various Parts of the Continent* (1799) by Friedrich von Matthisson, *Physiognomical Travels* (1800) by J.C.A. Musaeus, and "Stanzas to a Valley" from the German of J.G. von Salis.[24]

Four final translations followed the publication of *Something New*: Bertrand's *A Historical Relation of the Plague* (1805), Henry Lichtenstein's *Travels in Southern Africa 1803-1806* (1812, 1815), François Charles Pouqueville's *Travels in the Morea, Albania, and other parts of the Ottoman Empire* (1813), and *Voyages and Travels to Brazil, the South Sea, Kamschatka, and Japan* (1813, 1814). As well, Plumptre worked with Robert Bland to translate Friedrich Melchior's *Historical and Literary Memoirs and Anecdotes* (1814) which went to a second edition in 1815.

In the final decade of her life Plumptre produced four original works including the accounts of her visits to France and Ireland, a novel, and a book of stories. In 1810 the three-volume *A Narrative of a Three Years' Residence in France, 1802-5* offered the public practical advice for the visitor to France. Although this was praised as "useful information" by at least one critic,[25] the sympathetic portrayal of Napoleon in a section entitled "Remarks on the Character of Bonaparte, and on the present Situation of France" incensed a number of readers. In this section Plumptre defends Napoleon against a number of contemporary accusations, including charges that he had ordered the massacre of Turkish prisoners in Jaffa, allegations that he had proscribed religious expression, and rumours that he was allowing English visitors to be mistreated in France. According to Plumptre, British denouncers of Napoleon were being misled both by the reports of French émigrés and their own prejudices; she argues that an unbiased assessment of Napoleon and his achievements would prove him to be an exceptional leader:

> In all the governments where Bonaparte has any influence, he has uniformly been the means of procuring relief to the people from some of the most grievous of their oppressions. He has carried on a determined warfare against feudal and ecclesiastical tyranny, and this has rendered him odious among those whose exclusive privileges have been abrogated: but it has rendered him popular among the orders relieved; and if their voices were as much to be heard as those of the other class, we should from them probably hear a very different representation of his character. (3: 384)

Narrative of a Residence in Ireland published in 1817 by Henry Colburn, met with an equally mixed reception: The *London Quarterly Review* condemned it as "trash," calling it "pedantic and dull ... gross and vulgar"[26] while the *London Literary Gazette* praised it as an "agreeable volume" that acted as an "industrious and discriminating mirror" of Ireland (May 17, 1817).

Plumptre's last novel, *The History of Myself and My Friend*, was published in 1813 by Henry Colburn. In this novel the "Myself" is Samuel Danville, the son of a parish clerk who spends a good deal of time watching over and protecting his friend, Walter Armstrong, the rector's son. Walter, who in the novel is associated with weakness, instability, and emotion, is a "mere creature of impulse" whose chief misfortune is that "he [can]not think" (2: 12, 9). He is one of a series of feminized male characters in Plumptre's novels, a series that includes Charles in *The Rector's Son* and Lionel in *Something New*.

The focus on a male point of view in *The History of Myself and My Friend* is part of an on-going pattern in Anne Plumptre's fiction. At a period when the bulk of novels concentrated on the perceptions and experience of female protagonists—often reflected in titles such as *Belinda*, *Rosella*, or *Camilla*—Plumptre increasingly focused on exploring the male perspective. In *Antoinette*, for example, the narrative focus wavers from the nominal subject of the novel to Theodore's problems and adventures; in *The Rector's Son* the reader's interest is directed to Charles rather than Amelia; and in *Something New* the bulk of the novel is written with Lionel as epistolary subject. The first-person narration with a male protagonist that Plumptre uses in *The History of Myself and My Friend* is a further step in this pattern.

Plumptre's last work was published the year she died and written with her sister Annabella. *Tales of Wonder, of Humour, and of Sentiment; Original and Translated* (1818) is a collection of didactic stories which are surprisingly engaging. The Plumptre sisters exploit a number of exotic locales in these tales, including Spain, India, Hungary, Burgundy, Peru, and China. One of the stories, "The Fair of Beaucaire," is particularly interesting for the similarity of its themes and motifs to those of *Something New: or, Adventures at Campbell-House*. Like *Something New* "The Fair of Beaucaire" utilises a number of the elements of the popular "Beauty and the Beast" folk tale including a monstrous suitor, a beautiful girl who is pressured to marry him, a parent as initiator of the action, and an enchanted castle. In this tale the heroine, Alexis, is forced by her domineering mother to marry the Marquis de Montalon, a man who is "a mass of ugliness and deformity" and more than three times her age (2: 209):

> Figure to yourself a man more than sixty years of age, low in stature but large in bulk, with short legs, high shoulders, a small head, a mouth from ear to ear, an immense long nose, hollow cheeks, and red sunk eyes which squinted exceedingly. (2: 208)

The bridegroom also stammers, is deaf, and suffers from gout. Alexis, the epitome of passive feminine virtue, obeys her mother and marries this appalling suitor despite the fact that she loves the young and handsome Monsieur de Chalante. After the marriage Alexis figures as an imprisoned Beauty:

> The place she inhabited was … a real enchanted palace; but like many another was rendered inaccessible, not by a dragon, but by the ill-humours of its owner. (2: 206-7)

Like any good hero, de Chalante would attempt his lady's rescue, but Alexis sends him away. Like her fairy-tale prototype, she is determined to keep her bargain with the beast: "whether I am given to a monster or a man, I am his," she tells her lover (2: 215). Unlike the beast in the tale, however, the Marquis is not transformed by her devotion; Alexis is freed only upon his death.

Something New: or, Adventures at Campbell-House

The plot of *Something New: or, Adventures at Campbell-House* hinges on the value placed on feminine appearance by society—a value reflected in the beauty of fictional heroines. Beauty is, in fact, the sign that marks the heroine; it is what entitles her to a story at all.[27] From Cinderella to Anna Karenina, from chivalric romance to Harlequin Romance, heroines, and particularly eighteenth- and nineteenth-century heroines, are physically attractive. Admittedly there are exceptions: Fielding's Amelia has a nose that is "beat all to pieces"; Anna Maria Bennett's Rosa is a rickety, emaciated, dirty little girl in the opening passages of *The Beggar Girl and her Benefactors* (1797); Frances Burney's Eugenia is undoubtedly unattractive; and Jane Austen offers a trilogy of less-than-handsome heroines: Fanny Price is mousy, Anne Elliot is faded, and Catherine Morland is quite remarkably ordinary. But these exceptions are merely variations on the beautiful heroine theme. Amelia remains disfigured only long enough for Booth to demonstrate that he loves her for more than her looks, Rosa is transformed into a stunning beauty once she is adopted, Eugenia is relegated to secondary character status, love returns Anne Elliot's bloom, and time works wonders with Fanny and Catherine (Catherine grows up to be "quite a good-looking girl" and Fanny as a woman is appealing enough to attract a man as shallow as Henry Crawford). Even Sarah Scott in *Agreeable Ugliness; or, The Triumph of the Graces* (1754)[28]—a work predicated on the ugliness of the heroine—ameliorates her main character's unattractiveness by the end of the novel.

It is the stranglehold of the beautiful heroine convention upon the novel that Plumptre addresses in *Something New*. In a spirited prefatory poem, she declares that the convention of the beautiful heroine has exercised its tyranny for too long:

... still, in spite of ever-varying Chance,
Has BEAUTY held o'er Novel and Romance,
One undivided, unmolested rule,
And was the Heroine, witty, wise, or fool;
Still she was lovely, still in form and mien,
The rival e'en of fair Idalia's Queen.

Plumptre challenges the primacy of the beautiful heroine convention boldly:

No, we'll the RIGHTS OF AUTHORS here defend,
And in these pages place before your view
An UGLY heroine—Is't not SOMETHING NEW?

Although we only see Olivia Campbell through the eyes of other characters, these reports are consistent: while Olivia is blessed with every important virtue ("her equal is scarcely to be found on earth for true benevolence, strength of understanding, and cultivation of mind"), she is not blessed with physical beauty; she is at best considered "uncommonly plain," at worst "damned ugly." It is the task of the novel's male protagonist, Lionel Stanhope—a man who has "always been the devoted slave of beauty"—to develop the perception to see and value the woman behind the face, to discover and love the real Olivia Campbell.

The problem of distinguishing between appearance and reality is the controlling trope of *Something New*. When Lionel and his cousin Harry Edgeworth enter Campbell-House nothing is what it seems, themselves included. Harriot Belgrave is who she says she is and yet is not; there is a ghost that is not a ghost and a betrayed woman who is not betrayed; there is a wedding that is not a wedding, and jokes and challenges to duels that are neither. Above all, Lionel must sort out the problem of Olivia. Is she "a piece of deformity" or a "truly admirable woman"? A "fiend" or an "archangel"? A "tormentor" or a "treasure"? In this "castle of wonders" Lionel must decide what is real and what is only appearance.

It is through such language, the trope of appearance and reality, and various elements of plot that *Something New* is linked to fairy tale. As in "The Fair of Beaucaire," in *Something New* parental pressure is being brought to bear upon a young person to marry someone considered monstrous, a plot with a clear affinity to that of "Beauty and the Beast." The "Beauty and the Beast" fairy story was well known in Plumptre's time[29] and, indeed, continues second only to "Cinderella" in popularity and range of dissemination. Both stories have archetypal resonance and both have informed the early romantic and gothic fictions associated with women: "Cinderella" has been replayed with countless Evelinas and Fanny Prices, while various Gothic monsters have exercised the courage and discernment of numerous Beautys. Both are tales of transformation, differing mainly in the object transformed and the initiative required of the heroine. In "Cinderella" the heroine's role is essentially passive; she waits for her goodness and worth to be recognized and rewarded. Her transformation is really a change in how she is perceived and a change in her status from "worthless" or "unworthy" to "treasure." In "Beauty and the Beast" the heroine is subject, rather than object; it is she who must learn to perceive what is real and what is mere appearance, who is the villain and who is the hero. In both cases, however, the transformation merely reveals what is already in existence; it is the seeker—Beauty or the Prince—who must learn to perceive the Beast or Cinderella correctly.

In *Something New* Lionel plays male "Beauty" to Olivia's female "Beast," male "heroine" to her female "hero." In this novel it is the hero who blushes like a "fair maiden" and feels "silly and abashed" when his stratagems are made obvious; it is the heroine who acts as a wise and discerning mentor, guiding the hero through the shoals of choice. It is the hero who opens his heart in a series of letters, who is presented as a "creature of feeling" forced to choose between reason and emotion, and who struggles with the traditionally feminine moment of choice. In Plumptre's hands and with the gender of the main characters reversed, the focus of the original fable shifts from an expression of female fear of marriage and male sexuality to male fear of transgression of social boundaries; Lionel fears ridicule if he marries someone so far removed from the societal norm. In effect, by shifting the genders of the characters in the "Beauty and the Beast" archetype to male subject/seeker and female object/monster, Plumptre returns to the "Cinderella" paradigm that has structured so many courtship novels. Lionel, like the Prince, must seek the true Olivia/Cinderella. The important difference is in the representation of the heroine. Whereas Cinderella's physical beauty, temporarily obscured by her social condition, is an outer manifestation of her innate goodness and purity, no such direct equivalency exists with Olivia.

Olivia's lack of beauty creates a number of difficulties in the narrative, which is not surprising since the plot of the courtship novel is predicated on the beauty of the heroine. This predication is generally taken for granted, an invisible thread binding together literally thousands of novels. In very early narratives, and especially in folk and fairy tale, physical appearance functions as a type of narrative shorthand which associates beauty with such desirable ethical and social conditions as goodness and nobility. In the early novel beauty continues to act as a narrative signal, alerting the reader that a particular female character is worthy of the hero's interest. Beauty can also function as a form of currency, allowing women to trade access to their beauty for social status and financial security through marriage. In such cases the sign of beauty discreetly elides into a signal of sexual attractiveness and availability. Although one would expect heroines who engage in such trade to be criticized by the narrative, they generally are protected from censure by the beautiful heroine trope's conflation of the aesthetic, moral, and social: because their attractiveness signals their inherent virtue and nobility (in spirit if not in blood), their social rise is naturalized, becoming a recognition of their authentic condition rather than an unmerited elevation.

In *Something New* Plumptre illustrates the lack of narrative space for an unattractive heroine. Lionel, who comes to truly care for Olivia, has a great deal of difficulty positioning himself in relation to her. In fact, he becomes lost in a no-man's-land of generic scripts, none particularly appropriate in addressing a non-standard heroine. Olivia cannot be treated within the standard paradigms of gullible ingenue, romance heroine, victim of gothic horror, or sentimental subject—although Lionel and Harry successively attempt to fit her into each of these models. Nor can she be addressed with the standard language and gestures of love; for example, Lionel finds it impossible to write the passionate love poem he had envisioned to welcome her to London, remarking that he can "scarcely find any appropriate language in poetry to express [his] admiration of the charms Olivia really does possess." Instead, Lionel produces verses with "a philosophical turn of reflection in them" in a mode "far removed from the impassioned tone in which [he had] intended to write." Lionel does indeed care for Olivia, but he finds his emotion disguised and distorted by the very form that he utilizes to enhance its expression.

Just as Lionel finds love poetry to be frustratingly recalcitrant to his purpose, so too does he struggle with expressing his feelings for Olivia in other forms of verbal and written discourse. In an attempt to find a suitable mode in which to address or discuss Olivia, Lionel repeatedly represents her as something other than or more than woman: she is a saint, an angel, a pure soul, an enchantress. These expressions, while not uncommon in romance, are suspiciously asexual. Because the language of desire is centred on beauty, Lionel is unable to address Olivia as he would wish. The very language thwarts his purpose, making what he would attempt to say in all seriousness appear ironic. Frustrated and racked with indecision, at one point Lionel longs to simply eliminate the romantic aspect of his relationship with Olivia:

> ... how gladly I would even yield up privileges so important, could I make Olivia my sister. Oh that this were possible! This would be indeed to form to myself a little paradise upon earth! What a delightful intercourse of fraternal attachment should we then maintain, how affectionately might we participate in each other's joys and sorrows, and administer to each other's happiness ...

This is Eden before the serpent, where concern with looks would be as foreign as fig leaves.

The problem is really a structural one. Plumptre has predicated *Something New* on Olivia's ugliness. To ameliorate that ugliness would be to surrender to the tyranny of the convention. Yet the structure of the courtship novel—informed by such narrative archetypes as "Cinderella" and "Beauty and the Beast"—renders Olivia as reward. Given Olivia's lack of beauty and the power of the beautiful heroine convention, however, it is difficult for her to be regarded as a proper prize. Figuratively stuck between the plot and the convention, Lionel writhes in an agony of indecision. As Patricia Howe has noted in relation to German literature, lack of beauty in the heroine confronts the hero with a new and painful dilemma:

> For, whereas the hero reacts with delight to the conjunction of beauty and virtue, indeed comes to expect them to be synonymous, he is confused and embarrassed by the combination of ugliness and virtue. The ugly heroine confronts him with a new dilemma, internalizing his struggles and implicating her in them, so that she is no longer simply his goal and reward. The separation of beauty from other criteria thus challenges the marriage plot as the source of the heroine's identity.[30]

If Olivia is not Lionel's goal and reward, if her identity is not affirmed by marriage, then what is her narrative position or function? As Plumptre grapples with the requirements of opposing conventions in *Something New*, the constraints on the courtship novel become increasingly more apparent.

Plumptre is interested in more than just challenging the conventions of the courtship plot, however. Her touch is light, but her novel takes part in the contemporary debate about the role of women. In *Something New* the proper education of both sexes is seen to be of primary importance to their emancipation from the prejudices of the past. Olivia, of course, is the principal example of the benefits of a good education; she weds in one form the qualities of rationality and practicality, intelligence and benevolence. Lionel is the negative example. The indecision and character faults that result in so much trouble and pain to everyone involved are ascribed to parental over-indulgence and a faulty education. Plumptre's critique of Lionel's upbringing is doubly pointed since she has gendered him female in the text. In a passage that might be mistaken for Wollstonecraft on the importance of female education, Olivia reflects that Lionel's weaknesses may well defy correction since "a mind not trained from its earliest infancy to the exertion of its powers, scarcely ever attains the full possession of them." Plumptre is criticizing both a female education that leaves women unprepared for meaningful labour and a male education that results in an endless pursuit of pleasure and in an unthinking adoption of societal norms and mores.

Lack of proper education is seen to harm all society, not just the individuals involved and certainly not just women. The "hoaxes" and gossip that fill the empty days of a woman such as Mrs. Harrison spread their poison indiscriminately. We see, for example, gossip dogging the reformed Lucy Morgan, Ryder being plagued by rumours of past sexual misconduct, and the near-tragic results of a "hoax" involving a false challenge to a duel. In the latter incident, only chance keeps the female "hoax" and the thoughtless male adoption of codes of honour from combining into an incident with a potential for serious injury or even death.

Just as Plumptre offers no easy solution to the problems inherent in Lionel and Olivia's relationship, so she offers no utopian or simplistic solutions to the problems of women in general. In *Something New* female community and education are presented as key elements in women's emancipation, but Plumptre does not discount ideological and practical difficulties. We see Olivia offering a haven to a number of distressed women of different backgrounds: Harriot Belgrave and her mother become part of the Campbell household; the dwarf Fanny who was formerly "obliged ... to gain her livelihood by exhibiting herself as a sight" is given meaningful employment; and Lucy Morgan, the fallen daughter of a poor Welsh curate, is rescued and employed as a schoolmistress. But Olivia is also seen to draw much of her power and authority from male culture, and other women—such as the censorious and hypocritical Mrs. Harrison or the foolish Peggy Perkins—are presented as being the most likely saboteurs of their fellow sex's efforts.

Plumptre takes many of the standard tropes of the popular novel and ironically transmutes them. She offers us, for example, that rarest of all creatures, a male epistolary subject. Equally unusual is the psychological complexity of her heroine; Olivia's difficulties and self-division, as well as her assertive attitude, are credibly realised and distinguish her from the hundreds of passive cardboard-cutout heroines found in the popular literature of the period. Plumptre, however, does not discount the difficulties women encounter in a world that privileges looks and presence over inner worth and intellect. Olivia may be the epitome of "true benevolence, strength of understanding, and cultivation of mind," but the pain she experiences as a result of her lack of looks is severe and rendered more realistic by Plumptre's understatement of it.

Within the confines of Campbell-House Plumptre offers a utopian vision of a society where internal, rather than external, beauty is celebrated. But Plumptre's awareness of the importance of beauty for women is apparent in the fairy-tale imagery she employs: Campbell-House is presented as a "castle of wonders," Olivia as a "treasure," and Lionel as intoxicated or enchanted—held by a "magic spell" that keeps him at Olivia's feet. Lionel, however, cannot stay at Campbell-House forever, and the question is whether he has the strength to stand against the common values of his society. In the fairy-tale version of this story Olivia would be magically transformed into a beauty, thus sidestepping the problem; in the *Bildungsroman* version a reformed Lionel would scorn societal pressures and receive Olivia as his reward. In either case Olivia would function as a barometer of Lionel's success or failure rather than as a heroine in her own right. In *Something New* Plumptre neither discounts the power of societal norms nor objectifies her heroine by reducing her to a virtual loving cup, a silent symbol of masculine success. Instead, in the gap between fairy-tale expectation and the actual resolution of the novel,

Anne Plumptre exposes the force of the beautiful heroine trope and the power of the conventions of the courtship novel.

Notes

1　In *Narrative of a Residence in Ireland* (1817) Anne Plumptre indicates that her surname is often incorrectly pronounced "Plum-tree." During an excursion to the Upper Lake of Killarney Plumptre's Irish guide suggests that one of the unnamed islands on the lake be named after her. Plumptre refuses, writing that "I would not, however, permit my name to be given: as the habit of the world has been ever to pronounce it as if it were a *Plum-tree*, I was sure that the island would never be called any thing but *Plum-tree Island*; and a tradition would soon be affixed to it that it was once covered with Plum-trees" (II 279). Instead she has it named "KEAN'S ISLAND" in honour of the well-known tragic actor Edmund Kean.

　　Although Plumptre gives no indication of the correct pronunciation of her surname, she may have valued the aristocratic ring of a French pronunciation. According to Patrick Hanks's and Flavia Hodges's *A Dictionary of Surnames* (Oxford: Oxford UP, 1988), "William de Plumptre, mentioned in documents of 1330 and 1335 is an ancestor of a family associated for centuries with Notts. Their name is derived from the village of Plumptre in the county, now spelled Plumptree" (424). The original William, being Francophone, would have read the Anglo-Saxon "Plumptre" as French and pronounced it accordingly. It seems, then, that the most likely eighteenth-century pronunciation was the French "Plumpter" for the name and the English "Plumtree" for the village. Thanks to Brycchan Carey for this information.

2　There is some confusion about the number of children in the Plumptre family. *The Dictionary of National Biography* and Roger Lonsdale (*Eighteenth-Century Women Poets: An Oxford Anthology*, 1990) indicate a family of ten children. *Burke's Landed Gentry* (1894) lists eight children, missing Mary, the fifth daughter. In a letter to John Hay dated Monday, August 30, 1813 [Cambridge MS Add 58649B], however, James Plumptre lists nine children: Diane, Joseph, Anne, Annabella, Lydia, Robert, Mary, Jemima, and James. It is possible, of course, that he has omitted a brother or sister who died at an early age.

3　Memoirs of Henry Crabb Robinson, Dr. Williams's Library, London. Later references are also to this manuscript. See Edith J. Morley's edition of *Henry Crabb Robinson on Books and Their Writers* (London: Dent, 1938) for an abridged version.

4　In a letter dated February 27, 1813 [Cambridge MSS Add 5864(B)], John Hay asks James Plumptre to clarify a point he has made concerning this rupture:

One expression of yours I do not quite understand. After saying that your Mother and two eldest Sisters receded from the Church, you add "and soon after a separation of the opposite side[s?] of the family took place"—I always thought [unclear] had been in Orders when you first came to my Lectures …

James Plumptre's eldest sisters were Diane and Anne but, given Anne and Annabella's shared radicalism and the fact that Diane married a clergyman, James may have been referring to Annabella rather than Diane. What is certain, however, is that there was a family rupture over religion with Anne and her mother on the anti-church side.

5 *The Love-Letters of Mary Hays (1779-1780)*, ed. A. F. Wedd (London: Methuen, 1925) 238.

6 Roger Lonsdale, ed., *Eighteenth-Century Women Poets: An Oxford Anthology* (Oxford: Oxford UP, 1990) 492.

7 *The Feminist Companion to Literature in English: Women Writers from the Middle Ages to the Present*. Edited by Virginia Blain, Isobel Grundy, and Patricia Clements (New Haven: Yale UP, 1990) 861.

8 Margaret Eliot Macgregor, "Amelia Alderson Opie: Worldling and Friend," *Smith College Studies in Modern Languages* 14, no. 1-2 (Oct. 1932-Jan. 1933): 14.

9 John Busse, *Mrs. Montagu "Queen of the Blues"* (London: G. Howe, 1928) 304.

10 Walter Graham, "The Authorship of the Norwich Cabinet, 1794-5," *Notes and Queries* 162 (1932): 294.

11 A portion of "Ode to Moderation" is reprinted in Roger Lonsdale's *Eighteenth-Century Women Poets: An Oxford Anthology*. The poem was published anonymously and the attribution to Annabella made from a marked copy. Lonsdale notes that, given the similarity of the sisters' names, it is possible that Anne was the author (492).

12 Plumptre is mentioned in "Memoirs of Mrs. Jebb" (*The Monthly Repository*, Oct. 1812, 670) as being "long and intimately acquainted" with Mrs. Jebb and "frequently an inmate of her house." Ann Jebb (1735-1812) was a well-known dissenter who under the name "Priscilla" answered the arguments of Dr. Randolph and Dr. Balguiy for the Thirty-Two Articles of Faith in the newspapers.

13 Cecilia L. Brightwell, *Memorials of Amelia Opie*. 2nd ed. (Norwich, 1854) 97.

14 *The Monthly Magazine* also mentions her visit to France. In 1803 it is noted that "Miss PLUMPTRE, who is passing the winter in the South of France, is preparing for the press a Sketch of her Excursion into those parts, which will

be enriched with private anecdotes respecting the events of the revolution" (Vol. 15, i., 61). No mention is made of her travelling companions.

15 Although Plumptre never refers to her travelling companions as "Monsieur and Madame Barthelemy," when she first introduces "Monsieur and Madame B—" to the reader she notes that "The name of Barthelemy, and a relationship to the celebrated author of Anacharsis, were a natural attraction towards persons coming under that description, and an acquaintance with their many amiable qualities soon converted those feelings into the warmest friendship and esteem" (1:3-4).

16 Anne Plumptre to Mr. Dulau, Soho Square, London, 12 June 1806 [Bodleian 25435 (ff. 165) MS. Montagu d.9].

17 Richard Hey to James Plumptre, 30 October 1815 [Cambridge MSS Add 5864(B)]. This address is confirmed in a letter from Anne Plumptre to Francis Douce, Dec. 23 n.d. [Bodleian MSS Douce d.31, fo. 67].

18 Ann Plumptre to [Henry?] Colburn, 4 June 1818 [Bodleian 254359 (ff. 165-70) MS Montagu d.9].

19 The will of Ann [sic] Plumptre, spinster of the parish of St. Peter Parmentergate parish, Norwich, was proved in the Norwich Consistory Court in 1818. I am grateful to Miss Jean M. Kennedy, Norfolk County Archivist, for this information.

20 *Gentleman's Magazine* (1818): 2: 571.

21 *A Biographical Dictionary of the Living Authors of Great Britain and Ireland* (1816) 277.

22 Janet Todd, ed., *A Dictionary of British and American Women Writers 1660-1800* (Totowa, N.J.: Rowman & Littlefield, 1987) 257.

23 Plumptre's fiction generally was not as well-known or as well-received as her translations. In 1800 *The Monthly Magazine* still seemed unaware that she had published two novels previously, noting in its "Literary and Philosophical Intelligence" section that "Miss PLUMPTRE is preparing a novel for the press [likely *Something New*]; and the public may expect as much pleasure in this lady's original work, as it has already received from her translations" (Vol. 10, 48). Although *Antoinette* had been welcomed by the reviewers, *The Rector's Son* and *Something New* both met with unenthusiastic responses. *The Critical Review* was mildly approving of *Something New*, but noted that given the immaturity of novel readers, few authors would choose to imitate her (April 1802). The reviewer for the *Monthly Catalogue* was even less impressed, remarking that "we have looked in vain for novelty and entertainment" (May 1803).

24 "Stanzas to a Valley" appeared in *The Monthly Magazine; or British Register* 2 (Part 1, 1801): 514-15.

25 *Stevenson's Catalogue of Voyages and Travels*, no. 439. Quoted in Allibone's *Dictionary of English Literature*, vol. 2 (1874) 1611.

26 Vol. 16: 337-44. Quoted in *Allibone's Dictionary of English Literature*, vol. 2 (1874) 1611.

27 For a discussion of beauty as the sign of the heroine see Isobel Grundy, "Against Beauty: Eighteenth-Century Fiction Writers Confront the Problem of Woman-as-Sign," *Reimag(in)ing Women: Representations of Women in Culture.* Edited by Shirley Neuman and Glennis Stephenson (Toronto: U Toronto P, 1993) 74-86.

28 *Agreeable Ugliness; or, Triumph of the Graces* is Scott's translation of the French novel *La Laideur Aimable* by Pierre de la Place. For further details see Betty Rizzo's edition of Scott's novel *The History of Sir George Ellison*, forthcoming from the University Press of Kentucky.

29 Gabrielle-Suzanne Barbot de Gallon de Villeneuve (1695-1755) wrote the first known literary version of the "Beauty and the Beast" folk tale in 1740. A shorter version by Jeanne-Marie Leprince de Beaumont (1711-80) appeared sixteen years later in *Magasin des enfants, ou dialogues entre une sage gouvernante et plusiers de ses élèves de la première distinction* (1756). This shorter version was translated into English and was published with a collection of didactic conversations in *The Young Misses Magazine, Containing Dialogues between a Governess and Several Young Ladies of Quality, Her Scholars* (1761). A play based on the tale was written by the Comtesse de Genlis in 1785. For a history of "Beauty and the Beast" see Betsy Hearne *Beauty and the Beast: Vision and Revisions of an Old Tale* (Chicago: U of Chicago P, 1989).

30 Patricia Howe, "Faces and Fortunes: Ugly Heroines in Stifter's *Brigitta*, Fontane's *Schach von Wuthenow* and Saar's *Sappho*," in *German Life and Letters* 44:5 (October 1991): 426-442.

Anne Plumptre: A Brief Chronology

1760   Born third child of Robert Plumptre and Ann Newcome of Norwich. Christened 22 February at Cathedral Church, Norwich.

1791   Appears with sister Annabella and friend Amelia Alderson [later Opie] in a private theatrical production of *Adelaide*, a tragedy written by Alderson.

1794   Anne and Annabella support Alderson while she gives a political speech to a large party of Jacobins assembled against the Whig MP William Windham.

1796   Plumptre's first novel, *Antoinette*, published anonymously in two volumes by the Minerva Press, acknowledged in a later edition. *Antoinette* was also published in a Dublin edition of 1796 and as *Antoinette Percival* in a Philadelphia edition of 1800.

1798   A second novel, *The Rector's Son*, published in three volumes by Lee and Hurst. R. Phillips publishes translations of two plays from the German of August von Kotzebue: *The Count of Burgundy* and *The Natural Son*. Living in London according to the preface to *The Natural Son*.

1798-9 *Seven Plays from the German of Kotzebue.*

1799   Living in Bedford Square, London, with Annabella. Friendship with Eliza Fenwick. Longman and Rees publish *Letters Written from Various Parts of the Continent, Between the Years 1785 and 1794; containing a variety of anecdotes relative to the present state of literature in Germany, and to celebrated German literati. With an appendix. In which are included, three letters of Gray's, never before published in this country*, a translation from the German of Friedrich von Matthisson. Five more translations of plays by Kotzebue are published by R. Phillips: *The Force of Calumny* (also Dublin, 1799); *La-Peyrouse; Pizarro. The Spaniards in Peru; or, The Death of Rolla; The Virgin of the Sun* (also Dublin, 1799): and *The Widow, and the Riding Horse. The Count of Burgundy* is adapted to the English stage by Alexander Pope and produced in a benefit for him on 12 April at Theatre Royal, Covent Garden. Plumptre paid £25 on 14 May for use of *Pizarro* in a Drury Lane production.

1800   *Physiognomical Travels, preceded by A Physiognomical Journal .... To which is prefixed A short sketch of the life and character of the author, by his Pupil Kotzebue*, Plumptre's translation from the German of J. C. A. Musaeus, is published in three volumes by Strahan. Publication of Plumptre's translation of Kotzebue's *Mein literarischer Lebenslauf*

(1790): *Sketch of the Life and Literary Career of Kotzebue, with the journal of his tour to Paris* (also New York, 1801). Advertisements in both works place Plumptre in London.

1801   *Something New: or, Adventures at Campbell-House* published in three volumes by Strahan for Longman and Rees. Publication of another translation of Kotzebue, *Miscellaneous Writings*. "Stanzas to a Valley" from the German of J. G. von Salis appears in *The Monthly Magazine; or British Register*.

1802   Plumptre travels to France where she remains for three years. Although Plumptre is generally understood to have travelled to Paris in the company of Amelia and John Opie in August, by her own account she left in February in the company of "Monsieur and Madame B——." She remained in Paris for eight months.

1803-4 Plumptre spends two years in Provence as well as considerable time touring the French countryside.

1805   Returns to England in late January. Mawman publishes translation of Jean Baptiste Bertrand, *A Historical Relation of the Plague at Marseilles in the year 1720.... With an introduction, and a variety of notes by the translator.* In the introduction dated "Hamstead, June 1, 1805," Plumptre indicates that she had discovered the manuscript during a twelve-month stay in Marseilles.

1806   A letter to a London bookseller places Plumptre in St. Martin's Stamford in June.

1810   *A Narrative of Three Years' Residence in France, principally in the southern departments, from the year 1802 to 1805; including some authentic particulars respecting the early life of the French emperor, and a general inquiry into his character* published in three volumes by Mawman.

1812   First volume of *Travels in Southern Africa in the Years 1803, 1804, 1805, and 1806 ...*, translated from the German of Henry Lichtenstein, is published by Colburn.

1813   Colburn publishes Plumptre's fourth novel, the four volume *The History of Myself and my Friend* and her translation from the French of François Charles Pouqueville, *Travels in The Morea, Albania, and other parts of the Ottoman Empire ....* First volume of *Voyages and Travels to Brazil, the South Sea, Kamschatka, and Japan* from the German of Langsdorff is published in London.

1814   First tour of Ireland from early July to early September. Travels to Dublin where she meets Sir Charles and Lady Morgan, then to Belfast and Carrickfergus. Second volume of *Voyages and Travels to Brazil, the South Sea, Kamschatka, and Japan* published. Colburn publishes *Historical & Literary Memoirs and Anecdotes, selected from the correspondence of Baron de Grimm and Diderot with the Duke of Saxe-Gotha, between the years 1770 and 1790* from the French of Friedrich Melchior Grimm which Plumptre translated with Robert Bland.

1815 Second summer trip to Ireland; returns to London in September where she lives at No. 17 Percy Street. Second volume of *Travels in Southern Africa, In the Years 1803, 1804, 1805, and 1806 ...* published.

1817 *Narrative of a Residence in Ireland during the summer of 1814, and that of 1815* published by Colburn.

1818 Colburn publishes Plumptre's final work, a three-volume collection of stories written with Annabella: *Tales of Wonder, of Humour, and of Sentiment; original and translated*. Dies in Norwich on 20 October at the age of fifty-eight.

A Note on the Text

The three volumes of *Something New* were printed by A. Strahan for T.N. Longman and O. Rees in 1801. I have used square brackets to indicate any changes to this text with the following exceptions: obvious printer's errors have been corrected silently, running quotation marks have been removed, and the long "s" has been modernized. I have left in place irregularities of spelling and punctuation.

SOMETHING NEW:

OR,

ADVENTURES

AT

CAMPBELL-HOUSE.

IN THREE VOLUMES.

BY ANNE PLUMPTRE.

Man is but man, inconstant still and various!
There's no to-morrow in him like to-day!
Perhaps the atoms rolling in his brain
Make him think honestly the present hour,
The next a swarm of base ungrateful thoughts
May mount aloft. [1]

DRYDEN.

VOL. I.

LONDON:

PRINTED BY A. STRAHAN, PRINTERS-STREET;
FOR T. N. LONGMAN AND O. REES, PATERNOSTER-ROW.
1801.

PROLOGUE.

The man who oft turns o'er th' historic page,
To mark th' events of each succeeding age,
Must still observe, as he pursues his course,
That though, while aw'd by pow'r's superior force,
States, empires, cities, provinces remain
Supinely yok'd by Tyranny's fell chain,
That love of freedom which in ev'ry breast
Resistless rules, nor e'er can be suppress'd,
Indignant bursts its bonds, or soon, or late,
When despots in their turn must yield to fate.

    Here long fair Liberty has rear'd her head,
And choicest blessings over Britons shed.
Restricted only by the laws' decree,
'Tis our proud boast that we indeed are free.—
Are free indeed?—Ah 'tis an empty boast!
For deep within our sea-encircled coast,
Though Freedom long has gen'ral empire held,
Though Slav'ry's inroads have been oft repell'd,
One branch of tyranny has still retain'd
Its pristine force, unshaken still remain'd;
And held o'er Learning's sons imperial sway,
From earliest times till e'en the present day;
While through our Island's wide-extended bound,
No high-aspiring soul has yet been found,
Who dar'd magnanimously spurn these chains,
And rearing Freedom's staff on Learning's plains,
Invite thy more enlighten'd vot'ries, Sense,
Resistance' task tremendous to commence.
No! still, in spite of ever-varying Chance,
Has BEAUTY held o'er Novel and Romance,
One undivided, unmolested rule,
And was the Heroine, witty, wise, or fool;
Still she was lovely, still in form and mien,
The rival e'en of fair Idalia's Queen.[2]
The hapless female, whose irradiant eyes
Ne'er struck beholder's heart with soft surprise;
Who shew'd no symmetry of form, or face,
Though richly stor'd with ev'ry mental grace;
Nor in the Novel's or Romance's walk,
Has dar'd presume as heroine to stalk,
But far from wounding observation flown,
To live retir'd, unnotic'd, and unknown.

But shall our breasts, by love of freedom warm'd,
Still bow to laws by Despotism form'd?
When from the civil throne, where long the world
She rul'd at will, we see the monster hurl'd;
Shall Learning's sons still at her altar bend?
No, we'll the RIGHTS OF AUTHORS here defend,
And in these pages place before your view
An UGLY heroine—Is't not SOMETHING NEW?

LETTER I.

LIONEL STANHOPE
TO
HENRY EGERTON.

Kilverton, August 1.

Importunity is at length triumphant, Harry!—Obstinacy at length has vanquished resolution!—Lionel Stanhope at length has yielded to his father!

Lift up your hands and eyes in astonishment, if you please, my good cousin, yet 'tis even so. I have this very moment solemnly pledged myself to Sir Francis to pay my respects to my long-destined wife, Olivia Campbell, in my way to Scarborough. But, mistake me not—I have promised nothing more than merely to see her; I have not insinuated even the most distant hope that my visit will be productive of the consequences wished, though, in spite of my assurances to the contrary, the worthy Baronet seems to think that in gaining my consent to an interview he has gained every thing.

Yet though such may be his ideas, formed on his own wishes, those who know me better, and who can take a dispassionate view of the question, will be convinced how much he deceives himself. Can it be rationally supposed that I, who have always been the devoted slave of beauty, who have so often sworn even by the mighty Jupiter himself, that the woman who could fix my roving affections must be lovely as an angel— that I can on a sudden be so changed as to harbour an idea of uniting myself with a woman proverbially plain?—That I, who have vowed no less resolutely never to submit to the tyranny and superciliousness which in a female are the inseparable companions of a large fortune, but that the wedded partner of my heart should be poor as lovely—that I can think of paying my addresses to one of the richest heiresses in the kingdom?

No, Harry; in consenting to this interview I am actuated by far other motives; I have merely yielded to necessity, and taken the only possible method of rescuing myself from importunities which have long been the torment of my life. Vainly have I flattered myself that my steady resolution would at length weary out my father's obstinacy: often as I have parried his assaults, he has still returned undaunted to the charge.

"Do but see her, Li.—that cannot do you any harm—that does not pledge you to any thing. And what can be more unjust and unreasonable, than to reject her unknown?"

"Would it not be a much greater affront, my dear Sir, to reject her when known? And this I am very confident would be the case, since you yourself, notwithstanding your strong prejudice in her favour, have been frequently obliged to confess that she is uncommonly plain."

"No, no, Li.—don't say so—I never confessed that.—I allow indeed that she is not handsome, but she is so amiable, so sensible, so accomplished"—

"That it would be a great pity to throw herself away upon a being so insensible, unamiable, and unaccomplished as Lionel Stanhope. Adieu, my dear father, my horse waits, I am going to take a ride."

"Ah! Li. Li.! thou art a sad boy. 'Tis true indeed that she would be thrown away upon thee—thou art unworthy to possess such a treasure. But since I do not know any man worthy of her, thou may'st as well—Damn the boy; there he goes, and won't even stay to hear me!—Yet what a fine handsome, spirited young fellow it is!—Curse him, I can't help loving him in spite of his folly."

And what, after all, are these accomplishments to which my very affectionate father would sacrifice my inclinations, my happiness?—Miss Campbell's mind he says is so highly cultivated: that is, I suppose, so abundantly stored with novels and romances, that she would expect from a lover no less devotion and adoration than the tender sentimental heroes of such works are accustomed to pay to the heroines—and such attention she would be little likely to receive from me. Perhaps too she is an adept in all works of fancy, so that the house is littered from top to bottom with the productions of her ingenuity; and I should be afraid of moving, lest I might rend her fair bosom with agony unutterable, by disturbing or injuring some painted table, box, screen, or cabinet, the labour of many an anxious moment.

Yet, hold!—An idea suddenly strikes me!—You, Harry, are in want of a fortune—I want to get rid of one. Why then should we not accommodate each other, and by making this visit together, under an exchange of names and characters, accomplish our reciprocal aims?—By heaven 'tis a glorious idea!—it fires my blood!—it exhilarates my heart!—I feel new life!—Transports till now unknown trill through my veins!—Olivia wedded, I have nothing more to dread from parental importunity; and this single object of contention between Sir Francis and myself removed, we shall become the best friends in the world—while you, Harry, will be relieved from those embarrassments by which you are now so cruelly tormented.

But I am called away—adieu therefore for the present. Write to me immediately, and tell me that you will meet me at Doncaster on Thursday next, ready to perform your part in this drama; then how jocund will be the heart of
　　　Your faithfully affectionate

LIONEL STANHOPE.

LETTER II.

HENRY EGERTON
TO
LIONEL STANHOPE.

Bath, August 3.

Never, oh never, Lionel, could such a proposal as yours have been otherwise than acceptable to me, but never could it have come more opportunely than at the present moment. A powerful stimulus was indeed wanting, to rouse me from the state of torpor into which I have been plunged by recent disappointment—some new object of pursuit to occupy my soul, and chace from it that gloom—that worse than gloom—those images of horror, by which it has been overpowered for several days past.

Look at the date of my letter, and when you read BATH, your hands and eyes will surely be no less raised in astonishment to heaven, than you expected mine to be at finding that you had consented to visit at Campbell-House. You will then also see clearly what has occasioned that more than usual agony of mind to which I alluded. I once thought that no mortal power could again draw me into this city, the grave of all my happiness; but, alas! I knew not then the omnipotence of necessity!—Born to affluence, not accustomed to find any wish ungratified, I had no idea, till taught by cruel experience, how far the pressure of want, and the goading recollection of that enormous load of debt by which I am overwhelmed, could supersede all other feelings in my bosom.

Though stung almost to madness at the repeated disappointments I have experienced in endeavouring to repair my fortune by marriage, so desperate was my situation, that another opportunity of making an effort for that purpose presenting itself, I was resolved even to incur the hazard of another refusal, rather than have to reproach myself with pusillanimously yielding to my adverse fate. This new object was the daughter of a rich West-India merchant, whom I met with accidentally at an assize-ball at Dorchester. I immediately began once more to run that career of flattery and attention which had hitherto, to my utter astonishment, proved so unsuccessful, and now had soon reason to hope that a better fortune awaited me. In short, within ten days from the commencement of our acquaintance every thing was arranged, not only with her but with her father, who, though not extremely pleased at hearing the state of my affairs, yet was too entirely managed by his daughter to make any strong objections to her wishes. One thing alone occurred as an alloy to my transport, that Bath was fixed upon by the lady as the place at which our union should be completed.

I started at the very mention of that idea, and was about to entreat an alteration of the plan, yet, overpowered as I was by an arrangement so unexpected, what excuse could I frame for my objections to it?—A sigh burst involuntarily from my bosom but a second which was rising I had resolution enough to suppress; and apprehensive lest, by trifling, I might risk a change in my fair one's disposition, which I plainly saw was versatile and capricious, I resolved to subdue my feelings, and rush at all hazards to the appointed rendezvous.

A journey to my own estate was however necessary, before the settlements preparatory to our marriage could be finally adjusted. I was concerned at being obliged to lose sight of my intended bride, but the thing was unavoidable, and I departed for Arrenton, while she and her father proceeded to Bath. I dispatched my business with all possible expedition, and hastened to join them. But, oh! Stanhope, judge what must have been my feelings at the first sight of those spires and turrets to which were annexed such agonizing associations?—Clasping my hands together, I exclaimed, "Ah! wherefore are not the waters of Bath endued with a Lethean virtue![3] Why can they not

> Pluck from the memory a rooted sorrow,
> Rase out the written troubles of the brain;
> And, with some sweet oblivious antidote,
> Cleanse the charg'd bosom of that per'lous stuff
> Which weighs upon the heart?[4]

Soon, however, recurring to my new engagement, I roused the slumbering energies of my soul, and clothing my face in smiles, while my heart was a prey to the severest torture, I was prepared to meet my beloved with becoming transports, when—oh! cursed fortune—the first news I learned on entering Bath was, that she had eloped the preceding night with the son of an indigent Earl, whose title I suppose she considers as a sufficient excuse for her infidelity.

Thus foiled in my plans, bereft once more of the hope of emancipation from my distresses, at such a moment, and in such a spot, all my former wounds seemed again torn open. Three days did I remain shut up in my own apartment, a perfect recluse amid surrounding dissipation; while the sainted spirit of my long-lost Emily seemed to hover about me, tenderly reproaching me for the degrading life I have so long led, and pathetically exhorting me to break my chains, and become once more the same Henry to whom her pure and artless heart had been so ardently devoted. Oh yes, Lionel, I felt all this so forcibly, that I had actually resolved on making a vigorous effort to shake off the enervating tyranny under which I groan— but at that moment your letter arrived; it recalled too powerfully to my recollection my true and genuine situation, and convinced me that, bankrupt as I am both in fortune and reputation, the resolution was made too late, and not till 'tis become impracticable to carry it into effect.

Be your plan then pursued!—it was surely the inspiration of heaven itself!—Ill-fated Bath, in one hour more I quit thy walls for ever!—Hail, Yorkshire! hail, scene of my hopes, my wishes!—Before I reach thy borders, gloom shall be banished from my brow, and sorrow from my heart;

and thou, Lionel, shalt embrace once more the gay, the volatile, the dissipated

HENRY EGERTON.

LETTER III.

LIONEL STANHOPE
TO
HENRY EGERTON.

Kilverton, August 4.

Scarcely knowing whether this will reach you, I yet think it better just to write a few hasty lines, to mention a circumstance which has occurred. Within an hour after I had dispatched my last letter to you, Orlando St. John arrived here very unexpectedly, and learning that I was to set off for Scarborough in a few days, proposed to accompany me. This, considering our long intimacy, I knew not how to refuse, so I thought it better to impart our scheme to him. He interests himself deeply for our success; and, to promote it as far as lies in his power, has agreed to take Jerry on with him to Scarborough, since I am afraid of his accompanying me to Campbell-House, lest, good soul, he should think it necessary, in duty to his old master, to betray the proceedings of his young one.

Orlando insists upon an exact and minute detail of our adventures. He once saw Olivia at Doncaster races, and says that you can have no idea of any thing not deformed so uncommonly plain. Do you not shrink, Harry?—Weigh the matter well—remember that when her husband, the pursuit of beauty must be relinquished for ever. If your self-command can comply with such terms, you have much more than

Your very affectionate

LIONEL STANHOPE.

LETTER IV.

LIONEL STANHOPE
TO
ORLANDO ST. JOHN.

Campbell-House, August 10.

Retired to my apartment for the night, Orlando, I sit down to give you the first chapter of my promised narrative.

I quitted Doncaster within a quarter of an hour after you, leaving directions for Harry to follow me to the Campbell Arms at Maxstead, where I arrived about nine o'clock. I had not been there many minutes, before I was informed by the bar-maid that a young man was enquiring for me. I ordered him to be introduced, when, announcing himself as Mr. Egerton's servant, he said that his master might be expected in an hour, and that he was in the mean time himself sent forwards, in case he could be of any use to me.

Having previously heard much of Harry's dashing valet, and knowing that he received his education at Cambridge as a college hair-dresser, I was well prepared for the sort of person I might expect to see, but had no idea that I was to recognize in him an old acquaintance. Orlando, you have frequently heard me mention Arthur Williams, who had the honour of being operator in ordinary and extraordinary* to the head of my poor deceased friend Arabin, when I was upon a visit to him at college. In Egerton's valet I beheld this very man. We immediately recollected each other, and expressed mutual surprise at a meeting so unexpected. He was full of regret for the loss of Arabin, who he said was one of the best masters he ever had; and declared, that if he had lived, and I had become a member of the college, to which I had then a strong inclination, he never should have quitted his situation there.

These compliments paid, he began in his usual free and easy manner:

"I suppose you have heard of our disappointment at Bath?—Devilish hard to be sure!—We were cursedly unwilling to go thither, and 'twas too bad when we had summoned up resolution for it to find the bird flown. But now we seem to be after fresh game, and 'tis to be hoped we shall have better luck."

"How came you to be so well informed upon this matter, Mr. Arthur?"

"Lord bless you, Sir, why you know me pretty well, I think, and you can't suppose that I don't see the go of these things at once, without being told much about 'em. But Lord, Sir, they tell me that though she's devilish rich, she's damned ugly."

"Who told you so?"

"The folks at the inn at Doncaster. When they bid me go after you to the Campbell Arms, you know I of course asked directly what they meant by the Campbell Arms? They stared, seemed to think I ought to know all about the matter by inspiration, and at last said that the Campbell Arms was the sign of the inn at Maxstead, the parish that Campbell-House was in, the great rich heiress Miss Campbell's seat. Oho, the great rich heiress thought I—you are there or thereabouts, are you—and so I falls to pumping, and got it all out at last, that she's damned rich, damned ugly, and a damned fool."

---

*   *In ordinary* designated regular staff or staff in constant attendance. The addition of the designated *extraordinary* indicated supplemental services as in someone engaged for a special or temporary purpose.

"Did the people at the inn tell you all this?—Tolerably impertinent methinks."

"I beg pardon, Sir; I hope no offence. As for the information that she's ugly and a fool, I can't say that did come from the people at the inn. A brother of the livery who seemed upon the lounge there, overhearing my questions, put in, and added these two pretty little circumstances.— Damn it, thought I, rich and a fool is all very well, but how my master may like her being so devilish ugly is another story."

"And no concern of your's," said I, rather angrily.

"I'm sorry you're displeased Sir, but 'tis only my anxiety for my master's credit."

To put an end to his impertinent remarks, I wrote a note suited to the occasion, and dispatching him with it to the heiress, ordered breakfast. This my hostess, a goodly portly lady, brought with her own fair hands; when, judging by several observations she made that she was disposed to be communicative, and thinking I might by this means obtain some useful information, I began:

"I observed, as I came hither, Madam, a fine looking old house at a little distance; may I ask to whom it belongs?"

"Lawk, Sir, what don't you know who live there?—For sartin then you must be a great stranger hereabouts."

"A very great one. I never was in Yorkshire before."

"Well, to be sure, nor niver heard of Miss Campbell?"

"Miss Campbell?—what, Miss Olivia Campbell?—the rich heiress, the only child of the late General Campbell?—Oh yes, I have heard of her."

"Aye, aye, Madam Olivy as they call her. Well, Sir she live there."

"And that large house, then, is inhabited only by one solitary female?"

"Not so soluntary nather. She has two frinds as lives with her, Madam Belgrave and her darter; but old Madam is not there now, for she's gone to Lunnun arter a state as she was chated on a pretty time agone."

"But Miss Belgrave is at home?"

"Yes. And there's one Muster Baicham as lives here just by; he's staying there now bekays his own house is repairing. Nay, as for that matter, Madam Olivy's is always as much his home as his own house, for what I can see."

"What, he is some rich squire, or son of a lord, that goes a courting to her, I suppose?"

"Lawk, lawk, no such matter I promise you. Madam does not matter lords nor rich squires nather so over and above. If a man is but good, why lawk she say, what does it sinnify what he's called. And to be sure for that matter she has not much right, as you may say, to like your lords so vast, for folks says it was a lord as chated Madam Belgrave of her state, but he's like enough to be fitted now, thank God; and let every one have their own, I say, for right's right, whether the man's a lord or a beggar, that's my thought. And to be sure every body hereabouts was glad enough for to hear what the sarvent said t'other day when he bring'd a parcel to go by the Lunnun coach; for he said, says he, my lady hopes now, says he, that damned rascal of a lord"—

"How?—did Miss Campbell call the lord a damned rascal?"

"She?—Lawk, no, Sir, God love her; she wouldn't use no such words for niver so much. No, no, that was only the sarvent's word, and a damned rascal for sartin the lord is, if all's true as the sarvent said about him; and for that matter the sarvent's as honest a fellow as ever broke bread, and I don't believe would tell a lie for nobody. And to be sure he said that the lord fit with Madam Belgrave's husband and kilt him, and so got the state, and left Madam and poor Miss Harrit without so much as a penny in their pockets, and they must ather a starved or a gone to a workus; and lawk your honour knows that a workus is but a sorry place even for poor folks, crammed together, stiving and stewing, three or four in a bed like, God bless 'em, poor cratures"—

"I ca'nt say that I know much about a workhouse myself, but I can suppose that Mrs. Belgrave and her daughter would not have found it a very comfortable place."

"God bless your honour, and I pray God as you niver may know nothing about 'em, for your honour seems a main good kind of a gentleman. But to be sure nobody but what must wish as that there rascal of a lord may come to one at last, for 'tis but right that folks should have as good as they bring."

"True, Madam—but Mrs. Belgrave?"—

"Why for sartin if it had'nt a bin for Madam Olivy and the old Gineral, Madam Belgrave and Miss Harrit must a gone to a workus, and if its a bad place for poor folks its worser a deal for ladies. But his honour the Gineral axed 'em both to come and live with him, so that they liked mightily."

"And Mr. Beauchamp, Madam, whom you were mentioning, is not, then, a lord's son?"

"No, he's only a sort of a squire like, and has a little state of his own, as he looks arter himself. He was ommost a mind to be a lawyer, but somehow when he'd been arter it a little while, he did'nt seems to fancy it no matter, so he thought he'd be independant, as he calls it, and he comed to live at his own farm there, at yin little neat white house, as you see from the road just by the park gate, and there he have lived ever sin."

"But he is to marry Miss Campbell."

"Why to be sure when he first comed home, folks said it was acause he didn't like to be away from Madam, but now they does'n't much know what to think. His father and the old Gineral were great frinds, and so young Muster Baicham was always backwards and forwards, playing with young Madam, as thos they had been brother and sister; and to be sartin Madam and he are more likerer brother and sister now than any thing else."

"And has not Miss Campbell any lover?"

"Why there's a sort of folk they say as would be glad enough to have her, but she's so monsus difficle she won't have none on 'em."

"I understand her fortune to be very large."

"Aye, by my troth, and so it is."

"Then I suppose she has several elegant carriages, a great many fine horses, with forty or fifty servants, and is dressed all in gold and silver like a queen?"

"No such matter, I assure you. Madam is quite another guess sort of a lady from all that there. For sartin she have all them kind of things genteel enough, but she don't matter 'em like some folks. No, no, she spends a great deal of her fortin in charity; there is'nt a poor famaly for the Lord knows how many miles round but what's the better for it."

"Humph, I thought, how will this suit with Harry's taste?—I'm afraid he will think that charity begins at home, and chuse that it should stay at home too. What more information I might have obtained from my talkative landlady, had not our conversation been interrupted by the arrival of Egerton himself, I cannot say. His spirits were now no less elevated than they were depressed when last he wrote to me. Shaking me eagerly by the hand, he began:

"Well, Lionel, how go we on?—Have you seen my dog Arthur?—Are things in a prosperous train?—I am impatient till I clasp those beauties to my heart, the bare idea of which sets it all on fire."

"What sort of beauties is Harry Egerton so very eager to clasp?"

"The dazzling beauties of the fair Olivia—those golden beauties, more resplendent than the early rays of Phœbus,[5] when from the orient main majestic he ascends, gilding the lofty mountain tops, and, and, and,—But tell me truly, Li., hast taken any steps towards our introduction?"

"Yea, verily have I, my dear cousin. That bright ornament of the livery, Mr. Arthur Williams, is probably by this time on his return from Campbell-House with a very polite answer to a very polite note I sent, politely requesting permission for my cousin Henry Egerton and myself to throw ourselves at the feet of the illustrious heiress of the ancient house of Campbell."

"Pshaw, Lionel!—now I hope you did not write any of your strange inflated nonsense."

"Verily, no, my beloved Harry.—I did write such a note that thou thyself, hadst thou but seen it, wouldst have hung with rapture o'er a composition so highly-finished, so eloquent, so persuasive."

"Take care how you provoke me, Stanhope.—Tell me plainly what you have done?"

"Plainly then, and in most plain and concise terms, I have written such a note as I doubt not will procure our ready admission into the house and presence of the heiress. And faith, now I have done it, I almost repent me of my officiousness, since that busy babbler, conscience, has been so impertinent as to suggest strong doubts whether or not this scheme of ours is perfectly consistent with honour and honesty."

"Away with such idle suggestions. All scruples upon the subject should have been thoroughly canvassed before the idea was suggested to me.

Now, half my future bride's fortune is mortgaged for the payment of my debts—in idea at least, which is to me the same thing as though it were done in reality—have her I must, therefore, by some means or other. And, believe me, I intend to make her a most excellent husband. She shall have one thousand pounds a year entirely at her own disposal; and with that I shall leave her to follow her own inventions, while I, with the rest of her fortune, follow mine. One only thing disturbs me, and that is, a dread lest the plot should not succeed."

"And I only dread lest it should succeed—of which, indeed, I entertain very little doubt, since it will be no small recommendation to the lady that you pass for the son of Sir Francis Stanhope, whose elegant manners and amiable disposition are the subject of universal admiration. Indeed, he is such a prodigy, that to know and to be charmed with him are synonimous terms."

"The *pretended*, not the *real* Mr. Stanhope, I suppose you mean?"

"Certainly.—For, as I have often heard you say, Harry, you have such insinuating manners, and so fine an address, that 'tis impossible for any girl to listen to you with indifference."

"Confound your sneers!—I own indeed I did once think that I might have any woman to whom I would condescend to offer my hand; but experience has fatally convinced me of my error, refusal has followed refusal, till"—

"At length, after having repeatedly boasted that you would have beauty and fortune too, you are obliged to forego the former, and be content only with the latter."

"Too true. Indeed, so desperate is now my situation, that I would even marry the devil's daughter for money, aye, and consent too to live with the old folks."[6]

Our conversation was here interrupted by the return of Arthur, who brought a very gracious answer from Olivia, expressing great pleasure in the idea of seeing us, and hoping that we would pass some days at Campbell-House.

"Oh bravo!" exclaimed Harry—"some days!—In some days, I trust, I shall have made such a progress in gaining her affections, that she will never part with me more!"

"And so," said Arthur, fixing his eyes upon his master, sticking his hands by his sides, and lolling very coolly against the window, "that pretty creature I have just now seen is to be my mistress."

"You did get a sight of the heiress, then?" said I.

"I fancy I was there or thereabouts," he replied. "You know I'm not apt to use much ceremony, so finding the house-door open I marched in, and proceeded onwards till I came to the servants' hall, where the gentlemen and ladies of the lower regions were all assembled at breakfast. Never saw such a damned set of quizzes in my life—such liveries—wouldn't have put one of 'em upon my back on any consideration—no, damn me if I would."

"Pshaw, curse the servants," said Egerton, "we don't want to hear about them."

"With submission, my dear master, I think you need not have cursed the servants, neither; you'd have made noise enough if they had cursed you."

"Have done with your impertinence, puppy, and go on."

"Aye to be sure, servants must always be puppies, or dogs, or scoundrels, or whatever their masters please to call 'em."

"Never mind, never mind, Arthur," said I; "you know these are only words of course. So the servants were all assembled at breakfast?"

"Just so, Sir. Well, I gives your note to one of the footmen to carry to his mistress, and then down I sits me by the window. 'A sweet place this,' says I. 'If the owner be as beautiful as her house and gardens, she must be almost an angel.'—'She is almost an angel,' answered one of the fellows, not over and above politely, and as if he thought I was quizzing a bit or so—'She is almost an angel, and so you'd think too, if you knew her as well as we do.' I was forced to look out at the window, for fear he should see me laugh; when I beheld in the garden—mercy on me! I shall never forget her!—a little ugly, black-faced thing, with eye-brows in a strait line from one side of her face to the other. 'Damn it, brother,' says I, to a man that stood by me, 'you've a devilish ugly Abigail there to flirt with. By God, if I were in your place I would'nt stay in the house another moment, unless my mistress would get something better than she.'—I was going on, but happening to turn round, I saw the fellow lighting up his rushlights, as if he meant to set me and the whole house too on fire.—'That the maid!' said he, 'why that's my mistress herself, God bless her!—and if I hear any more of your impertinence, Sir, I can tell you I shall shew you the way out of the door a little faster than you came in.'"

Egerton, not less incensed than the man whose indignation Arthur had been so emphatically describing, now flourished his whip in the air, which had inevitably descended on the back and shoulders of the unfortunate valet, had he not dexterously escaped by a sudden spring to the other side of the room, exclaiming,

"Patience! patience! my dear master!—I own I was guilty of a sort of a *lapsus linguæ*,* but you shall hear how well I got upon my legs again. Instantly whipping out my glass, I gave a good stare through it; 'I beg pardon,' said I, 'a thousand times. I am so extremely short-sighted; but now I look again, I see she is not so very ugly.' I should have added more apology, but at that moment such a lovely little rosy-cheeked blue-eyed lady of the bedchamber entered, that she completely diverted my attention from every thing but herself. I swear my mouth watered plaguily for a kiss. Take care, my dear master, that you don't fall in love with the maid, instead of the mistress."

---

*   A slip of the tongue.

"I am not much afraid of that, for as 'tis not the lady's eyes, but her land, by which I am attracted, nothing but superior charms of the same kind could lead me astray, and those, I presume are not to be found in the maid. For the lady herself, I only take her, like the buildings, as an incumbrance to which I must submit, or forego the land."

Orlando, will you not readily suppose that I was here visited by a qualm which had well nigh made me give up the whole business. Yet I looked at Harry, when the dread of oversetting his mind by opposition, after having myself been inadvertently the means of embarking him in the scheme, suppressed all other considerations, and I determined to proceed, in the full conviction that I had now involved myself too far to retract. In this I was the more confirmed when, Egerton's watchful eye having perceived my momentary abstraction, he said, with a suspicious eagerness, "Lionel, I absolutely prohibit all hesitation. From this moment I am thee, and thou art me, or both are nothing."

Ah! too well he knew his power. We dressed, and repaired to Campbell-House; but what passed at our introduction must be reserved for another opportunity. At present, adieu! and believe me,

Faithfully yours,

LIONEL STANHOPE.

LETTER V.

LIONEL STANHOPE
TO
ORLANDO ST. JOHN.

Campbell-House, August 11.

Be this hour of leisure, Orlando, devoted to the continuation of my narrative, after premising a few words on the house and its environs.

The ancient possession of a very ancient family, all the characteristic features of its antiquity are still retained in the mansion itself, though without doors the reins have been somewhat given to the modern propensity for improvement. Nature, who, according to the taste of the æra when the grounds were laid out, was then entirely banished, has been in a considerable degree restored; and, in truth, her complete restoration is the great improvement wanted in the place. But though much has been done, much still remains undone. The little parterre, surrounded by the diminutive gravel walk, scarcely exceeding a foot in breath, the allotted residence of some god or hero, exists no more; yet the god, or hero, obstinately retains his situation, notwithstanding the barriers which guarded his dominions are thrown down. Thus, half ancient, half modernized, the place may be called in the crysalis state, between the crawling solemnity of remote ages, and the fluttering foppery of the present day.

The entrance to the house is by a large old hall, and through this we were conducted into a saloon. As we entered it, we caught a transient glimpse of a beautiful female going out at an opposite door. The servant said his mistress was in the garden, and he would let her know that we were come. Thus left alone together, Egerton seized my arm:

"Heavens, Stanhope!" he exclaimed, "was ever such an angelic vision seen!—Oh God! should that lovely creature who just quitted the room prove my intended bride, and should it but appear that all the reports circulated to her disadvantage were only pretexts to keep unhallowed gazers at a distance, would there be a mortal on earth so blessed as myself?—And why may it not be so?"

"Because if you had been less attentive to your angelic vision, and more to what the servant said, you would have learned that the heiress is now in the garden. No, no, doubtless that was Arthur's pretty Abigail; he warned you to beware of her, and, it should seem, not without reason."

"Well, no matter, I care little about her face, as long as report has but been faithful with respect to her fortune. But I say, Lionel, grand alterations must be made before a man of my taste can think of passing even a week at the place. That magnanimous knight, with his beauteous Dulcinea,[7] who greet all that enter the hall with such sweet condescending smiles, and who, I suppose, are ancestors of the illustrious house of Campbell, must doubtless be tired of remaining so long in the same spot, so they shall be permitted to relax themselves by a walk up into the garret."

"Whither, I suppose, the present owner of the house, if she have any inclination, will have free leave to follow them?"

"And a proper supply of money to defray her travelling expences. The fine tapestry too, which decorates the walls of this saloon, and which probably is the handy-work of that very Dulcinea, shall be of the party. That great masculine overgrown Fame, who blows her trumpet in the faces of all that approach the mansion, shall take herself to some distant region, to sound forth the elegant reformations carrying on at Campbell-House. Neptune and his tritons shall return to the waves whence they came.[8] Fair Venus shall retire to her own Idalian groves[9]—those hideous old-fashioned liveries"—

"But suppose, after all, Harry," said I, tapping him on the shoulder, "the heiress should reject your suit?"

"Reject *my* suit?—the suit of a man with such a person, such an address?—oh that's very likely."

"True,—experience has proved them perfectly irresistible."

"Confound your sarcastic tongue. But if they have not proved so irresistible as I once thought them, you must at least confess that I am never at a loss for words. Then, if I only admire the taste displayed in her house and grounds, and pay some well turned compliments to her beauty, since all persons are most gratified at being complimented upon qualities which they are conscious they do not possess, the game's my own. But, by God, she comes! behold her at this moment ascending the steps to this saloon!

Heaven and earth, Stanhope, what do I behold!—shield me, ye pitying powers, from so horrid a spectacle!—I am confounded!—struck dumb!"

And struck dumb no less was I. The heiress entered.— Notwithstanding all that I had heard I started at beholding her; I had no idea of a female face so plain. We looked like fools, stammered, hesitated. Egerton made a low bow, but though *never at a loss for words*, could not utter a syllable. She soon, however, somewhat relieved our embarrassment, by assuring us with a politeness, which I felt but too conscious was wholly undeserved on our part, that she was particularly gratified by our visit, and happy in being at last introduced to the son and nephew of a man whom she had so long known, and whom she so highly respected.

Somewhat encouraged by the ease and frankness of her manner, I was on the point of making my grateful acknowledgments for her hospitality, when she spoiled all again, by enquiring which of us she was to address as Mr. Egerton, and which as Mr. Stanhope. "Though" she added, turning to me, "I think that question almost superfluous, since your strong resemblance, Sir, to the worthy Sir Francis, speaks you at once his son."

I felt the blood instantly rush into my face, and was on the point of confirming her conjecture, when Egerton, alarmed, replied without blush or hesitation: "Pardon me, Madam, 'tis not surprising that such an inference should be drawn; yet, however natural it may appear, in this instance it is erroneous, since 'tis I who have the honour of being heir to Sir Francis Stanhope."

Now, I thought, we are embarked indeed, and nothing remains but to put the best face possible upon the matter. I therefore began making my acknowledgments, though very awkwardly, for the obliging reception given us; but Egerton, not satisfied with my performance, took upon himself to be spokesman, and with a kind apology for my awkwardness, observed that I was always shy before strangers, "and no wonder," he added, "that my cousin should at the present moment be more particularly embarrassed, by reflecting that he is in the company of a lady so highly and so justly celebrated as Miss Campbell."

I was really astonished at his assurance, and could not forbear earnestly surveying Olivia, to see what effect it produced upon her. She fixed her eyes upon him with a scrutinising attention, which, methought, seemed to say: "Can this really be the son of Sir Francis Stanhope? What a contrast are his manners to those of his father! If the latter may sometimes appear to want a higher degree of polish, yet how far preferable is his blunt unvarnished honesty, to this florid fulsome strain of compliment."

Whether such were in truth her sentiments, I will not pretend positively to determine; I only know, that they certainly were mine, and we are always very ready to suppose, that what we think ourselves must be the opinion of others. After duly surveying Egerton, she turned to me and said, "I am very sorry, Sir, that any one should find cause of embarrassment in my house; my wish and endeavour is to establish perfect ease among my guests. Of this I hope you will soon be convinced, and no longer experience sensations no less painful to me than to yourself."

Hitherto, I must confess, nothing had passed that bespake the absolute fool. I paused a few moments, expecting Egerton to pursue the conversation; but as he was silently surveying his future domains, and seemed totally absorbed for a while in the contemplation of them, I found I must take that upon myself, and I began to make various observations upon the country in general, to which I said I was till now a perfect stranger, and which appeared to me extremely beautiful. Then I proceeded to expatiate particularly on the environs of Campbell-House, and paid them some compliments, of which, indeed, I think them highly deserving. Olivia seemed pleased, and said, that when her plans were completed, she hoped the grounds would be pretty; "at present," she added, "I cannot say much in their behalf."

"How can you be so unjust, Madam," said Egerton awakened from his reverie, "to the sweetest spot that art and nature ever combined to form upon this habitable globe. Not the far-famed groves of the Hesperides,[10] not the little paradisaic island of the semi goddess Calypso,[11] no nor even the gardens of Elysium[12] themselves, could display a finer *coup-d'œil** than I behold at this moment, inferior in beauty only to its owner."

"You mortify me, Mr. Stanhope," she replied. "I had flattered myself that this spot was capable of great improvement, but you teach me in a few words the vanity of such an idea, by assuring me, that the place itself is less beautiful than its owner."

A reproof so severe, for a few moments abashed even Egerton; for myself, never did I feel so little in my own eyes, while our tormentor looked with a triumphant sneer, first at the one, then at the other. But Egerton's repulse was only momentary, and though a blush did overspread his cheek, he would not alter his tone.

"This humility," he said, "does but place exalted merit in a more amiable point of view. Perhaps I deserved some reproof, since through an involuntary impulse of admiration, I fear I had used expressions bordering upon extravagance. But who can be acquainted with the widely-extended circuit over which the sun of Miss Campbell's bounty sheds its genial beams, and not be ready, like the Persians, to worship what confers such blessings upon mankind."

"Mr. Stanhope, this strain of flattery may suit courts, but in the country we are vulgar enough to prefer the language of the heart."

"Which I truly use. Though till this moment not personally known to you, Madam, yet who can be a stranger to Miss Campbell's character? Her virtues, her accomplishments, her charity, her generosity, are the subjects of universal panegyric; they are known and admired in the remotest provinces of the kingdom; the trump of Fame—"

"Blew them in our faces as we approached the mansion," I whispered [to] Harry, whose harangue was suddenly interrupted by the entrance of

---

*   A view or prospect. Literally "a stroke of the eye."

Miss Belgrave, which gave Olivia an opportunity of turning away from us; and she did so, not without an appearance of extreme indignation, while I felt so chagrined, so mortified, that I could gladly have run away from myself.

Miss Belgrave started as she entered, and her face was in a moment suffused with the deepest scarlet, as if altogether abashed at the sight of two strangers. Timidity like this, if it increase not the lustre of beauty, at least gives it additional interest; but Harriot Belgrave wants not such adventitious aid to make an indelible impression upon every beholder, for she is loveliness personified. Olivia introduced us to her, of course calling me Mr. Egerton, and Harry Mr. Stanhope. Again the angelic creature started, and looked alternately at the one and the other, as if petrified with astonishment, but still she spake not. All this was to me utterly incomprehensible, and so tremblingly alive am I to the least idea of detection, that my fancy immediately tortured me with the apprehension of our being known to her, and that she was about to publish the imposture.

But this terror was momentary, and her subsequent behaviour convinced me that excess of timidity was the cause of all. Beauty in cities and courts inspires confidence, and challenges admiration; beauty in seclusion only increases diffidence, and shrinks abashed within itself, unable to face the attention it excites.

In a few minutes Mr. Beauchamp was added to the company, when Olivia proposed a walk, a proposal which I was very glad to embrace, since I hoped to breathe more freely in the open air; or, to speak more plainly, I felt so thoroughly embarrassed, that any change seemed preferable to remaining in the same situation another moment.

Harry here giving the reins to his imagination, began to indulge in even bolder flights of rhapsody and hyperbole than before. "Well," thought I, "thou certainly hast a mind, my good cousin, to be kicked out of the house before thou hast been in it two full hours." But, to my utter astonishment, the more his extravagance encreased, the less offensive did it appear to his fair auditor; nay, before the walk was at an end, she evidently listened with as much pleasure as he harangued; so that at last I could not forbear assenting to his favourite axiom, that there is no flattery too gross for a woman, provided a man understands the art of administering it properly.

Egerton and Olivia being thus engrossed with each other, I was compelled to attach myself to Mr. Beauchamp and Harriot Belgrave, both of whom I found conversible and agreeable, and I was pleased to find that the excessive timidity of the latter gradually subsided.

So much, Orlando, for my second dispatch from Campbell-House. 'Tis a heavy task which you have imposed on
    Yours very sincerely,

LIONEL STANHOPE.

LIONEL STANHOPE
TO
ORLANDO ST. JOHN.

Campbell-House, August 12.

Orlando, what a busy fool have I been! How I could curse the ill-fated planet that ruled my destiny when I planned our present adventure! In what a labyrinth of perplexities have I involved myself, from which I see no possibility of being extricated with credit, while, instead of alleviating, I have only increased poor Harry's sufferings.

An unfortunate idea has taken possession of his soul, that Harriot Belgrave is the living image of his long-lost Emily, and this sometimes tortures him almost to madness. Whether or not there be any foundation for the idea, I who never saw Emily, cannot judge; but I endeavour to persuade him, that the resemblance is the mere creature of his own imagination, like many others which he has at various times discovered. Alas! I urge this in vain!—All others he allows to have been ideal;* but this, this alone is real, nor can he live without her. Yet in a moment after he bursts into a rhapsody about Olivia and her fortune, dwelling wildly on the transports he shall experience when the latter is fully and absolutely in his possession.

Yesterday, when Olivia and Harriot quitted the room after dinner, I could not forbear making some passionate remarks on Harriot's beauty, which, I said, far exceeded any thing I had ever seen: Beauchamp immediately replied, "She is, indeed, the most lovely of women; and what enhances the value of her personal charms immeasureably is, that her manners and disposition may be pronounced, without exaggeration, as amiable as her face and form are enchanting. Two such hearts as hers and Miss Campbell's rarely meet."

"And if Miss Campbell be not absolutely her equal in personal attractions," said Egerton, "yet I must say that I think her plainness has been grossly exaggerated; for though she cannot be called strictly handsome, yet in the *toût-ensemble* of her countenance there is something extremely pleasing."

Beauchamp turned towards him hastily—he seemed to think that this could only be spoken in irony, and was disposed to be very angry; but as no appearance of sarcasm was to be perceived either in Harry's countenance or manner, the reproof quivering on Beauchamp's tongue was suppressed, and he said calmly,

"Can such be your real sentiments, Sir?—Yet wherefore not?—Tastes are various; nor can any thing be more absurd than for one person to pretend to judge for another in these matters."

---

*   Imaginary.

This observation was the prologue to a very long and elaborate discussion between Messieurs Egerton and Beauchamp, upon taste and opinion, their endless varieties and changeful forms, in which much able argument was produced on both sides, illustrated by a profusion of beautiful similies and appropriate metaphors. For all this at least I gave them credit; but I cannot say that I attended to them very closely, since my mind was so entirely occupied by the lovely object who had occasioned the discussion, by the angelic Harriot herself, that I could not attend to any thing else. Her appearance in the garden soon after, with Olivia, drew my person, as well as my attention, away from the rhetoricians; nor did they remain long together after I quitted them, but soon also joined the ladies.

Egerton immediately took his post by the heiress's side, and soon began talking in his usual strain. He ingeniously introduced several oblique hints that the place was too large for one solitary inhabitant, and that the fair owner was very cruel to his sex, in not selecting some worthy object to share with her the cares of managing so large a fortune; interspersing many sapient reflections on the forlorn and disagreeable situation of single unprotected females, particularly when they happened to be encumbered with a large property.

Olivia listened attentively, but replied not either to his hints or remonstrances. She sometimes smiled, but whether *at* or *with* her swain I was at a loss to determine. He, however, seemed well content with her reception of his advances, since, as we were left together for a few minutes between the conclusion of our walk and the entrance of tea,

"Don't you think Li.", he said, "that I go on well?—I play my part admirably, you must allow. If I can but keep up the farce for a week, I shall by that time be absolute master of all this fair Venus's rich domains. Then adieu to the bowers of love, and away to the delights of some elegant watering place."

"So then fortune has now the ascendancy?—'Tis not many hours since the lovely Harriot Belgrave was all in all—she was the sole object of your wishes—you would sigh out your soul at her feet; and, flying with her to some sequestered spot, sacred alone to love and soft desire, there, far from the unhallowed eyes of less enamoured mortals, live in transports that gods themselves might envy."

"Oh Stanhope! Stanhope! forbear!" he cried. "What a picture hast thou drawn!—how transporting, could it be realized!—how agonizing, since it can only exist in idea!—Why, why would you conjure up such a phantom to torment me?—Away with it!—I cannot pursue it—you know I cannot—for how then are the mouths of hundreds of gaping creditors to be stopped?—No; though I almost loath the sight of such a piece of deformity as Olivia, yet I must and will have her!"

"Loath her, Harry?—How can that be, when you know that, though not strictly handsome, yet the *toût-ensemble* of her countenance is altogether pleasing."

"Curse your sneers!—Oh fortune! fortune! thou art blind indeed, to shower thy blessings in such profusion on so uncouth a form, and leave in indigence one of the brightest gems that ever ornamented this lower world!"

"Upon my word that was a very fine flourish, but unfortunately thrown away here with nobody to listen to it. Treasure it up, however,—it will do admirably for Olivia, since a gem may have as rough and uncouth an outside as she has, yet 'tis a gem still, and there is no occasion to specify whether you mean the simile before, or after, it has passed through the hands of the beautifier."

"No more of this ill-timed raillery, I intreat, Lionel.—'Tis barbarous thus to goad a heart already tortured like mine, struggling between the intolerable pressure of bitter self-incurred necessity, and a passion which I could almost call a revival of what has cost me so many hours of misery. Oh God!—Oh God!—am I never again to know repose?"

He stamped with his foot upon the ground; he struck his hands upon his forehead; his whole frame trembled; he seemed overpowered with the conflict. I was vexed with myself, for I found that the matter was more serious than I had apprehended. Still I thought it was better, if possible, to laugh it off; and I said,

"Come, come, Harry, consider not the matter so deeply. This is not a time to give way to gloom and despondency. That long face will never do for a lover. Cheer up, then, and be not so like an April day, one moment all gloom, the next all sunshine."

"Stanhope," he replied solemnly and emphatically, "if my countenance and manner do sometimes wear the appearance of thoughtless levity, believe me they form an unfaithful index to a heart constantly racked with tormenting reflections. I flew to dissipation to chace from my bosom a poison that corroded it; but in extirpating that, I have planted a thorn which will rankle there for ever. What will be the end of all, the powers above only know—unless I succeed in my present attempt, there is but one step left, and that"—

* * * * *

The entrance of Beauchamp stopped him short, but I had heard enough to fill me with the most serious and dreadful apprehensions. There is but one step left if he fail of obtaining Olivia!—Oh! St. John, can we doubt what was then passing in his mind?

And yet, how was I astonished when, notwithstanding the agitation in which I had just beheld him—notwithstanding the fatal ideas of self-destruction over which his soul was evidently brooding, yet the moment that Beauchamp joined us he became perfectly calm and composed, and entered into conversation with him first, and afterwards with the ladies, with as much ease and vivacity as if his gaiety had never received a moment's interruption.

What wonderful self-command!—Yet I am by no means satisfied about him. The dark hints he threw out dwell upon my mind; and while I meditate only upon them, I seem justified to myself in suffering our project to proceed, as a last desperate effort to heal the wounds in his fortune, and, through them, those in his mind. At other times, when not wholly engrossed by this subject, I become a prey to the bitterest pangs of self-reproach; and, taking a retrospect of my situation, I can scarcely persuade myself that I am the same Lionel Stanhope who once piqued himself so highly upon his honour and integrity, and made it his pride and boast that, though the world might justly charge him with innumerable follies, he never could be accused of an act of deliberate baseness.

On one thing, however, I am firmly resolved; Olivia shall not be *deceived* into an union with Egerton. She seems pleased with his attentions, and I suspect already considers him with some degree of partiality. I will not therefore interpose immediately, but suffer the impression to gain strength for a few days, till I see reason to hope that attachment to the man may plead powerfully against indignation at the imposture. Then shall she know all; and if, after that, she yield to his suit, it will be done with her eyes open, while I shall have gone to the utmost length that conscience will permit for the service of my friend.

And oh that he may ultimately prove successful! for I do from my soul believe it might be a means of restoring him to the height from which he has fallen. 'Tis true that hitherto he has appeared to have no other idea but of squandering away Olivia's fortune, by the like course of dissipation that exhausted his own. Still I think, if freed from the pressure of his present incumbrances, that there are latent principles of goodness in his heart which might at length re-conduct him into the paths of honour and happiness. Then would I endeavour to persuade myself that the end obtained would sanctify the means used—though this, I own, is wretched morality, and will not bear to be dwelt upon.

But in the accomplishment of this very desirable alteration, much after all, must depend upon his wife, and what Olivia's real character is, I am at a loss to determine. In the world it is so various, that from common report nothing satisfactory can be collected. If I may believe my father, her equal is scarcely to be found on earth for true benevolence, strength of understanding, and cultivation of mind, all which is strongly corroborated by Beauchamp. Both these ought to be good judges; yet some things which have fallen under my observation lead me to doubt very much whether the superiority ascribed to her understanding be altogether just, or whether it may not principally originate in the undoubted superiority of her fortune. Of this I shall be a better judge upon a longer acquaintance. For the present, adieu! and believe me,

Your faithfully affectionate

LIONEL STANHOPE.

JEREMIAH SMITH

TO

SIR FRANCIS STANHOPE.

Scarborough, August 12.

Honoured Sir, my ever dear Master,

This is with my duty to you, and I hope your honour will not please to be offended with me for sending these few lines, hoping they will meet you and my lady in good health, as, thank God, I am at this present time of writing; and so I hope is my young master, but he is not here at present, God bless him.

Sir, I hope your honour will not be angry, but I don't like the goings on of Master Lionel at all, and I thought it was better to let your honour know on it, being that the longer it goes on the worser it will be. To be sure, your honour, there had been a great deal of writing between Master Lionel and his cousin, Harry Egerton, before he and Muster Sin-John set off together from your honour's at Kilverton, for to go to Scarborough; which, to be sure, I did not much like it, because your honour knows that your honour's nephew, Muster Harry Egerton, is but a slippery kind of a chap, and not fit company for my young master. I beg your honour's pardon for speaking so disrespectfully of your honour's nephew, but what's true is true; and your honour were always so kind for to like that all your sarvents should speak truth, which to be sure it was always a great pleasure to me, being that I hates to tell a lie, because, your honour, its my thought that a lie's a lie, let who's will tell it, and they as will lie about trifles, its odds if they don't do worser things some day or another.

And to be sure, your honour, I were grieved enough about Master Lionel, for when we were got to Doncaster he were all for shuffling me off, and it almost broke my poor old heart for to think that he should ever want to get rid of honest Jerry, as his goodness pleases to call me. For your honour knows that I and my poor wife that's dead and gone, God rest her soul! knew Master Lionel from the first moment as he was born; and we used to dandle him upon our knees, and loved him all to one as thos he had been our own child, being that your honour knows it niver pleased God that we should have none of our own. And Master Lionel always seemed to fare so fond of us like; and your honour knows that your honour would have set us up in one of your honour's farms, but that we did'nt chuse, being that I didn't like for to think of leaving Master Lionel, and so, bless his heart, he let me be his sarvent still; and it was always good Jerry do this, and dear Jerry do that, so kind and so effectionate like. And then he was always so careful about me when we was out a journeying together, and so fearful like that I should get tired with riding, being that I was growing into years; and your honour won't please for to wonder that I were almost broken-hearted for to think that he should send me on to Scarborough with Muster Sin-John, while he stayed behind at Doncaster to wait for that slippery chap, Harry Egerton.

And moreover too, your honour, Master Lionel seemed to fare as how he pretended he did not know as he should go at all to see Madam Olivia Campbell; and, your honour, it make me quite onket* for to think that he should pretend so, for to be sure, your honour, I know for sartin as he is now at Campbell-House, and therefore, to be sure, it were but a kind of a lie like for to pretend that he shouldn't go there. And to be sure I niver could have thought that Master Lionel would have done no such a thing, but its my thought that 'tis all Harry Egerton that's to be thanked for it; for, your honour, he's now along with young master at Madam's; and what is worsest of all is, that my young master, God love him, have changed names with Harry Egerton, that he may court Madam Olivia as your honour's son, and make a hand of her fortin like as he did of his own.

And this, your honour, I knows to be every word true, being that to-day, and I hope your honour will forgive me, when Muster Sin-John was out after a young lady that its my belief he goes a courting to, I happened to go into his room, and there I sees a letter upon the table, which I knowed it at once to be my young master's writing, because your honour knows that I can tell his writing equel as thos it were my own, being as I have knowed him from the first moment as iver he took a pen into his dear little hand. So I takes up the letter and kisses it; and to be sure I had such a longing desire to know how Master Lionel did, and how he were a going on, that I did peep into the letter, God forgive me, which I own your honour it were not right, and there I seed how that Harry Egerton hoped to be married to young madam very soon; so I thought it best to let your honour know all about it, hoping your honour will forgive me for peeping into the letter: which is all at present, and I pray God bless your honour, and my lady, and Master Lionel, who am your honour's

Faithful sarvent at command,

JEREMIAH SMITH.

---

*   Probably *unked* meaning "depressed" (*OED*).

LETTER VIII.

ORLANDO ST. JOHN
TO
LIONEL STANHOPE.

Scarborough, August 13.

En verité, my dear Stanhope, thy last communication favoured more of the sermon than the epistle: and I did give one, two, three, monstrous yawns, before I came to the conclusion. But I think, thou suffering saint, that I can administer a drop of balsam to thy agitated bosom—*ecoutez donc*.

In the circle of beauty and fashion now inhaling sea breezes in this northern latitude, is a *petite enchanteresse* from our sister kingdom of Ireland, Charlotte O'Brien by name, who is well acquainted with Olivia, and a relation of the Belgraves. She is in the party of a Mr. and Mrs. Tichfield, once persons of fortune, but now a little in the case of *le pauvre Henri*. So great a sympathy indeed is there between them and our friend, that they too have cast their eyes on Olivia's fortune, as the means of repairing their own, and for this purpose have planned an union between her and their only son, an officer in the guards. Not that a hint of this intention has yet been given to the lady, but, to render more perfect the resemblance between them and Harry, they too think that 'tis only "*ask and ye shall have*,"[13] so apprehend nothing farther necessary than to arrange matters for the wedding according to their own convenience, and then announce their intentions to the future bride.

When I heard these particulars, I asked Charlotte whether she thought this plan was likely to succeed or not?—She laughed at the very idea of its success, as she says that Olivia is uncommonly acute, and immediately penetrates all such designs, when she never fails to expose the planners of them to deserved contempt. So much for thee and Harry, Lionel. However, thou canst not fail of receiving consolation from the conviction that Harry is encountered on equal ground, and that Olivia will herself take care not to be *deceived* into the match.

I asked Charlotte farther, whether she did not think there was a probability of the friendship between Olivia and Mr. Beauchamp ending in a match? for in truth, Lionel, from your account, I thought him very likely to be the Jason who would at last carry off the golden fleece.[14] She says this is a question which she really cannot answer. She thinks that a strong attachment exists between them, but that 'tis rather the affection of a brother and sister than any thing else; 'tis probable indeed that a nearer connection is not the idea of either, since if it had been, no reason appears why it should not have taken place long ago. From many circumstances that have fallen under her observation, she inclines strongly to the opinion that Olivia never will marry at all, or if she should, that the person who stands the best chance with her is a half-pay ensign, by name Ryder, whom misfortune first introduced to her notice, and who is now a frequent visitor at Campbell-House.

Mais que vois je?—By heaven 'tis Charlotte herself walking upon the beach!—Stanhope, I go!—I fly!—adieu.

Yours most sincerely,

ORLANDO ST. JOHN.

Poor Jerry has been sadly downcast ever since his separation from you, and is perpetually enquiring when you will be here. I am sometimes apprehensive lest, in his anxiety to see you, he should give me the slip, and fly with the speed of a lover into your arms. 'Tis a worthy old soul as ever lived.

LETTER IX.

SIR FRANCIS STANHOPE
TO
JEREMIAH SMITH.

Kilverton, August 14.

Honest Jerry,

I received thy letter, and thank thee kindly for thy attention to my poor boy, who I am sorry to hear has disgraced himself so sadly. But I am determined to bring him to shame, and have been planning in my head how it shall be managed.

In the mean time, Jerry, I would have thee come to me at Kilverton, because I shall like to have thee with me, the more to shame my dear boy, that he could desert his old friend. I therefore wish thee, upon receipt of this, to set out from Scarborough, and I will contrive so that Li. shall not know why I have sent for thee.

But I cannot say it was right in thee, Jerry, to peep into a letter. I do not commend thee for that, honest Jerry; nevertheless, as thou didst happen to be guilty of such a fault, it was very right of thee to let me know of my boy's tricks. Ah! I have often warned him against his cousin Egerton. Li., says I, my dear child, take care of *evil communications*, for they *corrupt good manners*. But he was always willing to excuse his cousin's faults, and I thought he had such an honest heart himself that he never would do much amiss; and I hope now, Jerry, that we shall soon reclaim him.

Thy mistress and I, thank God, are both very well for persons of our years, and all the family desire to be remembered to thee: Poor Thunder is much better, and I hope at last he will rally again, but Roan I am afraid will never come out of the stable any more.

I enclose this in another letter, which may be shewn to Mr. St. John, as a reason for thy setting off immediately.

  I am, honest Jerry,
    thy sincere friend,

FRANCIS STANHOPE.

LETTER X.

LIONEL STANHOPE
TO
ORLANDO ST. JOHN.

Campbell-House, August 16.

Orlando, you cannot surely have forgotten a very amusing evening, which some three or four years ago, Harry, and you, and I, passed together at Coachmakers' Hall, when my youthful bosom burning for distinction as an orator, urged me to make a essay of my rhetorical powers in that celebrated school.

The question for the evening was in substance, for I will not pretend to remember the exact words, "Whether there be any reason, either from experience, or upon speculation, to believe that the Creator employs evil spirits as agents to incite men to the commission of crimes, for the accomplishment of important purposes of his own?"

Much talent for argument was on this occasion displayed by many of the orators, to whom I listened with attention, and even sometimes with admiration. At length I rose myself, in reply to a speaker who had been strenuously supporting the agency of the infernal ministers, and in a speech of considerable length refuted all his arguments with true logical precision, proving, to my own entire satisfaction, and, as I did not doubt, equally to the satisfaction and conviction of my audience, from whom I received unbounded applause, that to suppose a deity employing evil spirits to lead mankind astray, or even to conceive that he permits their interposition, was supposing a God as diabolical as the prince of darkness himself, or even more so, and that the thing therefore was in its nature impossible.

But now, without investigating how far it may or may not be consistent with our ideas of perfect benevolence, for the Deity occasionally to send the little winged Mercuries of his Satanic majesty,[15] to incite us, poor worried mortals, to some little snug piece of mischief, I do positively pronounce that this is done. Yes, confident am I that one of these agents must have been concealed at the bottom of my ink-glass, and, perhaps, another have lain perdue* within the hollow of my pen, when I wrote to Harry proposing this accursed scheme, otherwise an idea so base, so infamous, could not have entered my head.

For, oh St. John! 'tis an accursed scheme indeed, and the farther I proceed in it, the more accursed does it appear. What unaccountable apathy must have possessed my soul, that in the many days which intervened

> Between the acting of this dreadful thing
> And the first motion,[16]

It should never have been visited by any sensations of remorse, that no doubts should ever have been awakened in my mind as to the rectitude of our plan, nor even a distant suggestion have obtruded itself upon me, that though I might by this means be released from importunities I had long found so harassing and irksome, I should raise up to myself disquietudes ten thousand times more corroding, and never to be banished again by any time or penitence.

Yet is my mind in one respect less harassed than when I wrote to you last, since my alarms on Harry's account are nearly removed. Harriot Belgrave is gone to spend some time with a friend about ten or twelve miles from Campbell-House; and seeing her no longer, Harry thinks of her no more, but devoted to his pursuit of the heiress, is too much transported with the idea of possessing her fortune, ever to experience a qualm respecting the means by which 'tis to be obtained.

But though in this point of view I find Harriot's absence a great relief to my anxieties, in another it but increases them. Her departure was sudden and mysterious, nor was a hint of her intention given, till the chariot† was at the door to carry her away. In vain do I seek a reason for a procedure so abrupt; none can I find. I am only lost in a maze of conjectures, and am ready to surmise a hundred disagreeable private reasons for it, because no satisfactory public one appears.

Indeed, the loss of her society alone is to me a source of deep regret, for, upon my soul, she has made a most powerful impression on my heart, as well as upon Harry's. There is a soft melancholy about her, which adds a peculiar interest to features approaching to perfection, and gives the most enchanting tone of expression to a countenance almost too interesting without it. I have no doubt that my talkative landlady at the Campbell Arms, was accurate, in representing her as the child of misfortune! Lovely creature! why must she be thus persecuted? Among our sex, my friend, how often, how generally, are our distresses, our mortifications, self-

---

*   Hidden.
†   A light four-wheeled carriage with only a back seat and a seat for the coach-man.

incurred! Yet woman, lovely woman, guiltless herself, is commonly the greater mark for the arrows of affliction.

But if I go on thus, I shall be reproached again with having occasioned you one, two, three, or more yawns. To indulge in this sermonizing vein, was not what I intended on taking up my pen; my purpose was to have devoted my letter to narrative alone, but these reflections crossed me, and would not be suppressed. Not that I lack matter for narrative, I am rather overpowered with a super-abundance of it. I must tell you of my own distresses, of Olivia's virtues, of Olivia's follies; on all and each of these subjects I could fill whole sheets. Such a compound of the opposite qualities alluded to as my hostess, never fell under my observation before. The nonsense she talks to Egerton is inconceivable, and whoever listens to it must suppose her the fool he wishes; yet read, and then pronounce her a fool, if you can.

Unable to sleep, I quitted my bed early this morning, and was tempted by the delicious freshness of the air to enjoy it in a solitary and contemplative walk. I bent my course to a gate in the garden, which I had observed the day before, and which seemed to lead into a wood so charming and romantic, that I longed to explore it. After I had pursued a meandering path for about half a mile, I came to a lawn, one side of which was occupied by two very neat Gothic cottages, with each a garden and conveniences for keeping pigs, poultry, and a cow. They looked like the true abodes of simple rustic happiness; yet as I stood contemplating them, sounds of discord and fierce altercation seemed to issue from the nearest. I listened, and immediately distinguished Olivia's voice soothing some person in distress, and Beauchamp's saying in an authoritative tone, "Will you leave the house quietly, or must I be compelled to use force? for here you remain not another instant."

"Force me out if you can," answered a savage brutal voice. "What does such a baggage mean by making all this racket; she is mine, and I will have her."

On this a scuffle ensued, which occasioned a violent shriek from a female in a tone of mingled anguish and terror. I hesitated for a moment whether to interfere or not, but I thought I had heard enough not only to justify, but to demand my offers of assistance. I accordingly entered the house, when I beheld at the farther end of the room, a young woman, with a loose gown thrown hastily on, sitting in a chair in extreme agitation, while Olivia and an elderly woman were endeavouring to soothe and compose her. Nearer the door, were Beauchamp and another man trying to force out of the house a stout savage-looking fellow, the author of all the disturbance, and who so ably resisted their efforts, that without my interposition they had probably been foiled. With my assistance, however, he was soon dragged out upon the lawn, swearing and storming at us all the time for a pack of cowardly rascals, to set three upon one. But on me his rage was more particularly vented, as he said he was confident he could have managed the other two, spite of all their blustering and swaggering.

A little boy from the neighbouring cottage was now dispatched into the village for the constable, to whom the culprit was consigned, with orders that he should appear before the Justice at twelve o'clock, that the law might take its proper course against him; and this settled, Beauchamp proposed our walking home together by a very pleasant circuit he would shew me, to which I gladly assented.

We had not proceeded far before he began: "Among the numberless instances of Miss Campbell's benevolence, which all who know her are daily witnessing, none in my opinion does greater honour to her head and heart, than the patronage she has extended to those two unfortunate women."

"There is something particular in their story, then?" said I.

"Not very particular," answered Beauchamp, "the circumstance that rendered them objects of compassion, is alas! far from single in its kind. Mrs. Morgan and Lucy are the widow and daughter of a poor curate in Wales, and the man from whose brutality we rescued them, is a booby* squire by name Owen, who lived in their neighbourhood, and who, like many other squires, holds it as a principal article of his creed, that women were created only as toys for the men to sport with, and cast from them at pleasure. Under a promise of marriage, which he never intended to fulfil, he seduced this poor girl. He kept her for about half a year, frequently amusing her with fixing a day for the completion of their union, but before its arrival constantly deferring the marriage upon some trifling pretext, till at length tired of her, he turned her out of doors ruined and pennyless.

"In this deplorable situation she sought shelter again under her father's roof, who received his lost child with open arms, but with a breaking heart. The frowns of fortune he had borne with patience and resignation, but his philosophy was not proof against the keener anguish of wounded honour. Not a smile had illumined his features, nor a ray of pleasure beamed on his heart, since the moment he heard of his Lucy's disgrace.

"To see her return a penitent, was a balsam that soothed, though it came too late to heal his sorrows. It could not snatch him from the path along which he was hastening to the tomb, but it removed some of the thorns that were goading him as he passed on. He lived just to know that his unhappy daughter was delivered of a still-born son, and then expired in prayers to heaven that her fault might be forgiven, and not prove an obstacle to her gaining an honest livelihood in future.

"Vain prayers! A father might forgive such an error,—it could not be forgiven by the world. Lucy, recovered from her confinement, first endeavoured to get into service, but her *virtuous* neighbours unanimously agreed that it would be an impeachment of their own characters to admit such a woman into their houses. She then attempted to take in nee-

---

*   "A dull, heavy, stupid fellow; a lubber" (Johnson).

dle-work and washing, but who would trust their property with her, since as she had been once unchaste, her honesty must of course be suspected? Her next idea was to keep a little school, but this was worse than all. If the *property* of her neighbours would not be safe in her hands, how could she expect that they would entrust their *children* to her care?

"Finding herself thus debarred from all hopes of supporting herself and her mother in her own country, she had recourse to some relations at a distance, and entreated their assistance to enable her to settle herself creditably elsewhere; but among them also she found too nice a sense of *virtue*, to concern themselves about one whom they regarded as a disgrace to her family.

"In this situation, driven almost to despair, and seeing herself nearly reduced to the dreadful alternative of starving or prostitution, her story accidentally became known to Miss Campbell. She instantly sent for both the mother and daughter, and has proved a ministering angel of comfort to them. She established them in the cottage we have just left; and, after some months' probation, when convinced that Lucy's error was the lapse of one unguarded moment, not the effect of depravity of heart, she made them mistresses of a little school, to which they have paid the most unremitted attention; and the children have improved rapidly under their hands.

"To some of the neighbours, the introduction of such a woman into the parish was at first matter of great offence, and nothing but her being under Miss Campbell's immediate protection would probably have restrained them from commencing a persecution against her, similar to that from which she had been rescued. But Lucy's exemplary conduct has at length disarmed the tongue of calumny itself: her error is forgotten, or remembered only by the inveterately censorious; and she lives respected and respectably."

"Oh! would to heaven," I exclaimed, "that this example might prove a lesson to others, and teach them, that forbearance shewn to a first transgression may be the means of saving many an unfortunate fellow-creature from farther misconduct, while severity can only drive them into lasting shame and misery. We call the great charitable when they give ten guineas towards a subscription for feeding the poor; but how infinitely greater benefactors would they be to society, by extending their protection in such instances to rescue the penitent from the contumely* of a harsh and mis-judging world. Would that this were more universally considered!— Many there are who want not the heart to practise such benevolence—'tis omitted more from the absence of reflection, than of inclination."

"While they would receive a rich reward," said Beauchamp, "in beholding, as Miss Campbell does, the countenance on which once sat deep anguish and despondency, now illumined by the smile of cheerful-

---

*   Scornful contempt.

ness and heartfelt gratitude—in hearing the voice, once attuned only to notes of penitence and lamentation, now carolling the wild and artless lays that spring from an easy and contented heart. One circumstance alone has ever occasioned any alloy to Lucy's happiness, and that is, the discovery of her retreat by Owen, who has made many attempts similar to that you saw this morning, to get her again into his power."

I was here about to enter on some farther enquiries relative to Olivia, with a view to gaining a more complete acquaintance with her character, but we were unfortunately joined by a farmer, who, wanting to discuss some parish affairs with Beauchamp, walked the rest of the way home with us. We found breakfast ready, and I sat down to it, inspired with sentiments of the warmest admiration of my hostess; but I retired from it with feelings almost of disgust, from the insufferable nonsense she talked to Egerton.

But more of this hereafter. 'Tis now almost twelve o'clock, the hour appointed for Owen to appear before the Justice, and my heart has a grievous conflict to sustain. Beauchamp told the constable that I, as well as himself, would attend as witnesses against the culprit. And what now am I to do?—Must I be sworn as Henry Egerton?—Impossible! What then remains but to confess our fraud?—Oh God, St. John! how little can a man calculate in what scenes of anguish and perplexity he may be involved, if he deviate but a hair's breadth from the strait path of rectitude. But Beauchamp calls. Adieu! and believe me

Your unalterably affectionate

LIONEL STANHOPE.

LETTER XI.

LIONEL STANHOPE
TO
ORLANDO ST. JOHN.

Campbell-House, August 16.
Eleven at Night.

My morning's detail, Orlando, left me setting off on my own trial rather than on that of Owen, since I do not believe he felt half the terror at appearing as a culprit at the bar of justice, that I did at appearing there only as a witness. I quitted my room, half resolved fairly and openly to confess all my guilt in confidence to Beauchamp, and consult with him what was best to be done, fully convinced, even on our short acquaintance, that a firm reliance might be placed upon his honour and liberality of mind.

But this design was frustrated, by finding that the man who had assisted in rescuing Lucy was also, as one of the witnesses, to be the companion of our walk, so that any confidential communication with Beauchamp was effectually precluded. Nothing then remained but to act according to the pressure of the moment; and I at length resolved, if driven to the last extremity, to plead conscientious scruples about taking an oath—thus, as is very frequently the case, concealing baseness by a lie. Yet, as I pursued my way, I felt no scruples of relieving my soul by cursing heartily, though only internally, my father, myself, Egerton, and the world at large. My father, for having importuned me so often to see Olivia, which was the original cause of all the mischief—myself, for not having had sufficient resolution to resist his importunities to the last—Egerton, for being base enough to adopt the plan my baseness had suggested—and the world at large, because we constantly do curse all the world when we are out of humour with ourselves.

The magistrate, at whose tribunal we now appeared, was Doctor Paul, rector of the parish of Maxtead, a very sleek and courteous member of the body ecclesiastic, who received us with abundance of compliments on the courage and conduct we had shewn in our encounter with Owen; and expatiated in most elaborate strains on the obligations we had conferred upon Lucy, in rescuing her so gallantly from her persecutor. He then proceeded to entertain us with a very long and eloquent harangue on his perfect impartiality in all his judicial proceedings; assuring us, that in his eyes, as in those of the holy Founder of our religion, the poor were of equal account with the rich—nay, if ever he was inclined to a bias either way, which he hoped and trusted was not the case, it was rather to favour the poorer than the richer party.

This exordium* concluded, he began to question Beauchamp about the case before him. But though he endeavoured to give his enquiries all possible appearance of seeking nothing but the truth, his principal aim evidently was to discover Olivia's wishes with respect to the culprit, that he might in no way act contrary to them. From Beauchamp's answers, however, nothing was to be collected but the simple facts; and thus the poor Doctor was left to act solely upon his own conjectures. These led him very naturally to conclude, not that Olivia was desirous of seeing impartial justice administered, but that, as she patronised Lucy Morgan, she must, at all events, wish Owen to be committed to gaol, be the assault proved upon him or not.

Yet that he might, if possible, inform himself better upon the subject, before he proceeded farther, when he found that nothing was to be gained from Beauchamp, he thought he would try what was to be done with me; so addressing me, he said, "And you, Mr. Stanhope, I understand were one of the principal actors in repelling this outrage?"

---

*   "A formal preface" (Johnson).

Orlando, you well know that I am not much addicted to blushing, yet in a moment my face became a perfect scarlet. He had called me Stanhope, and I was in that blessed predicament, that nothing could have startled me so much as being addressed by my own name. I hesitated, faultered, and at last, with some difficulty, stammered out, "Yes, Sir."

Beauchamp eyed me very earnestly; my confusion encreased tenfold. Doctor Paul addressed me again; "You were present during the whole scene?"

"Ye—Yes, Sir.—No, Sir, no,—not the whole."

"At what part, then?"

"At the be—the beginning—I mean not till towards the conclusion."

"Mr. Stanhope had no other concern in the affair," said Beauchamp, "than assisting Atwood and myself to force Owen out of the house."

"Then your evidence it should seem, Mr. Stanhope," rejoined the Doctor, "does not include any part of Owen's assault?"

Good heavens, thought I, what dæmon can possess them!—both call me Stanhope!—Am I then really detected? or can this be merely accident?—But Beauchamp soon relieved me by saying,—"Not Mr. Stanhope, if you please, Doctor, but Mr. Egerton."

"Mr. Egerton!"—returned the Doctor, in a tone of surprise,—"I beg his pardon; but indeed, as I had heard that Mr. Stanhope was at Campbell-House, I concluded this gentleman, from his extreme likeness to Sir Francis, to be that worthy Baronet's son."

"He is certainly very like Sir Francis," said Beauchamp; "but that is not surprising, since he is his own nephew."

"Then 'tis accounted for most naturally, to be sure," said the Doctor. "So then you cannot swear to the assault, Mr. Egerton?"

"No, Sir."

"I should think," said Beauchamp, "that there can be no occasion to take Mr. Egerton's deposition, since Robin Atwood's and mine will be sufficient for Owen's conviction, and speak to the main point much more effectually."

"As you please, Sir," answered the polite Doctor.

Had I been walking over hot ploughshares, and come off safe from the last, I could not have felt a greater release. I could almost have fallen down and worshipped Beauchamp as my guardian genius.

The cause now proceeded, a breach of the peace was proved against Owen, and as he was not in a situation to procure bail, he was of course committed to Doncaster gaol, to take his trial at the ensuing sessions. The several parties were then dismissed, and after sitting half an hour with the Doctor, we returned home, I heartily congratulating myself upon my deliverance.

Yet Beauchamp's conduct relative to this affair perplexes me beyond expression. He made a great point of my accompanying him to Doctor Paul's, as he said that my evidence might prove of considerable importance, yet he was himself the person afterwards to suggest that it was wholly immaterial. Besides, he watched me so narrowly the whole time I was there, that I am almost persuaded he had something more in his mind than I am able to fathom. Were it not for a ridiculous scene going forward here, from which I hope to derive infinite amusement, and besides that Egerton's amour seems in so prosperous a way, that it would be cruel now to raise any obstacles to it, I believe I should mount my horse early to-morrow morning, and ride away unknown to any one.

In my morning's detail I alluded to the nonsense that passed between Egerton and Olivia at breakfast. The conversation turning accidentally upon the days of chivalry, Olivia immediately burst into a rhapsody upon them, and lamented in terms exquisitely pathetic, that they were past before the time allotted for her residence on earth.

Harry instantly caught the hint, and poured forth the most passionate expressions of admiration at times so glorious, and of rapture at finding another person in the world who would concur in his sentiments with regard to them.

"And are you then an admirer of chivalry, Mr. Stanhope?" exclaimed the transported Olivia; "Oh, how you delight my soul! Yes, the days when that flourished were days indeed!—days in which it would have been some satisfaction to live!—But how, alas! is mankind degenerated. Not an action is now performed worthy to be recounted in the same breath with the exploits of an Orlando, or a Rogero, a Tancred, or a Palmerin![17]—Not a hero has for centuries past existed in the world, entitled to hold a candle to a Godfrey, a Charlemagne, or an Arthur![18] or to latch the shoe of a Rodomonte, a Rinaldo, or an Astolfo!"[19]

"Still less, Madam, has a female appeared worthy to be mentioned with a Bradamant, or a Marphisa, and Erminia, or a Clorinda[20]—unless indeed—but you know, Madam, the present company is always excepted."

"Alas, Mr. Stanhope, you flatter;—I feel but too sensibly how little I merit such a compliment. Supinely educated but to those frivolous occupations, which, have alone of late years been allowed to my sex, the thimble and the needle are the only weapons I have ever been permitted to brandish. My unaspiring fingers know not to gird on the polished sword, or adjust the plumed helmet; my nerveless arm is unaccustomed to poising the mighty spear, or hurling the well-aimed javelin. My trembling foot shrinks from the manly spur and well-suspended stirrup; and if I dare to mount the mettled* courser, I vault not, alas! with vigorous stride into the rich caparisons† that valour claims, to traverse shapeless mountains and trackless deserts, regardless of the howling tempest's fierce assail, encountering beasts, and still more savage monsters in the human form— but tamely seat myself in a tame side-saddle, canter my steed for an hour or two over the smooth-shorn lawn, or along the even gravel-road, and then return home dull and indolent as I went out, again to betake myself

---

*   [mettled] Spirited.
†   [caparisons] Decorative trappings for a horse.

to my paltry feminine employments. Thus must I crawl through life, at the end of which I shall not have performed one exploit worthy to hand down my name to far-removed posterity."

I was astonished, mortified too, yet could scarcely refrain from laughing at a rhapsody so nonsensical. At first I suspected that she was only turning Egerton into ridicule, yet she wore an air of such perfect seriousness, and seemed so absolutely entranced by her subject, and absorbed in admiration of the martial prowess of ancient heroes and heroines, that I was constrained at length to give up the idea of jest. Indeed I was the more confirmed in my belief of her seriousness, from observing Beauchamp shake his head very significantly, and with an air of deep concern, as if the master-string of her foibles was touched, and the world united could not prevent its vibrating.

Egerton proceeded, clasping his hands in extasy, "Oh, Madam, how you transport me! Never did I meet with one whose ideas upon this subject so perfectly corresponded with my own. Now do I indeed begin to hope, since the fair are again disposed to smile upon them, that we may see those glorious days revived when every man was brave, and every female chaste; when castles were built of gold, not of beggarly brick or stone; when not condemned to ceaseless drudgery for gaining our daily bread, the enchanter's wand at one stroke produced whate'er was requisite to satisfy our wants, our wishes—when"—

"Oh! Sir, no more! no more! but hasten with me to a beloved little closet in my library, the repository of the choicest collection of archives of these worthies, that the kingdom perhaps can boast. 'Tis, I assure you, in my estimation, by no means the least valuable part of my family inheritance." Then tendering him her hand, which he pressed respectfully, they retired together, while I repaired to my apartment and wrote my letter to you, nor saw I more of Egerton, till my return from the hall of justice.

Going then to his room, I found him stripped of his coat and waistcoat, with his shirt-collar unbuttoned, his breast laid bare, and his sleeves tucked up to the very top of his arms, surrounded by soap, water, brushes, and towels, scrubbing and scouring himself, as if, like the poor barber's brother, he had been sentenced to a daily purification of forty washings.[21]

"Why heyday, Harry," said I, "what's the matter now? Olivia has not been rolling you in the kennel, I hope?"

"The kennel—no, damn her—I don't think a roll in the kennel would have made me half so filthy!—Curse chivalry, say I!—I don't believe the closet had been opened these twenty years, though she made such a sputter about her fondness for her damned knights-errant. Four whole hours did she keep me rummaging over heroes and princesses smothered with dust and cobwebs, the spiders all the time running about as if frightened at such intruders, after being suffered to live so long unmolested. 'And now, Mr. Stanhope, do reach down that Palmerin[22]—bless the dear fellow!—and now read me a page or two of that glorious Cassandra[23]—oh, and that beloved Amadis[24]—kiss the dear creature for my sake.'—

"Confound 'em all I say!—and yet I'll be shot if her dusty Amadis is not as good kissing as herself." And then again he fell to rubbing and scrubbing, as if he would have rubbed his very skin off, while I stood by laughing heartily.

"Curse your mirth," said he, "I don't see any thing so very laughable in all this; you would not have thought it such an excellent joke had you been in my place." Then ringing the bell violently for Arthur, "What can the blockhead be after," he said, "I've rung for him a dozen times already, I believe."

This time, however, the ringing was not without effect, for the valet soon made his appearance.

"And what was the reason you rascal," said Egerton, "that you were so long in coming, and gave me the trouble of ringing so often?"

"I humbly beg your honour's pardon," said he, admiring his legs all the time, "but I was lounging away an hour or two in looking over this venerable mansion, for, upon my soul, 'tis a devilish hard matter to know how to kill one's time here. Never saw such a parcel of countrified boobies as the servants. I swear 'tis quite a bore to be among 'em. Yesterday morning, being very gapish* and yawnish, and not knowing what to do with myself, I proposed a little sixpenny vingt-un in the servants' hall, and, would you believe it, the fools set up their eyes and stared, and did'nt know what I meant. So I explained, that 'twas a game at cards which I could teach 'em in five minutes, and then they all drew up their heads, and screwed up their mouths, and Lord bless 'em, they never played at cards in a morning, they'd play at *Put*† with me in the evening for a penny a game, if that would be agreeable. Curse me if it was not as much as I could do to forbear laughing in their faces."

"Confound you, Sirrah; be a little more guarded in your behaviour, or all my schemes will be blasted by you, you dog." Then turning to me, "We are to have a grand serenading to-night, Lionel," said he. "A pretty broad hint was given me this morning, that this was a piece of knighterrantry by no means to be dispensed with."

"Egad, a good thought," said Arthur, "and faith I'll avail myself of it to try and appease the wrath of my pretty Abigail."

"How," said I, "have Mrs. Jenny and you then quarrelled?"

"Tiffed a little bit, to be sure," said he, "and I'll tell you all how and about it. You must know I could not bear to see such a tight‡ lass, with whom one really should not be ashamed of being seen walking in the Park, were she but well-dressed, go such an old-fashioned figure. So I advised her to dress in a more dashing style, and particularly not to wear

---

*   To gape is "To open the mouth wide to yawn" (Johnson).

†   Also *Putt*. A game of cards for two to four players in which three cards are dealt to each player.

‡   Well-made, shapely (*OED*).

vulgar cotton stockings, for her ancles would look as neat again in silk ones, and I assured her there was'n't a lady's maid of my acquaintance but what dressed as well as her mistress. So forsooth she took huff, called me an impertinent puppy, and bid me mind my own business, and not be so free of making remarks upon other people; and then, when I told her I was only advising her for her own good, what does she do but hits me a swinging box on the ear that made reel again, 'and take that,' said she, 'that's for your good, and I hope 'twill teach you to keep your impertinent tongue within your teeth another time.' But I'm determined not to keep my tongue between my teeth, but to have at her again, and try if I can't bring her at last to hear reason."

"Why should you be so very anxious about this matter?" said I.

"Lord Sir," said he, "why now, if you had any thoughts of courting a lady, should'n't you wish, for your own credit, to make her look a little like other people?—And, to confess the truth, I believe I shall make up to Mrs. Jenny, for they tell me she's worth money, and I can't say but that Arthur is almost as much in want of a fortune as his master."

"Hold your impertinence, scoundrel," cried Egerton. "And for you, Mr. Lionel," said he, turning to me, "I desire you to walk out of the room. You are always encouraging that puppy to make himself one of the company, which I by no means chuse he should be."

I felt the justice of the reproof, and in my heart condemned myself for encouraging such impertinence, merely for the sake of a momentary amusement. I therefore obeyed Harry's commands, and retired. But as I thought the serenade promised the highest gratification to all who, like myself, have an extreme relish for the ridiculous, I urged Harry to permit my accompanying him on the occasion. To this he would by no means consent, as he said he was certain I should prove a Marplot;[25] but as I am very unwilling to relinquish so rich a source of entertainment, I have resolved to follow him at a distance, and am now only waiting till I hear him set out upon his expedition.

And, to fill up the remaining time till then, let me introduce to your acquaintance a lady, for the mention of whom I have not yet found a vacant corner in a letter. The same carriage that bore away from us the lovely Harriot, brought back in it an object not quite of equal loveliness, an old maid, by name Harrison, a distant relation of Olivia's, with a good fortune, and a very pretty villa on the banks of the Thames.

Orlando, thou hast been at Cambridge as well as myself; thou hast seen a painted window in Trinity College Library, the principal figure in which is our gracious Sovereign, to whom the artist has given a complexion of the deepest carmine, or, perhaps, rather of the tint of raw fresh-killed beef. Very similar to this is now the complexion of Mrs. Rebecca Harrison; though, as her Mama has often been heard to say, it rivalled in delicacy the snowy plumage of the swan, till it was unfortunately spoiled by that bitterest foe of beauty, the small-pox. Mrs. Rebecca herself, however, does not seem aware of this tragic circumstance, or that it does not still retain its pristine delicacy, since on the day of her arrival, as Olivia was drinking a glass of water, to which Rebecca has a mortal aversion, she said, "So, my dear, you will persist in that practice, though I've so often warned you against it; but take my word for it, you'll repent your obstinacy some day or another: why I'm sure if I had persisted in drinking water, I should by this time have had a settled redness in my face."

To what, then, the redness that certainly does now exist is to be ascribed, I will not pretend to say. She tells us for certain whence it does *not* originate; our own conjectures must supply the rest. Not that I mean positively to insinuate that she is a disciple of the Brunonian system[26]— she may have a convenient parlour closet* at home, for any thing I know to the contrary; but here I have never seen her drink any thing stronger than good old *English port*, as she calls it. When to the idea I have thus given you of the charms of her face, I add that her stature is somewhat under five feet, and her circumference somewhat above it, you will not suppose my heart in any great danger from that quarter.

As to her character, how shall I define what is absolutely indefinable? She is a true original; and I think the great Linnæus[27] himself would be puzzled in determining to what class, order, genus, and species of animals she ought to be referred. Her talents and powers of mind must be very uncommon, equal, if not superior, even to those of the *admirable Crichton*;[28] since there is no one individual thing attempted by the inge-nuity of man, in which she does not give instructions to whoever she sees employed in it; or, to use her own words, shew 'em a *better* way of doing what they are about. To the housemaid, in sweeping the room or lighting the fire—to the cook, in spitting and roasting the meat, or in making the pies and puddings—to the groom in rubbing down the horses, and to the coachman in driving them—to the gardener in pruning his trees and planting his cabbages, and to the park-keeper in managing his deer—to the bricklayer in arranging his bricks and mortar, and to the carpenter in cutting out his rabbets, his mortices, and his dovetails†—to Miss Campbell in doing the honours of her house, and to Beauchamp in the cultivation of his farm—to all and every of these she kindly gives such directions, that it will not be her fault if they do not arrive at perfection in their respective departments.

But let her actions and words speak for her—of both which more here-after; for by the great Jupiter himself I hear Harry's door open, and he must be going to the serenade. Adieu! then, and believe me
    Faithfully yours,

LIONEL STANHOPE.

---

*   A small room used for privacy and retirement (Johnson).
†   All types of joints used in carpentry.

LIONEL STANHOPE
TO
ORLANDO ST. JOHN.

Campbell-House, August 17.

Orlando, I was right; it was indeed the valorous knight's door that opened, and I instantly heard him,

—With stealthy pace,
With Tarquin's ravishing strides, tow'rds his design
Move like a ghost.[29]

The moon was just at the full, and, as in duty bound, while an affair of so much love and gallantry was carrying on, shone with even more than usual splendour. When I thought I might safely venture after the lover I also stole down, and reached the garden just as he turned round an angle of the house, near which were the chamber-windows of his mistress. I immediately concealed myself in a clump of shrubs, whence I could see and hear all that passed most admirably, and without the least hazard of being detected.

After a few moments pause, the lovelorn knight began to tune his voice; and then, with inexpressible passion and pathos, sung the following *beautiful* stanzas, composed for the occasion:

SONG.

Within my bosom hope and fear
    Maintain alternate sway;
While hope's bright beams my soul would cheer,
    Pale fear clouds ev'ry ray.

Bright hope still paints my fair one kind,
    Her face with smiles illum'd;
But then, to pallid fear consign'd,
    With grief my soul's consum'd.

Yet to thy arms, oh Hope, sweet maid!
    Thy willing vot'ry take;
For ah! without thy genial aid
    My wounded heart must break.

During the song, his fair princess appeared at the window, and, sitting down by it, reclined her head upon her hand in an attitude of serious and plaintive attention. When it was finished, she exclaimed: "What sounds are those which strike my ravished ears?—ah! sure 'tis some celestial harmony; for strains so soft, so sweet, ne'er could proceed from mortal voice!—Oh say, thou soul-enchanting songster, art thou indeed of human mould?—or art thou not rather one of those celestial spirits that rove invisible to mortal eyes in the pure realms of æther?"

Egerton listened with rapture—he started—he paused—he sighed—he clapped one hand to his breast, and struck the other on his forehead—in short, went through all the passionate lover-like evolutions proper for the occasion, and at length, in a transport of extasy, burst forth:

Oh heavens! what light through yonder window breaks?
It is my lady!—oh! it is my love?—
Oh that she knew she were!—
Two of the fairest stars in all the heavens,
Having some business, do intreat her eyes
To twinkle in their spheres till they return.[30]

"Pardon, divinest excellence, the presumption of a slave, who dares thus to intrude with unhallowed sounds on the calm hours sacred to soft repose!—Yet consider that transport, no less than misery, is foe to sleep, and then let any one who has a heart to feel, judge if 'twere possible that I could rest. No!—admitted to the contemplation of charms and excellence so far exceeding the feeble powers of mortal comprehension, the trammels that in common cases restrain our bosoms, were all incompetent to repress the ardent ebullitions of my feelings."

"Mr. Stanhope, if my ears do not deceive me!—or, as he henceforth shall be called, my valiant Palmerin."[31]

"Yes, fairest Polinarda,[32] 'tis your devoted slave!—'tis your love-stricken Palmerin!—Cursed indeed, if by this presumption he should incur his princess's displeasure, but blessed above mortality's frail lot, could he but hope her favourable attention to his vows; while he swears, even by the sacred altar of beauty's queen herself, that he was never till this moment sensible to the power of female charms, and that life will henceforward be to him but a lingering death, unless he obtain permission to indulge in the fond hope of one day possessing such perfection."—And here he drew forth a deep and lengthened sigh, so soft, so piteous, that it seemed to rend in twain the bosom whence it issued.

A sigh responsive burst from the bosom of the gentle maid, and in a trembling, yielding accent she replied, "Ah! my Palmerin, may I give credence to these fair-seeming words?—Oh! my boding heart whispers that you woo thus but to betray me!"

And truly, I thought, those bodings are not altogether without foundation.—But Egerton was in a different story.

"Betray thee?" he cried; "Oh! can my Polinarda suffer a thought so injurious to her Palmerin to find a harbour in that gentle bosom!—Banish, banish such ideas, lovely princess; and believe that your knight, your devoted slave, is truth itself."

Heavens! thought I, what cannot mortal man have the assurance to affirm!—And, indeed, so monstrous was this falsehood, that it seemed for a moment to confound even the daring spirit by which it was uttered, for Egerton immediately began to hesitate and stammer, as if not knowing how to proceed. At length, however, he recovered, and burst forth again:—"Betray thee!—Oh no!—thou art my soul's best, only treasure!—Speak comfort to me then; bid me hope, and live."

"Alas! I must believe you!—My heart, itself unpractised in deceit, knows not to suspect falsehood in another. Yet, that in so short a time you should be so devoted to me—"

"Cannot surely appear extraordinary.—Was it not ever thus in ancient days?—one glance alone from a bright eye, was then sufficient to confirm irrevocably the mighty empire of Love's all-powerful deity; and though from the supineness of modern times, instances of this nature are become uncommon, believe not, fair princess, the thing absolutely impossible!"

"'Tis true! Palmerin of England was instantly subdued by the bright eyes of the angelic Polinarda; so was it with the accomplished maid to whom the heart of the valorous knight Belianis[33] became a captive; nor did Durandarte[34] longer withstand the glances of the fair Belerma.[35] Why then should I doubt the truth of like professions?—Yet, my Palermin, there is one thing that I fain would ask—"

"Oh name it!—Can there be any proof of my sincerity that I would for one moment hesitate to give!—Speak but the word and behold me ready—"

"Not here, we are too public, and may be overheard. But if for my sake you can defy danger, and ascend to the window by a ladder of ropes, we can then converse without reserve."

"Oh kindness and condescension unparalleled! This is indeed happiness almost too great to bear!—where, where is my blessed passport to such transcendent bliss!"

"'Tis close at hand." The princess then retired for a few moments, and returned in the true spirit of romance clad in a long veil. The ladder was fixed, the knight skipped up in an instant, the window closed on them, and I saw him, in idea, happy in his fair one's arms.

Thus precluded, as I imagined, from being a farther spectator of this ridiculous farce, I thought only of returning quietly to my own chamber, and betaking myself to repose. I was accordingly stealing up to it as gently as possible, when, just as I arrived at the top of the stairs, I heard Olivia's voice in the gallery, saying, "This way, if you please, Mr. Beauchamp. I am certain I saw a man ascend by a ladder into my dressing room."

I was all astonishment, nor could divine how Olivia should come there, but, circumstanced as I was, I thought it best to make my appearance as her champion. Entering the gallery I beheld her at her dressing-room door with a candle in her hand, and accompanied by Beauchamp. "What did I hear, Madam," I said, "your house attacked by robbers? Oh, let me offer my assistance."

She made no reply, but opening the door, we beheld—Oh all ye Gods and Goddesses!—Egerton kneeling at the feet of a woman, and pressing her hand with extasy to his lips.

"Good heaven!" cried Olivia. "Mr. Stanhope at Jenny's feet! What can this mean?"

In an instant both started up, Jenny throwing aside her veil, and casting her eyes bashfully to the ground, while Egerton looked first at her, then at Olivia, with mingled emotions of astonishment and confusion.

An awful silence of two or three minutes ensued, when Beauchamp addressed the knight: "I can scarcely express, Mr. Stanhope, how much I am confounded at what I see. Is such a gross violation of decorum a proper return for the hospitality you have experienced here? Can a more flagrant insult be offered to the mistress of the house, than thus to attempt seducing her domestics?"

Egerton hesitated, stammered, muttered, and at length began: "Madam I, I—pardon me, Madam——Yes—I—I—I must own Madam—that—that—that appearances Madam—"

"Speak your intentions pretty plainly, Mr. Stanhope—leave no room to doubt that you were basely seeking the ruin of that poor girl."

"Condemn me not so hastily, I entreat Madam!—I own that appearances—that appearances, Madam—that appearances but too well justify your inference—yet Madam—believe me Madam—I hope and trust—yes Madam—I hope—and I trust—"

"That your invention, though somewhat tardy, will in time furnish you with some plausible story, by which to varnish over this outrage against decorum."

"Oh, for heaven's sake, Madam, do but hear me, and I trust that I can soon remove suspicions so injurious to my character."

"Well, Sir, as 'tis rather late at present, your vindication shall, if you please, be deferred till to-morrow. I only request the company now to retire, and I trust that for this night, at least, I shall hear no more such disturbances."

Her request was instantly complied with, nor was Harry, I believe, at all sorry to have so much time allowed for preparing his defence. I accompanied him to his chamber, whither Arthur, who had quitted it upon hearing the confusion, was returned just before us. "Why Harry," said I, clapping him on the shoulder, "this was rather an unfortunate mistake. The adventure, it seems, more properly belonged to your Esquire Arthur, than to yourself. But I wonder that you did not ask to see your mistress's face,—entreat that the odious veil might be thrown aside."

"Curse her ugly face, I did not want to see it; I was glad enough that it was concealed."

"And then not to distinguish the maid's voice from the silvery tones of your princess."

"Curse her croaking voice too, I did not attend to it."

"Nay, Harry, 'tis not croaking surely. I should rather say 'tis more than usually melodious."

"Well, damn her voice, I don't care whether 'tis melodious or not. I thought nothing about it, and was only studying how to be sufficiently upon the stilts.* The devil's in that baggage Jenny too, I believe, for she made such fine high-flown answers to my rhapsodies, as I could not possibly have conceived to come from any other mouth than that of Olivia herself. The girl's brains must be stuffed as full of romances as her mistress's. I suppose, during the old General's life they did nothing but sit and read them together in that damned dusthole of a closet."

"Why, indeed," said Arthur, "my little Abigail has some shrewdness. And to say the truth, my dear master, I'm glad to find that this is all mistake on your part, since I was not extremely pleased at hearing that you and she had been caught together. I was cursedly afraid you had been bamboozling me all this time, and pretended to make love to the fortune, only as a blind to get poaching on my manor."

"Insolent wretch," said Egerton, "who bid you speak! But this impertinence will pass no longer. Get out of my sight this moment, and take notice that you quit my service this day month."

"Is this the thirtieth, or only the nine and twentieth time that I've had warning," said he, with a coolness and impudence that really astonished even me. Then turning upon his heel, he said to me with a wink and a nod as he quitted the room, "What would he do now were I to take him at his word?" I had almost followed to give him a hearty caning.

I stayed not long after Arthur's departure, but left Egerton preparing to retire to bed, though not, as he said, to sleep, since he must meditate upon what was to be pleaded in the morning in his vindication. Nor did I retire with any hopes of rest. I knew too well that I was only going to encounter the torment of those reflections, with which amid the silence and solitude of night I am constantly assailed. Yes, Orlando, at such moments I feel most poignantly that the day of our detection must inevitably arrive; that we may be detected at any moment. No less sensibly do I feel that this discovery were better anticipated by a full and frank confession of our guilt, and yet I cannot summon up resolution to make this confession. But such is the inconsistency of our nature. We are eternally repining at the ills which surround us; we cannot forbear seeing that our calamities are in, perhaps I may say with truth, ninety-nine instances out of an hundred, self-incurred, and might be greatly lessened at least, if not entirely removed, by a trifling exertion of our own; yet rather than rouse ourselves from that torpor of indolence in which we all delight, to make such an exertion, we supinely languish on from day to day under

---

*   To use high-flown or condescending talk. To be bombastic.

the pressure of a grievance that must, if the truth of my axiom be allowed, be considered rather as imaginary than real.

But I am summoned to breakfast. Farewell, and believe me with great sincerity
Your affectionate

LIONEL STANHOPE.

LETTER XIII.

ORLANDO ST. JOHN
TO
LIONEL STANHOPE.

Scarborough, August 18.

Though I am perfectly of opinion, *mon cher ami*, that thou wouldst be rightly served were I never to address another epistle to thee, yet is my temper far too sweet and benignant to allow me to inflict punishment so severe on any human being. Three monstrous long letters have I received bearing the signature of Lionel Stanhope, yet in no one of them does he condescend to make the least acknowledgement for favours received from his Orlando, or to enquire how he goes on? whether he finds Scarborough *a son gout*? or what company he may have seen besides those already mentioned?

What aileth thee, Li.? Thou wert not wont to be so dull and insensible when a pretty girl was in question, yet dost thou not utter a single remark upon the fascinating Charlotte, dost not utter one expression of envy at my being blessed with such sweet society, while thou art immured within the walls of an antiquated castle, yawning away thy days with only old Mrs. Harrison and ugly Miss Campbell. *Ma foi*, I think thou too must have been making love to Jenny, otherwise thy insensibility is wholly unaccountable. I thought thou wouldst have been madly in love at the bare mention of Charlotte; but thy letters only ring changes upon Olivia, Beauchamp, Egerton, and thyself, as if the world contained but those four personages.

But though thou wilt not enquire, I will impart; and the first piece of intelligence I must communicate, I fear will not prove very grateful. Jerry yesterday received a summons from Sir Francis to repair immediately to Kilverton, without any reason whatever being assigned for so hasty a movement. This makes me fear that some storm is gathering over your heads. If all had been right, why should the summons be addressed to Jerry himself, without his young master's name being so much as mentioned. What to infer from this I know not, but I thought it better that you should be informed of it, that should any thing be amiss, you may not be taken wholly unprepared.

Now then let me try once more whether thy insensibility is capable of being roused. For my own part, I live in a delirium of extasy. Added to the society of the lovely Charlotte, I am become now the sworn follower of a most enchanting little widow, the relict of a French nobleman, and the intimate friend of my bewitching Hibernian.*

But Madame de Clairville is not a *Françoise* by birth. She is the daughter of a gentleman of property in this kingdom, and was sent to a convent in France for education. In this situation she became acquainted with her late husband, who was a frequent visitor at the convent to a sister of his, also a pupil there. Nor was it long before the acquaintance grew into a warm attachment on both sides. This was made known to their respective parents, and as the old people made no objection to the union, the young ones were married as soon as the lady was of an age to be released from her confinement.

Three years did Monsieur and Madame de Clairville live together in undisturbed happiness, when the former was seized with a violent fever, which carried him off in a few days, and left the gay and elegant Eliza, at only nineteen years of age, a widow, with two daughters to educate and establish in the world. For them, however, as well as for the widow, a handsome provision had been made by the marriage settlement, though the family estate went of course, with the title, to the next male heir. Soon after her husband's death, Madame de Clairville, accompanied by her children, came over to visit her father and mother; and the latter dying during the time of her proposed stay, her father became extremely unwilling to part with her again, and has therefore prevailed with her to remain in England ever since.

But the ease of manners she has acquired from the society to which she was accustomed in France, has unfitted her extremely for the more precise and demure conduct expected in her sex in this country; and thus she exposes herself but too frequently to their extreme and inveterate censure. She often invites a party of gentleman home with her from the rooms, or the play, to a *petit souper*, where, perhaps, oh! outrage against all decorum! she is the only female present. More commonly indeed, Charlotte is there to keep her in countenance; but still as the parties consist principally of gentlemen, and are out of the common routine of receiving company, they cannot obtain public sanction. Besides, as the company sometimes sit late, and Madam de Clairville does not like to keep her servants up, she dismisses them to bed, and actually lets the company out herself when they go away.

All this however might possibly have been passed over with only some slight animadversions, had not the unfortunate widow, a few days ago,

---

*   Irishwoman. *Hiberia* is the Latin name for Ireland.

been guilty of another offence of a nature so heinous, so absolutely unpardonable, that she has forfeited every shadow of a claim to lenity in less atrocious matters. She was walking out with Charlotte, a Miss Perkins, a cousin of Mrs. Tichfield's who had joined her party the day before, Captain Tichfield, a Mr. Peters, and myself. The Captain and Madame de Clairville were the first in the procession, when I observed the latter's garter drop, which I picked up, and presented to her. She stepped aside into a cottage, replaced the zone,* and joined us again with perfect composure; not having sufficient grace even to blush, or betray the least confusion, but seeming to regard the accident as a common every-day occurrence, unworthy of notice.

Not in so unimportant a light was it considered by Miss Perkins, who is one of the most modest of her sex, and a rigid adherent to even the minutest principles of decorum. She was all confusion, blushed, concealed her face behind her fan, and, in short, took every possible method of evincing how trembling alive she was to the delicate distress of being present at a circumstance of so embarrassing a nature; rendered ten times more shocking by the want of shame betrayed on Madame de Clairville's part. This incident soon became the general talk of the place. The ladies assembled in groupes of four, five, and six together, at the rooms, at the public breakfasts, on the walks, scanning it over in a half whisper, with gestures expressive of all proper horror at the wound given to the delicacy of the sex in general, by such gross behaviour in an individual. Many of the fair creatures even took the opportunity of blushing whenever Madame de Clairville appeared; while from me they turned aside with the utmost indignation, as the aider and abettor at least, if not the principal cause, of the poor widow's delinquency.

But while she was thus made a mark for the arrows of rigid censure, compassion was no less liberally extended to Miss Perkins, who was so unfortunate as to be present at the transaction; and who certainly was the only person that appeared properly impressed with it, unless Mr. Peters be excepted, who politely turned away his face, and stuffed his pocket-handkerchief into his mouth to conceal a laugh, or to conceal that he could not force one on an occasion which so eminently called for it. With some persons, indeed, astonishment that a woman of Miss Perkins's delicacy of mind, and strict propriety of conduct, would be seen walking with such an impudent hussey as Madame de Clairville, was mingled with the compassion expressed for her. Some excuse for this was however to be made, as she was unfortunately in the same party with Miss O'Brien, whose intimacy with the widow led Miss Perkins almost unavoidably into her company.

Many more anecdotes could I give you of these two bewitching sorceresses, would it not detain me too long from their company; and I trust

---

*   A girdle or belt. In this case, the garter.

that no more is wanting, Mr. Li., to fill thy bosom with the most corroding envy of

Thy very affectionate

ORLANDO ST. JOHN.

LIONEL STANHOPE
TO
ORLANDO ST. JOHN.

Campbell-House, August 18.

My last, St. John, concluded with a summons to breakfast on the morning after the serenade. As I approached the breakfast room, the door being open, I heard Mrs. Harrison's voice as if in earnest conversation; and not doubting but that anything said by her must be well worthy of attention, I was induced rather to listen at an awful distance, and unseen by her, than to hazard the putting any check upon her oratory by my sudden appearance. I soon found that she was questioning Beauchamp about the adventures of the preceding night, of which she said she had got some *inkling*—I use her own word—from her maid Nanny as she was a dressing of her. "Aye, well," she proceeded, "I thought that Mr. Stanhope seemed one of your clever folks, and they're always a doing something odd. Thank God, I a'n't clever!"

And certainly if that be a subject for gratitude to heaven, I know of no person on whose gratitude the Creator has stronger claims than on Mrs. Rebecca Harrison's. She concluded with saying;—"But I'll tell you what we'll do—we'll have a little fun with Mr. Stanhope. I'll *hoax* him" (again I use her own word, her very favourite word); "I'll *hoax* him about his knight-errantry."

Beauchamp made no reply; and as I heard footsteps, I thought it better to join them. On seeing me, the fair virgin immediately began:—"Oh, Mr. Egerton, I've been a hearing all about your cousin Stanhope's"—

But unfortunately my cousin's entrance put a stop to her imparting all that she had been a hearing; and Olivia coming in almost immediately, we arranged ourselves round the breakfast table, Egerton looking extremely chagrined and mortified at the recollection of the last night's adventure.

We were scarcely seated before Mrs. Harrison addressed our hostess:—"Marm, I hope you was'nt frighted last night with the fellows that got into your bedchamber?"

"You mistake, Madam; there was but one man, and he got no farther than my dressing-room."

Mrs. Harrison made no immediate reply. She seemed to wish to be extremely funny, yet to be at a loss how to set about it. She looked vastly important; winked at Beauchamp, as if to say, now I'll be severe indeed; and then turned again to Olivia—"Oh!" said she, "why I thought you was waked by two fellows, each poking a pistol into your bed."

"You quite misapprehend the affair then, Ma'am. The man carried no offensive weapon about him but his tongue; nor did he appear to have any intention of seizing my property by force. Undermining seemed rather to be his aim."

"Pho now!—Why Nanny told me that Arthur said they was two of a gang of housebreakers that he's often seen at the Old Bailey;[36] and that they was just a breaking open of your bureau, when Mr. Egerton came behind 'em, *wrinched* the pistols out of their hands, and was a going to bind 'em to the bed-post, when they darted away, bounced down the ladder like a couple of monkeys, and was out of sight before you could say Jack Robinson."

This fine description was accompanied with so much action, particularly flourishing the hands, that a knife and fork with which they were armed as instruments of offence against the many good things upon the table, unfortunately struck, one the coffee-pot, the other the cream-jug, and fairly overturned both. The cream-jug, comparatively inoffensive, in its fall only inundated a plate of rusks, and then the cream pursued its course quietly along the table. But the more ponderous coffee-pot, striking against the bony end of a cold ham, occasioned that to take a sudden spring into the air; yet not having been properly trained to such exhibitions, it did not, like a Sadlers-Wells rope-dancer,* light again upon the same spot, but descended among a plate of rolls, and set them skipping this way and that, like the figurantes attendant upon himself, the principal performer in the ballet. One of these inferior gentry jumped into the midst of a glass with butter and water, and made the latter ascend in a fountain; this, in its descent, united its stream with those from the coffee-pot and cream-jug; and altogether they formed a torrent which threatened to sweep away knives, forks, plates, dishes, and in short the whole apparatus on the table, had not fortunately the alarum-bell, which was rung at the commencement of the disaster, at that moment brought in a footman, who instantly raised a mound with dusters and pocket-handkerchiefs, that stopped its further progress.

Scarcely could any thing have happened more unfortunately, since Mrs. Harrison, though so frequently offering up her thanks to God that she is not clever, is continually boasting of her own dexterity, and arraigning others for their awkwardness. At this moment too it was more particularly ill-timed, by coming at the conclusion of a speech so replete with

---

* A rope-dancer is someone who dances or performs on a rope suspended above the ground. In the eighteenth-century Sadlers-Wells was known for its music hall entertainments.

wit and humour, and turning the attention of the company from that to the scene of anarchy and confusion before them.

Order however was soon restored, the table fresh spread, and the conversation resumed by the very person whose ill-fortune it had been to interrupt it, and who seemed very unwilling to be deprived of the least atom of her premeditated *hoax.* "And so Marm," said she, "that was'nt true as Nanny was a telling of me?"

"No indeed, Madam, Mr. Arthur and Mrs. Nanny were both extremely inaccurate in their information. I acknowledge with gratitude the gallantry of Mr. Egerton's behaviour; but I should have been very sorry to see him hazard his life, by attempting to wrench a loaded pistol from the hands of a desperate villain."

"Trifling and insignificant as my services were, Madam," I said, "they scarcely merit gratitude. I could almost wish indeed that there had been some real danger, to have afforded me an opportunity of evincing by my actions, that there is no danger I would not joyfully encounter to serve Miss Campbell."

"You are gallant indeed, Mr. Egerton. The bravest knight that ever poised lance, could not have shewn more ardour in the service of the fair. You really are scarcely inferior to Mr. Stanhope himself."

My friend must not be offended, Madam, if I assure you that I shall always consider his mistake as a circumstance of peculiar good fortune to me, since it has furnished me with an occasion of recommending myself to your favour."

"Nay, now you are quite cruel to your cousin, Mr. Egerton; you shew him no mercy at all."

"What then shall we say of you, Madam," said Beauchamp. "You surely are not very lenient in thus dwelling on circumstances which Mr. Stanhope cannot particularly wish should be made the subject of our morning's entertainment. I protest I absolutely pity him."

This was too much. Egerton had for some time sat writhing and twisting in his chair, scarcely able to restrain his impatience, but to pity him was past all bearing, and starting up he muttered, "curse your pity," and went to lean out of the window.

There was a wildness in his look and manner that alarmed me, and seemed to make a deep impression upon Olivia. I went to him, "for heaven's sake, Harry," said I, "take care what you do." He instantly recollected himself, and returning quietly to his seat, made an apology, but said he was apprehensive that a choaking in his throat, to which he was extremely subject, was coming on.

But as if all the fiends of Pandemonium* had conspired to torment him, after the company had been silent for two or three minutes, Olivia,

---

*   The abode of all demons. The word was first used by Milton to represent the principal city of Hell (*Paradise Lost* 1.756).

to recommence conversation, told Beauchamp that she had that morning received a letter from Mrs. Trelawney, who would be down in a few days.

The name of Trelawney was like an electric shock to poor Harry, and affected him the more strongly, from his spirits having been previously so much ruffled. He struggled with himself for a few moments—in vain,—again he started up—again went and leaned out at the window. I followed him, "for God's sake," I said, "have more command of yourself." He cast a look of agony upon me;—"be not thus your own enemy," I continued. "What is become of your usual self-possession?"

This enquiry seemed to restore it, and he made one effort more to resume his seat. I saw that both Olivia and Beauchamp were struck with his agitation, and perplexed in what way to attempt restoring conversation and hilarity. In this dilemma Mrs. Harrison proved of essential service. Unobservant of what had passed, she remained absorbed in her breakfast, for eating is with her one of the most important concerns of life, but that finished, her next care was to devise some means of killing the morning, so she addressed Olivia: "Suppose, my dear, you was to offer the gentlemen to go to shew 'em *them* mills."

"The Cotton Mills at Gresley do you mean, Madam?"

"Aye, I believe it was Gresley. *Them* Mills I mean, where they work up the cotton from its first coming off the sheep's back, till its fit to wear."

"I beg your pardon, Madam, they are *Cotton* Mills."

"Aye, my dear, I know that; *were* we saw the rough *Cotton* just as it comes off the sheep's back."

Don't suppose me guilty of rhodomontade,* Orlando. She literally repeated the "*Cotton off the sheep's back*," a second time. I can scarcely imagine how we all refrained from laughing, but we did hear it with tolerable composure. Olivia replied,—"The gentlemen will do as they please, Madam. My guests know that my carriages and horses are always at their command; but for myself I must beg to be excused, as I have letters to write which will occupy me for the whole morning."

"Well then," said Mrs. Harrison, "Mr. Beauchamp shall take Mr. Egerton in his *wiskey*."† Pray observe the proper pronunciation, here, Orlando, for the good lady in question always drops the *h*, when associated with a *w* because she says 'tis so confounded pedantic to pronounce it.—"Mr. Beauchamp shall take Mr. Egerton in his wiskey, and Mr. Stanhope shall drive me in Miss Campbell's phaeton."‡

"I should think," said Beauchamp, "that there will be no occasion for the whiskey. If Miss Campbell will permit the two gentlemen to accompany Mrs. Harrison in the phaeton, I can mount my horse, and then we need not take a servant."

---

*   Empty bluster. From Rodomonte (see explanatory note 19).
†   *Whiskey* or *whisky*: a light one-horse gig.
‡   A light, four-wheeled open carriage usually drawn by four horses.

"Pho now," returned Mrs. Harrison, "that's cramming one up so. But you're always for sparing the servants trouble."

"Rather, Madam, for sparing myself being troubled with their attendance."

"Aye, that's one of your independent ways, as you call it. But I hate your notions of independence, so let it be as I settled."

"Well then," said Beauchamp, "perhaps Mr. Egerton will have no objection to riding also."

I was about to remonstrate strenuously against this arrangement, and plead for Mrs. Harrison's, as I wished extremely for some private conversation with Beauchamp, and thought the whiskey would afford an excellent opportunity for it. But Doctor Paul coming in unexpectedly, Beauchamp invited him to join the party, and proposed his accompanying me in the whiskey, and then he could himself pursue his plan of going on horseback.

To this proposal, which I verily believe was made on purpose to teaze me, the Doctor readily assented, only lamenting extremely that we were not to have the pleasure of Miss Campbell's company. At the same time he suggested, that as we should be within half a mile of Mr. Donellan's at Flaxland Place, we might as well include that in our ride, as his grounds, though very confined, were laid out with such exquisite taste, that they were well worth the attention of all strangers. The idea met with Mrs. Harrison's warm approbation, as she seemed apprehensive that the mills might not occupy the whole morning, consequently that there might be an hour or two which she should not know how to get rid of, and no objection being made by any other of the party, the thing was soon settled. All matters being therefore at last arranged, we set off, Mrs. Harrison instructing Egerton how to hold the reins and manage the horses, to my no small amusement, and his no small chagrin, since he values himself upon being one of the most *knowing whips* in the kingdom.

My companion seeming determined if possible to make himself agreeable, began the conversation with an elaborate eulogium upon the virtues and accomplishments of the heiress, and then by a very natural concatenation, adverted to the great intimacy that had long subsisted between the Stanhope and Campbell families. He observed what a prodigious favourite the late Mrs. Egerton was with General Campbell, and that probably if he had known her before she was married, she would have been Mrs. Campbell. Then he remarked again upon my uncommon resemblance to Sir Francis, and that I had quite a Stanhope face, even more so than my cousin Stanhope himself. Next he proceeded to say that he never saw a young man so prepossessing at first sight as Mr. Stanhope, and expressed his warmest wishes that he and Miss Campbell might form a mutual attachment, as it would be a match in every way so suitable, and would give so much satisfaction to their friends on both sides.

To all this common-place nonsense I answered not a word; but the Doctor indeed did not appear to want any answer, since he continued to entertain me in the same strain, till at length he introduced Mrs. and Miss Belgrave, and observed how noble had been Miss Campbell's conduct towards them. This induced me to break silence. I earnestly wished to know more of their history, as I was fully convinced from many things which had fallen under my observation, that there was some mystery attached to it, and I thought if I could learn the secret from the Doctor, that it would be some small compensation for having him forced upon me as a companion.

I therefore replied, that I was totally unacquainted with the extent of Miss Campbell's kindness to these two unfortunate ladies, since I had never heard it mentioned but in general terms, and I should be much obliged to him if he could favour me with the particulars. But how noble soever had been Miss Campbell's conduct, I observed, I did not doubt but that Miss Belgrave had shewn herself deserving of it, since she appeared one of the most amiable of women.

To this Doctor Paul readily assented, and extremely regretted that he could not give me the information I wished. But he said he had been only six years rector of the parish, and all he knew was, that at the time of his coming Mrs. and Miss Belgrave had long been inmates of Campbell-House. He always understood that they had been entirely supported by General Campbell during his life, and since his death by his daughter, but that an uniform secrecy was observed as to the circumstances which reduced them to this state of dependence. He had lately however, heard, that they had some prospect of recovering an estate in Ireland which had long been litigated, and which would place them in affluence.

By this time we had reached the mills, whence, after we had sufficiently surveyed them, we proceeded to Mr. Donellan's. Here Rebecca mounted indeed upon her hobby-horse. She particularly prides herself on her knowledge of trees and plants, and on her taste in the picturesque, consequently she is a great critic in gardening and laying out grounds. Whether or not she had not found Harry altogether as gallant as she expected I cannot pretend to say, but deserting him, she now seized upon my arm, and dragged me hither and thither at a most unmerciful rate. First I must see a *cactus grandiflorus*, then I was pulled another way to look at a *deciduous cypress*, then at a view, then at something else, yet all the time she arraigned me very severely for not appearing pleased: I assured her I was highly delighted, and that I had never seen a place which for the size displayed more taste and variety. "Aye, but," said she, "you never *express*—I hate your folks that never *express*, for there's no telling wether they're pleased or not; now you may always tell when I'm pleased, because I *express*." And then she peered through her glass—"What a noble larch! that's a cedar of—of—Lord bless me, I forget the name. I dare say you never see one of *them* trees before, they're such great curiosities—isn't it a beauty?—What a lovely peep that is through *them* what d'ye call 'em's, Weymouth pines I believe they are, into that valley."

Thus did she go on, *expressing* and *expressing*, till my patience was well nigh wearied out, and I was heartily glad to be released by Mr. Donellan's politely inviting us into the house to eat Sandwiches.

The little I had collected from Doctor Paul relative to the Belgraves, only made me ten times more anxious for a private conference with Beauchamp, to learn, if possible, farther particulars from him, and I therefore determined, when we were setting off on our return, to make a second attempt at being his companion in the whiskey. But this was not to be accomplished. The fair spinster not having yet tormented me sufficiently, insisted that as Mr. Stanhope had driven her thither, Mr. Egerton should drive her back. In reply I urged that this would be making an unequal distribution of her favours; that as I had been honoured with her arm in walking about, Doctor Paul's turn was now come, and I thought he ought to be her charioteer. But my remonstrance was of no avail; nothing would content her but my accompanying her in the phaeton, and to this I was obliged, however reluctantly, to submit.

I therefore seated myself by her side, when she began a long and eloquent series of observations upon *them* mills, and *them* grounds, that we had been *a* seeing, and *them* birds *a* singing so sweetly, and *them* people at work in the fields, *a* looking so picturesque, and sundry other *thems*, too tedious to enumerate; but since I was not particularly pleased with my situation, and was too much interested by the mysterious Harriot to pay much attention to any thing else, I made no more answer to her than I had done for a long time to Doctor Paul.

But she did not take my silence quite so contentedly as the Doctor, for tired at last with not being able to obtain a single reply, she said rather angrily—"Why you don't talk, Mr. Egerton. But mayhap you're one of *them* kind of people that don't like talking in a carriage."

"Oh yes, Madam," I replied, "I have no kind of objection to it, if any subjects for conversation occur."

"Aye," said she, looking very wise, but that's the art now—to make occurrences." Mrs. Harrison is certainly a very agreeable companion in a phaeton, whatever she might be in a post-chaise.

Orlando, had I time, I have a vast deal more to impart of a very unaccountable nature indeed; but at present I must lay down my pen, though with an assurance that it shall be resumed the very first opportunity. In the mean time let me suggest, that as Charlotte O'Brien is related to the Belgraves, you might perhaps be able to learn their story from her. Bear this in your mind, and whatever discoveries you make, be sure to transmit them faithfully to me.

I had almost forgotten to say that we have heard no more of the proposed investigation into the affair of last night. Perhaps Olivia thinks it better dropped, conscious that she herself, no less than Egerton, would make but a ridiculous figure in it.

   Farewell; and believe me now, as ever,
    Yours most faithfully,

            LIONEL STANHOPE.

LETTER XV.

LIONEL STANHOPE
TO
ORLANDO ST. JOHN.

Campbell-House, August 20.

I told you in my last, Orlando, that I had strange things to communicate. They appear to me now more unaccountable than ever; and I am daily, nay hourly, more and more perplexed what opinion to form of Olivia's character. Combating as she does, in many instances, the absurd prejudices of the world, and acting in general in such perfect conformity with the dictates of sound reason, can it be possible that such a mind should give way to any kind of superstition?—Yet 'tis no uncommon thing to see persons rising superior to all other prejudices excepting those which attach to some religious belief, yet clinging to them with a folly and weakness totally inconsistent with the general firmness of their character.

That Arthur entertained a belief in ghosts, excited in me no surprise. It was the natural effect of the ignorance and credulity so prevalent among his class of society, acting upon a conscience by no means clear of reproach. But I was exceedingly astonished to find that Olivia not only did not condemn such a belief among her servants, as contrary to all reason and experience, and endeavour immediately to convince them of their folly in fancying that they heard super-natural noises in one part of her house, but that she even countenanced and supported them in so gross a superstition.

Thus I reasoned, when first I learned that one wing of this mansion was reputed to be haunted, and that Olivia had not sufficient resolution to investigate the cause of the noises heard there, but rather suffered it to be shut up and totally neglected. Yet for a moment, I must confess that my own faith was staggered, and no small exertion of my reason was necessary to convince myself that all was deception.

On the morning after the serenade, Arthur did not attend as usual at his master's toilette, but one of the footmen of the house answered his bell when he rang, and informed him that his own valet was still in bed. After we returned from our excursion, we went up together to Harry's room, where we found Arthur waiting for us.—"Lord, Sir," said he, "I have been wanting so to see you, to tell you that I can't stay another night in this house, for 'tis haunted, and I've seen the spirit, and I'm afraid of my life every moment I stay here."

"Prithee no more of this nonsense," said Harry. "What new vagary is in your head now?"

"Oh pray don't call it nonsense, my dear master," said the affrighted valet, "for fear you should be served as I have been. I never used to believe in ghosts, not I, but talk as lightly about 'em as you do, and say, damn 'em I should like to see the ghost that dares to face Arthur Williams, I'd teach 'em the odds on't, that's what I would—I fancy I should be up to a thing or two of that kind—I'd cut him a nice neat stroke across his bare ribs with my cane, till I made his bones ring again. But now I wouldn't for the world say such things, for as sure as can be 'twas all along of my talking in that way that I met it last night as I left your room."

"How?—as you left my room?"

"Yes to be sure, at that very time. I had got pretty near the door that goes out from the gallery to the great staircase, when puff comes a great gust of wind and blows out my candle, though 'twas as still and calm a night out of doors as ever mortal eyes should see; and then looking up, there stood an old man full in the moonshine, just by one of the windows, with a head like a skeleton, hair as white as snow, and the monstrousest great beard. Well, I've often heard that beards grow in the coffin, and now I believe 'tis true, for I can't conceive else how the ghost could have come by one all that length. He never could have had it when he was alive, that's a sure thing, for I verily believe that it trailed upon the ground, and he must have trod upon it in walking."

"Well, don't plague us about his beard, but go on with your story."

"All on a sudden, just as I turned my eyes that way, the window shutters clapped to without being touched, and then I was left so entirely in the dark that I could see nothing more, but I had scarcely a heart to stir for fear the ghost should be after me. I was thinking once to come back to your room, my dear master, for a light, but I thought you'd be angry, as we hadn't parted the best friends in the world; and besides, thinks I, if Mr. Ghost there's spiteful, he'll only raise a wind and blow it out again. What to do I didn't know, but at length I bethought myself that I'd pull off my shoes to prevent making a noise, and then have a run for it. Off I sets, therefore, scampering down stairs fit to break my neck, but as sure as you're alive I heard it pat, pat, pat, after me, as hard as it could go; however, I never stopped till I got into my own room, and then I clapped the door to, and locked it fast. 'Tis a wonder how I got along so well in the dark, but I've heard that one can do any thing if one is but frightened enough. Well, I wouldn't stay to undress, but skulked under the quilt directly, and there I lay trembling and shaking till day-light. Then, as I was sure that the ghost must be gone I ventured to get comfortably into bed, and got a good nap, and that was the reason that I was not awake when your honour rung in the morning. But if you'll believe me though, while I lay under the quilt I felt a cold, cold hand, groping about for me several times, and 'tis a wonder how I escaped being found out."

"And what did you suppose the ghost wanted with you?" I asked.

"Oh Lord, Sir, there's no telling; a hundred things, perhaps."

"Possibly had heard that you were famous for handling a razor, and wanted you to help him off with his long beard."

"Pray, dear Sir, don't make a joke of him, for then 'tis odds but he's after you too. You may think if you please that there's nothing in it, as I did when first I got an inkling about it from the servants, but now I've seen it, and know better."

"The servants of the house then have seen the ghost as well as you?" said I.

"As for *seeing*, I can't say," he replied, "but they know very well that it does walk, for they've been shaking their heads and looking wise about it ever since we came here. I used to quiz 'em a bit or so, because I did not believe in such things, but now mum shall be the word with me, and I hope in God, my dear master, that march will be the word with you, for I shall never be able to stir again after dark, for fear of what may happen."

"What did the servants tell you about the ghost?" said Egerton.

"Why, you must know, as I was one day looking about me, I comes to a door at one end of the long gallery that runs through the middle of the house. I tried to open it, but found it fast locked. So as I had seen all the rest of the castle, I'd a mind to see that wing too, and I went and asked the butler if he could help me to the key of that door. I can to be sure, said he, but whether I will or not, is another story. And why so? says I. Why, says he a little savagely, for your honour must have observed that the butler is but a crusty kind of a chap, because my mistress doesn't choose that part of the house should be seen. And what's the whim of that? says I. Whim, says he, please to hold your impertinent tongue, you'd best not speak so disrespectfully of my mistress. Well, damn it, says I, you need not be so very uppish about the matter, I don't care whether I see the musty old house or not. For all there's so much of it, 'tisn't half so well worth seeing as a lodging in St. James's Street. With that the fellow ups with his foot to kick me, so I thought it high time to vote myself scarce, and away I ran.

Well, then I applies to Will Beckford, one of the footmen, and asks if he could get me the key of the door. He didn't snap indeed like the butler, for Will is a tolerably civil fellow, but he puts on a long wise face, shakes his head, and said no, that was impossible, his mistress never suffered that wing of the house to be shewn. And what's the joke of that? says I. No joke, says he, there's things in that room she doesn't choose should be seen. What things? says I. Why, you fool, says he, you might as well see 'em yourself, as I tell you what they are; besides, what if I don't know no more than you. But you can guess perhaps, says I, and there's no harm in guessing. Mayhap not, says he, but suppose I don't choose to guess, and at that minute the bell rang, and off he marched.

Next I thought I'd try what was to be done with my pretty Abigail, for you must think now, my dear master, I began to have a mortal desire to know all about it. But no, she was in the same story, her mistress did not choose that part of the house to be seen. Why, what the devil can she keep locked up there? says I. Layer-overs for medlars,* replies the lass,

---

*   An answer often given to children as a rebuke for their impertinent curiosity when they ask what is in a box or bundle (Grose, *Dictionary Vulgar Tongue*, 1785). Forby identifies "layer-over" as a gentle term for some instrument of chastisement (*Vocabulary of East Anglia*, 1825).

and you happened to be the first. Lord, says I, you are mighty sharp. Serve you right, says she, what business have you to be prying into my lady's secrets. Well, says I, be as close as you please, I only asked to see what you'd say, for I know fast enough that your beautiful lady shuts up the room, because her old father's ghost walks there; for I thought this would put Madam Jenny in a passion, and then out it would all come. And it did partly answer; for says she, well, and if you knew all that, what occasion was there to ask me about it?——but I beg to know, Sir, who told you this, for my lady shall hear of it, and the servant that blabbed shall be turned away directly. What then, it is the old gentleman, says I. If it be my master, says she, he never does harm to nobody, and that's more than can be said of every body's master."

"Still however I couldn't be quite satisfied, but wanted to know whether all the servants thought the same about it. So I goes up to Coachy, as he was putting to his horses, for he's a mighty steady chap, and says I, so Mr. Jenkins, says I, they tell me that your old master walks of a night? He shook his head. But always keeps in the old wing, says I; does not come among the company?—Shake went his noddle again. Makes a little noise though now and then, with lumbering about in the dark? Another shake. Well, 'tis mortal strange of the old fellow, says I.—Shake went his upper story once more, and then he whips upon the box, and away he drives.

To be sure I did think all this mortal odd, yet I scarcely knew how to believe that the old gentleman could give his coffin the go by in such a way; but I thought that the servants wanted to keep that part of the house for themselves for some damn'd sly purpose or another, and so made their lady believe that the ghost had got there. But now I've no such thoughts, and once more I tell you, my dear master, that I wo'n't stay another night in the house, lest his honour the ghost should take it into his head to do something more than frighten me."

"But how happened it," said I, "that the spirit had got to the other side of the house? for, according to the servants account, he keeps entirely in the old wing."

"Aye, but your ghosts are such slippery kinds of things, that when once they've got into a house, there's no knowing what part they'll come to next; and if he has a grudge against me, he'll have me one way or another you may be sure. And finally to make short of the matter, here I wo'n't stay."

"Go then, if you please," said Egerton, "I certainly *shall* stay."

"Why 'twill all be to no purpose, for neither the lady, nor the *rino*, for aught I can see, appear to be come-at-able."

"Cease your impertinence, and begone. I shall stay as long as I please, but you are perfectly at liberty to go."

Arthur was about to reply, but Harry said in such a peremptory tone, "begone this instant," that he walked off with a gloomy countenance and sullen air.

I was not a little struck with this detail, and I must confess thought with Arthur, that the whole story was a fabrication among the servants to impose upon their mistress, and serve some private ends of their own. As to the apparition which he affirmed he saw, that might easily be accounted for from the effect of his own fears, since he probably was deeply impressed with what he had heard, though affecting to turn it into ridicule.

But to investigate the affair thoroughly, became from that moment my most ardent wish, and I resolved to take the first opportunity of questioning Olivia about that part of the house, so as to arrive at her reasons for keeping it shut up, since I could by no means suppose Arthur in possession of the truth, and that the servants really had duped their mistress so grossly, as to persuade her that her father's spirit actually made it the scene of his nocturnal rambles.

Fortune favoured this design, by bringing the heiress and myself into the drawing-room at tea time, a quarter of an hour before any other of the company appeared. I immediately availed myself of being thus tête-à-tête with her, to say that I hoped I had not been guilty of impertinence, but as I was extremely fond of exploring old houses, I had been endeavouring to pass into the old wing which appeared uninhabited, but had however found the entrance barred against me.

"Those apartments have not been inhabited for several years," she replied. "Indeed the house is so large that they are not wanted."

"But might I not be indulged with a sight of them? I should surmise from the appearance of the great window at the end of the wing, that the whole, or a part of it at least, must formerly have been a chapel."

"There was once a chapel there."

"In the times of Catholicism, perhaps?"

"I believe so."

"And possibly it may contain many curious and interesting relicks of that extraordinary superstition?"

"None of any consequence."

"Does the chapel occupy the whole wing?"

"Not much more than half."

"There are apartments then between the long gallery and the chapel?"

"One very large room."

"But not to be seen?"

"'Tis seldom opened."

"Is it impertinent to request admission both to that and the chapel?"

"'Tis better not asked, refusal is unpleasant."

"I am sorry I have transgressed."

"No offence, Mr. Egerton; you could not know my reasons for keeping them closed."

"Excuse me, Madam, there seems some mystery?"

"I have been unwilling to think so—yet 'tis wonderful."

"How?—you astonish me, Madam."

"I am myself astonished."

"Heavens, what can you mean?"

"Unaccountable noises are heard there."

"Rats perhaps. They will often make very unaccountable noises."

"Rats, Mr. Egerton!—Would I could be satisfied of that!"

"Nothing easier, surely."

"Than to be convinced 'tis something more; as you would be, had you seen and heard what has been witnessed by the eyes and ears of others."

"The ghosts then have been seen as well as heard? That is indeed extraordinary, since they are seldom so obliging as to shew themselves."

"Talk not thus lightly I entreat!—Reason would persuade me that the spirit rests with the body."

"Reason certainly does not teach that to all, else had the idea of ghosts never gained credit in the world."

"But does any person of sound reason believe in the departed soul's still hovering about the spot it loved on earth?"

"Not of *sound* reason, I believe. That is rather the creed of a heated imagination."

"So I have been accustomed to think.—But yet—"

"Think so still. Trust me, Madam, that if your house is reported to be visited by departed spirits, the story has been circulated for no good purpose."

"What would you insinuate, Mr. Egerton?"

"That such a report probably originated from the servants, to answer some sinister views of their own."

"Oh no!—My life upon the honesty and integrity of every domestic in my house. Not one among them but has lived many years irreproachably in the family, and I should esteem myself culpable were I to entertain a momentary doubt of their fidelity."

"It may be then people of the village, who, as that part of the house is shut up, have found means to gain an entrance for private purposes of their own, and have raised false alarms in the family to screen themselves from discovery."

"You would not say so, were you yourself to hear the noises."

"I have no doubt that I should hear some imposture, and I would omit no effort for its detection."

"I would not wish you to make the experiment."

"And wherefore not, Madam?"

"Because as the nephew of Sir Francis Stanhope, I place some value upon your life."

"Can I risk my life in a better cause than in seeking to render a service to Miss Campbell?—-Let me watch in that room to-night, Madam."

"No, Sir.—*You* may be fool-hardy, *I* am not."

"I do not mean to shew myself fool-hardy. I will be properly armed against mortal powers—of immortal I have no fear."

"I own this is being the true hero of romance—but take care what you are about, Sir."

"You mistake me, Madam. It is not fame I seek, 'tis only my own satisfaction. Do not then refuse my request."

"I confess it is much my wish to have this matter more fully investigated;—yet should any thing unfortunate happen"—

"Away with such fears!—Only grant my request, and leave the rest to me. Believe me, I shall ever gratefully acknowledge the obligation."

"There is no bed in the room."

"If there were, I should not lie down."

"No furniture but an old table and chair, and the room is wainscotted with dismal old cedar."

"'Tis but the more romantic."

"It contains many old arms, and some suits of armour."

"I shall be the better defended."

"And you really wish to pass the night there?"

"So ardently, that I could not be easy elsewhere."

"Well then, be it so. But understand, Mr. Egerton, that no preparation can be made for your reception; and the door must not be unlocked till the moment of your entrance. You may be armed if you please."

"Oh, I freely consent to all."

"And you must be silent as to your intention, though after all is over you may freely relate what you have seen."

"Agreed."

"Then come with me to my room for the key, only give me your honour that it shall not be used till we separate for the night."

"You may rely upon me."

I attended her to her room, and received the key with a fresh injunction to silence till the morning. This settled, we went down to tea.

Had I been to fly to the arms of an adored mistress, I could not have expected night more eagerly, or with greater anxiety. Yet I suffered not the thoughts of my adventure to engross me so entirely, but that I watched Olivia very narrowly. I observed her to be more thoughtful than usual, yet she never left the room for a single moment, so that I could not suspect her of making any preparations to alarm me with strange visions or noises. I never lost sight of her for a moment after I received the key; I accompanied her up stairs when she retired, and then charging my pistols, hastened with them, a candle, and a book, to the scene of my adventure.

I entered the room; all was dark, dismal, and dreary. I locked the door carefully, and put the key in my pocket; then laying my book and pistols upon the table, I applied myself to a strict examination of my new abode. On one side of it was a large high canopy, from the back of which hung to the ground a tapestry, ornamented with a variety of armorial bearings. I endeavoured to search behind this, but found it fastened to the wainscot; I however rapped against it with my hand, and was convinced that it could conceal nothing corporeal, however it might serve as the hiding-place for a *spirit*.

On another side of the room was a very large old-fashioned looking-glass, which reached to the ground, and completely displayed the whole figure. I confess I was surprised to find this remaining here useless, since the plate must be of great value, though it was encumbered with an immense mass of frightful, heavy ornaments. When I had satisfied myself with speculating upon the mirror, I proceeded to examine the arms and armour, of which I found a great profusion. At length I came to a gigantic figure of a knight *"in complete steel,"* * with the helmet unbraced, so that the countenance was visible, and I beheld two large glaring black eyes fixed directly upon me. I gave an involuntary start, but instantly recovering myself, examined the warrior as carefully as I had before examined the tapestry, and was soon fully convinced that the eyes which had given me a momentary feeling of terror belonged to no animate form, but that the figure was a mere senseless block, or lump of wax.

My next care was to examine what avenues to the room there might be, by which pretended ghosts might gain admittance, but no door could I find excepting that to the gallery, which on my coming into the room I had carefully locked and bolted on the inside; and as to the windows, they were at so great a height from the floor, that no danger could be apprehended from that quarter, and they were besides covered with long thick tarpaulins. Another side of the room was occupied by a large old-fashioned chimney, capable of burning up a whole load of wood at one blaze, but now filled with rusty helmets, swords, battle-axes, and various relics of martial prowess. These I turned over, to assure myself that nobody was concealed beneath them, and then looking up the chimney, I perceived a grating of iron two or three feet above my head, which must effectually preclude a descent that way.

Thus satisfied that I was safe from the intrusion of flesh and blood, and not apprehensive of other visitors, I ventured to sit down at the table and take my book. It was Young's Night Thoughts; I opened it, when the first thing that met my eyes was that exquisite passage, *"The bell strikes one."*[37] Instantly the solemn sound of one struck upon the great clock of the castle, in a turret directly over my head. Never shall I forget the impression it made upon me!—I dropped the book involuntarily upon my knee—I paused—I looked around me—there was a something so awful in the gloom and desolate appearance of the apartment, and the dreary silence that reigned around, broken only by the single solemn sound I had just heard, that I felt a momentary impulse to rise and quit a scene, where even my stout heart began to be appalled. But instantly my attention was roused to other matters, on hearing a violent crash, resembling the firing

---

* In full armour. See *Hamlet* 1.4.52.

off a large cannon. I started, I turned towards the door, when a rushing wind came from the other side of the room, and blew out my candle, leaving me totally in the dark. I was half mad with vexation, since, deprived of light, I felt myself powerless to investigate the cause of this extraordinary phænomenon. I was not however suffered to remain long at leisure to torment myself with this idea, but was harassed by a succession of wonders, each of which almost obliterated all sense of the former. A light of a very uncommon nature darted along the room, in a direct line with my eyes, in the midst of which I beheld, standing directly before me, a figure in a long white garment, in whose features I instantly recognised, oh God! the perfect resemblance of my father.

My feelings are not to be described.—Armed, as I thought I was, against whatever might happen, yet a sight so awful, so unexpected, absolutely for some moments petrified me with horror. I soon, however, recovered myself, and catching up one of my pistols, advanced towards the figure. It did not move, and I seemed to get close to it, but stretching out my hand to seize it, I found that I grasped at vacancy. Still I beheld it; I could even observe a variation in the features, which at one moment frowned upon me with an awful severity, at the next were illuminated with that smile of benevolent affection which I had so often seen overspread the venerable Baronet's countenance, when after a transient storm we shook hands again as friends. This extraordinary vision continued for about the space of two minutes, and then vanished, leaving me once more in total darkness.

I stood for some moments in the same spot, transfixed with astonishment, when I was again startled by a voice that said in a deep, solemn, and emphatic tone, as if it came from the inmost recesses of the darksome tomb itself, "IMPOSTER, TREMBLE!!!"

Overwhelmed with confusion and vexation, I staggered back to my seat, and throwing myself into it, laid my folded arms upon the table, and buried my face in them, when I soon perceived a faint odour in the room, unlike any thing to which my senses had ever been accustomed, and which gave me sensations I am unable to describe. Again I started up and looked around me, in hopes that something more might be seen; but all was dark as the grave, though not equally silent, for I now began to hear the thunder rolling at a distance.

I could almost have cursed the elements for thus interposing, and lending their aid to add force to the strange and unaccountable deceptions practised upon me; for as deceptions my reason still endeavoured to consider them, though my senses strove no less forcibly to convince me that they were realities. Here however there could be no delusion: the thunder still continued to roll, each clap growing louder and louder than the former. I buried my face again in my hands, for I felt overpowered with a propensity to sleep, apparently the effect of the odour which still continued to scent the room. So powerful indeed was this effect, that notwithstanding the continued and increased noise of the storm, I soon fell into a most profound nap, from which I awoke only to hear the great clock strike seven.

It being now broad day, I would gladly have entered upon an investigation of the causes of all I had seen and heard; but the tarpaulins precluding any light from coming in at the windows, and being so high that it was impossible for me to remove them, I had no other light to assist me but what I could procure by opening the door, and that was altogether insufficient for my purpose: I therefore quitted the room, and rushed with a bosom tortured by a conflict of passions into my own apartment.

I had just thrown myself upon my bed, and was beginning to take a hated retrospect of what had passed, when I heard a gentle tap at my door. I enquired who was there, and was answered by a voice which I knew to be Olivia's, "'Tis I, Mr. Egerton. I wish to speak with you."

I opened the door. "I beg your pardon for this interruption," she said; "but I was anxious to hear the event of your last night's adventure. Did you see or hear any thing extraordinary?"

"Assuredly, Madam, I did both see and hear things which have astonished and perplexed me beyond expression."

"Oh, what did you see?—my father?"

"No, Madam; my—my—It was a human form indeed to all appearance, but its features were those of Sir Francis Stanhope."—I did but just recollect myself in time, Orlando, for in my eagerness I had almost said "*my* father."

"Sir Francis Stanhope!" exclaimed Olivia. "Heavens, I hope he is not dead!—But are you sure that it was him you saw?—It has always been supposed my father."

"Oh! Miss Campbell, pardon me; but I am confident that some wicked deception is here practised upon you, which, if you will permit me, I am determined to investigate to the very bottom. An unfortunate gust of wind blew out my candle last night, and disabled me from making the researches I wished; but if you will only allow me to watch there again to-night I will be better prepared against such contingencies, and I trust I shall be able to lay this ghost without the aid of charms and incantations."

"Ah! no, Mr. Egerton, this must not be."

"How, Madam! would you wish still to remain the dupe of villains—for that some villainy lurks beneath the strange appearance I saw, I am confident."

"What villainy can there be?"

"That is what I would examine."

"Oh no; I dare not permit it."

"Dare not, Madam?"

"To what good purpose could it tend?—and should this really be my father, I would not for worlds do any thing that might offend him. Besides, it has always been the same; the candle has blown out, and thunderings have been heard in that room when the air was perfectly calm, and the elements entirely at rest. Can it then be doubted that my father wishes to remain there unmolested? and would it not be a gross violation of filial duty to repeat these attempts at intruding upon him?"

"Good God, Madam, how much you astonish me!—But believe me, the figure I saw was Sir Francis Stanhope. Is not this variation of the form then, a sufficient proof of the imposture?"

"Alas! no.—I fear it only indicates a new calamity, and that the worthy Sir Francis is even now no more."

Orlando, I cannot describe the horror I felt at this suggestion. Though convinced of the frail foundation on which the idea rested, yet a momentary chill ran through my veins, as if I had actually seen the messenger of my father's death. Nay, even now, so much more powerful is feeling than reason, I cannot help experiencing a painful anxiety to hear of that kindest of parents, and to be assured under his own hand that I am not gifted with second sight. Perhaps this feeling is the stronger from my having received only one letter from him since I left Kilverton, and that on the very day of my arrival at Campbell-House.

Yet, unwilling to give up my point, several times in the course of the day did I urge my tormentress to grant me another night's lodging in the *Chamber of Spectres*. But this was not to be obtained, and I was at last interdicted from mentioning the subject again.

What perplexes me more than any thing in this strange business is, that nobody seems to have heard the storm but myself. Not that I have made even Harry the confident of my last night's adventure, nor shall I ever acknowledge to any one but yourself how egregious a dupe I have been made, unless I succeed in detecting the fallacy. But when I talked to Harry of a storm between one and two o'clock, he said I must have been dreaming of one, for that he was not in bed till near two, and he never saw a more clear and beautiful night.

Oh that I had but enquired farther particulars respecting the former appearances of this vision, since Olivia alluded to others who had both seen that, and heard the thunderings; and could I arrive at some communication with them, a clue might be furnished for unravelling the mystery. At least by knowing who these persons are, I should be able to judge of the exact measure of credit due to their testimony. But interdicted as I am from mentioning the subject again, how am I to obtain the information I wish?

And now, Orlando, what do you think of the matter?—Is Olivia really weak, and therefore easily imposed upon by artful persons, who have some unknown purpose of their own to serve by thus sporting with her credulity?—or she is a malicious fiend, fertile in devising means of tormenting all whom she can entice within her magic circle? One of these she must be; and yet, upon the faith of a gentleman, she is the pleasantest woman in conversation that I ever met with—that is to say, when she is only plain Olivia Campbell; for when she chooses to be the heroine of romance I cannot say much in her commendation.

I thank you for informing me of Jerry's summons to Kilverton. I could almost say let Sir Francis come; he can hardly sink me lower in my own

esteem than I am at present, and a fair opportunity would then be presented for making the dreaded disclosure. I know not what to think of Harry's ultimate success; I am sometimes afraid that his princess grows weary of him. Heaven only knows what will become at last of him, and of
Your very affectionate

LIONEL STANHOPE.

LETTER XVI.

HARRIOT BELGRAVE
TO
OLIVIA CAMPBELL.

Kirby, August 20.

Is it really that, among the various calamities which alternately agonise the human mind, none is so severe as to have an old wound which had occasioned years of smart, and been healed at last with difficulty, again violently torn open?—or is it that we always suppose the present suffering the most acute?—Whichever of these may be the case, certain it is, my dearest Olivia, that my heart seems to have experienced even greater torments during the short interval which has elapsed since my departure from Campbell-House, than in those horrible moments when I first became convinced that the connection to which I had looked forward as the balm to assuage my sorrows, and in which I hoped to enjoy no common degree of happiness, was irrevocably dissolved.

Indeed, the events which occasioned our present separation were such as to wound a mind, not lost to all feeling, in the most sensible part, inasmuch as no anguish can be inflicted equal to that given through the bosom of a beloved friend and benefactor. My own injuries I had felt deeply; they for a while entirely destroyed my peace, and impaired my health—but that time was past, and the kind counsels of an excellent mother, united with the still kinder treatment of two friends, who more resembled angels than mortals, had taught me to rise superior to misfortune; nor could the mere sight alone of the author of my sorrows have affected me so deeply as to make me endeavour, or even wish, to shun the interview. But to behold one who had interested me so tenderly, and whom I had allowed myself fondly to hope might one day reform, and return to the paths of virtue, so sunk in degeneracy as almost to preclude the possibility of reformation, was a stroke against which my heart was not guarded, and I was obliged to fly the conflict.

Yes, my dear Olivia, friend of my bosom, consoler of my troubles, notwithstanding the many instances I daily heard of my former lover's profligate conduct, I was still weak enough to hope that at some future period he might be reclaimed. I thought that the flame of honour and virtue which had once glowed so ardently in his breast, could not be entirely extinguished, and trusted that the smothering embers would in time blaze forth again with their original vigour. This idea was soothing to my fancy, although I could never hope myself to profit by the change. Alas! I am now fatally convinced that his heart is too entirely depraved ever to recover its former tone.

But enough on this subject—Would that I could blot it entirely and everlastingly from my memory!

My mother joined us yesterday. She is in high spirits about our lawsuit, but it will occasion us a journey to Ireland, and that probably very soon. Oh! what painful recollections will re-visiting that country awaken in my bosom!

Among the letters you have forwarded to me since my departure, was one from Charlotte O'Brien at Scarborough. She has become much acquainted with a Mr. St. John, the intimate friend and constant correspondent of one or both of your guests, who, since he found that she was related to me, has frequently made both you and myself the subject of his conversation, and been extremely inquisitive with respect to your fortune, character, opinions, and various other particulars. He appears to be acquainted with your person, from having seen you at Doncaster races.

As soon as I learned all this, I wrote to Charlotte, requesting her to be very careful never to mention, or even in the remotest way to allude, to those circumstances in my life which I have always so cautiously concealed from the public attention, and which I now feel more anxious than ever to bury in the faithful bosoms alone of the few to whom they have hitherto been confided. I thought, till put to this severe trial, that my heart had been stronger; but, alas! experience shews me but too plainly, that its old impressions are very far from being erased.

But I will lay down my pen, for I perceive that I cannot write without perpetually reverting to this subject. Pardon this weakness in

Yours most affectionately,

E. H. BELGRAVE.

LETTER XVII.

ORLANDO ST. JOHN
TO
LIONEL STANHOPE.

Scarborough, August 21.

In compliance with thy request, Mr. Li., yesterday evening, when a large party of us were walking together upon the sands, I contrived to draw Charlotte apart from the rest of the company, and very ingeniously leading the conversation to Campbell-House, I asked, after a few other trifling questions, how long Mrs. and Miss Belgrave had lived with Miss Campbell?

"Several years," she replied.

"Miss Campbell then must have been very young when they settled there?"

"She was."

"I suppose Mrs. Belgrave first came into the family as governess to Miss Campbell?"

"No, as a friend only."

"I presume, however, that Mrs. Campbell was not then alive?"

"Recently dead."

"So that Miss Campbell was principally educated by Mrs. Belgrave?"

"Principally."

"Miss Campbell and Miss Belgrave, therefore, have been brought up together like sisters?"

"Excepting the difference of age and fortune."

"I thought they had been very nearly of an age?"

"Miss Belgrave is the oldest by some years."

"I should not have supposed that, as I understand Miss Campbell to be five-and-twenty?"

"Within a few weeks."

"And Miss Belgrave does not look more."

"She looks young."

"Her father, I think, was a clergyman?"

"Oh no."

"You surprise me! I always understood that she and her mother were reduced to their present state of dependence by the loss of income upon Mr. Belgrave's death?"

"Incomes may be lost in various ways."

"The ladies are not very nearly related to Miss Campbell, I think?"

"They are not at all related."

"But have nevertheless been for some years entirely supported, first by the General, and then by herself?"

"Entirely so."

"Miss Belgrave is very beautiful."

"Yes."

"And I am informed very sensible and accomplished."

"Yes."

"Mrs. Belgrave must be very clever to have educated both these young ladies so well."

"Yes."

"'Tis very extraordinary that a woman so beautiful and accomplished as Miss Belgrave should still remain single."

"Hum!"

"She must doubtless have had many admirers?"

"Hum!"

"Her cruelty must have occasioned many a heart-ach[e] to our sex."

"Hum!"

Make your best of this interesting intelligence, *mon cher ami*. For my part I could support such a conversation no longer. The little abrupt answers at first were sufficiently repulsive, but when they dwindled down to a *yes*, and the *yes* at length to a mere *hum*, 'twas past all endurance.

And what could make the bewitching Charlotte thus cautious and reserved, is far beyond my comprehension, for *croyez moi*, this excess of phlegm, is extremely foreign to her general disposition, which is perfectly frank and open, I might even say to a high degree unguarded. Is it not then a natural conclusion, that if such a character be reserved upon one particular subject, it must be for some very particular reason?

I know thou lovest an ingenious conjecture to thy heart, Lionel. *Eh bien donc*, thou shalt have one. What if Harriot should be another of that unfortunate class of females who has once in her life made a slight *faux pas*, and has likewise found a protecting angel under the form of thy benevolent heiress? *Ma foi*, I think this a very probable case, and it solves the whole matter at once, for thence arose the *hums* when I began upon the subject of lovers, marrying, and so forth.

And now since I have amply supplied with speculation, my deficiency in fact, no more at present from,

Thy most obedient,
Most devoted,

ORLANDO ST. JOHN.

LETTER XVIII.

LIONEL STANHOPE
TO
ORLANDO ST. JOHN.

Campbell-House, August 21.

Orlando, you threatened us with an approaching storm. One has indeed burst upon us, but it came not from the quarter you apprehended. Sir Francis is not the Æolus[38] who has raised the wind. Indignant though he might be, did he suspect our treachery, no tempest of so rude a nature could originate from a source so benevolent. Oh! that I could at this moment fly far hence to some obscure asylum, where, remote from the observation of my fellow-creatures, I might seek in penitence and seclusion to atone for the infamy of my conduct, and whence, as a first proof of my contrition, I would write a full and free confession of my guilt, to her against whom I have sinned so deeply.

But I am spell-bound here, and the more ardently I wish to escape from the magic circle, the more firmly do I find myself rivetted to the spot. With still greater ardour do I wish that Harry were away, since each day, each hour, I dread seeing him driven to absolute distraction. Yet, if under our present circumstances it would be *difficult* for me to escape, for him it is *impossible*. His flight would be pleading guilty to a new charge against him, of which I trust he will prove himself innocent; but at any rate he must stay and face it, even at the hazard of his reason.

St. John! St. John!—I could almost swear that this house must be the abode of evil spirits, who assume any form at Olivia's command. In no other way can I account for the phantom I saw, nor can I conceive that aught but a fiend could utter the circumstantial falsehoods I have this day heard. Yet hold!—am I so certain that they are falsehoods!—Oh yes!—yes!—they must be so!—Harry could not be guilty of deceit when he asserted to me his innocence; he was too much heated to be capable of it. Intemperance is generally sincere; cool recollection and self-possession are essential to supporting deceit with consistency.

This morning while we were at breakfast, a letter was brought to Olivia, which the servant said he was desired by a young woman to deliver into her hands, with a request that she might see her when she had read it. Olivia read the letter instantly, and ordered the servant to shew the lady into the library, where she said she would wait upon her in a few moments.

She then turned to Harry and myself: "Gentlemen," she said, "it is not easy to express how much I am shocked and astonished at the charges here brought against you. So deeply should I be concerned to find them substantiated, that I never can credit them but upon the most irrefragable proof. I shall therefore give you a fair and full opportunity for your mutual vindication, by desiring that the letter may be publicly read. May I trouble you, Mr. Beauchamp;" and she put the paper into his hands. It was as follows:

MADAM,

To be addressed by a perfect stranger upon a subject of so delicate a nature as the present, may appear extraordinary, yet I could not have felt acquitted to my own conscience, had I remained silent at such a moment. Yes, Madam, I feel it no less a duty to you than to myself, to warn you of the frightful precipice on the brink of which you stand, and into which you might otherwise rush unawares.

The gentleman who is now staying at your house under the name of Stanhope, I can safely assure you is not the son of your late father's old and respected friend. He is a libertine of ruined character and broken fortune, who has assumed a name of respectability in hopes of obtaining your hand, that he may squander away your property in the same dissipated and profligate manner in which he wasted his own. But, Madam, over the hand he offers you, believe me he has not himself any right; it is mine by every claim of faith and justice, and had not perjury been a trifle in his eyes, ere this the plighted vows we have exchanged, had been solemnly ratified at the altar.

I ask not in a matter of this importance to be believed solely on my own assertions. Fortunately for me and for the world, to which it is but proper that such a character should be exposed in its native deformity, I have evidence of a much stronger nature to bring against him, evidence that must overpower even effrontery like his.

I have no doubt that he will deny any knowledge of me. Let him do so; it will but compel me to produce the stronger evidence of *my* wrongs, and *his* guilt and folly.

I am, Madam, with all respect,
Your obedient humble servant,

JANE RIVERS.

St. John, at this moment I could gladly have seen the earth open and swallow us and our shame together. Abashed and confounded, I had no power of utterance, but sat motionless as a statue, in mute expectation of what was next to follow. A solemn pause succeeded, when at length Olivia addressed Egerton, "What have you to say to this accusation, Sir?"

He hesitated for a moment, but then adroitly evading the first part of the charge, his change of name, adverted at once to the latter, which he could more easily answer, and said, "Indeed, Madam, I am so astonished at the audacity of this imposture, that I scarcely know in what manner to attempt its refutation. I can only swear by all that's sacred, that till this moment I never heard of such a person as Jane Rivers."

"I must then bring her hither," said Olivia, "and we shall see how far she can really substantiate her charge. You will be so obliging as to wait my return, gentlemen;" and she arose and departed.

After an absence of a few minutes, she returned accompanied by a smart looking young woman, whose features were in great measure concealed by a long muslin veil, and a profusion of dark hair hanging about her face and shoulders. "Now, Madam," said Olivia, "it will appear whether or not you know the gentleman whose hand you claim, since he denies any knowledge of you."

"Oh false-hearted man," she exclaimed, going immediately up to Egerton and seizing one of his hands, "can he dare to deny a promise that he knows I can so fully prove!—Ah traitor! traitor!—well you know that I ought ere this to have been your wife!"—Here she quitted her hold as if altogether overpowered, and throwing her hands upon the table concealed her face in them.

Egerton started up, and stamping furiously upon the ground, cried, "False, false as hell!—I swear then once more by all that's sacred—"

Here I interposed, and going to him, "Swear not so vehemently, Harry," I said. "This surely cannot all be false." Indeed, St. John, I will own, that from the general tenor of his life for some years past, I thought there was but too much reason to apprehend it true.

"'Tis false, by heaven!" he said. "Yes, though I knew that this were to be the last hour of my life, I would swear that I never till the present moment beheld that vile woman. Heaven and earth, is such treatment to be borne! This house is the abode of fiends, and I will not stay in it one moment longer!"

He was then rushing towards the door, but I stopped him. "No, Harry," I said, "you leave it not thus. Whatever may be the truth of the present case, you must be conscious that on other grounds we stand here two guilty wretches, nor must depart without acknowledging our treachery with humility and contrition."

Olivia paid no attention to what was now passing between us, for she had drawn Miss Rivers aside to one of the windows, where they were engaged in close conversation. Beauchamp looked on, but spake not a word, nor appeared sensible of my having twice called Egerton by his own name of Harry. As for Egerton himself, I saw him so violently agitated, that I thought it better we should retire for a while; so taking his arm, I drew him gently with me to a seat in the garden.

"Oh Stanhope!" he exclaimed as we sat down, "whither can we go!— what can we do!—where hide our guilty heads!—To what a situation am I reduced!—how am I fallen, even below contempt! become the sport, the mockery, of a malicious woman, who affects folly herself only to draw others into the grossest absurdities!—And I to become her dupe!—Oh 'tis too much!—Teach me, Lionel, how to support myself in a situation so degrading!—Yet you seem no less agitated than myself."

"And with no less reason! Am not I equally fallen and degraded? Nay, am I not more so, since I was the accursed origin of this detested scheme? But why waste our time, and exhaust our fortitude in unavailing complaints! Let us rather instantly throw ourselves at Olivia's feet, acknowledge our guilt, and then become voluntary exiles from the world. Yet first I would be satisfied on one point, Harry. Too well I know the lightness of your conduct towards the female sex; tell me truly, then, has not Miss Rivers been its victim?"

"Can you suppose it probable, Lionel, that I who have long pursued my pleasures with a licentiousness so unbounded, so unrefined, that I sought no higher gratification than what was to be purchased at a stated price; that I would employ so much circumvention for the possession of one object, and she too not one of particular attraction? Still less does it appear credible, that I would give a promise of marriage with no view at all; and she does not even pretend that it was given for the purpose of seduction."

"This is but evading the question. I am not investigating probabilities, I seek to ascertain a fact."

"Hear me, Lionel. Once I could boast of principles more pure, and practice more conformable to them, than is usual among young men in my situation. That one overwhelming calamity led me to renounce those principles, and abandon myself to vice and dissipation, is, alas! but too true! My guilty conduct towards the female sex in particular, I will not pretend to disguise or palliate, I acknowledge its criminality in the fullest extent. Then surely, after a confession so explicit, I may expect to be believed when I solemnly assure you, that in the present instance 'tis Jane Rivers, not myself, who is forsworn."

"Harry, I must, and do believe you. Yet there is something in the affair wholly inexplicable. 'Tis evident she knows you, since she singled you out from among the three men present."

"She had been instructed for the purpose by Olivia, whom from my soul I believe the contriver of the whole business."

"The truth of that suspicion I have no doubt I can learn from Beauchamp. When he sees the agony you suffer from this affair, his benevolence, I am confident, will induce him to tell me all."

"His benevolence!—his!—Curse him! pander as he is to this infernal woman's malicious machinations."

"I cannot believe that he has any share in the plot, if plot it be. I have seen proofs of the goodness of his heart that would render any doubts of it unpardonable. Nay, I have witnessed such instances of benevolence in Miss Campbell, as render some apparently darker shades in her character altogether incomprehensible."

"I wish I were acquainted with them. But for my part, since I entered the doors of Campbell-House I have seen no disposition in either but to sport with the follies they themselves excited. Let us hasten, then to our confession, and when once I am out of this detested place, may curses greater than any I have now experienced, light upon my head if ever I approach it again."

Anxious, however, to spare him as much as possible, I persuaded him to go for a while to his own apartment, and endeavour to compose himself, while I would prepare the way for the dreadful task we had to perform. To this he with some difficulty consented, and I went immediately to enquire for Beauchamp, persuaded that by opening my heart first to him, the moment of disclosure to Olivia would be softened. But, to my infinite mortification, I found that Olivia had gone out in the chariot a few minutes before, taking Miss Rivers with her, and that nobody knew any thing of Mr. Beauchamp.

What was now to be done I knew not. I went to Beauchamp's own house, thinking he might be there, but did not find him. He had been with his workmen before breakfast, but they had not seen him since. I returned, and walked about the garden for some time, but still as neither he nor Olivia appeared, I was obliged to go and tell Egerton how we were circumstanced. He was extremely irritated at this delay, and I with difficulty restrained him from setting off directly. He swore he would not thus wait Olivia's pleasure, but would write the hated confession from some distant part, which would be less humiliating than making it in person.

With much soothing, however, and suggesting that Olivia was probably gone to seek further information relative to Miss Rivers, I did at last obtain a solemn promise that he would not quit the house before her return.

But of her we saw no more that day. Beauchamp did not return till late in the evening, when he made an apology that Miss Campbell was obliged to be absent all night, but hoped to be at home by dinner on the morrow. Not a syllable transpired of the occasion of her absence, not did Beauchamp, during an hour that he and Harry and myself sat together, make the remotest allusion to Miss Rivers, or her claim.

When Harry retired for the night, I lingered behind, resolved to break the important matter to Beauchamp, and accordingly began: "I hope I shall not be deemed intrusive if I request half an hour's conversation, Mr. Beauchamp, before we separate. I wish to make you the confident of an affair which oppresses my mind very severely, and which I shall feel less reluctance in disclosing to you than to any other person."

"Excuse me, Sir. It is a principle with me not to be the confident of any man. I hold the office of confident to be one of the most difficult in the world to discharge conscientiously. Perhaps I might see reason to think that your secret ought to be made public, and then I should certainly consider my duty to the world at large, as superseding that to you as an individual. Besides, I have rode a great many miles to-day, and am extremely fatigued. I must therefore wish you good night;" and so saying he hastily and abruptly quitted the room.

Surprise and mortification kept me fixed to my seat for some moments. Alas! thought I, is this an earnest of what we are to expect from Olivia! At length I rushed up stairs, and threw myself upon the bed, a prey to unutterable torments. From these, after a while, I roused myself, to relieve my soul by unburthening all its troubles to you, Orlando. And now I go to seek rest, though little hoping to find it. But sleeping or waking, I shall still be

    Unalterably yours,

LIONEL STANHOPE.

LETTER XIX.

LIONEL STANHOPE
TO
ORLANDO ST. JOHN.

Campbell-House, August 27.

'Tis all over, St. John, the whole story is known, and yet we are not turned out of doors. This morning after breakfast, perceiving Beauchamp leave the room, I followed him, resolved to try whether a night's rest might not have brought him into better temper. "Will Mr. Beauchamp," I said, "still refuse to listen to the confession of a penitent? Will he not now grant me the privilege of a hearing? I was perhaps too obtrusive in asking it last night."

"You distress me, Sir. If you wish to ask any questions upon the subject of Miss Rivers, say on. If, as I suspect, you wish to mention another subject, I must beg to be excused listening to you. I am not insensible to your cousin's pretensions with regard to Miss Campbell; but if he wishes me to interfere in his favour, that I must absolutely refuse."

"Believe me you mistake, Mr. Beauchamp. Far other things at present occupy my bosom. My friend indeed—"

"Not a word of him if you wish me to hear you, unless, as I said before, your enquiries have any reference to Miss Rivers. On that subject, and on that alone, can I answer your questions."

"Nor is it my object to ask questions. I only wish to impart to you a matter of deep concern, both to my friend and myself."

"And I, like yourself, am ready to give information, not to receive it."

"Oh that you would listen to me!"

"With what view can you seek this confidence in one, for whose faith you can have no adequate security? Our short acquaintance precludes the possibility of your having a sufficient knowledge of me, to be assured that the trust you repose would not be misplaced, and I must suspect therefore, that there are secret motives for this confidence, which would render my yielding to it embarrassing to myself."

"A very short acquaintance is sufficient to attract my confidence in some men; with others I might have frequent intercourse for my whole life, yet never be disposed to make them sharers in my heart."

"I will not arraign such feelings, because they are precisely my own. But however you may be disposed to number me among the chosen few to whom you are thus instantly attracted, though I may feel grateful for the compliment, I must not the less decline listening to the communication."

"I do not wish to impart a secret that must be locked up in your bosom for ever, nor even for many hours. I only wish to confide to your generosity some perplexities in which I am at present involved, and intreat your advice how best to extricate myself from them."

"I still less like the office of a counsellor than of a confident. And allow me to observe, that a person with a tolerable share of common-sense is always the best judge of his own concerns. No one can be so well acquainted with all the minute circumstances, the thousand intricacies interwoven with the affair in question as himself—and these should all be thoroughly understood before it can be possible to judge impartially upon a matter of any difficulty."

"I must then be silent?"

"Or else importunate."

"Which I by no means wish."

"Therefore let us drop the subject. And on that condition I shall be very happy in your company if you will join me in a walk."

This proposal I declined, for as I had now no other resource but to address myself immediately to the heiress, I wished not to be absent at her return. She did not arrive till very near the dinner hour, and then went up to dress, so that I had no opportunity of seeing her till we were all assembled round the dinner table. She then apologised very politely for her absence, but did not give the least hint of what had occasioned it.

Never have I seen her more animated or brilliant in conversation since I came into the house. I could not help looking at her with astonishment, for it seemed to me wholly unaccountable that any thing so plain should be so eloquent. This amenity was, however, peculiarly grateful to me, as it inspired me with confidence for the task I had to go through; since I could scarcely conceive it possible, how grievous soever the provocation, that such unaffected ease and good humour could be changed in a moment to sourness and severity. I was considering how best to solicit a private audience, but she prevented my application by requesting, as she rose to retire after dinner, to speak with me in the library.

I followed like a culprit to execution, when desiring me to sit down, she began: "Much as Mr. Stanhope appeared agitated yesterday, at the interview with Miss Rivers, I wished, Mr. Egerton, to put some questions to you before any thing farther was said to him upon the subject. I intreat you to answer me sincerely, whether you know of any connection between your cousin and this young lady?"

"Upon my honour, Madam, I do not. Indeed, I am myself fully convinced that she is an impostor; and I think the more minutely the matter is investigated, the more clearly this will appear."

"I own that the circumstances she has related to me are very extraordinary, nor do I know absolutely what to think about them. That she has a claim somewhere, however, I can scarcely doubt; but many things she has mentioned in support of the truth of her story, I should have thought more applicable to you, Sir, than to your cousin."

She paused—I thought that here was a fair opening for me to enter upon my confession, as I had no doubt, from what Olivia said, that she thought the woman's claim referred rather to Henry Egerton than to Lionel Stanhope. Summoning together, therefore, all my resolution, I began, though still with a great mixture of hesitation and confusion,— "Madam—I—Madam"—but she prevented my proceeding, by resuming the conversation again herself, and saying, "Yet she may, after all, be right, and have addressed her claim to the proper person."

"Pardon me, Madam, but my cousin has so solemnly disavowed to me any knowledge of this woman, that I must suspect her of being an impostor, who has only urged this claim in hopes of being bought to silence."

"Well, Sir, be this as it may, I presume you will concur with me in opinion that there is only one way of deciding the matter—to hear both sides fairly. If then it shall clearly appear that your cousin has engaged his faith to Miss Rivers, I trust he will not deny her that justice which the case requires. Can you persuade him to meet her here?"

"'Tis what he earnestly wishes."

"Will you then request his attendance?"

"At what time, Madam?"

"Immediately, if you please. Miss Rivers is now below with her witnesses; I will desire them to come up."

I instantly hastened to Egerton, who returned with me to the library, where we already found the claimant. Olivia addressed Harry:—"This is an unpleasant affair, Mr. Stanhope; I am sorry to trouble you farther about it, but justice must take its course. Will you now acknowledge your engagement to this lady?—or will you compel her to produce witnesses of her wrongs, whom perhaps you may not be much pleased to see?"

"She can have no witnesses that I need fear, Madam. Conscious of my own innocence, I am certain that no respectable person can appear against me; and for a parcel of perjured knaves, their testimony may disgrace her, but cannot injure me."

"I would have spared your confusion, Sir, but since you do not chuse to spare yourself, the witnesses must appear. Will you call the first, Madam."

Miss Rivers went out of the room, and returned in an instant, leading in—oh astonishment past all expression!—Beauchamp himself. "Now, Sir," said she, "will you be so obliging as to relate what you once heard pass between this gentleman and me."

"A solemn exchange of vows of unalterable fidelity, with an agreement on a day then named, to ratify those vows, even at the sacred altar of heaven."

"How, Sir," exclaimed Egerton, "do you dare to assert this?—Can a man of your character and respectability stoop to support so gross an imposture?"

"I speak but what I heard, Sir. Would to God that every person present detested imposture as much as I do!"

Struck to the soul with this implied reflection upon us, Egerton fixed his eyes wildly on Beauchamp, nor could utter a word in reply. I, though at the first moment scarcely less confounded, yet soon recollected myself sufficiently to take up the matter:—"Mr. Beauchamp," I said, "it seems so extraordinary to find you, whose acquaintance even with the person of my cousin is of so short a date, thus appearing as a witness against him, that I cannot help suspecting some unaccountable misapprehension—"

"The mistake is on your side, Sir, in supposing that because my personal acquaintance with your cousin is so recent, I cannot have been sufficiently acquainted with his actions to be a competent witness in this case. I affirm nothing but what is strictly true; and would readily, if required, take my oath that I heard vows of unalterable fidelity exchanged between that gentleman and lady."

"Death and damnation!" exclaimed Egerton, almost frantic, "here is some vile collusion; and I call upon you, Miss Campbell, who make such eager professions of your impartial justice, to extend it to me, by unfolding the whole of this mysterious affair, which, I have no doubt, is in your power."

"Call not on me, Sir," replied Olivia, "as an evidence on your behalf. I must confirm what Mr. Beauchamp has advanced."

"Oh God of heaven!" cried Egerton, "is then all truth and honesty banished from the world? But by the sacred name of justice itself I swear, that not all of you combined shall compel me to yield to this infernal claim. For you, Madam," he continued, addressing Olivia, "I know that I stand before you a guilty wretch, not entitled to your pardon or compassion; but I am not quite so fallen, so degraded, as that I will submit to be made your sport, your laughing-stock. I know not whether to leave your house with tears of remorse or denunciations of vengeance, but leave it I will at this moment, and for ever. For you, abandoned wretch," he added, turning to Miss Rivers, "may all the dæmons of hell!—yet no!—be the torment of disappointed villainy, and hopes for ever crossed, your bitter punishment, as it will still be mine!"

He was now rushing towards the door, when Olivia interposed: "No, Sir," she said, "you do not leave us thus. We have yet another witness to produce, who must be heard ere you can be suffered to depart."—She then opened a door, when in walked—oh God! never shall I forget my sensations at that moment—Sir Francis Stanhope.

I started, exclaiming with a tone of mingled horror and astonishment—"My father!!!"

"Sir Francis Stanhope!!!" cried Egerton, in a tone of equal consternation.

"Yes, Sir," replied the venerable man, "Sir Francis Stanhope, come to expose your treachery and villainy, in bearing testimony to your engagement with that lady."

Egerton threw himself at Olivia's feet, and clasping her hands in agony, cried,—"Tell me, tell me, I conjure you, unless you are resolved to drive me to distraction, the meaning of all this. Do I dream?—or am I awake, and is there really any truth in magic?—for without witcheries and sorceries I know not how this matter can be explained."

"It may be explained much more simply," said Olivia.—"But rise, Sir; this groveling attitude becomes neither me nor yourself.—Miss Rivers, will you be pleased to unveil?"

Miss Rivers advanced; she pulled off her bonnet, and with it a large bushy wig, and a pair of thick black eyebrows, while before us stood confessed, Jenny, *fille de-chambre* to the lady Olivia. "Now, Sir," said the latter, "will you persist in denying your engagement with that lady?"

Egerton looked surprised, confused, half angry, half pleased, and at length stammered out—"No, Madam—no—it—it cannot be disowned any longer. She has an undoubted claim upon my hand."

"Which from this moment," said Olivia, "I have no doubt she will cheerfully resign. Am I not right, Jenny?"

"Yes, Madam," replied the damsel; "and I hope the gentleman will forgive me for reminding him of it."—Then, with a curtesy, she withdrew.

This business dispatched, our fiery trial for our real offences was next to come on. But this was a subject of a nature so singular, so unprecedented, that scarcely did any one of the company know how to enter upon it. We all looked at each other for some minutes; all seemed to feel that something remained to be settled, yet no one knew how to give his feelings utterance. Sir Francis fixed his eyes upon me; I once or twice stole a glance at him; I saw him endeavouring to be very angry; I thought that I ought to begin with throwing myself at Olivia's feet, and that this was what he expected of me—but when it was done I knew not what to say.— At length seeing me still mute and motionless, he approached me, and said, "Young gentleman, by what name would you please to be addressed?"

"By any that you please, Sir."

"Rascal, then—I know of none that you deserve so well."

"Nor I neither, upon my soul, Sir."

"Are you not ashamed to look me in the face?"

"Perfectly so."

"Oh! Li. Li. that ever it should come to this!—that ever your poor old father should be ashamed of owning you for a son!—Have you nothing to say in your defence, imposter?"

"Nothing at all, Sir—except that I came hither solely in compliance with your entreaties."

"But I did not entreat you to take name of Egerton, Mr. Scape-grace."

"Granted, Sir, that was entirely my own idea. The guilt of that is exclusively my own."

"And guilt enough on my conscience, guilt that even the benevolence of Miss Campbell can never pardon."

"Or if she could, that I never can forgive myself." I paused—I thought these answers were in a strain of levity ill-suited to the occasion, and though such as I had been too much accustomed to make to my father in our petty contentions, yet now but adding tenfold to my offences. Assuming therefore a tone of seriousness and remorse, I turned to Olivia:

"Do not suppose, Madam," said I, "that I shall add to the guilt I have already incurred, that of seeking by paltry excuses to extenuate treachery and baseness, of a nature far too black and heinous to admit of extenuation. That I was urged to it by strong motives is needless to urge, for who can act without motives?—but however forcible they might be, a man with any principles of honour or honesty never would have yielded to them, even in thought, for a single moment. I do not therefore ask forgiveness. A youthful lapse from the strict path of virtue may receive pardon—deliberate baseness admits of none. I only ask permission, now that I have acknowledged my transgressions, to fly this place, and hide myself and my shame for ever, in some remote and obscure corner of the world."

"A permission which I shall certainly refuse."

"Madam?"

"By your conduct towards me, Mr. Stanhope, you have given me a power of controul over you to which I had otherwise never made pretention; and since the law cannot take cognizance of your offence, I shall take upon myself to be your judge, and sentence you to at least a month's imprisonment in Campbell-House."

"Oh heavens!—what do I hear?"

"You think my sentence then severe?"

"I think it one that no heart but your own could have been capable of inflicting."

"And one to which you will submit with reluctance?"

"I acknowledge it, Madam. The injured party is not wounded by the sight of the offender, but how can the offender support the presence of those whom he has injured?"

"That must depend entirely upon the dispositions of the respective parties, and I trust that in this case you will not find your confinement painful, nor your gaoler harsh."

"Indeed I fear so. But the more mild my treatment, the more severe will be my punishment, since your lenity will but make my conduct appear in much darker colours. Oh! then, Madam, I conjure you to let me depart!—Keep me not constantly on the rack, by compelling me incessantly to contemplate my own conduct in the most degrading and mortifying point of view."

"Yet let me intreat your stay. We have hitherto been all playing at cross-purposes; let us not separate the moment we are come to a right understanding."

"How can you solicit a deceiver, an imposter, to remain under your roof?—'Tis scarcely knowing what is due to yourself."

"You have not deceived or imposed upon me. You only deceived yourself in imagining that I could be imposed upon by so shallow an artifice. Your features alone, Mr. Stanhope, had been sufficient to betray you; for could that strong resemblance to a face so well known, leave me any room to doubt whose son you must be. But I rested not my conviction of your intended imposture merely upon that evidence—I had other means of information upon the subject, in which I could not possibly be deceived. Believe me I have felt—yes, with the deepest regret, have felt, how much both you and Mr. Egerton were degrading yourselves. Instant exposure and disgrace was what I was conscious such treachery deserved, yet I had powerful motives for delaying that exposure to the present moment. Time and circumstances alone must determine whether those motives ever shall be explained. Even now I will not pretend to perfect disinterestedness in soliciting your longer stay here. I own that as the son of a much-respected friend, I have long wished for your acquaintance, yet my own wishes alone would not be sufficient to influence me in requesting a moment's prolongation of your stay—but I have other reasons for urging it which must remain concealed. Will you not then grant my request?"

Orlando, what answer could be made to such solicitations, but that I was entirely at her disposal. I bowed assent, adding grateful acknowledgments for her kindness and lenity. She then addressed herself to Harry—"And on Mr. Egerton," she said, "I wish to inflict a like sentence. I have equal motives for requesting his stay at Campbell-House, and trust that he will rely upon me when I faithfully promise not to require his playing the knight-errant any longer. Come, gentlemen, let us all shake hands in token of reconciliation. You endeavoured to impose upon me, and I, in return, really did impose upon you—let pardon then be the word on all sides."

It was not for the parties who were to receive the greatest benefit from the proposed amnesty to offer any opposition to it, and accordingly the hands were held out, and we were all sworn friends in a moment. Sir Francis was the only person, however, who could exert any eloquence upon the occasion, and he made so many compliments and fine speeches to the heiress, that in good truth I thought she had no loss in being deprived of Harry's gallantries.

The evening passed off as well as could be expected, considering the extreme awkwardness of our respective situations. Few women would have conducted themselves so well as Olivia did under circumstances equally embarrassing. As for Harry and myself, it was impossible that we could shake off the feelings of disgrace and humiliation necessarily attached to the consciousness of exposed treachery. Indeed I feel every moment more and more acutely how severe is the punishment of being condemned to the society of a person we have so grossly injured. Not all Olivia's truly generous endeavours to remove this restraint can inspire with any confidence the heart of

Your sincerely affectionate

LIONEL STANHOPE.

LETTER XX.

LIONEL STANHOPE
TO
ORLANDO ST. JOHN.

Campbell-House, August 26.
That the lamented days of chivalry were over in this house, as well as in the world at large, was sufficiently explained by my last letter, Orlando. With them, of course, the ghost too has vanished—Arthur need no longer fear walking along the gallery, even at the solemn hour of midnight, and

I might watch in the great room unmolested. Campbell-House is become like any other place, excepting that I know of none where time passes so pleasantly.

Yet no!—I am still almost persuaded that Olivia deals in magic, since by what other means she could obtain any knowledge of the disastrous loves of Harry and Emily I am at a loss to conjecture; but so it is!—not that she had heard the story accurately, since she was ignorant of Emily's death, and supposed the match to have gone off from some fault of Harry's. All this appeared in a private conversation with her yesterday, and as I found that she had heard the story told so erroneously, I thought it but right to state every thing as it really happened, and vindicate poor Harry from any culpability in this instance.

But to his ghostship. On that memorable day when Harry first took upon himself the order of knighthood, just as the tea was concluded, Beauchamp was called out of the room to a gentleman who desired to speak with him at his own house. The incident was in itself so common and insignificant, that it was scarcely noticed by any of the company, and indeed I could not without difficulty recal it to my remembrance. But it now appears that the gentleman was no other than Sir Francis Stanhope, summoned into these parts through the officiousness of honest master Jerry, who peeping into one of my letters, Monsignor Orlando, which you had left upon your table while you were amusing yourself with the fascinating Charlotte, had there fully informed himself of the tricks then playing at Campbell-House, a faithful account of which he immediately transmitted to his dear old master. Curse your carelessness, Mr. St. John!—Could you not have spared one moment's attention from your enchantress to put your letters into a place of safety?—Yet no; I retract my curse, for had not Sir Francis been thus made acquainted with my transgressions, I must now have written him a long explanatory apological epistle, which I am very glad to be spared.

Beauchamp found the old gentleman in what he himself, who is wont to deal in plain and forcible terms, would call a damned passion, and in the short space of about five minutes he did most lamentably transgress the Christian precept of "*swear not at all*,"[39] for he thundered out almost every oath contained in the catalogue of Ernulphus,[40] making over both me and my unfortunate cousin to every dæmon that inhabits the infernal regions, concluding his denunciations with rubbing his hands desperately hard, and asking how Miss Campbell liked Li.?—Beauchamp replying that she did not think him absolutely the most disagreeable man in the world, he gave another rub and said, "Aye, aye, the women all like him; and to be sure he is a fine, handsome, spirited young fellow, though damn him I'll never own him for a son again."

He was then very anxious to burst in upon us immediately, and consign us over to the disgrace we merited, only he wanted first to devise some new and terrible mode of punishment adequate to our offences, since even the severest tortures ever invented by inquisitorial ingenuity were all too mild for such offenders. But Beauchamp, who knew that his so sudden appearance would frustrate Olivia's schemes, prevailed upon him to remain incog.* for a while, upon promise that some means should be contrived for him personally to torment the two graceless truants.

Accordingly, at that silent and enchanting hour when Cynthia[41] began to array herself in her brightest robes, to attend the impassioned Henry Egerton to the windows of his mistress, Sir Francis quitted the humble roof of Reginald Beauchamp, and by the postern gate entered the ancient and more spacious mansion of Olivia Campbell. Here, in a conference with the heiress, he was informed of the expected serenade, at which anxiously wishing to be present, he was permitted to remain in the dressing-room till it was proper that Jenny should be left alone to receive the knight, when he retreated into a closet, and Olivia with Beauchamp retired into the gallery. Thus did he become a witness to Harry's solicitations of the fair Miss Rivers's hand, and to her promise that it should be his on the very next day.

He had just quitted Olivia's apartment, when hearing a door open in the gallery, and fearful of being discovered, he blew out his candle, and concealed himself behind a statue; but as Arthur passed him, still apprehensive of detection, he contrived to blow through the hollow of a truncheon in the statue's hand, which gave the puff sufficient force to extinguish Arthur's light, and leave him in darkness to his no small astonishment and terror. Sir Francis then proceeded boldly on to his own apartment, but as he was obliged to pass a window into which the moon shone very bright; in passing it, he clapped to the shutters, lest his form should be too distinctly seen. The flannel night-gown which he wore assisted to give him a ghost-like appearance, and Arthur's fears were sufficient to supply all the rest.

The ghost I encountered was of a very different nature, and proceeded from one of those optical deceptions which have of late been so much the rage. The large mirror I mentioned in the haunted room had been fixed there some time before, for the express purpose of making experiments in this way, and it was owing to a concatenation of circumstances that it was now used for playing me a not unfair trick. The first refusal on the part of the servants to let Arthur see the room, originated entirely in a determined dislike to him and wish to teaze him, and as they found this purpose effectually answered, they carried on the joke, and in consequence of his suggesting that the General's ghost walked there, encouraged the idea. This had reached Olivia's ears by means of Jenny, and my inquisitiveness concerning the room convincing her that I too had heard of its being haunted, she gladly availed herself of the circumstance to teaze me also. Little preparation was requisite to answer her purpose, and that little she contrived, unnoticed by me, to give Beauchamp a hint to

---

*   Incognito or unknown.

make, while Sir Francis was delighted at playing the part of a ghost, the better to torment his poor boy. The loud crash which so much astonished me, and the thunderings I heard afterwards, were no more than theatrical thunder; for be it known to thee, that the ci-devant chapel was in the old General's time converted into a theatre, where private plays were frequently performed for his amusement; for he being so much of a cripple with the gout that he never could stir from home, his affectionate daughter always contrived every means in her power of entertaining him beneath his own roof.

Tarpaulins were fixed over the windows to exclude the moonlight, as it was necessary for the success of the scheme that I should be left in total darkness; and at the appointed signal, the clock striking one, a small door in the tapestry which I did not perceive, was opened just sufficiently to admit the end of an enormous pair of bellows, with which my candle was blown out—through this also Sir Francis entered very gently, and without shoes, to play the phantom. At departing he left a gum smoking in the room, the effluvium of which operates as a powerful soporific, and it was that which occasioned the odour I mentioned. With this, perhaps you will think somewhat tedious, explanation, I take my leave of the spiritual world, and proceed to other matters.

A not very pleasant effect of our general pacification is, that my good papa has recommenced his importunities on his darling subject of a matrimonial alliance between the ancient and illustrious houses of Stanhope and Campbell. He took an early opportunity, after the amnesty was signed, of seeking a private conference with me, when, after abusing me heartily for the tricks I had been playing, he enquired how I liked Miss Campbell now I had seen her?

"Upon my soul, Sir, I think her extremely plain and extremely pleasant."

"What?—do you really, Li.?—do you really think her extremely pleasant?—do you really like her, Li.?—Well, well, and I promise you I don't think she has a very bad opinion of you, though you are such a good-for-nothing scoundrel."

"Is not that an impeachment either of Miss Campbell's taste, or principles?"

"Hey?—how?—what d'ye mean, Li.?—Pooh, pooh, I only meant to say, that as she has been so good as to forgive you—why there's no knowing—and perhaps if you were to try, Li.—Ladies, you know, have odd tastes sometimes."

"But a lady of Miss Campbell's accomplishments and elegance of mind cannot be supposed to have an odd taste."

"I don't know that, Li.—I am not so sure of that. The most accomplished people have their peculiarities—and 'tis but trying—for after all there's no harm done, supposing you should not succeed."

"I must beg your pardon, Sir, but I do not consider it as so very unimportant a matter to be refused."

"Li. thou art a conceited puppy."

"But what if I have not merely an utter aversion to this match, but to matrimony in general?"

"Then thou art a greater puppy, and fool too, than I thought thee."

"That is my misfortune, Sir. Our wisdom or folly is not in our own power, and if I have not a proper feeling of the sweets of a wedded life, my nature is to be blamed, not I. But let us drop the subject if you please, since we never shall agree upon it."

"And whose fault is that?"

"'Tis not for me positively to decide that question, but I should think the fair thing is to share the fault between us. I am not covetous, I do not wish to keep the whole to myself, I shall be perfectly content with half."

Thus we go on with reply and retort, till at the end of a debate of half an hour we leave the matter just where it was at the beginning. And thus we are likely to go on, since I do not yet find so perfect a transformation in myself, as that I can like a plain face as well as a pretty one.

Among other reconciliations, let me not omit to mention that between Jerry and myself. He was stationed at Doncaster while his old master was playing the ghost here, but now that his ghostship is dispatched to the Red Sea, Mr. Jeremy has resumed his attendance upon my person. I had determined to be very angry with him, but before I recollected my intention, my hand was held out, which he gently pressed to his lips, and bursting into tears, "that was a favour," he said, he "never counted to have received no more," considering what he had done. Thus did he so effectually disarm my resentment, that without another word being said upon the subject we became as good friends as usual.

Adieu! Orlando; and believe me
Unalterably yours,

LIONEL STANHOPE.

LETTER XXI.

OLIVIA CAMPBELL
TO
HARRIOT BELGRAVE.

Campbell-House, August 26.

The plan I imparted to you, my dear Harriot, on the day I passed at Kirby with Miss Rivers, succeeded to my wish, and to the detail I then gave you of all that has occurred since your departure from Campbell-House, I could now add that of the final exposure and contrition of the two cousins, had I not matters of a much more important and interesting nature to impart.

Ever since the morning that I observed Mr. Egerton's extreme confusion upon hearing the name of Trelawney, I have anxiously wished for an opportunity of questioning Mr. Stanhope in private on the subject of his cousin's former engagement; but none could I find till yesterday afternoon, when, as I was walking by myself in the garden, he came and joined me.

After conversing for a short time upon indifferent subjects, he once more mentioned his own and Mr. Egerton's past misconduct, and as he seems to think that sufficient atonement for it can hardly be made, he again assured me, in very eloquent terms, of the deep shame and remorse by which they were overpowered, and of the lively emotions of gratitude and admiration excited in their bosoms by my lenity. I entreated him to be silent, and observed, that heartily as I detested and despised every species of imposture, adverting to this subject so frequently, was particularly painful to me; and the rather as the persons, who had been guilty of misconduct so flagrant, were two, whom, from their connections, I ardently wished to respect and esteem. "And I cannot forbear flattering myself, Mr. Stanhope," I added, "that they will yet allow me to esteem them as I wish, though there are circumstances in Mr. Egerton's conduct prior to this affair, which lead me to fear that he has always been too much inclined to duplicity and treachery."

"Good heavens, Madam! to what can you allude? Among all Harry's faults, I cannot charge him with any deliberate act of baseness, except in the present instance: and even in this he must be considered rather as an instrument than an agent."

"Is it possible, Mr. Stanhope, that you, who have always lived with him upon terms of intimacy, can be ignorant of a secret engagement he formed many years ago with a very amiable girl, whom he afterwards, without any apparent reason, basely and ungenerously deserted?"

"A secret engagement!—Good God, Madam, you surely cannot mean to allude to his affair with Miss Trelawney?"

"Ah! Mr. Stanhope, why mention that affair, if it were not suggested by conscience?"

"But not by a troubled conscience. Your alluding to this engagement, Madam, as a thing clandestinely carried on, suggested to me indeed the idea that you must refer to Miss Trelawney; but believe me, in that affair Harry's conduct was perfectly blameless. Honour and ardent affection dictated every step he took in it, nor could any thing but the unfortunate Emily's untimely death have prevented its being brought to a happy conclusion."

"Miss Trelawney's death, Sir?—Pardon me! but this is the first syllable I ever heard of such an event."

"Is it then possible that you can have heard the affair mentioned, and not know of its tragical termination?"

"I have always been informed, as I said before, that Mr. Egerton, after being for some time engaged to Miss Trelawney, deserted her, without assigning any reason for his infidelity."

"How cruelly then has my poor friend been slandered! No, Madam, believe me that in this instance he was guiltless, though unfortunate. I thought the story had not been known, except to myself and another friend of Harry's; but since you have heard it related in a manner so mutilated, and with misrepresentations that reflect so much upon poor Harry, I should think it great injustice to him, not to set you right."

"Believe me, I shall listen to any vindication of Mr. Egerton with the sincerest pleasure. As I have heard the story, he certainly appears to have been very culpable."

"You probably know, Madam, that at the time when he and Miss Trelawney became acquainted at Bath, it was his father's intention to marry him to his cousin Miss Atkins, a rich heiress. Harry was consequently obliged to conceal his attachment to Miss Trelawney, till some opportunity should arrive more favourable for its disclosure."

"All this I know, and for the rest have heard that your cousin was soon after set at liberty by Miss Atkins's eloping with a man of her own choice, but that by the time this obstacle was removed, Mr. Egerton's mind was changed, nor did he concern himself farther about that Emily, to whom he had so often declared his affections were wholly devoted."

"Oh, not so! When Harry quitted Bath, he left Miss Trelawney and her mother about to depart for Ireland upon business of importance, which they expected would detain them for several weeks. From that time Harry's mind was solely occupied in devising plans for disclosing to his father the attachment in which his soul was absorbed, and for procuring his consent to his wishes, that his engagement with Emily might be fulfilled at her return. Letter after letter did I receive from him, full of these projects, and of the most passionate expressions with regard to Emily. His soul seemed incapable of admitting any other idea, and at length he earnestly entreated me to come and pass some time with him, as he thought we could better consult together upon his various plans by personal intercourse than by correspondence.

"I immediately complied with his request, and hastened to Arrenton, his father's seat. When I arrived there, I found Harry almost wild with extasy, for his father had that very morning received an account of Miss Atkins's elopement. Harry however resolved to delay the mention of Emily for a few days, as he thought the first moments of chagrin at this disappointment, not a propitious time for disclosing his wishes to his father, and this delay was the cause of the whole affair being ultimately concealed for ever from Mr. Egerton's knowledge.

"For, alas! the next day brought the fatal account of the Cornwall Packet, on board of which Emily and her mother were passengers, being lost in a very heavy gale of wind near the entrance of Dublin harbour, when every soul on board perished. It was my lot to impart this dreadful catastrophe to Harry, and never, no never, can I lose the recollection of that moment. No one who has not been a witness of similar scenes can have an idea of his agony; I thought indeed at the first moment that I had given him his death's wound. After these transports began somewhat to subside, he entreated, that since the affair had terminated thus fatally, it might remain for ever a secret from his father. 'He cannot enter into my feelings,' he said, 'and to see the apathy with which he would consider a loss that harrows up my soul, would be even more horrible to me, than the efforts I must make to controul myself in his presence. You alone, Lionel, can truly sympathise with me; be you alone, then, the repository of this unhappy secret.'

"Having made such a determination, all his resolution was exerted to appear tranquil before others, and he did command himself to a degree that often excited my utmost astonishment. But when I alone was present, and he could give full vent to his feelings, the conflicts I witnessed were such, that I thought they must at last inevitably overturn his reason. Alas, I was but too right! He was soon seized with a raving phrenzy, in which he remained lost to the world and to himself, for more than a year. Indeed, I may say but too truly, that he never has been perfectly restored to either.

"For, Oh! Madam, the Harry Egerton you now behold, is but a miserable wreck of the cherished friend of my youth, and 'tis only at transient intervals that the bright effulgence of those amiable qualities which first united my heart so firmly to his, bursts forth from amid the clouds by which it is obscured. Yet deeply as I have been interested by his misfortunes, can I be otherwise than indulgent to his frailties, and though I feel most sensibly the degraded state to which he has reduced himself, I never can relinquish the pleasing hope, that if he could but again ardently attach himself to a woman equally amiable with her he lost, he might yet be reclaimed, and become the respectable character his early years promised.

"During the period of his phrenzy, both his father and mother died, and thus at his emancipation from the necessary restraint in which he had been kept, he found himself sole master of a very affluent fortune. But, alas! since with reason returned recollection, he flew to dissipation as the most effectual means of banishing that bitter enemy to his repose. Intoxicated by the momentary relief he found in each new scene of pleasure, he soon became the slave of that licentiousness and extravagance which have ultimately depraved his mind, and ruined his fortune. In these scenes, I must own with confusion, I have but too frequently shared; yet did I suffer myself to be enticed into them principally from a fond hope, that by a temporary compliance with his inclinations, there would be a greater probability of reclaiming him at last, than by uniformly opposing them.

"Such, believe me, Madam, is the truth, the strict truth, with regard to this unfortunate affair. Judge then yourself, whether Harry is not rather an object of pity than of censure, or whether any thing can have been more cruel than the conduct of those who have circulated the story with such gross misrepresentations. Alas! often have I regretted the fatal resolution he took never to mention it himself, since I believe the efforts he made to controul his feelings were in great measure the cause of his subsequent calamity. But if ever I hinted a wish to be allowed to mention the affair, he uniformly opposed it, always urging that he could not bear the idea of the name of his departed saint becoming a common topic of discussion for a babbling world. Particular circumstances did indeed lead to my imparting the story to our mutual friend Mr. St. John, as they have now led to my relating it to you, Madam; but never had either Harry, or myself, an idea that it was known to any person besides. And now, may I not trust, Madam, that my friend stands wholly exculpated in your eyes, in this instance, and that even the really faulty parts of his conduct appear not altogether without excuse."

Harriot, I was so affected with what I heard, that I could not make any reply, and we walked on in silence for some time, when farther conversation was precluded by a summons to tea. I felt almost sorry for this interruption, since I wished to ask a thousand additional questions, though perhaps it was as well that they were prevented, as I might thus have betrayed more than I wished. I could have wept with transport at finding Mr. Egerton not the guilty wretch he has been supposed, and still constant to his first attachment. I could have wept with anguish at reflecting, that though acquitted of this great offence, his situation is still such as almost to preclude the possibility of his being received back into that heart from which error, not alienation, has kept him so long a stranger.

I shall say no more at present, as it is my intention to see you in a few days. But information so interesting as the above, I could not withhold for a moment. Adieu, my dearest Harriot, and believe me with great sincerity,
Your very affectionate

OLIVIA CAMPBELL.

LETTER XXII.

ORLANDO ST. JOHN
TO
LIONEL STANHOPE.

Scarborough, August 28.
And after all, Li., I think your affair has terminated better than could possibly be expected, and your not being kicked out of doors may fairly be reckoned among the *negative successes* of your summer's campaign.

Verily, *mon cher ami*, I can tell thee, that if thy heiress has through the medium of dæmons, cacodæmons, witches, wizards, or spirits,[42] become partially acquainted with poor Emily's story, then must Charlotte also hold communication with the same kind of beings, since I am confident that she too is possessed of the history of that tragedy. Not that she has owned as much, but from a hint she dropped in conversation the other day, I was led to suspect it. Struck with the idea, I ideot like, don't scold, Sir Lionel, entered with more haste than judgement upon a succession of questions, by the answers to which I hoped my suspicion would be fully confirmed, or absolutely confuted. But alas, 'tis my hard fate not to be successful as a questionist, for here again was I foiled; she at once perceived my drift, her mouth was instantly closed, nor could I obtain even a *yes* or a *hum*.

Oh! how did I inwardly rail at my own loquacity, that could not let her go on without interruption, since I might then have learned all I wished. But now she is shy, and I am shy, and we seem reciprocally afraid of communicating what I suspect would not make either of us a jot the wiser. One thing particularly distresses me; I am apprehensive that Charlotte may have heard the story with the same misrepresentations that Olivia had, and if so, it were equally proper that the whole matter should likewise be explained to her. *Mais cependant*, I do not like to transgress my injunction of secresy, unless upon full conviction that my suspicion is not erroneous, or upon receiving free leave from Harry to impart all that I know.

But though I dare not at present confess myself upon this subject to Charlotte, I must confess myself on another to thee, Mr. Li.—upon the subject of my two divinities, with whom, upon my soul, I am more and more in love every day. Most fortunate is it for me that there are two of them, since by this means my inclinations are held in such exact equipoise, like those of the poor ass so often celebrated,[43] that not knowing in favour of which to decide, I may perhaps at last escape from both— at least I must leave the matter to Providence, since he is the general referee when we are unable to determine for ourselves. *La belle veuve* sings so enchantingly!—ye gods! how she does sing!—And Charlotte writes such enchanting poetry!—ye gods! what poetry she does write!

Take a specimen. The other day an ingenious discussion happened to arise among our party, upon writing from the impulse of feeling, when Charlotte advanced, that she believed all animated writing to be a mere *essor de l'imagination*,* as she did not conceive it possible for any body to write well, she even doubted whether they could write at all, upon a subject by which, at the moment, their feelings were powerfully agitated. The mind, she said, in such circumstances, was too much engrossed by that particular subject to admit the varied attention necessary to form a tolerably correct and polished work.

"Oho," said Madame de Clairville archly; "then I see how we are to account for the present silence of Charlotte's muse. The time has been when scarcely a day passed that she did not produce some offering to the Nine,[44] breathing the most impassioned strains of love and tender sentiment, though at the same time she constantly affected to ridicule the lit-

---

* Flight of the imagination.

tle mischievous deity,[45] and all his votaries. I have several times wondered why this should cease all on a sudden, since I don't believe for the last six weeks she has produced so many lines, but now I perceive the inference to be drawn from her silence."

Many jokes flew about in consequence of the fair widow's discovery, and Charlotte was earnestly pressed to declare the happy object of this new passion. She parried our wit with the most enchanting good humour and vivacity, half disowning her friend's suspicion, and half encouraging us to believe it true. But after a while she took an opportunity of absenting herself from the company, and at her return presented Madame de Clairville with the following verses:

THE TRUE STATE OF THE CASE.
ADDRESSED TO A FRIEND.

'Tis true I long doubted the influence of love,
 And have oft, in the frolicks of mirth's gayest hour,
When others his sway have been lab'ring to prove,
 Made a jest of his arrows, and slighted his pow'r.
When I heard of the torments by lovers endur'd,
 I laughing enquir'd what such jargon could mean?
I believ'd that such anguish was easily cur'd;
 But alas! then my Albert I never had seen.

I could talk with the witty, could laugh with the gay,
 With the learned be wise, with the thoughtful be grave,
With the pensive could muse, with the sportive could play,
 Encourag'd them all, but to none was a slave.
Unmov'd I beheld each attraction of grace,
 Unmov'd view'd the dignified figure and mien;
With indifference regarded each soul-inspir'd face,
 But alas! then my Albert I never had seen!

I oft was assail'd by the glances that dart
 Through the languishing softness of Frederick's eye,
But though they play'd round, they ne'er fix'd on my heart;
 I confess'd they had pow'r, yet their pow'r could defy.
Oft too was I charm'd by young Ferdinand's tongue,
 As together we walk'd o'er the daisy-pied green;
I admir'd the soft sounds on each accent that hung,
 Yet lov'd not, for Albert I then had not seen.

I wrote of the passion, unsway'd by its pow'r,
 For love was my muse's most favourite theme,
But while in my lays to obey him I swore,
 My heart still denied that his pow'r was supreme.

No gloom then o'ershadow'd the sun of my days,
  Each morning was tranquil, each ev'ning serene;
'Twas in fancy alone I trac'd sorrow's dark maze,
  Till that fatal hour when my Albert was seen.

Then the merciless god, who had long been incens'd
  At a mortal's resisting his powerful shaft,
Double poison to each barbed arrow dispens'd,
  That Albert's keen eyes to the bosom might waft.
Too soon was my heart by that poison subdued,
  Soon did clouds betwixt me and my peace intervene;
Then with thorns the smooth path of my life was o'erstrew'd,
  And I mourn'd that my Albert I ever had seen.

For, alas! to the flame in my bosom that burns,
  To the poison his eyes have instill'd in my veins,
He only the coldness of friendship returns,
  Nor breathes for my sorrows soft sympathy's strains.
And those who their vows had long paid at my shrine,
  And receiv'd with a tranquil indifference had been,
Now behold their keen suff'rings avenged by mine,
  And rejoice in the moment when Albert was seen.

Nay, by passion so wholly my heart is engross'd,
  That my lyre is forgotten, my pen thrown aside,
And the strains that so long were my pride and my boast,
  With the passion you fancied had rais'd them, have died.
For since I've been fetter'd by love's potent chain,
  What most used to please me produces the spleen;
And all that I seek, is alone to complain
  Of the anguish I've felt since my Albert was seen.

Cease then, dear Eliza; ah! cease to suppose
  That, while on the transports and sorrows of love,
So many soft stanzas my head could compose,
  My heart e'er those transports and sorrows could prove!
Ah no!—when twas fancy alone felt the dart
  I could sing of the passion unmov'd and serene;
But now since my bosom's oppress'd with the smart,
  In silence I mourn that e'er Albert was seen.

Good heavens! thought I, what if I should be the happy Albert?—and surely this may not be impossible, since it appears that the passion is of a recent date. Peters too seemed by his looks to indulge in an equal degree of self-flattery; while Captain Tichfield, not behind either of us in vanity, heaving a pretty languishing sigh, and surveying his elegant figure in an opposite looking-glass, plainly shewed that he had no doubt who was the favoured though cruel lover. But I fear we are all equally mistaken, for when Madame de Clairville was rallying Charlotte upon the subject, and complimenting her own discernment, the fair poetess in a moment suppressed all our rising hopes, by observing that the poem was in itself a contradiction, since she had been absolutely writing on a subject on which she declared she could not have written had she really felt all that she professed. I must therefore only console myself with the hope, that though this divine creature does not particularly favour any lover at present, she will not long remain insensible to the merits of her new adorer.

A profusion of compliments and fine speeches were however bestowed upon the verses by all present, excepting Miss Perkins, who sat drawing up her head and screwing up her mouth, and evidently listening to what passed with no slight degree of impatience. She however said nothing, till one of the company requested to hear the verses again, but that was too much to bear; colouring as red as scarlet, she said, if they were to be read a second time she must beg to be excused hearing them, as she for her part was so old-fashioned in her notions, that she thought it extremely inconsistent with the proper reserve of the female character, even in fiction, to profess a passion for a man, and she believed few people besides Miss O'Brien would have thought of writing any thing so indelicate.

This was prudery with a vengeance—or rather, to call things by their proper names, envy with a vengeance. But though heartily despised by us all, it was impossible in politeness not to yield to it so far as to drop the subject. And with the subject shall drop the pen of

Your faithfully affectionate

ORLANDO ST. JOHN.

LETTER XXIII.

LIONEL STANHOPE
TO
ORLANDO ST. JOHN.

Campbell-House, August 30.
And you really think, Orlando, that we had but been treated according to our deserts if we had both been kicked out of doors?—But this is not strange—persons of the same description are wont to hold the same sentiments; and yours correspond exactly with those of an *old maid* at Doncaster, to whom I beg leave to have the honour of introducing you.

Yesterday, as Beauchamp and I, who are become very dear friends, were out upon a ramble, the conversation insensibly led to his mentioning Olivia's lenity to us in strong terms of admiration, though he said he must apologise for alluding to the subject in my presence.

"Indeed, Mr. Beauchamp," I replied, "such an apology was unnecessary. Believe me 'tis a subject on which, however it may recal to my mind a painful remembrance of my own criminality, I can never sufficiently dwell. The astonishment and admiration with which Miss Campbell's conduct has inspired me, is past expression. That knowing our imposture, as I understand she did, even from its commencement, she could yet permit us to remain in the house, is an instance of unparalleled forbearance and self-command."

"She had sufficient reasons for acting as she did—yet 'tis almost needless to say that, since she never acts but upon reasons the most solid and substantial. She was not, however, insensible to the unworthiness of your conduct—and while in her heart she properly reprehended it, she had powerful motives for not immediately exposing you."

"And permit me to ask, Mr. Beauchamp, whether you also were acquainted with the important secret?"

"I was, but was strictly enjoined silence upon the subject; only Miss Campbell gave me full permission to embrace any opportunity that might be presented for terrifying and tormenting you with the apprehension that you were, or might be, detected. Of this licence I availed myself in making you accompany me to Doctor Paul's upon Owen's affair. I knew that your evidence was in fact nugatory, but was determined to alarm you with the idea of being sworn. And to torment you still farther, when the Doctor called you Stanhope by a real mistake, I took the hint, and called you so likewise by a pretended one. I saw your confusion, and enjoyed it highly."

"Oh you do not know what I suffered at that moment, or what a relief it was to the agonies of my soul when you said that you thought my evidence unimportant."

"I observed that too. It was as fine a theatrical change of countenance as ever was beheld, and would have been invaluable upon the stage. But the admiration I feel at Miss Campbell's behaviour to you is by no means a general sentiment. Some of her neighbours condemn, as warmly as I applaud it."

"Has then our shame become a topic of public discussion in the neighbourhood? But I feared it would be so."

"Your fears might have been certainties."

"Good God!—and what is said about us?"

"You are not spared. It was with the view of amusing you with a dialogue between our amiable friend and one of her outrageously virtuous female acquaintance, in which Miss Campbell's conduct was very severely reprobated, that I introduced this conversation."

"Mrs. Harrison, I suppose?"

"No.—Wonderful to relate, I do not believe Mrs. Harrison has delivered an opinion upon the subject, or, what is still more extraordinary, recommended a *better* mode of proceeding in it. The lecturing lady was a friend of her's, a Mrs. Stapleton of Doncaster, of the honourable sisterhood of old-maids. She called here yesterday, evidently to collect particulars of your exploit, that she might retail them in the evening at the card-table; for you know by coming thus to the fountain head for intelligence, her authority must of course be of greater weight than that of her neighbours. After vainly endeavouring to entice Miss Campbell into a voluntary relation of the story, she was at length compelled to enter upon the subject herself."

"So, Miss Campbell," she began, "I hear you have had a fine kettle of fish in your house, with a couple of flashy London bucks coming to make love to you under feigned names. I think you served them very rightly in kicking them both out of doors."

"I kick them out of doors, Madam?—I am sorry to hear that I am suspected of having done any thing so unbecoming my sex and situation."

"Lord, I declare there's no such thing as talking to ladies who are so precise about their expressions as yourself. I did not suppose that, literally speaking, you yourself kicked them out of doors, but only that you dismissed them your house with a flea in their ears."

"That would have been almost as feminine as kicking them. But indeed, Madam, you have been misinformed. The gentlemen to whom I suppose you allude, are with me still, and I hope will continue here some time longer."

"Well, so I heard, but I would not believe it. No, said I, though Miss Campbell has done many things very improper in a young woman who has any regard for her character, yet I'm sure that not even she could countenance such a couple of cheats. No, no, I'm sure she turned 'em out of doors the moment they were detected."

"Another time I hope you will form a more just opinion of me, Madam, since you see that I have not so grossly violated the laws of hospitality and humanity."

"Hospitality and humanity indeed, to a couple of cheats!—Well, I should have thought of that!—Humanity to cheats!—This is the first time I ever heard of humanity to cheats!—But if this be your way of going on, Miss Campbell, I must give you up entirely, I cannot pretend to defend you any longer."

"Indeed, Madam, I am not aware that in this instance my conduct wants defence. It surely defends itself."

"Defends itself!—Humph!—curious, indeed!—Why, I don't believe that there's half a dozen women in the king[dom] would have acted in such a manner."

"Possibly, Madam. But I always regulate my conduct by what I think is right to be done, not by considering what others would be likely to do."

"Well, Miss Campbell, I've taken a great deal of pains to correct your mistaken notions upon many subjects, because I had a great regard for your poor aunt Lætitia, who has so often lamented to me the strange manner in which you were educated by your father. But I may as well have done, for any good that I can see my kindness produces."

"I am always very ready to confess my great obligations both to yourself, Madam, and to my aunt Lætitia. She certainly did take some pains to make me as censorious as herself, but I was a very incorrigible scholar. And really, Madam, I am sorry you should concern yourself farther with me, or my affairs, since you probably will never find them other than an endless source of uneasiness to your mind."

"And I can assure you Madam, but for your good aunt's sake I should not concern myself about them; but I know not absolutely how to give up a niece of hers, especially as I have defended you so long. Many's the battle I have fought for you about that baggage you have set up here as a school-mistress, and that beggarly Ensign that's so often coming after you. I have been forced to tell a thousand lies in your behalf, and protest that you did not know what sort of a woman Lucy Morgan was when she came into the parish, and before you found it out, she had gained a settlement, and could not be sent away again, else you would have got rid of her directly."

"Indeed, Madam, you have done me great injustice in thus misrepresenting the case. It was because I knew of Lucy's misfortune, and of the persecutions she had undergone in consequence of it in her own country, that I sent for her hither, and took her under my protection."

"But it was as well for your own credit, that the world should not know the nature of her *misfortune*, as you are pleased to call it."

"As I am not ashamed of having rescued a penitent from too severe contumely, and restored a valuable member to society, I would by no means wish for my own sake that the nature of her misfortune should be concealed. Delicacy to her alone, would prompt such a wish."

"Then there's that Ryder. Every body says you are going to be married to him, yet you shew no indignation at the report, and encourage him still to come to your house. 'Tis in vain therefore for me to say that I think I know Miss Campbell too well, to fear her degrading herself so far as to marry a little shop-keeper's son; while he's still suffered to come after you in this way, how can people disbelieve the report."

"And if they find any gratification in believing it, I should be very sorry to deprive them of such a source of pleasure. As Mr. Ryder is a man of the highest worth and talents, I should certainly not think an alliance with him degrading to me, therefore the idea really does not excite indignation in me, and the reports to which you allude, believe me, will not in the smallest degree either accelerate or prevent the match."

"But let me tell you, Miss Campbell, that whatever you may think about being degraded by the match, if you do stoop to such a fellow as Ryder, you wo'n't be quite so much respected in the world as you are now, or find people very ready to keep up an acquaintance with you."

"I care very little, Madam, whether they do or not. But trust me, while

I can afford to give them good dinners, though they may allow their tongues unbounded licence behind my back, they will not absent themselves from my table."

"Do you mean to insinuate, Madam, that this is my practice? But I despise your reflections."

"As much as I despise the meanness to which I alluded. And if I should marry Mr. Ryder, I do not desire the company of those who think they would degrade themselves by visiting the wife of a little shop-keeper's son."

"Well, Miss Campbell, if you will be so headstrong, you must follow your own way, and take the consequence." And here she rose up and departed, not with much complacence on her countenance, or appearance of satisfaction in her mind.

This dialogue, related by Beauchamp solely for the purpose, as he said, of amusing me, yet awakened other emotions in my bosom. Till now I had paid little regard to a hint mentioned in one of your letters as thrown out by Charlotte, that she was of opinion if ever Olivia should marry, "*a half-pay Ensign of the name of Ryder would be the Jason to carry away the golden fleece.*"[46] 'Tis true I had occasionally heard the name of Ryder quoted both by Olivia and Beauchamp, but never with that kind of interest or distinction that led me to notice it particularly. Enough had however now been said to excite my curiosity upon this subject in no small degree, and I therefore asked several questions relative to the truth or falsehood of the reports alluded to by Mrs. Stapleton, which ultimately led to the disclosure of the Ensign's history—a history I think, Orlando, well worthy of a place in our correspondence. Had I known it sooner, I should have heard with concern that Harry had so formidable a rival to oppose; but since his pursuit is relinquished, I learn with satisfaction that there is another person in the world to whom I may look up as the probable means by which I may at last be released from parental importunities.

Richard Ryder is the only child of Anthony Ryder, who some years since kept a country shop, and was parish-clerk in the village of Blakeney near Sheffield, the seat of a Mr. Barry, who also had an only son about the same age with little Ryder. Nor was this the only circumstance in which a similarity of fates attended these two boys; when they were not above four years old, they were both deprived of their mothers, who fell victims to the small-pox, which at that time made great ravages in the parish.

Now since in infancy we are apt to overlook those distinctions of rank on which we afterwards place so high a value, so at George Barry's tender age he could see no reason why Dick, the clerk's son, should not be a proper companion for him, though heir to the Squire. In short, George having accidentally seen Dick as he was upon a visit with his father to the gardener, was so delighted at having found a playfellow of his own age, that he never ceased importuning Mr. Barry, till leave was given for his new favourite to be invited to the Hall. Perhaps the Squire was the more easily prevailed upon to comply with this request, from his heart being then softened by affliction for the death of a wife whom he tenderly loved, and from feeling glad of any thing that could compensate in the smallest degree to his infant child the loss of an affectionate mother's fond attentions.

But though Georgy was not so deeply impressed with a sense of the inequality of condition, as to think the clerk's son altogether beneath his notice, he yet had sufficient ideas of his own superiority to expect the latter's patient acquiescence in any impositions in which he chose to indulge himself at play, such as reckoning four at Trap-ball,* when he had no claim to more than three, and the like petty encroachments. These however accorded so ill with a certain loftiness of mind which seemed almost inherent in Dick, that he warmly remonstrated against them, and would even sometimes carry the matter so far as to declare that he would not come to the hall any more, unless Master Barry would promise to play fairly. This spirited conduct generally kept the young squire in good order, though he did occasionally resent it; yet as Dick always adhered steadily to his purpose, George at length submitted rather than lose his companion, and he was consoled by the servants persuading him that Dick was a child, and knew no better.

As the two boys advanced in years, however, these petty contentions became less frequent, and at length were heard of no more. The decided superiority of Ryder's talents gave him an ascendancy over young Barry, which the latter insensibly ceased attempting to resist—nay, he even gradually acquired such a habit of respect for this superiority, that he soon began to make Ryder his principal guide and counsellor, till in time no affair of moment was determined without his advice; a confidence which the latter never abused, and of which, by such moderation, he proved himself fully deserving. At the age of twelve years a friendship was thus established between them, and which has been proof against the strongest efforts made at various times to alienate them from each other, and which remains unshaken even to this moment.

Mr. Barry saw this increasing attachment not without serious uneasiness, and often endeavoured to impress his son with the idea, that though Dick's inferiority in rank might be overlooked while they were both infants, yet at a more advanced age the distance between them would form an insurmountable obstacle to their keeping up any intercourse. This was, however, urged in vain—George's heart was affectionate, though his mind was not strong; his attachment to Ryder was irrevocably fixed, and if any opposition was ever made to the latter's visiting him, he made his escape from the Hall, and became himself a visitor at his friend's more humble abode.

Convinced at length that to separate the boys was impossible, Mr. Barry began to entertain different views. So much as he had seen of

---

*   "A play at which a ball is driven with a stick" (Johnson).

Ryder, he could not be insensible to the powers of his mind, and to these he turned his attention, as the best means of extricating himself with tolerable credit from the embarrassing situation in which he was placed. He rightly judged that talents so eminent, if properly improved by education, would one day raise their owner to such distinction in the paths of science and literature, as would in great measure supply the defect of birth, and render him a not altogether unworthy associate of the more affluent George Barry; and he therefore resolved to bestow upon Ryder those advantages of education which his own father's confined means never could have procured. In this resolution he was the more fully confirmed, from Anthony Ryder's dying shortly after, which threw Dick upon the world an unprotected orphan, when any favour shewn him consequently became the greater act of charity—added to which, his parents being now no more, the obscurity of his origin would thus be more easily glossed over. Richard was therefore immediately placed by his self-elected protector and benefactor, at a very good school, from which, at the age of eighteen, he was removed to the university of Cambridge; and as his patron could best provide for him in the church, he was destined in future to deal out food to the souls of those, to whose corporeal wants his father had long administered, or, in other words, to be rector of the parish in which the good Anthony had for so many years sold his ounces of tea and pennyworths of cheese.

But even from the commencement of his academical career, it seemed *ecrit là haut*, that Ryder should not become a parson. Not that he was idle, or inattentive to his studies; he was rather over studious, and from this disposition soon grew so unpopular among his fellow-collegians, that he was universally distinguished by the most odious of all appellations, according to their ideas,—that of a SAP. To his patron, however, the rapidity of his progress in his academical exercises recommended him very strongly. Mr. Barry repeatedly wrote to him, commending in the warmest terms his industry and application, and assuring him, that upon their continuance would depend the continuance of his patronage,—indeed that his future liberality would be proportioned to the honour he should obtain at taking his Bachelor of Arts degree. A more unfortunate criterion for poor Richard could not, alas! have been fixed upon, for ere the time of taking his degree arrived, he had been guilty of offences to his superiors, by which he became no less obnoxious to them, than by his studious turn he was to those of his own standing.

It was his fortune to be placed at college under a tutor who entertained so high an opinion of his own learning and importance, that it was impossible for the pupils to hold them in equal consideration; and since mankind are prone to hesitate in believing the existence of qualities which their limited faculties cannot comprehend, so because Mr. Bounce's learning was far too deep to permit of its being fathomed by the pupils, they had even the audacity to doubt whether he had any learning at all.

As he was one day holding forth, very eloquently, in a lecture upon morals, after laying down many striking axioms, enforced by an equal number of appropriate illustrations, he at length put the following question to his audience:—"*Suppose I were all alone upon an uninhabited island, and were to meet a baker with a basket of bread upon his shoulder, should I be justified in taking a loaf from him?*"

Now since Ryder had not always fully comprehended the tutor's lectures as they were delivered, he had recently come to a resolution constantly to take down minutes of them in short hand, in hopes that when he could consider and reconsider them in his closet, the mist that obscured his mind would disperse, and that they would appear as clear and comprehensible to him, as he had no doubt they were to others—and this resolution he had that day, for the first time, begun to put in practice. Eagerly employed therefore on his notes, he had not hitherto looked at the lecturer; but when the above profound question was proposed, he started from his attention to his own paper, and involuntarily turning his eyes, in which a smile of sarcasm was but too visibly depicted, towards Mr. Bounce, he unfortunately met his directly, as they were making a circuit round the room, to look for the admiration he thought due to a proposition of such profundity. To behold the smile of sarcasm in a countenance in which he expected to meet the uplifted eye of admiration, was a trial far beyond Mr. Bounce's fortitude to support, and with eyes flashing fire he exclaimed—"*And pray what may excite your mirth, Mr. Ryder?*"—To this the other unhesitatingly replied, "*I was only thinking, Sir, how the baker could get custom there.*"

An obvious speculation this, no doubt; yet it somehow or other so happened, that it did not find favour with Mr. Bounce. He started up, and in a very irascible tone exclaimed, "Do you mean to insult me, Sir?—but I won't bear it, Sir.—You are always treating me in this insolent manner, Sir, and endeavouring to render me contemptible in the eyes of the other pupils, Sir!—And what business have you to be scribbling there, Sir? I suppose 'tis for the purpose of turning what I have been saying into ridicule, Sir, when you get among your young companions.—But I won't be treated thus, Sir!—I'll teach you to know who I am, Sir!"—So saying, he snatched away Ryder's hapless notes, and throwing the paper on the fire, declared that he would instantly go and complain to the master of his behaviour, for if such insolence were to pass unnoticed, there was an end of all authority over the pupils.

The consigning [of] Ryder's paper to the fire was contemplated with deep regret by all the scholars, who doubted not that it contained much excellent matter for future mirth. One of them, by name Croftes more particularly concerned at the idea of losing it, as he had long owed the tutor a grudge, had watched it with especial anxiety, from the moment it passed from the hands of Ryder into those of his antagonist, and saw, with some degree of consolation, that the latter, in the irritation of his bosom, had not been careful to thrust it directly into the flames, but that it had lighted upon some fresh coals, which protected it from being immediately consumed. It became instantly the great object of his wishes, and the considerable one of his hopes, that a favourable moment might yet occur to rescue it finally from the jaws of destruction; and seeing Mr. Bounce turn his back to go out of the room he caught at it eagerly, and was just bearing it off in triumph, when, oh cursed fortune!—the tutor unluckily turned round again, for the purpose of dismissing the pupils, which, in his eagerness to lay his complaint before the master, he had not at first recollected was necessary; and the first object that met his eyes was Croftes, in the very act of delinquency.

A rage, if possible more vehement than what he had felt at meeting Ryder's sarcastic smile, now glowed in his breast and flashed from his eyes; and darting upon Croftes, he snatched away the paper, which he thrust immediately into the very fiercest of the flames, where he beheld it, with a look of exultation, instantly consumed;—then bidding the pupils begone that instant, and denouncing the bitterest vengeance against both the culprits, he proceeded to the master, where he painted, in the warmest terms his indignation could inspire, the indignities he had received—declared that never tutor was so treated by persons *in statu pupillarii*, and demanded that the most exemplary punishment should be inflicted upon both. The master owned that the young men were very much to blame, and ought to be reprimanded, and said that a meeting of the Fellows should be held in the evening for that purpose—a promise which somewhat appeased the tutor, who returned to his room to prepare his charges in form against the appointed hour.

The Fellows accordingly met; the charges were laid before them, and were discussed with due gravity and solemnity, when sentence was unanimously passed that Ryder, as the principal offender, should get a thousand lines of Homer by heart, and Croftes, as the subordinate one, five hundred—both the tasks to be repeated to the tutor on that day fortnight, upon pain of incurring a year's rustication. Ryder said not a word; he perhaps thought the sentence somewhat severe, but as no appeal could be made against it, that it was the wisest plan to acquiesce in it quietly.

But Croftes was not quite so acquiescent. He warmly remonstrated against a punishment which he said was extremely disproportioned to the offence, and finally declared that he never would submit to such flagrant injustice. "As you please, Sir," said the tutor haughtily, "only remember the penalty, Sir, the year of rustication."

But the Master, who knew that the incurring [of] this penalty must be a very essential injury to the young man, as it was a great object with him to obtain a fellowship, to which an almost insuperable obstacle would thus be raised up, detained him after the meeting was dissolved, and mildly expostulated with him upon the folly of his conduct, representing in forcible terms the serious consequences that must inevitably attend his not submitting to the punishment, and exhorted him to weigh them well, and to relax in his contumacy. But his expostulations were vain; Croftes still adhered to his resolution, to resist oppression, as he said, in every shape, and declared that he would sooner even be expelled the college, than comply with the sentence.

The Master finding the young man thus deaf to remonstrance, and really feeling interested in preventing, if possible, his being so much his own enemy, wrote to his father, fully stating the case, and strongly recommending to him to use his influence with his son to induce him to submit, shewing him plainly what an obstacle the rustication, if incurred, must be to his future views.

The father was a man of low extraction, having been originally only footman in a nobleman's family, from which post he was afterwards advanced to that of gentleman, and at length, upon his Lord's coming into power, was made a clerk in one of the public offices. From that moment his great ambition was to educate his son as a scholar, and by a prudent management of his affairs, he contrived to spare the money requisite for giving him an University education. Totally illiterate himself, every step his son advanced in the acquisition of knowledge, excited in him the utmost astonishment, and though the young man's attainments never rose above mediocrity, he was considered by his father as a perfect prodigy of science and literature. The idea therefore of his being punished only filled him with excess of indignation, and instead of regarding the Master's conduct as the effect of kindness and lenity, he rather considered it as encreasing the indignity, and accordingly sat down immediately and wrote him the following curious answer:

D——Street, 24th March.

Revnd. Sir,

I have recd. your letter; my son acknoledges himself guilty of the folly imputed to him; he is a judge of the propiety of the punishment, and I shall leave it to him to act as his discretion shall lead him. Late experence tells me justice dos not always govern the decisions in —— College.

I see with pleasure that you testifye under your owne hand, that this is the first fault he has commetted.

I am, Sir,
Your obedient
Huble servant,

WILLIAM CROFTES.

The woman that was brought before our Savour (for adultry) said, goe thy way and do so more. He that is without fault thro the first stone.

The young man's discretion, however, did at length get the better of his obstinacy, and at the appointed time the five hundred lines were repeated. Here therefore let us dismiss him, and return to Ryder.

Though in passing sentence the Court had been particular as to the *day* on which he was to appear with the allotted task before the offended tutor, no notice whatever was taken of the *hour*, and the choice of this therefore Ryder considered as left entirely to his own option. Before the time arrived, he had accidentally learned that on that very day a turtle-feast was to be given at a neighbouring college, to which Mr. Bounce had been invited, and that three o'clock was the hour appointed for dining. At about half past two then, just as the tutor was dressed in a fresh powdered wig, and a new silk pudding sleeved gown, ready to sally forth, Ryder appeared before him.

"Well, Sir, what do you want?" said Mr. Bounce rather impatiently.

"I come, Sir, to repeat the thousand lines of Homer, allotted me as a punishment, the time allowed for getting them expires to-day."

"I can't possibly hear them now, Mr. Ryder; I am just going out to dinner."

"At what time then, may I attend you, Sir?"

"Oh, it will probably be late before I am at home. To-morrow morning you may come again."

"I beg your pardon, Sir, but you will be so good as to recollect, that unless they are repeated to-day, I incur a year's rustification."

"Pshaw!—Why did'n't you come in the morning then?—This is the most inconvenient time you could have chosen."

"I was coming, Sir, only that I found Mr. Croftes was with you."

The poor tutor was reduced to a sad dilemma. If he refused the hearing required by Ryder, he must take upon himself to be responsible to the superiors of the College for the young man's omission, and he was conscious to himself that the going out to dinner, even though to partake of a turtle, would appear but a paltry excuse for foregoing his duty as tutor of the College. Hard therefore as was the case, he dared not decline the hearing, and taking the book, though not very complacently, he said: "You will be as quick as you can, Mr. Ryder."

But before two hundred lines were repeated, Mr. Bounce's impatience to be gone became absolutely insupportable, and hastily closing the book, he said, "You seem astonishingly perfect, Mr. Ryder; this diligence is highly commendable, and I think I may spare you the trouble of going any further."

"I beg your pardon, Sir, but is not the penalty incurred unless the whole be repeated?"

"No, no, Mr. Ryder, I'll take care of that.—I'll take care that you shall not come into any trouble, and so, Sir, good morning."

Ryder bowed and retired, and the tutor went his way to the feast, but, Oh, terrible to think on!—he did not arrive till the delicious animal was so nearly demolished, that nothing remained for him but a few contemptible scraps scarcely worth eating, and he was compelled to make out a dinner as well as he could upon a dozen or two of other highly seasoned dishes. After such an aggravation of his former offence, who will say that any steps afterwards taken by Mr. Bounce for Ryder's ruin were not perfectly justifiable?

Whether the tutor however singly might have been able completely to crush his devoted victim, may be doubtful; but ere the time for the fiery ordeal that was everlastingly to decide Ryder's fate arrived, his evil genius, ever in action, had raised him up another antagonist even more formidable, because clothed with more power, than the great Mr. Bounce himself. At a public exercise in the schools preparatory to taking his degree, Ryder so completely foiled the Moderator of the year, Mr. Bertram, at his own weapons, that the latter was forced to retire from the rostrum degraded and abashed, while the superior talents of the young Soph became the universal theme of applause and admiration.

This was in itself a crime that never could have been passed over; but this was not all; the Moderator had yet, if possible, a greater mortification to experience. In an evil hour a wicked wit was inspired to make the circumstance the subject of the following epigram, which was instantly handed about the schools, and received with no slight degree of approbation:

Why turn all eyes astonished to the chair?
Can Bertram's want of learning make us stare?
He only proves he's fit for his vocation,
'Tis his to shew in all things MODERATION.

Nor was this formidable lampoon confined to the schools alone, to which it owed its birth; it soon got into such general circulation throughout the University, that poor Mr. Moderator was crossed by it at every step he took. Did he call on an acquaintance? as surely was it lying upon the table. Did he take his afternoon's lounge at the Coffee-house? as surely were several copies scattered about. Nay, one evening when he had a party of ladies at his rooms, on opening a fresh quarter of a pound of tea purchased for the occasion, behold a copy of the detested epigram written in the envelope. He saw, he blushed, or rather *reddened* with anger, and inwardly devoted to destruction the guiltless cause of all. Mr. Bounce's wrongs were not unknown to him, he had however hitherto concerned himself little about them; but now smarting himself under wounds which originated from the same quarter, he sought him out as a fellow sufferer, and they soon entered into a solemn covenant never to shrink from the support of each other till they had obtained the revenge after which they both so eagerly panted.

Ryder, unconscious of the obstacles thus raised to his views, looked forward to his fiery trial, with some anxiety indeed, but with flattering hopes, both from the success he had already obtained, and from the assurance in his own mind that he had omitted no efforts to deserve those honours on which his future fortunes were to depend. Ah, how could he conceive, that to possess too much knowledge was no less dangerous, perhaps even more so, than to possess too little! Those who could not contend with him upon the equal ground of argument, could crush him with the strong arm of power; and his persecutors, by the authority they acquired from their stations, so effectually prevented his talents and acquirements from being brought into notice, that instead of the high honour he had good reason to expect, he found his name wholly excluded from the list of honours.

This was a stroke upon which it was impossible for him to calculate, and the injustice of which he strongly felt. Yet conscious that his disgrace was unmerited, he hesitated not a moment to write a full and fair detail of the whole affair to Mr. Barry, relying upon obtaining that justice from him he had in vain expected from others. But the demons who had vowed his destruction, resolved to leave no arts unessayed for effecting their purpose, had fortified themselves also in this quarter, and anticipated him, by writing their own statement of the affair to the Squire. Thus before Ryder's apology reached him, his mind was too much prepossessed against this child of his adoption to admit of his listening to reason, and he wrote him in reply a very angry letter, forbidding him his presence for ever, and enclosing a bill for two hundred pounds, as the last mark of his favour he must ever expect to receive.

And since it was to be the last, Ryder had too lofty a soul to retain it. It was instantly returned with a warm and spirited remonstrance against the injustice of Mr. Barry's proceedings, and some pretty severe animadversions on his choosing rather to give credit to the accusations of persons unknown to him, and of the respectability of whose testimony he was therefore no adequate judge, than to the defence of one with whom he had been intimately connected from his infancy, and whom he had never found deceiving him in a single instance. Yes, his mind rose superior to accepting his quondam patron's money, when his friendship was withdrawn, though at that moment his prospects were as dreary and desolate as even his most inveterate enemies could wish them. He was without a home, without employment, almost without money, and destitute of all resources for ameliorating his condition except what were to be found in his own talents and industry, and he was in some danger of starving before it was possible to determine in what way they could be employed to the best advantage. To obtain any effectual assistance from his relations was out of the question, since the only ones he had were two aunts, sisters of his father, who, both pretty girls, had married greatly, considering their birth and situation in life, yet they were by no means in such circumstances as to have any superfluities to impart to others. One was then the wife of a Mr. Deacon, a country curate, with a large family, and an income of only a hundred pounds to support them; and the other was the widow of an Excise-officer at Pontefract, who with a small house there, had left her an annuity but just sufficient for her own maintenance. Doating however upon her nephew Richard, whom she considered as absolutely of a superior order of beings, she no sooner heard of his distress, than she wrote to him begging him to come to her, and assuring him, that rather than he should want or be driven into any servile occupation, she would herself seek a service, and leave him her annuity, till he was settled in some means of gaining his livelihood not degrading to a man of his learning and talents.

To George Barry indeed Ryder might still look up as a friend, ready and willing to serve him to the utmost of his power, but he was kept by his father so very strict in money matters, that a few guineas just for present support was all he could offer, and this he did offer in a very kind and affectionate letter, which went by the same post that carried his father's unjust and severe one. He expressed the deepest concern at the ill-treatment his friend had experienced, and at the prejudice Mr. Barry had conceived against him, adding many assurances of the real happiness it would give him should he ever be able in any way to serve him, and regretting severely that during his father's life his means of assisting him must be so extremely confined.

Ryder immediately resolved upon quitting Cambridge where he had nothing more to hope, and where, as the theatre on which he had experienced so much injustice and unmerited disgrace, he could have no great inclination to remain. The little property he had to dispose of, just sufficed to enable him to pay the small remains of his college expences, and to leave the place free of all claims, and then with five shillings in his pocket in a dreadful snowy morning, early in the month of February, he set out on foot for Pontefract, intending so far to avail himself of his aunt's kindness, as to take up his abode with her for two or three weeks till he could settle some plan for his future support. On the road he wrote to George Barry, acknowledging his kindness, and informing him of his intention of staying a short time at Pontefract, where if he could contrive to meet him, it would afford him very great satisfaction.

George lost no time in complying with wishes so conformable with his own inclinations, and dropped the silent tear of affection and regret upon the hand of his friend, as he mournfully pressed it beneath the humble roof of Mrs. Symonds at Pontefract, instead of shaking it eagerly in his father's mansion at Blakeney. Various plans were suggested for Ryder, but money, money was requisite for carrying any one into execution, and where was that to be procured? At length, as George was walking about the town, he met a young Ensign of his acquaintance, who was passing through in his way to London, and who, as he was just then going to dinner at the inn, earnestly pressed George to come and eat a steak with him. Here in the course of conversation it appeared that the Ensign wished to part with his commission as soon as a purchaser could be found, since otherwise he must join his regiment, which was upon garrison duty at Gibraltar, a service he by no means liked.

This was enough for George. He thought the very circumstance which created the Ensign's objection to retaining his commission, would render it the more agreeable to Ryder, who would thus have an opportunity of enlarging his ideas, by becoming acquainted with other countries and other manners, and who, in whatever station he was placed, would prefer an active to an inactive life. He therefore, without a moment's hesitation, agreed with the Ensign for the purchase, determining by some means or other to raise the money requisite for it, even though he should be compelled to have recourse to a trading money-lender; and he only waited for the completion of the business to announce what he had done, and present the commission to his friend.

Transported with the idea of thus in some measure repairing his father's injustice, he immediately applied to a manufacturer at Sheffield, with whom he was well acquainted, and from whom he hoped the money might be procured, only requesting that the affair might be kept a profound secret, as the most fatal consequences would ensue, should it ever come to Mr. Barry's knowledge. The manufacturer happening unfortunately at that time to be very short of cash himself, mentioned the circumstance to Beauchamp, who was then staying at his house for a few days, asking if he could by any means assist in raising the money. He told him likewise all the particulars of Ryder's story, which was no secret in the neighbourhood, but had been made the subject of very public discussion, and Mr. Barry's conduct had been severely reprobated.

Beauchamp was so much struck with what he had heard, that without a moment's delay he imparted all to Olivia. With her accustomed generosity she instantly desired that the commission might be purchased in her name, which would preclude any danger of George Barry's being known as an agent in the business, and she hoped, she said, that he would not refuse her the pleasure of making the intended present instead of himself.

But when the commission was put into Ryder's hands a difficulty arose, which in the ardour of arranging the plan had never suggested itself to any of the parties concerned. Miss Campbell was a person wholly unknown to Ryder, she might be one from whom he should not choose to accept an obligation, and with many acknowledgments for the intended kindness, he begged leave to decline it. Beauchamp upon this only requested him to see her, when he did not doubt that these scruples would instantly be at an end. To this he was at first very reluctant, but at length by much persuasion he was prevailed upon to consent, and accompanied Beauchamp to Campbell-House. Here Olivia's easy and engaging manners soon won so much upon the heart of the high-spirited young man, that his objections vanished, the commission was accepted, and he shortly after embarked for the place of his destination.

Perhaps it had been better had Ryder been himself consulted upon the business before it was finally arranged; but it never occurred to George in his eagerness to make some provision for his friend, that the army might be a mode of life not altogether suited to his manners and pursuits. He thought of nothing but the danger of his making objections upon the score of the difficulties to be encountered in raising the money, as he felt sensibly that Ryder would absolutely prohibit his binding himself in any way that might hereafter prove embarrassing to him, and he wished to spare his delicacy, by not suffering the engagements he must enter into to be known till it was too late to prevent them.

Not that George Barry was mistaken in the idea that his friend would like visiting foreign countries, that part of the plan was extremely agreeable to Ryder, but there were other circumstances attending his situation, that made his stay at Gibraltar not altogether pleasant to him. The dissipated lives led by people in his profession, had no charms for him; the bottle and the noisy mirth it occasions could not interest a mind devoted as his was to the pursuit of science and literature. It was besides the primary object of his soul to preserve his independence in the world, and as he felt that nothing was more essentially necessary towards attaining this object, than to avoid, with the most scrupulous caution, incurring any debts, so it was always his determined resolution, how small soever might be his means, never to live beyond what they would support. With this resolution it must be obvious that he could not pretend to associate with those who regulated their expences only by their wishes, and thus he found himself absolutely excluded from society, and compelled to place his sole reliance, both for amusement and employment, on the resources of his own mind. In consequence of this he soon obtained the character of a misanthrope, and though to withhold respect from him was impossible, yet he felt himself a solitary being, without an object he could love, or by which he could feel himself beloved. In this situation he remained near four years, when his regiment was recalled, and, at its return to England, disbanded. The officers were consequently put upon half-pay, and thus was he once more thrown out of employment, with a considerable reduction of his before small pittance. As in his hours of solitude at Gibraltar he had applied himself principally to the study of Physic, and every science connected with it, as Anatomy, Chemistry, Botany, Natural History, &c. he had thought of commencing the practice of Physic immediately on his return. But from his not having been regularly educated to the profession in either of the Universities, he found there were obstacles to pursuing this plan of which he was not at first aware. And at length, after forming various other projects for his subsistence, it has lately been determined that he is to take a large farm of Olivia's, the lease of which will expire in about half a year, when the present tenant goes to a farm of his own in a distant part of the country, recently come to him by inheritance. With this plan he is extremely pleased, as he thinks he shall thus be able to preserve that high-toned independence which forms the leading feature in his character, while he looks forward to making himself extremely useful among his poorer neighbours, by the medical pursuits in which he has lately been engaged.

Such, Orlando, is the Ensign whom Charlotte thinks likely to carry off the heiress; such the little shop-keeper's son whose intimacy at Campbell-House is matter of such high offence to the card-tables at Doncaster. As he is expected here shortly, you will then learn what opinion is entertained of him by

Yours with great sincerity

LIONEL STANHOPE.

END OF THE FIRST VOLUME.

VOLUME I

1 (titlepage) "*Man is but man . . .*" Dryden, *Cleomenes* 3.1.16–21.

2 *fair Idalia's Queen.* Venus.

3 *endued with a Lethean virtue.* With the power to make one forget the past. In Greek mythology Lethe was the River of Forgetfulness in Hades; souls forgot their previous existences when they drank from it.

4 "*Pluck from the memory a rooted sorrow . . .*" *Macbeth* 5.3.41–45.

5 *Phœbus.* In Greek mythology, Apollo as the god of the sun.

6 *I would even marry the devil's daughter for money, aye, and consent too to live with the old folks.* Robert Forby records this expression in *The Vocabulary of East Anglia* (1830) and comments that "[t]his strange saying is commonly applied to a person who has made unpromising connections in marriage" (434).

7 *his beauteous Dulcinea.* Dulcinea del Toboso was Don Quixote's mistress. Her name is used here as a general term for "sweetheart" or "inamorata."

8 *Neptune and his tritons.* Neptune is the Roman god of the sea; tritons are lesser sea-deities, often depicted as half-human and half-fish or dolphin.

9 *Fair Venus shall retire to her own Idalian groves—.* Venus is the Roman goddess of beauty and love. The mountain of Idalus was sacred to her.

10 *the far-famed groves of the Hesperides.* The garden from which Hercules stole the golden apples as the eleventh of his twelve labours. These apples were guarded by the dragon Ladon and a number of nymphs (3–7) known as the Hesperides.

11 *the little paradisaic island of the semi goddess Calypso.* Ogygia, the island on which Ulysses was shipwrecked in the *Odyssey*. Calypso, the queen of the island, promised Ulysses eternal youth and immortality if he would remain with her forever; she was heartbroken when he left after seven years.

12 *Elysium.* Paradise. In Greek mythology, the abode of the blessed dead.

13 "*ask and ye shall have*" See John 16:24: "ask, and ye shall receive, that your joy may be full."

14 *the Jason who would at last carry off the golden fleece.* In Greek mythology Jason, a prince of Iolcus, led the Argonauts in search of the golden fleece, which he secured with the help of the sorceress Medea.

15 *the little winged Mercuries of his Satanic majesty.* Evil spirits. The use of Mercury is particularly appropriate since Mercury was both the messenger of the gods and the patron of rogues, vagabonds, and thieves (Brewer's).

16 "*Between the acting of this dreadful thing | And the first motion*" *Julius Caesar* 2.1.63–64. (slightly misquoted)

17 *the exploits of an Orlando, or a Rogero, a Tancred, or a Palmerin!—* All heroes of chivalric romance. Orlando (or Roland) was the most famous of Charlemagne's Paladins. His exploits are retold in Ariosto's *Orlando Furioso* (1532) and Boiardo's unfinished *Orlando Innamorato* (1487). Rogero is another young knight; his marriage to Bradamante takes place at the end of *Orlando Furioso*.

Tancred was a great hero of the first Crusade as told by Tasso in the epic poem *Jerusalem Delivered* (1581). Palmerin was the hero of a number of sixteenth-century Spanish chivalric romances including *Palmerin of England* and *Palmerin of Gaul*. Many of the characters of classical romance became popularized with the translation and dissemination of French heroic romance in England during the 17th century. For a discussion of this process and its effects on English literature see Paul Salzman, *English Prose Fiction 1558-1700: A Critical History* (Oxford, Clarendon P, 1985) 177-190.

18 *a Godfrey, a Charlemagne, or an Arthur!* Godfrey de Bouillon, the leader of the First Crusade, appears in Tasso's *Jerusalem Delivered*. Charlemagne, king of the Franks, was crowned Emperor of the West by Pope Leo III in A.D. 800. He and his Paladins are the centre of a series of chivalric romances beginning with the *Historia de Vita Caroli Magni et Rolandi*. King Arthur, often considered the ideal Christian knight, was the romantic central figure of a cycle of legends as told by Malory in *Le Morte d'Arthur* (1485).

19 *a Rodomonte, a Rinaldo, or an Astolfo!* All three of these chivalric heroes appear in Ariosto's *Orlando Furioso* and Boiardo's *Orlando Innamorato*. Rodomonte, or the "Mars of Africa," was arrogant and boastful but also brave. Rinaldo of Montalbán, a principal character in *Orlando Innamorato*, was Orlando's cousin and a rival for Angelica's affections. Unfortunately for Rinaldo, Angelica detested him. Rinaldo also appears in *Jerusalem Delivered* where he is a victor in the battle for Jerusalem. Astolfo was a generous and courteous knight; he went to the moon to retrieve his cousin Orlando's lost wits.

20 *with a Bradamant, or a Marphisa, and Erminia, or a Clorinda—.* All heroines of romance. Bradamante was the sister of Rinaldo and a warrior in her own right. Rogero's sister Marphisa was also a female knight of great skill. Both characters appear in *Orlando Furioso* and *Orlando Innamorato*. Erminia falls in love with Tancred in Tasso's *Jerusalem Delivered*. Tancred, however, is in love with Clorinda, the Ethiopian princess who leads the pagan forces; he unwittingly kills her one dark night.

21 *scrubbing and scouring himself, as if, like the poor barber's brother, he had been sentenced to a daily purification of forty washings.* Unidentified.

22 *reach down that Palmerin—.* See note 17.

23 *that glorious Cassandra—.* The ten volume French heroic romance *Cassandre* (1644–50) was written by Gauthier de Costes de la Calprenède. It was translated into English in 1652.

24 *that beloved Amadis—.* Amadis was the central figure of Spanish and Portuguese chivalric romance. The earliest version of *Amadis of Gaul* was written in the late fifteenth century by Garcia de Montalvo. It was translated into English by Munday around 1590. An abridged version in English appeared in 1702.

25 *I should prove a Marplot.* A meddlesome but well-meaning character from two of Susanna Centlivre's plays: *The Busie Body* (1709) and *Mar-Plot; Or, The Second Part of The Busie-Body* (1711). In *The Busie Body* Centlivre describes this character as "A sort of a silly Fellow, Cowardly, but very Inquisitive to know every Body's Business, generally spoils all he undertakes, yet without Design."

26 *a disciple of the Brunonian system—.* The theory of medicine developed by Dr.

John Brown (1735–1788) which classified disease into two categories: those diseases that were the result of too much stimulus and those produced by too little. The former he treated with sedatives, the latter with stimulants. Lionel is hinting that Mrs. Harrison is stimulating herself with alcohol.

27 *the great Linnæus.* Carl Linnaeus (1707–1778), Swedish naturalist and taxonomist. He developed a binomial system to scientifically classify plants and animals.

28 *the admirable Crichton.* James Crichton, known as "the Admirable Crichton," a sixteenth-century Scottish prodigy who took his Master of Arts degree at the age of fourteen.

29 *"— — With stealthy pace, . . . Move like a ghost." Macbeth* 2.1.54–56.

30 *"It is my lady! . . ." Romeo and Juliet* 2.2.2,10–11,15–17. Harry's memory of the text is imperfect. He misses a number of lines and makes a few small errors.

31 *my valiant Palmerin.* See note 17.

32 *fairest Polinarda.* Palmerin falls in love with Polinarda in *Palmerin of England.*

33 *the valorous knight Belianis.* Don Belianus of Greece, the hero of an old chivalric romance modelled on *Amadis of Gaul.* It was one of the books in Don Quixote's library not burnt by the Curé.

34 *Durandarte.* A hero of Spanish legend and ballad. When he fell at Roncesvallês, his last request was to have his heart cut out and taken to Belerma.

35 *the fair Belerma.* Durandarte's beloved. See above note.

36 *the Old Bailey.* The seat of the Central Criminal Court of the City of London, so called from the ancient *bailey* or *ballium* of the city wall between Lud Gate and New Gate, within which it was situated (OED).

37 *"The bell strikes one."* Edward Young. *Night Thoughts*, Night 1.54.

38 *Æolus.* The god of the winds.

39 *"swear not at all"* Matthew 5:34.

40 *catalogue of Ernulphus.* In *Textus Roffensis*, a compilation of laws and other church documents said to have been compiled by Ernulphus, Bishop of Rochester (1040–1124), there is a form of excommunication involving a comprehensive curse. This series of curses is read out loud in Laurence Sterne's *Tristram Shandy* (Book 3, chapters 10 and 11).

41 *Cynthia.* A name of Artemis or Diana used to poetically represent the moon.

42 *the medium of dæmons, cacodæmons, witches, wizards, or spirits.* A *dæmon* is a being midway between the gods and man; a cacodæmon is an evil spirit; a witch is "A woman given to unlawful arts" (Johnson); a wizard is "a he witch" (Johnson); and a spirit is an "apparition" (Johnson).

43 *like those of the poor ass so often celebrated.* A proverbial figure of indecision commonly known as Buridan's ass, but which cannot be found in his works. See John Byrom's *Fight between Figge and Sutton* (1763) "Dame Victory . . . remain'd like the ass 'twixt two bottles of hay, without ever moving an inch either way."

44 *to the Nine.* In Greek mythology the nine daughters of Zeus and Mnemosyne (Memory). They were the inspiration of the sciences and arts, particularly music and poetry.

45 *the little mischievous deity.* The god of love, known either as Cupid or Eros.

46 *the Jason to carry away the golden fleece.* See note 14.

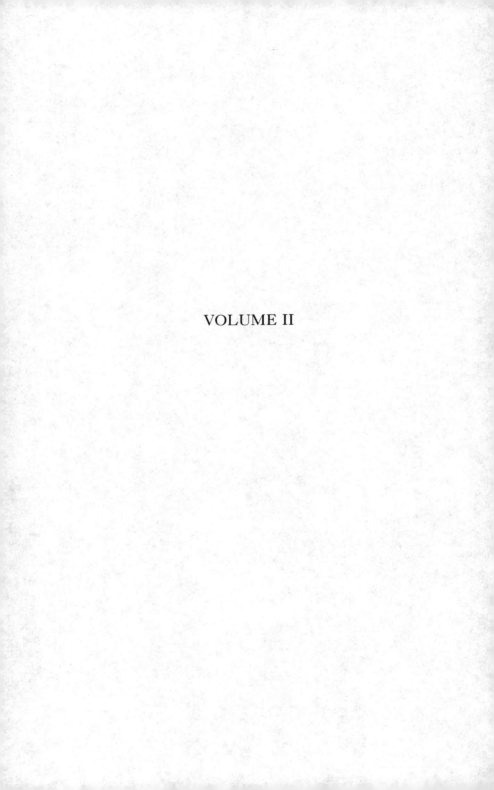

VOLUME II

LETTER I.

LIONEL STANHOPE
TO
ORLANDO ST. JOHN.

Campbell-House, September 2.

Oh! St. John! I am at length in possession of Harriot Belgrave's story. Read, and wonder.

Her father was an officer in the East India Company's service, and had amassed a tolerable fortune, with which he was coming over to settle in England. But very imprudently trusting the whole of his property on board the same ship, the savings of many years were all lost in one luckless moment. In a violent storm the vessel went to the bottom, and with it foundered Captain Belgrave's golden hopes of passing the remainder of his days in an easy tranquility, in the bosom of his family. But to console him for this loss, soon after his return to England, by the death of a distant relation, whose youth and excellent constitution gave little reason to expect a fate so premature, he inherited a considerable estate in Ireland, which promised to place him once more in affluence, and preclude the necessity of his making another voyage to India, to repair his former imprudence.

Not having any determined place of residence, he, with Mrs. Belgrave and Harriot, their only child, then about seventeen years of age, went to Bath, with the idea of settling there, should they find it a place suited to their habits and dispositions. But they had not been there many weeks, before they received the disagreeable intelligence of their right to the Irish estate being contested by a person who claimed to be nearer of kin to the deceased, than Captain Belgrave, consequently, as the deceased had died without a will, to be the legal heir.

Captain Belgrave's immediate presence in Ireland thus became indispensably necessary, though it happened at a moment when it was peculiarly distressing to him to be separated from his family. Mrs. Belgrave had been so unfortunate as to break her leg in a very dreadful manner, and from the effects of this accident, great apprehensions were entertained for her life; thus the Captain was forced to leave her, under the agonizing impression that perhaps the very next post after his arrival at Dublin might bring him the account of her death.

From the first intimation he had received of this affair, he was led strongly to suspect that the whole business was a combination of iniquity, and the more he investigated the matter, the more fully was he confirmed in his suspicions. The claimant was a man in a very indigent situation, who was known indeed to belong to the family, but who had always been considered as of so very remote a branch that there were many others besides Captain Belgrave, whose claims to the estate would have superseded his; besides, from his poverty it was obvious that he could not support his claim himself, but that he must be supported in it by others. In fact, it plainly appeared that the man was entirely instigated to the business by a rascally lawyer, who was to be well paid for his roguery if his client should at last get possession of the fortune. Nor was this all. It appeared too almost equally certain that the lawyer was supported by a Peer, who had long been at variance with the Belgrave family from an opposition of interests in electioneering concerns, and who joyfully embraced this opportunity of gratifying a paltry pique, though his malice fell upon one who could not possibly have had any share in the offence given.

In consequence of this conviction, Captain Belgrave one day, when he was particularly exasperated against the Peer, by some fresh circumstances relative to the affair which had just then come to his knowledge, very indiscreetly threw out many very severe reflexions upon him for connecting himself with such a dirty fellow as the lawyer, who, he said, deserved to be kicked out of society by every body that pretended to call himself a gentleman. All this was faithfully reported to his Lordship by one of those good-natured persons whose chief occupation it is to set others at variance—his noble blood was fired at the relation—a challenge was instantly sent to the Captain—they fought, and the Captain received a wound in his side, of which he died in a few days.

A situation of more complicated misery than Harriot's at that moment can, perhaps, scarcely be conceived. Her father's life thus fatally thrown away—her mother still confined by her accident, and her recovery rendered even more doubtful than ever by this additional weight of sorrow— while, from the situation of their affairs, it was probable that they were destitute of every means of support, and that at a time when the state of Mrs. Belgrave's health necessarily occasioned them many and heavy additional expences. This, altogether, formed such an accumulation of calamity, as must probably have overpowered a mind inclined, like Harriot's, to excess of sensibility, had she not, in the midst of her sorrows, found a most unexpected source of consolation in the kindness of some friends, attracted to her merely by the knowledge of her misfortunes.

Not many days after Captain Belgrave's departure, a gentleman and lady, with their son, took lodgings in the very same house where Harriot and her mother resided. A hint from the mistress of the house, that one of her lodgers had been for some time in great danger from the effects of an accident, occasioned the lady to enquire farther particulars respecting them, and when she heard the whole story, she immediately became deeply interested for the sufferers, and sent them, through the landlady, the kindest offers of rendering them any assistance in her power. Harriot, in consequence, the first minute that she could spare from her mother's bed-side, waited upon the lady to make her personal acknowledgements for her kindness, when her artless and pleasing manners fixed irrevocably the interest her situation had at first excited. A constant intercourse between the two parties commenced from that moment, and by the relief

Harriot thus found for her sorrows, she was enabled the more effectually to bear up against them. Nor was the kindness of these friends confined to mere words of consolation. Understanding the state in which Mrs. Belgrave's affairs were left at the Captain's death, they made her the offer of any pecuniary assistance she might want, and were constantly attentive to procuring for her numerous little comforts which she would have been scrupulous of providing for herself, yet which were very essential to her recovery.

With the account of Captain Belgrave's death, came a summons to his widow and daughter to repair to Dublin with all possible expedition; and accordingly, as soon as Mrs. Belgrave was able to undertake the voyage, they set out. The friends to whom they were so much indebted quitted Bath a few days before them, and the two families separated with the warmest expressions of gratitude on one side, and reiterated assurances of continued friendship on the other. The lady gave Harriot a strict injunction to write to her frequently, with particular accounts of her mother's health and her own, and of the probable termination of the unpleasant affair that occasioned their journey.

But the compassion which in the breasts of the father and mother had excited only a strong friendship for Harriot, and an earnest anxiety for her welfare, created a much more tender interest in the bosom of the son. His situation under the same roof with the object of his devotion, afforded him many opportunities for private conversation with her, and of these he availed himself so well, that he soon had the satisfaction of finding his passion returned with equal fervour. Both young, ardent, and enthusiastic, their whole souls were absorbed in each other, and hours seemed to pass but as moments, as they exchanged their vows of unalterable love and constancy. The young man, however, frankly told Harriot, that he knew his father had other views for him, consequently that skilful management would be necessary in the disclosure of his own wishes. Yet, he said, he could not but flatter himself that if matters were not precipitated, they might ultimately be brought about, to the satisfaction of all parties, and he be blessed with the only object who could ever make him happy. He entreated Harriot in the mean time to write to him very frequently, as he said her letters alone could enable him to support the many dreadful hours of suspense to which he must look forward; and he instructed her how the letters might be sent, so as to preclude all danger of their correspondence being detected.

In compliance with these injunctions both of the mother and son, Harriot, immediately on her arrival at Dublin, wrote long letters to each, pouring out profusely to the latter such pure effusions of artless affection, as their relative situations seemed fully to authorise. To these she received no answer, but she nevertheless soon wrote again to both. Still no answers came; however, as she knew the uncertainty of winds and waves, this appeared not strange, and while she could not absolutely control her impatience, she yet almost chid herself for yielding to it. A fortnight thus passed on, she became uneasy, yet still she endeavoured to persuade herself that all was right, and that the so much wished-for letters, though long delayed, would come at last. She wrote once more both to the mother and son, regretting that she had not heard from England since her arrival, expressing her apprehensions that letters must have failed, and entreating that she might hear from them without delay. With anxious longing did she watch the arrival of every packet, still expecting that each in succession would put an end to her torments; but she watched, alas! in vain—no letters arrived; till at length, unable any longer to delude herself with hope, she yielded to the fatal conviction that she was forgotten both by her lover and her friend, and sunk for a while into that state of despondency which was the inevitable consequence of a conclusion so fatal. From that time to this she has never heard any thing of the family but by common report, and all she knows concerning them is, that the father and mother both died within a year after her acquaintance with them, and that the son has turned out such a profligate, that his desertion of her must be considered as a subject of thankfulness, not of regret.

For the rest, as the affair of the estate was referred to Chancery,[1] Mrs. Belgrave was satisfied that a speedy decision was a thing not to be expected. She well knew the tedious nature of proceedings in that court, and that the suit might not improbably be protracted even beyond the life of either herself or her daughter, especially as the affair was rendered still more intricate by the death of Captain Belgrave, and the validity of a will he made on his deathbed, by which he bequeathed the estate to Harriot, subject to a jointure for her mother's life, being contested. From this, therefore, nothing was to be hoped, and it became necessary that she and Harriot should seek some other means of subsistence. Perhaps this necessity was a fortunate circumstance for the latter, since nothing less might have proved sufficient to rouse her from the state of morbid melancholy in which she had been sunk by her lover's falsehood.

As their presence in Ireland was not likely to accelerate the determination of the law-suit, they had no motive for remaining there, and they therefore resolved upon returning into England, where it was their idea to endeavour to establish themselves in a school. This plan Mrs. Belgrave immediately mentioned to General Campbell, with whom she had always lived on terms of intimacy, requesting his opinion as to the general expediency of it, and if he thought it eligible, his advice in what part of the kingdom they had best settle. This letter found the General in great affliction for the loss of his wife, who had died not many days before, and Mrs. Belgrave's being in want of a situation, suggested to him the idea of proposing her coming to live with him as mistress of the house, and superintendant of the education of his daughter, till she should be old enough to preside in the place of her deceased mother. This was a proposal too acceptable to be refused, and Mrs. Belgrave, with her daughter, in a very short time became inmates at Campbell-House.

In this situation they both conducted themselves with such propriety, and the General and Olivia became so warmly attached to them, that when the proposed limits for their stay expired, they could not bear the idea of parting with them again. Sensible, however, that the change which must take place in Mrs. Belgrave's situation, in becoming only a guest in a house where she had so lately been mistress, might be a little revolting to her feelings, some delicacy seemed requisite in proposing such a scheme. In the first place then, to leave the matter as much as possible to her own free choice, the General resolved to arrange pecuniary concerns with her in such a way, that her continuance with him should be no object of convenience to herself upon that ground, and he therefore added another hundred pounds a year to an annuity of two hundred, which it had been previously stipulated she was to receive at her quitting him, and to Harriot he presented three thousand pounds. Then making known his own and his daughter's wish that they should continue to live together, he requested her to take the matter into her serious consideration, assuring her, that if she should determine on not complying with their wishes, though they might regret, they should not be offended at her determination.

Mrs. Belgrave indeed strongly felt that this was an affair of extreme delicacy, and one which required ample consideration. Experience had taught her, that connections like that offered to her choice, however they might for a while pass on smoothly and amicably, often terminated in petty discontents and jealousies, if not in settled and deep-rooted aversion; and she many times questioned herself whether or not it would be justifiable in her to put such friendship as she and her daughter had received from the General and Olivia to so great a hazard. On the other side, after five years passed in uninterrupted harmony and happiness under the General's roof, and the conviction so long an experience had given her of his excellent domestic qualities, his benevolent, cheerful, and social disposition, and still more how truly amiable and affectionate was the heart of his daughter, it seemed almost criminal to doubt the continuance of their happiness, and to think of a separation in opposition to the wishes of persons to whom she was so deeply bound in gratitude.

Thus yielding a little to judgement, and a great deal more to feeling, she at length consented to remain at Campbell-House,—a decision she has never for a moment had reason to repent. Not a single spark of jealousy, or the remotest tendency to animosity or dissention, has ever appeared in any of the parties, but they have continued to live in the same uninterrupted harmony as before. So exemplary indeed has been Olivia's conduct with regard to both her friends, that they have repeatedly been heard to declare it was impossible for them to feel the difference of their own situation and hers. Every thing belonging to her has been as perfectly at their command as at her own, and she has uniformly made them of as much consequence in the eyes of the servants, and of all visitors at the house, as herself.

When I heard this detail, I could not forbear exclaiming in extasy, "Oh admirable woman! by heaven then she wants not beauty, not could the brightest eyes, or the loveliest form, add one ray of lustre to a soul like hers!" Nay, I could even in the transport of the moment have gone and thrown myself at her feet, humbly to solicit that hand I had so long despised, since no paradise appeared equal to passing the remainder of my days in constant intercourse with such a mind. Nor, believe me, St. John, was this a mere transient emotion that flitted through my heart in the first impulse of admiration excited by her noble conduct, and then vanished for ever; it still lives there, and by reflection gains added vigour. Oh God! how vain, how idle is beauty, when compared with qualities so exalted, so sublime! The one is fleeting and transient, adored for a while, then regarded no longer; but a soul like Olivia's is an inexhaustible mine of attractions, ever varying, ever new. Nay, even the tomb itself cannot deprive us of charms like these, for the heart of him who has been united to such perfections, can never lose the impression they have made, but must for ever dwell delighted on the recollection of what when living constituted its pride and glory.

And now tell me, St. John, what think you of the story above related? Can you not discern in it strong features of resemblance, in the commencement at least, if not in the catastrophe, to a tale of woe, long, alas! but too well known to us. One only thing is wanting to convince me that 'tis not merely a resemblance that may be traced between them, but that they are individually the same, and that is to know the name of the persons who are reputed to have treated Harriot with such mingled kindness and cruelty; but the knowledge of this is denied me. As Beauchamp related the story, I observed that the name was never once mentioned; this I noticed when he had concluded, and said, "Is it impertinent to ask to be favoured with it?"

"There is certainly no impertinence in making the request," said he, "but I am sorry to say that your curiosity must remain ungratified. Treacherously as her lover behaved to her, Harriot has never been able to banish him from her heart; he was the first, and will ever remain the only object of her affections, and from motives of delicacy she keeps both his name, and the story, concealed as much as possible. Accident alone led me to the knowledge of them, but I consider myself as no less bound in honour not to reveal them without permission, than if they had been imparted to me in the strictest confidence. 'Tis not without permission that I have now revealed the story to you, but in disclosing that, I have gone to the utmost limits granted me; the name must still remain a secret."

Ah does not this secrecy speak as plainly as the revealing the name at once? Yet much as I wish to reconcile all differences, there are some circumstances I know not how to get over. Time may perhaps disclose more; unless it does, I shall never venture to tell our poor suffering friend what I already know, since it is enough to set his unsettled brain a madding.

Orlando, thou know'st that 'tis ever the practice after a Tragedy, to give a Farce. The Tragedy you have above, let the curtain then draw up for the Farce, and behold it discovers* Rebecca Harrison spinster, making her first appearance among the company, after a confinement of some days to her own apartment.

Whether you may have regretted her absence from my letters for some time, I cannot say, but this I can say, that I certainly have not very much regretted her absence from our society. "And what has been the cause of her absence?" you will perhaps enquire. Why she hath been, as she herself expresseth it, *a little queer*, that is to say, somewhat indisposed; but being far advanced in a state of convalescence, she yesterday came down again to dinner.

It so happened that I was the only person in the room when she first made her appearance. I very politely accosted her: "How do you do, Madam, I am extremely glad to see you here again; we have been deprived of your company for a long time."

"Thank' ye."

"I hope you find yourself perfectly recovered?"

"Thank' ye."

Beauchamp now entered.—"Mrs. Harrison here—this is quite an unexpected pleasure. I hope it may be considered, Madam, as a proof that your health is entirely restored."

"Thank' ye."

Next came Sir Francis. "Ha Cousin Becky," for be it known to thee Sir Francis always calls Mrs. Harrison cousin, though for what reason I cannot tell, I only know that 'tis not because she is his relation. "Ha Cousin Becky! why we have not met before, though we've been under the same roof. But I hope all's set to rights now with you as well as with us."

"Thank' ye."

Fourthly appeared Edgerton, but a dry "How do you do, Madam?" was all that his politeness could bring forth. It received the same answer, however, as the more elaborate compliments of the rest:

"Thank' ye."

Fifthly, and lastly, came Olivia. "I am extremely happy in seeing you down stairs again, Madam, and hope you will not suffer from leaving your room."

"Thank' ye."

"Anon, anon, Sir," said Shakespeare's Francis,[2] and so he would have said had he been called twenty times more. "Thank' ye," said Mrs. Harrison, and this and no more, I believe, she would have said had twenty more persons made like enquiries after her health. What parrots can some people be. We mortals are strange animals, as I have often observed, Mr. St. John, and Mrs. Harrison is certainly not an exception to this general rule.

---

*   Reveals, discloses.

So much for the first act of the Farce. The second was played in the evening, when the spirit moved us to pass away a leisure hour in looking out some of the constellations upon the globe. At this employment our learned spinster found us, and understanding what we were about, "Well," she said, "but do you know how to *set* the globe?"

No answer was made, as it was a question, the meaning of which I believe we none of us clearly understood. She however proceeded, "My dear, hav'n't you got Guthrie's Introduction to Geography;[3] every body should have that book that has globes, it's so useful, it teaches you to do every thing with the globe."

"Oh yes, Madam," said Olivia, "here it is," and she immediately handed the book to her fair cousin.

The latter opened it at *Problems performed by the globe*; she read three or four of them, twirled the globe first this way, then that, and at last said with most profound satisfaction and self-complacency, "And now, my dear, I take it you see all them stars," pointing to half the stars in the southern hemisphere.

"I am sure, Madam," said Olivia, "we are much obliged to you for your instruction."

"Aye," said the good lady, "its always *better* to do things right at once."

She is to be appointed Astronomer royal to his Majesty, on the first vacancy.

Orlando, I wish you could see one of this lady's letters. The inaccuracy of writers in pointing their compositions has been often, and perhaps justly, a subject of complaint. To reduce this matter to a greater certainty, and prevent all possibility of mistakes, Mrs. Harrison never uses but one sort of point, and that of interrogation. Whether the matter of the period be a round assertion, a humble petition, or a simple narration, still it terminates with a point of interrogation. Perhaps the proper meaning of this is, that 'tis a question whether she ever knows what she is about.

You, I hope, will not question my sincerity, when I subscribe myself
Your truly affectionate

LIONEL STANHOPE.

LETTER II.

ORLANDO ST. JOHN
TO
LIONEL STANHOPE.

Scarborough, September 4.
And dost thou really think, Mr. Lionel Stanhope, that thou wilt be permitted to call me an *old maid* with impunity?—Oh know me better, *mon*

cher ami, know that I am not made of such passive materials, for I do call upon thee—yes, Monsignor Lionel, I do call upon thee—against the next time I write I will determine what satisfaction to require, for the common mode of settling differences between gentleman and gentleman is totally insufficient for expiating an insult so atrocious.

Truly thy biographical memoirs of Richard Ryder did surprize me much. Slightly as Charlotte mentioned him, I had no idea that he was to prove any thing above the common class of half-pay ensigns; and, indeed, her mentioning him at all as belonging to that class of beings, I thought a sufficient indication that nothing better was to be said of him. But in good truth, from what I now know, I think that since Harry has given up his pursuit, your heiress could not do better than to bestow her ample property on one who seems rich in all gifts save those of fortune.

Mais passons cela, for be he ever so richly gifted by nature, or improved by cultivation, who could bestow a thought on him, blessed in the society of Charlotte O'Brien and Eliza de Clairville, and amused with the humours of Francis Peters and Margaret Perkins? And yet, I must for one moment step aside from them to remark upon Harriot Belgrave's story. It has excited my anxiety and interest beyond expression. Oh that all may turn out as you wish!—I will redouble my assiduities to collect information from Charlotte, though I own without much hopes of success, as I suspect the little witch sees how I am devoured by curiosity, and, delighted with it, is determined to torment me.

So much for my apostrophe—let me now revert again to the subject from which I digressed. Lionel, since biography is so much the fashion, I think I can in no way so well repay the obligations I am under for the interesting details contained in your two last letters, as by sending you anecdotes of Peggy Perkins, whose misfortunes have, in her own opinion, so far exceeded any ever yet sustained by a child of Adam, that Richard Ryder's and Harriot Belgrave's cannot be put into comparison with them.

Some nine or ten years back, at the death of her father, she went to live with a rich old uncle, a widower, who about the same time lost a sister that had long kept his house. Here Miss Peggy remained for four years, when the old gentleman died, leaving her a very pretty *fortin*. That her situation with him was not very comfortable, and that her fortune was dearly earned by a four years subservience to his caprices, is, I believe, indisputable; but, at the same time, it may well be doubted whether her own temper be not sufficient to destroy her peace of mind wherever she may live.

Deeply impressed with ideas of her own importance, wherever fate has cast her, she has always supposed herself the principal object of attention in the little world around, and since she could not be regarded with indifference, that from each individual of that world, she must experience either warm attachment or inveterate aversion. Accordingly she has uniformly divided her neighbours into two classes, her *dear friends* and her *bitter enemies*, the same person being placed alternately, and perhaps with equal reason, both in the one class and the other. Friendships like hers, formed she knows not why, may be transformed in a moment, she knows not wherefore, into the most implacable enmities; and it has been her peculiarly hard lot, as she has often been heard to say, to find people as smooth as oil to her face, who, behind her back, have done every thing in their power, to traduce and calumniate her.

But at no period of her life was the friendship and enmity of her neighbours carried to so great a height as during the four years that she passed with her uncle. Accordingly, to her *dear friends* she was always lamenting the malignity with which she was pursued by her *bitter enemies*, and detailing the calumnies they circulated against her—calumnies which commonly had no existence but in her own perturbed imagination, and which certainly had never come into general circulation but through the pains she took, by deploring, to spread them.

One day visiting an acquaintance who had known her when she lived with her father, and who was then recently come to settle in the neighbourhood of her uncle, she began earnestly to caution this newly-arrived friend against believing the stories he heard of her; she assured him that they were all *bitter calumnies*, invented by her *bitter enemies* to traduce her character; "but believe me, Sir," said she, "I am not the woman they represent me."

"Indeed, Miss Peggy," he replied, "you need not make yourself so uneasy upon this account. I can assure you I have never so much as heard your name mentioned since I came into this country."

Oh mortifying consolation! To be a mark for the shafts of malice she could bear with fortitude; but not to be mentioned at all was too much to endure, and she incontinently burst into tears.

Since her uncle's death she has lived at half the towns and villages in the kingdom. At one time she was settled for life at Bristol; but though

> She meant to live there all her days,
> She felt she could not live there long;[4]

Since she was certain she was in a very rapid consumption, and must there shortly find her grave.

Nor did she *live there long*—but Weymouth, not the grave, was the next place of her abode. There she had truly found a Paradise, and no power on earth should ever induce her to quit it. And, indeed, this important matter was not brought about by any earthly power extrinsic of herself, but somehow or other, in about half a year she discovered that this place was not quite so Paradisaical as it at first appeared. She found herself still pursued by the implacable tongue of calumny, and if she hoped for repose she must seek some other situation.

Bath, Brighton, Cheltenham, Southampton, have all had their turns of being her heaven and her hell, for all have been awhile the place of her residence. At other times she has travelled about for several months by herself, or accompanied only by her maid—occasionally indeed she has taken a *dear friend* as the companion of her wanderings, till from some trifling subject of disagreement the friendship has on a sudden been transformed into the bitterest enmity. At length hearing that her relation, Mrs. Tichfield, was at Scarborough, she requested permission to join her party there, as she said her health continued very bad, and she had tried so many southern watering places without success, that she now wished to try the effect of one more northwards.

Mrs. Tichfield, though not very fond of her cousin's company, complied with her request without any hesitation, as it was extremely convenient to her thus to get another person to share in the expenses of her summer establishment. At first Peggy found Scarborough the most delightful place that ever was known, and there she should certainly fix for life. She accordingly looked at various houses and lodgings that were likely to be vacant by the winter, but could not find one that suited her taste; and now she thinks the place so much less pleasant than she once thought it, that she does not intend staying beyond the end of the season.

Such, Lionel, is Peggy Perkins, the cousin of Mrs. Tichfield—such the enchanting maid whose bright eyes seem mortally to have wounded the heart of Mr. Peters. You will not suppose they have made an equal impression upon that of

> Your affectionate

> ORLANDO ST. JOHN.

LETTER III.

LIONEL STANHOPE
TO
ORLANDO ST. JOHN.

Campbell-House, September 5.

Orlando, I am daily more and more perplexed with all I see and hear in this castle of wonders. Since I learned the lovely Harriot's story, I have had a very interesting conversation with Olivia, in some passages of which I can scarcely persuade myself but that "*more was meant than met the ear.*"[5] Fain would I adjust these to the purpose I am so anxious to effect, of reconciling the story I have recently heard with that I have so long known; nor do I think this impossible—I even think it may be done without violence, or putting forced constructions upon questions asked without any particular meaning.

This morning I was taking a solitary saunter in the garden before breakfast, when I was unexpectedly joined by my hostess. After walking together a few minutes she began:—"I have been uncommonly impressed, Mr. Stanhope, with the particulars you imparted to me the other day respecting Mr. Egerton and Miss Trelawney. I can scarcely doubt that your friend must have been extremely cautious to assure himself of the truth of Miss Trelawney's death, before he could relinquish all hope of her having escaped the peril she encountered—a hope to which he must have clung, even with a sickly eagerness, till its fallacy was too palpable to admit of its being longer cherished. Were I not fully assured of this, I should, from other circumstances, be led strongly to doubt whether he had not fallen into some unfortunate mistake upon the subject."

"Would to God that this admitted of a question!—Would to God the shadow of a hope remained that Miss Trelawney might be still in existence!—then might Harry's soul once more know repose! then might he once more rise to that height from which he has fallen!—But reflect, Madam,—do you think it possible that if Emily had escaped a peril so imminent she would not instantly have written to a man she so much loved, to set his mind at ease, and assure him of her safety?—Or supposing she could have been so negligent—so worse than negligent, so inhuman, as to omit this—had any of the hapless crew of the Cornwall been saved, must not an event so nearly approaching to miraculous, soon have been well known?"

"I own the justice of your reasoning; yet 'tis very extraordinary that though I have often heard Miss Trelawney's story mentioned, I never heard her death so much as hinted at. She was always represented as alive, and deserted by Mr. Egerton."

"You surprize me much, Madam, by saying that you have heard the story frequently mentioned, since Harry, as I told you before, has always cautiously avoided even the remotest allusion to it. But believe me, whoever has reported Miss Trelawney to be now alive, must have done it either through gross ignorance or gross malignity. Oh, Miss Campbell, ask yourself whether it be probable, supposing Emily to be still alive, that the name of Trelawney never should have met the ear of one so eager as Harry must be, to catch at the sound of a name so beloved?"

"She may perhaps have lived in perfect obscurity, since I understood from you that she and her mother were left in very indifferent circumstances."

"Pardon me, Madam, but surely this is not a supposition much to Emily's credit. If she be alive, she must studiously keep herself concealed from her distracted lover; and by what other motive could she be induced to a conduct so extraordinary, except by a failure of her own constancy, or doubts of his—doubts so injurious to him, that they would render her scarcely less culpable than inconstancy in herself. But away with the idea!—Emily never could suspect his faith; and had she been still in existence, could not have permitted him to suppose her dead. Oh God! severe as have been his sufferings at losing her, they would be nothing to the more dreadful pang of knowing that she was alive, yet not living for him."

"You really think that if she were alive he still would love her?"

"Love her!—Gracious heaven! who can have witnessed all he has endured, and see him still suffer as he does for her sake, yet doubt that he still would love her?"

"But are the sufferings you lament, and the constancy of which you boast, reconcileable with the profligate course of life he has so long led?"

"They are united in the indissoluble link of cause and effect. To dissipate corroding care has been Harry's sole object; and though he may have mistaken the proper means for obtaining his end, and in flying one uneasiness created himself a thousand others, still the passion he cannot conquer has been the cause of all."

"Has constancy to his Emily led him to seek so many other matrimonial connections?"

"Still links of the same chain. The wish to fly from reflection drove him into scenes of dissipation, by which his fortune was wasted, while his principles were undermined; and thus he scrupled not to seek relief from his own immediate embarrassments by involving others in his ruin. But his unprincipled conduct has carried with it its own punishment, in the endless disappointments and mortifications he has experienced. Refusal has followed refusal, till—"

"As a last desperate resource, he would have made my fortune subservient to his purposes?"

"Alas! Madam, it is but too true!—Yet, to my everlasting shame be it recorded, the means employed for attaining his purpose were my planning, not his. Oh God! Oh God! what an indelible stigma have I thus affixed to my character!—one that no time, no remorse, can ever obliterate!—I could almost say that my very existence is a curse, since I must be eternally tortured with such recollections. The only thing that can be urged to palliate so detestable an imposture, and even that perhaps may be too contemptible to mention, is, that the idea was suggested in a hasty moment, for reasons I now detest to think on, and acceded to by Egerton solely from the pressure of pecuniary embarrassments."

"You astonish me, Mr. Stanhope; this scheme was your planning, do you say?"

"Oh yes, yes, Madam!—it was!—it was!—Cursed be the hour that ever I could admit into my bosom a thought so base!—Wretch that I was!—Yes, it was planned to rescue myself from importunities with which I had never been assailed, could I have listened to reason—it was planned to preclude the possibility of an union which I ought to have thought of with transport, but from which my headstrong folly and ignorance made me shrink with affright. Oh! Miss Campbell, that I did but dare to talk freely with you on this subject!—that I had but courage to lay my whole heart open before you!—I have often wished to make a more ample confession of my folly and guilt, yet how enter on a subject of so delicate a nature?"

"Go on, Sir; I am ready, nay anxious, to hear all you would say.

Sincerity is a quality I prize beyond all others; and however unpleasant the truth may be, I never shrink from hearing it. But in this instance I suspect I could anticipate your story; however, proceed if you please."

"Well then, Madam, I will summon resolution to confess all my guilt, all my insensibility. Often had I heard my father descant on the treasure General Campbell possessed in a daughter whose merits might justly be said to beggar all encomium, and as often had he urged me in the most impressive manner to accompany him hither to see that treasure. Yet much as this plan was for my advantage, I was so blind—my headstrong folly was such—but alas, Madam, young men will be perverse—young men will be perverse, Madam—and they make it a sort of pride not to be governed by their fathers; for the idea of bondage you know, Madam, is a thing we none of us love; and I had always been over-indulged, and suffered to have my own way till I knew not how to submit to any kind of controul; nay, though my father had never attempted to exert his paternal influence except in this one instance,—but I believe that contributed to render me more obstinate, though undoubtedly—undoubtedly it made my resistance the more culpable; but you well know, Madam, as I was saying—that young men, Madam—"

"Like to choose for themselves. I believe I must help you out, Mr. Stanhope, as you seem not to get on very well by yourself."

"Why, indeed, I must own, Madam—I must acknowledge—I must confess, Madam, that—that—"

"You do not however seem very ready with your confession, so I believe I must assist you again. You confess, then, that you had heard reports in the world concerning my person, and which in this instance were more accurate than is usual among common reports, that did not particularly induce you to accompany Sir Francis, lest that should be considered as a tacit consent to his obvious views."

I felt myself blush and look extremely foolish; no fair maiden at the first pressure of a lover's hand, could have blushed more prettily, or felt more silly and abashed. I hesitated, I stammered, I essayed to speak again and again, and at last in this awkward way did I endeavour to extricate myself from the cleft in which I was enclosed: "Ye—ye—yes—Madam,—'tis true indeed, Madam—that—that—since you so kindly encourage me to frankness by speaking so unreservedly yourself, that I was possessed with that absurd, that nonsensical idea, that—that be—be—beauty—that beauty—"

"Was the sole thing needful in a woman: that you were averse even to the idea of seeing one you were well assured was not handsome."

"But indeed, Madam, I do not think so any longer; henceforward I shall be of a very different opinion, I shall consider beauty as a very secondary—"

"Consideration, undoubtedly, or worse, as perfectly contemptible, a mere snare with which 'tis impossible virtue or sense should ever be united."

"Oh yes, Madam, believe me I sincerely think all this."

"Ah, Mr. Stanhope," said she, tapping me familiarly on the shoulder, quite familiarly indeed, Orlando, "Ah, Mr. Stanhope, you don't perform your part well at all; you should have conned your lesson better, before you ever thought of coming to confession."

"I own 'tis true, Madam. But I believe 'tis perfectly needless to say more. Your excellent judgment, and deep discernment, have penetrated into the most secret recesses of my heart, and you there see the temptations by which I was led into this accursed scheme. But believe me, oh Miss Campbell! when I solemnly assure you, that 'tis impossible for any one to hold it in greater abhorrence than I now do myself! Would to God that I could blot the guilty recollection from the pages of my life! It seems indeed scarcely credible, even to my own mind, that I could form such a plan, and still more that I could for a moment entertain an idea of its success."

"Yet I will tell you upon what that idea and hope were founded. You had heard me represented as an inexperienced girl, educated in the country, and unacquainted with the world, and you therefore presumed that I should become your easy dupe."

"But I now see that common report is a senseless blockhead, that knows not what it says, and that the world has no conception of the inestimable value of a truly cultivated and accomplished woman. Whoever therefore can be weak enough to pay any attention to the nonsensical babble of the world, will to his cost commonly find himself thus deceived."

"In the world 'tis a commonly received, though a very absurd idea, that a country education necessarily implies ignorance of life; nor can people suppose it possible that a woman who, like myself, has lived constantly at such a distance from the capital, the great centre of knowledge, taste, and science, can have any acquaintance with mankind. But though my father's infirm state of health, martyr as he was for the last ten years of his life to a malady which confined him wholly to this spot, prevented my visiting distant parts, and that even now I have never been in London, yet I have perhaps scarcely seen less variety of company than if I had passed my whole life there. My father's infirmities never affected his mind or temper, the former retained its full vigour to the last moments of his life, the latter was uniformly hospitable and cheerful. Never was he so happy as when he could collect around him men of science and intellect, and as they always found his house a pleasant place of resort, we were seldom without visitors of this description. Thus I had opportunities of improvement which fall to the lot of few young women, and I had been unpardonable had I neglected to avail myself of them. Yet I know that the world in general has persisted in reporting me ignorant and uncultivated."

"And to my shame I chose to listen to the world rather than to my father, who has often endeavoured to correct my error. Happy am I that my eyes are opened at last, while I feel myself deservedly punished in the remorse I now experience, and in the loss of so many hours of the highest intellectual enjoyment, in which I might otherwise have participated."

"I can scarcely blame you. The views of the old and young are commonly, and indeed almost necessarily must be, at variance. PRUDENCE is the goddess at whose shrine the one sacrifices, while INCLINATION is the deity worshipped by the other."

"But if youth be not censurable for refusing obedience to commands arbitrarily imposed, it surely is indefensible in resisting entreaties founded on reason."

"That I allow; and I think you were wrong in absolutely refusing to come hither when Sir Francis pressed it so earnestly. But I also think that he fell into an error in urging the matter to such lengths, since this must inevitably create disgust where he wished to excite interest."

"You are truly candid and benevolent, Madam, in thus seeking excuses for me. But it is not so much for resisting my father's importunities that I so deeply condemn my conduct, as for the means which I afterwards employed to release myself from them. All that can be said in my excuse is, that I was betrayed into so much treachery and baseness from a sudden and hasty impulse, on which I did not allow myself a moment's time for reflection. The idea started into my mind as I was writing; I inserted it hastily, and by the time reflection came, I had embarked so far in the affair, that on Harry's account I knew not how to recede. His mind was then, from a peculiar circumstance with which I was unacquainted when I wrote to him, in a state of such uncommon agitation, that I dared not attempt to thwart him in a plan into which he had entered so eagerly."

"Is it impertinent to enquire the nature of this circumstance?"

"By no means, Madam. From the time of Miss Trelawney's death he never could endure the idea of going to Bath. Such indeed was his horror at the recollections which that place called up in his mind, that I have even seen him tremble in every limb at only hearing it mentioned accidentally in company. But urged by the necessity of his affairs, he had actually at the time of my writing so far overcome his feelings, as to go thither in pursuit of a lady with a large fortune, of whose hand he thought himself secure. By her however he was deserted; and it was amid the vexation of this new disappointment, and the horrors in which his mind was enveloped from the associations that surrounded him, that he received my letter. A new pursuit was started, the idea relieved his oppressed heart, and he posted from Bath in an excess of spirits proportioned to the weight of agony from which he was exonerated."

"Mr. Egerton's fortune is then extremely embarrassed?"

"So much so, that I fear his debts far exceed his property."

"And is there no possible means of his affairs being retrieved?"

"Not without exertions beyond what he is perhaps capable of making. Yet at this moment I have stronger hopes of his reformation than I have ever hitherto dared to entertain. 'Tis impossible to describe the powerful impression made upon him by all that has passed here, and the anguish of soul with which he has, within the last two days, frequently expressed his wishes that some honourable means could be devised for freeing himself from his embarrassments, and reinstating himself in the height from which he has fallen. Dare I—dare I tell you all, Madam?"

"I hope you do not doubt my honour?"

"I were a monster could I be capable of it!—Yes, all shall be confessed. In your friend, Madam, in the lovely Miss Belgrave, he fancied, even at the first moment he beheld her, that he saw the perfect resemblance of his long-lost Emily: and his heart, which no woman since her death has been capable of interesting, became a prey to agonies not less tumultuous than it would have experienced at the actual sight of the object of his adoration risen from her watry tomb. The conflicts I saw struggling in his bosom during the time she continued here, gave me the most serious and alarming apprehensions for his reason; and I rejoiced to see that at her departure his mind, wholly occupied by another pursuit, seemed to think of her no more. But that guilty pursuit being now at an end, and having terminated in exposure and disgrace instead of triumph, new ideas are awakened in his soul. Miss Belgrave's image has again wholly taken possession of it; in that all his ideas center; and he is now almost as much distracted at reflecting that he can never hope to obtain her, as he has long been with dwelling on the loss of Emily."

A tear stole down Olivia's cheek at the picture here drawn—she seemed struggling against emotions difficult to be repressed, yet which she wished to conceal, and a dead pause ensued till we advanced towards the house. Fain would I have broken this silence, but I knew not how to ask all I wished to know. The possibility of making farther enquiries was indeed soon precluded, since upon our arriving at the house Olivia went in without saying another word. She disappeared for about a quarter of an hour, when she came into the breakfast-room perfectly composed, nor did she, during the whole time of breakfast, betray the least symptom of remaining agitation.

Oh! St. John! would that I had not suffered the conversation to drop at that moment!—would that I could find some favourable opportunity for renewing it!—how earnestly do I wish to know the motives that induced Harriot's departure so soon after out arrival! There must have been something particular in it, as she had been then only returned about a fortnight from a visit to the very same lady. Perhaps I may learn something more from Beauchamp—I will try at least what can be done, for I find myself so much attracted to him, that I can talk to him without reserve almost upon any subject. And oh! I must try once more if he is not to be prevailed upon to impart the name of Harriot's false lover. I cannot rest without the knowledge of it.

The state of Harry's mind is explained in the above conversation. It wounds me to the soul. But on one thing I am fully resolved, to abandon the means I have hitherto pursued to dispel the gloom that oppresses him. No longer will I endeavour to soothe him like a child with a toy or a rattle, I will rather seek to rouse the slumbering energies of his mind, and excite him to employ against his sorrows the only remedy that can heal them effectually—the only one consistent with the dignity of our nature to employ, REASON.

Yes, I behold Reason here omnipotent, and both he and myself shall bend to its sway. Thus firmly resolves his, and your

Very affectionate friend,

LIONEL STANHOPE.

LETTER IV.

LIONEL STANHOPE
TO
ORLANDO St. John.

Campbell-House, September 8.

The motives for Harriot Belgrave's sudden departure still remain a secret, but she herself is restored to our society, and in as hasty and unexpected a manner as she left it. The very day on which my last letter was written Olivia went over to Kirby, and brought back with her, to our utter astonishment, both Mrs. Belgrave and her daughter.

But upon this renewal of our acquaintance I have not felt the same impression from Harriot's charms that I did at our first interview. Whether it be that there seems a kind of sacredness about her, from her devotion to the man who has used her so cruelly, which places her far above the reach of all other mortals—or that knowing Harry's sentiments I cannot think of interfering with him?—or lastly, whether my soul be not so entirely absorbed in the exquisite delight of listening to Olivia's conversation, in which every one who has the least spark of intellect himself must find an inexhaustible source of entertainment—whichever of these may be the cause, or whether it may proceed from all combined, yet certain it is that I now contemplate her with no other idea than that of admiring one of the most highly-finished pieces of nature's workmanship, without a wish of becoming its possessor.

Harry does not regard her with like indifference. He hangs on every look, on every word, with an adoration that absorbs his whole attention, as much as Olivia's magic tongue absorbs mine—yet he pays her not this adoration without some mingled feelings of self-reproach, as if it were a breach of that constancy he has vowed to his departed saint, and he only strives to vindicate himself by dwelling eternally upon her perfect resemblance to Emily.

"'Tis the same features, Stanhope," he cries, "the same complexion, only with a more matured form, and the animated smile and *naïveté* of seventeen exchanged for a cast of melancholy, the effect of worldly cares and calamities!—Oh Stanhope! would that you had known my Emily, that you might see and confess a likeness so extraordinary!—No, it is not Harriot Belgrave I adore, 'tis Emily revived in her!"

That I have not arrived at a knowledge of the mysterious motives which occasioned both Harriot's departure and her return, is not however owing to any relaxation on my part in my eagerness for investigating them. Yesterday morning at breakfast, a hint being dropped as if there was now a prospect of Mrs. Belgrave's law-suit being determined, I took advantage of it, as a pretence to ask Beauchamp, when we were afterwards walking together, whether this were really the case.

He replied in the affirmative: that a spirited remonstrance on the part of Mrs. Belgrave's agent, united with the detection of a long succession of rogueries on the part of the lawyer who first took up the affair against Captain Belgrave, seemed at length to have roused the tardy spirits of the great law officers, and a decision was shortly expected, which there was no doubt would be in Mrs. Belgrave's, or to speak more properly, in Harriot's favour. In consequence of this the two ladies must go over to Ireland, and it was probable that they would set out upon their journey before the expiration of many days.

"What a satisfaction it is," said I, "under any circumstances to see knavery thus exposed, and the injured restored to their rights; but how doubly satisfactory, when in the victim of injustice we behold one of the most lovely and amiable objects in the creation."

"To the first part of your position I most heartily assent. Does not the latter clause favour more of the man, than of the philosopher?"

"I make no pretensions to the character of a philosopher. Yet let me ask whether, even in the eye of philosophy, the magnitude of the crime be not increased in proportion to the merit and situation of the object aggrieved? and whether it does not betray greater depravity of heart, systematically to defraud a lovely and defenceless female, than one of our sex, who, if injured, has powers of redress, denied, alas! to hapless woman?"

"This is a delicate point to decide. But if you think treachery so much aggravated by being practised towards a woman, though unknown to her persecutors, what shall be said of the man who beholding Harriot, lovely as she is, could engage her affections, and then by forsaking her, ruin her peace of mind for ever?"

"That he was not a man, but a monster!—" I paused a moment. "Oh Mr. Beauchamp," I added, "may I without being deemed impertinently intrusive and importunate, advert again to a subject on which we were conversing not many days ago. I told you then how much I wished to know the name of this monster; every thing I see, every thing I hear, but encreases this anxiety. Nor does it proceed, believe me, from a mere idle curiosity, 'tis urged by a painful apprehension—"

"Mr. Stanhope, I must interrupt you, pardon the rudeness; but whatever may be your motives for wishing to be admitted to share in this secret, 'tis impossible you should be gratified without my being guilty of treachery; and that I think you will not require."

"I have done; pardon my having urged the matter thus far, but from this moment I am silent."

And silent we both remained for some minutes. At length somewhat recovered from this repulse, I ventured to hazard another. "Mr. Beauchamp," I said, "perhaps I am going to transgress again, but I would fain ask whether there was not some particular reason for Miss Belgrave's going to Mrs. Howard's so soon after our arrival?"

"Why this question, Mr. Stanhope? Was not the meeting her mother a sufficient reason for going thither?"

"Undoubtedly. Yet the plan seemed hastily settled, and, pardon me, I suspected from appearances, that she had taken some strong prejudice either against Harry or myself."

"You may be perfectly satisfied upon that account. Such capricious dislikes form no part of Harriot Belgrave's character."

Beauchamp might be right there, but since I saw plainly that he wished to evade the question, I would not press it farther. Quitting this subject therefore, I soon adverted to another on which I was scarcely less anxious to obtain satisfaction, and asked whether he thought there was any foundation for the report that Olivia had a partiality for Ryder?

He replied, that he thought he could safely say there was not. "A strong friendship, and a high esteem," said he, "two such people cannot but feel for each other, but I suspect the Ensign's affections to be otherwise engaged. That while paying all due respect to his benefactress's virtues and accomplishments, his heart is more susceptible of impression from a pretty face, and has become captive to the rustic charms of Lucy Morgan. When staying here he is very assiduous in his visits to the two cottages."

"Good God, you astonish me! From your account of Mr. Ryder, I should have supposed that understanding and cultivation of mind, were the qualities to captivate his heart, not mere prettiness of features."

"And had I not formed the same opinion of him, I should not hesitate a moment in considering the thing as settled. The ostensible reason for his going so often to the cottages, 'tis true, is to visit a little girl whom he placed under the care of Mary Atwood, Lucy's neighbour, not long after his return to England. But I suspect that for one minute passed with the child, ten are devoted to Lucy."

"A child of his own?"

"That I will not pretend to decide; 'tis not however acknowledged as such. All I know is, that about a year and a half ago, happening to call one morning upon Lucy, I found her nursing this little creature, which seemed then about six months old. With any body not in so awkward a predicament as Lucy, I should probably have begun joking, and asked if it was her own, but that was too tender a point for a joke with her, so I simply asked whose child it was? 'One that Mr. Ryder has placed under Mary Atwood's care,' said Lucy. 'A child of his own?' said I. Lucy blushed, and Mary Atwood smiled and said, no, only one to whom he was guardian. I saw plainly from her manner that she thought this story a mere fabrication, and suspected that the young soldier had in fact been somewhat indiscreet. But Olivia assures me that she is satisfied upon the subject, as Ryder has imparted the child's story to her, only with a request that it may never be mentioned to any one. Her parents, she says, are persons of fortune, though from some untoward circumstances they are compelled to this temporary estrangement from their infant daughter."

"Surely then if Miss Campbell be satisfied, there can be no ground for farther hesitation upon the subject. She is not a woman easy to be deceived, nor would, but upon sufficient reason, have given credit to the story related."

"I allow your position in its fullest force. But so many people have discovered a strong resemblance between Mr. Ryder and the child, that they have almost persuaded me it cannot be mere fancy. Of this you shall yourself judge when you have seen her suspected father. Some people go so far as to think the infant also like Lucy, and are certain that she is the mother. But of this she stands fully acquitted, since the babe must have been born before Ryder's return to England. Perhaps some *belle Espagnole* found her way to the heart of the solitary misanthrope."

As we were at this moment not far from the cottages, Beauchamp proposed our returning home that way, "and then," said he, "you can see the mysterious babe. "Besides," he added, "you have not yet been introduced to all the members of Lucy's domestic establishment, and you must see my little Fanny." To this proposal I very readily assented, as my curiosity, which thou knowest well, Orlando, is not an inactive principle in my composition, began to be much excited about the child.

We called first upon the school-mistress, where we found Olivia with the little nurseling, in whom she takes a very great interest, and, as I supposed, a little girl about five years old teaching the child its letters. "Aha, Fanny," said Beauchamp, "so you have taken Maria as your pupil." Then turning to me, and patting Fanny on the cheek, "This," said he, "is Lucy's assistant, and a very good little girl she is, I can assure you. You would not suppose that such a child could be of so much use in the school; she can read as well as Lucy herself. Come, Fanny, give us a specimen."

Fanny immediately took up a little book of stories, and read us a page. I listened with astonishment, little expecting to hear such a child as she appeared, especially in her class of life, perform so well; but looking in her face, I began to suspect the truth. "And I assure you she can sing too," said Beauchamp; "come, Fanny, you must shew off again, now for a song."

"Must it be a *song*?" said Fanny.

"What," said Beauchamp, "I suppose you would rather sing your own hymn to gratitude, as I know you are very vain of it. But, however, you shall be indulged."

Fanny cast a glance at Olivia, so expressive, that the most studied piece of oratory could not have said half as much, and then sung her hymn, not without taste, and with a feeling that drew the tear of sensibility from Olivia's eyes. "Is not that pretty well for a child of five years old?" said Beauchamp as she finished; "but it shews what may be done with children, provided they have tractable dispositions, and are under good management."

"Ah, Sir," said the little assistant, smiling, "you are always bantering poor Fanny." And then turning to me, she said, "if Mr. Beauchamp had added twenty years to the five, he would have been much nearer the truth."

She then proceeded to say, that she was the daughter of a reputable farmer, but her parents falling into misfortunes, and not being able to maintain her, she was obliged for a while to gain her livelihood by exhibiting herself as a sight. A situation than which few more miserable can be conceived. Coming at length to Doncaster, Olivia's compassion was excited, and she offered to take her under her protection, when finding that she could read and work very well, she made her assistant to Lucy, by which means the school could be considerably enlarged. It will be easily supposed that the little assistant found herself now in a paradise, and the effusions of her soul were poured out in a hymn to gratitude dedicated to her benefactress, a composition which, if it does not entitle her to a first seat among the daughters of Parnassus,[6] at least does credit to the goodness of her heart.

St. John, this is again an anecdote of Olivia,—of the woman whom we have so frequently heard represented in the world as little better than a fool! But perhaps 'tis these very things constitute her folly; for sad to say, yet not more sad than true, there are but too many among the sons of men, who would consider it as no small degree of idiocy to prefer pensioning dwarfs and the unfortunate victims of seduction, to adorning her person with jewels, and spreading her table with plate, expences in which Olivia finds no gratification. The family jewels are locked up in an iron chest whence they never emerge, for this admirable woman's judgment is shewn no less in her mode of dressing than in matters of more importance. Her study is to avoid making herself conspicuous by wearing any thing that might attract notice; and she unites the true elegance of a gentlewoman with a simplicity equally removed from every thing showy, or affectedly plain.

This short episode with regard to her dress came in my way, and I could not help inserting it. To return to the subject from which I set out, the mysterious child,—for Fanny's story too was but a sort of episode,—I can only say that whoever, or whatever, may be its parents, I heartily pity them in being separated from it, for 'tis one of the most lovely babes eyes ever beheld. When we had made our visit of a sufficient length, Olivia accompanied us home, and I cannot say that I thought the latter end of our walk the less agreeable for such an addition to the party.

Doctor Paul spent the evening with us. 'Tis indeed no uncommon practice with him to drop in upon the heiress thus self-invited—a practice I believe more agreeable to himself than to her.

Uncongenial as his manners are to Olivia's, or to what I conceive to have been the old General's, I at first wondered extremely how the latter could ever have given him the living of Maxtead, which placed him so much in his own neighbourhood. This difficulty was however solved to me, upon learning that he came into possession of the living,* not by the General's choice, but merely by his permission, in order to accommodate the then rector of the parish, a Mr. Burlington, a great friend of the General's, who by changing livings with Doctor Paul, could take some other preferment† not tenable with Maxtead—while the Doctor, who has a prebendal stall‡ at York, by this means also got his preferment more concentrated.

He has now been for some years a widower, and would, I believe, very gladly make himself agreeable to the heiress, as thinking the hall far preferable, as a place of residence, to the parsonage, and the fee-simple§ of the lands in Maxtead parish infinitely more desirable than a life interest only in the tythe of their produce. Yet should she prove invulnerable to his attacks, his heart is sufficiently susceptible to admit any other woman who has money enough to pay well for admission into a corner of it. When therefore he finds Miss Campbell pre-occupied, or not disposed to lend him a favourable ear, he can content himself with a flirtation with Mrs. Harrison, who has a very pretty *fortin*, and keeps her chariot. Since there has been a hope of Mrs. Belgrave's recovering her estate, he has indeed been rather more attentive to her than to Mrs. Harrison, but he makes so little progress there, that I believe he may as well give up the matter at once, as hopeless.

Yesterday, when he first came in, Olivia was so much occupied with Sir Francis, with whom indeed she does flirt most unmercifully, that he found it was vain to think of being favoured with her attention. Seating himself, therefore, by Mrs. Harrison, he began:—"Well, Madam, what say you to the anecdote respecting Mrs. Stapleton, just furnished by the scandalous chronicle?"

Rebecca's eyes sparkled with delight. Mrs. Stapleton is her dear friend, and a scandalous anecdote of her, was consequently a most choice

---

* A position as a vicar or rector with its attached income or property.

† Superior appointment or promotion.

‡ A cathedral stall or benifice.

§ Property held by a person in his or her own right, free from condition or limitation.

morçeau, a very ortolan* in the anecdotic way. "Lord! why you surprise me, Doctor!" she answered; "why what can you mean?—why I never heard any scandal of Mrs. Stapleton."

"You doubtless have taken notice of the young woman who lives with her—a pretty smart-looking girl, whom she educated from a child."

"Oh aye!—well, I was always a wondering about that maid."

"She has, you know, Madam, obtained great credit with the world for her kindness to that girl; and to be sure it does sound like a very good and Christian spirit to take a poor friendless orphan into the house to educate and provide for. But behold it appears that this seeming generosity was something less than justice—that the poor girl has a claim to live with her upon a very different footing from that of a servant—that there was a handsome footman in her father's house—"

"Absolute scandal, I have no doubt," said Mrs. Belgrave; "and 'tis surely very hard that she cannot have extended this kindness to a friendless creature without drawing an impeachment upon her own character."

"If there be any justice in the *lex talionis*,† Madam," said Beauchamp, "this is no hardship at all. Mrs. Stapleton propagates scandalous reports of others with so much industry, that she has little reason to complain of being made the subject of one herself. However, few people who know Mrs. Stapleton will believe the story, unless the tastes of other men differ very widely from mine."

"Pho now! that's your way," said Mrs. Harrison; "you're always a thinking that every body must be of your opinion. But I dare say the story's true. Lord, why I don't believe that there ever was twenty maids buried in the world."

Doctor Paul bowed obsequiously, and hoped that, for the sake of his sex, *Mrs. Harrison* would not be one of the twenty.

"Why to be sure," said Sir Francis, cousin Becky judges of others by herself. But I dare say," he added, "that Mrs. Stapleton is one of the twenty, and that's the reason she's so splenetic and censorious against all women whom she thinks have attracted the notice of the men more than herself. Now there's my good cousin, you see, as she is less virtuous, is a thousand times more candid."

"But," said I, "with all due respect for Mrs. Harrison's opinion, what will she say to Saint Ursula and her eleven thousand virgins?"[7]

Mrs. Harrison looked *wise*, and seemed excessively desirous of saying something more than usually *funny*, yet knew not how to set about it— probably because she did not understand to what I alluded. Doctor Paul however came in to her assistance—

"True, Sir," he said. "But you will recollect that though these eleven

---

*   Delicacy. An *ortolan* is an edible bird native to North Africa which summers in southern Europe. It is considered a great delicacy.

†   The law of retaliation (i.e., an eye for an eye, a tooth for a tooth).

thousand fair ladies were virgins at the time their pilgrimage was undertaken, it no where appears that they remained so to the end of their lives."

"And 'tis to be hoped they did not," said Sir Francis. "I'm sure women are much better employed in looking after their families and educating their children, than in going [on] silly pilgrimages to silly saints. So, my dear cousin Harrison, if you are now one of the twenty, the sooner you diminish the number the better. If I were not unluckily encumbered with a wife, I'd instantly throw myself at your feet, and I've no doubt but Li. would be very happy in such a mother-in-law. But since Doctor Paul fortunately is not so shackled, what say you to him?"

Mrs. Harrison was too much delighted with the idea that there was only one small obstacle to her becoming the wife of a Baronet to attend to the offer of Doctor Paul; but assuming a very important, yet facetious look, she replied—"Take care what you are a saying, Sir Francis, for fear I should be a using of a *sledge hammer* to poor Lady Stanhope."

On taking his leave, Doctor Paul announced that he hoped at his next visit to have the honour of introducing a nephew of his to Miss Campbell. "He is a Cantab,* Madam," said he, "and is coming to pass the remainder of the summer vacation with me; and since he is himself *a little bit of an author*, I trust he may prove not an unacceptable addition to the circle of talent and intellect always to be found at Campbell-House. He has indeed just published three little volumes, works of imagination, which I intend myself the honour, Madam, of requesting you to accept—though I am sensible that in thus soliciting a place for them in so extensive and valuable a library as Miss Campbell's, I look forward to their being honoured even beyond their deserts."

Olivia received this pompous notification of the Doctor's intended present only with a bow, and he departed, whether satisfied or not at this coldness I will not pretend to say. The volumes arrived this morning, but I do not know that any one of the party has yet been induced to seek edification by examining their contents. It certainly has not been sought by

Yours very faithfully,

LIONEL STANHOPE.

---

*   Of the University of Cambridge. *Cantab* is a colloquial abbreviation of *Cantabrigian* (*OED*).

ORLANDO ST. JOHN
TO
LIONEL STANHOPE.

Scarborough, September 10.

I have been in perils the most imminent, Lionel, since last I wrote to thee. Perils, compared with which all the dangers thou didst encounter in the haunted chamber, or any other that thou or Harry have faced, in your various adventures at Campbell-House, are but as the achievements of a Marlborough in the fields of Blenheim and Ramilies,[8] compared to the glorious campaigns of an Uncle Toby, and a Corporal Trim in the bowling-green.[9]

Oui, mon cher cousin, I have been even on the brink of offering a surrender of my liberty, my property, nay of my own dear self, with all my *"perfections on my head,"*[10] either to the bewitching Charlotte O'Brien, or the fascinating Eliza de Clairville; nor did any thing snatch me from the precipice but the exact equipoise in which my heart is held between them, so that I could by no means decide to which of the twain this same own dear self should be offered. And *foi d'honnête homme,* I do still think that it will be impossible for me to escape from the delightful town of Scarborough, without playing the fool, after this fashion, either with the one or the other, though it must remain for some chance, accident, or unforeseen occurrence, to determine towards which the handkerchief shall be thrown.

And this chance, accident, or unforeseen occurrence, will probably be when I can convince myself that a tolerable prospect appears of my being accepted by either—for never does a man look so cursedly foolish as when he is refused—and not even self-flattery (and I don't think I am upon the worst of all possible terms with myself) can delude me so far as to think that there is at present the smallest hope from either quarter.

In truth I believe my heart would be decidedly in favour of the widow, but that, fascinating as she is, I must reprobate her conduct extremely in one very essential point. I hold it to be the most sacred and indispensable duty of every mother, however elevated her rank or affluent her fortune, to attend herself to the education of her daughters; and if, from the negligence of her own parents, she be not at the time of her marriage, sufficiently instructed to be capable of the task, her first care and attention should be to supply that deficiency, and acquire those qualifications which she must afterwards impart. Yet de Clairville, early accustomed to the homage paid by our Gallic neighbours to persons of her sex and situation, thinks only of upholding the empire she has obtained over mankind; and while studying to eternize, if possible, her own attractions, leaves the important task of forming the minds and hearts of her children to one bound to them only by the ties of venality.

Thus far, however, must be acknowledged, that the governess she has placed over them is much better qualified for the task of education than are most of those who undertake it. She is a woman of polished manners, of decided talent, and, I sincerely believe, of excellent principles, who does instruct them in things of more value than merely to hold up their heads, and embroider a bad rose, the very caricature of that nature it was intended to imitate. Sometimes, in my impassioned reveries, I am sanguine enough to believe that were the bewitching Eliza once mine, I could reform all that is amiss in her, and make her no less exemplary as a mother than she is fascinating as a woman. Perhaps on this idea thou wilt saucily observe, Mr. Li., "Physician first cure thyself."

Charlotte's muse, once roused from its lethargy, grows extremely prolific. A few days ago she, with de Clairville and myself, were sauntering upon the beach, admiring the varied tints of the glassy ocean, as the shadows of the flitting clouds above, swept along its surface. On a sudden the fair Hibernian made a pause—a poetic vision seemed instantaneously to take possession of her soul—wrapt in the delicious trance, she started away from us, sat down on a piece of rock hard by, and taking out pencil and paper began writing.

"What is Charlotte about?" said the widow.

"You shall know presently," replied the maiden; "don't interrupt me now."

De Clairville grew impatient—Charlotte wanted to revise and correct—for that the other could by no means wait, so snatching the manuscript jocosely she read aloud:

THE EBB OF THE TIDE.

When the glitt'ring moon-beams at eve softly play
O'er ocean's green waves, as the light fades away,
'Tis sweet to descend from the mountain's steep side,
And trace the still shore at the ebb of the tide.

Tho' bards have oft sung how the raptures of love
'Tis charming to breathe in the gay myrtle grove,
To me greater charms in those vows would reside
Were they breath'd on the shore at the ebb of the tide.

While others admire too the flute's dulcet strains
From the rustics at eve on the smooth-shav'n plains,
To me more enchanting its notes when applied
To the echoing shore at the ebb of the tide.

The belles of the court may delighted advance
With their airs, and their graces, to fashion's gay dance,
But, like the brisk Scot on the banks of the Clyde,
I would trip on the shore at the ebb of the tide.

> Let the vot'ries of pleasure still throng with delight
> Wherever the idols they follow invite;
> But let me, remov'd from the mansions of pride,
> Still rove on the shore at the ebb of the tide.

> Let me rove with the man who has won my fond heart,
> Whose presence to all fresh delight can impart,
> When we'll own that no joys could in Eden reside
> Like those that we taste at the ebb of the tide.

"Rove with your Albert I suppose," said Madam de Clairville, as she finished reading. "But you know, my dear Charlotte, that the heart of this same Albert is of a nature so flinty, that 'tis incapable of receiving any tender impressions, and he would probably leave you to rove by yourself. Let this then be followed by a dirge, lamenting his cruelty and your despair, that you are left in the state of Tantalus, upon the shore indeed, yet deprived of all enjoyment of its delights, since the senseless animal refuses to share them with you."[11]

"I do not think," said I, "that Miss O'Brien has much to apprehend upon this account. If a companion to share her joys is all that is wanting to make the shore a complete paradise, who will not think himself but too happy in being permitted to become her Albert? Were solitude her wish, the case would be otherwise."

Indeed, Lionel, there is something so exquisitely romantic in falling in love by the sea-side, so much more poetical than by the fire-side, that I believe this has had considerable influence in awakening me so sensibly to the charms of my two fair companions. I am not much surprised at this effect in myself, but I have seen another from the sea breezes that speaks them nothing less than omnipotent. They have actually so far subdued the rigid purity and chastity of Miss Perkins, that she gives Mr. Peters such encouragement as is totally inconsistent with the vestal character she has hitherto sustained. Though perhaps I ascribe too much to the sea-breezes when I consider this change as entirely effected by them, for probably the propriety of her lover's behaviour in the garter affair might be the first thing to win upon her virgin reserve.

But so it is, that all the flirtations of Charlotte and Eliza are nothing to that now carried on between Francis Peters and Margaret Perkins. Messieurs Adam and Eve in their lovely garden, while yet the sole inhabitants of earth, were not more effectually *tête-à-tête* than are these languishing lovers in the most public companies of this public watering-place. Seated together on a sopha, abstracted from all present, whole evenings are passed in whisperings behind the lady's fan, in which the gentleman's face appears to come so much in contact with his fair companion's, that if no tender pressure from his lips be imprinted on her rosy cheek, 'tis not for want of their being sufficiently approximated.

Yet while she indulges her *inamorato* with these public *tête-à-têtes*, think not she has relaxed so far from the rigidity of her former notions as to allow even him a private interview. No; she still makes it her pride and boast that she never in her life was alone in a room with a man excepting with her papa or uncle. She will certainly never be solicited to break through this reserve in favour of

Yours most sincerely,

ORLANDO ST. JOHN.

LETTER VI.

LIONEL STANHOPE
TO
ORLANDO ST. JOHN.

Campbell-House, September 12.

Justly do you observe, St. John, that a man never makes a more silly figure than when he is refused; and in that predicament do I, the *fine, handsome, spirited* Lionel Stanhope stand at this moment. Curse on my forwardness!—why must I thus rush into disgrace!—You are perfectly right, St. John, in proceeding more warily.

Yes, I have been refused!—rejected by a woman whom I expected would have rushed with transport into my arms, and only thought herself too happy that my former reluctance, nay aversion, to the idea of appearing as her suitor, was subdued. But it shall teach me caution in future— no second woman shall have it in her power to boast that she has refused Lionel Stanhope. Never more, in a matter so momentous, will I be caught acting with such precipitation. Before I set about whining and praying again, I will be well assured that the lady is desperately in love with me— nay, I am by no means certain that I shall not now leave it to her to make the first advances.

Fool that I was, to be thus deceived!—I felt so confident of success, that I never paused a moment to consider whether or not that confidence were well-grounded. And by what motives my refusal has been influenced I am wholly at a loss to conceive. It cannot be that Olivia is attached to Ryder, since a hint might easily be given to him, and 'tis not very likely that an Ensign upon half pay would reject the good fortune thus laid at his feet. Neither can Beauchamp be the object of her affections, since all things might be settled with him with equal facility. Still less can I conceive that she is actuated by a general dislike to the thoughts of matrimony, since her whole manner evinces the contrary; and a heart capable of such ardent affections can scarcely fail of fixing them upon some definite object. Sometimes I have indulged in a speculation whether she can have sported with Egerton's pretended passion till she is herself become the victim of a real one. That were now a thing so little consonant to his wishes, and so unfortunate for herself, that I sincerely hope it is not the case.

There must be something more in the affair than I can comprehend, and the more I reflect upon it the more I am convinced of this. Though she has refused the hand I condescended to offer, she evidently likes my company, and is desirous of detaining me here. On receiving her very unexpected answer, I was going away in a huff and a hurry, urging that it was impossible after what had passed either party could find it agreeable to remain together in the same house. She laughed, and asked why it should be otherwise?—assured me it was perfectly agreeable to her, and begged I would not be sulky or give myself airs upon the subject, as if I were terribly aggrieved. I had pleased *myself*, she said, in making the offer, and she had pleased *herself* in rejecting it—why then should we quarrel because we had each followed our inclinations?—was she not to be allowed a choice in the affair, but must she be compelled to like me for a husband because I had done her the honour of thinking I could like her for a wife?—And all this was said with so much good nature and unaffected pleasantry, that it was absolutely impossible to refuse complying with her; so here I remain. Yet 'tis too much, after having received such an indignity from her hands, that she can still mould me entirely to her own pleasure. Confound these women, I say!—ugly or handsome they somehow or other get an ascendancy over us that we cannot resist.

Yet, after all, my pride is much more wounded than my love. Though feeling a very strong prepossession in her favour, and well convinced that I still could ardently love her, I am not so entirely absorbed in my passion but that I shall be able to resign myself to my fate, and live contentedly without her. Indeed I had not at last been so forward in the business, but to gratify my father, whose mortification I can say with truth I feel yet more severely than the wound given to my *amour propre*; though I will frankly own that I had not shewn so much compliance, even towards him, could I have foreseen the consequences. How bitterly does he abuse Harry and myself, as he says he is fully convinced my failure is to be ascribed to the ill impression made upon Olivia by our damned frolick. Alas! perhaps he is not altogether mistaken, since it is surely impossible for two persons to have exposed themselves more completely, or to make a more contemptible figure than we do. It may well be questioned whether we appear the greater fools or knaves, for never was a rascally scheme planned with less probability of success, or worse executed from beginning to end. But away with a recollection so hateful!

In one respect however I may consider myself as a gainer by what has passed, since now I have an obvious answer to Sir Francis should he ever renew his importunities. At some moments I am disposed heartily to regret my ill success, for upon my soul every hour that I continue here I grow more and more enchanted with Olivia's manners and conversation, while the daily testimonies of her unbounded benevolence and generosity that I see all around me, command a species of adoration that may be felt, but that no words can express. 'Tis not mere esteem or respect, they are words too cold to apply to a soul so truly noble; it is in short a feeling only to be experienced in contemplating a heart like hers. Can there be on earth a spectacle more sublime than a person with powers so extensive, employing them to the noblest purposes, and becoming the organ through which plenty and happiness are dealt out to thousands; or can one hear unmoved the blessings that are invoked upon her by all her tenants and dependents, among whom there is scarcely one that I believe would not literally sacrifice his own life for the preservation of hers.

Yes, Orlando, when I think only on these things, I heartily regret that I must not hope to possess this treasure, since one of equal value is not to be found over all the habitable globe. But at other times pursuing a very different train of reflection, I am disposed to believe that all is for the best. While we remained in the country I should have felt no alloy to my happiness, I should have seen a homage paid to my wife that would have satisfied my vanity, and all would have been well. But when she came to be introduced into the gayer circles of high life, where, in appreciating the worth of a character the qualities of the heart are not taken into the account, and I saw all eyes attracted to her, not by her beauty, but by her plainness; when I heard all around me enquiries who that little ugly woman could be, and heard her described as Mrs. Stanhope, the *ci-devant**. Miss Campbell, the celebrated Yorkshire heiress, *celebrated* said with a sneer, excited by the idea of the personal imperfections to which she so much owes her celebrity—oh I could never have supported all this, but should have shrunk abashed within myself, and wondered how I could ever be so infatuated as to think of such an incongruous union.

No, St. John, she must beware a man of the world, one who is anxious that public admiration should sanction his taste in the wedded partner of his heart. Her husband's breast must be guarded by a thick coat of mail, impenetrable to the senseless sarcasms a face like hers will unavoidably excite in the gay world, or all her virtues and accomplishments could not ensure him from many painful moments of disgust and repentance. *She* must be all to her husband, *public opinion*, nothing, or woe to them both.

And am I this man? Ah that question had better not be asked. I can despise those jokes as I sit writing here by myself, but I feel that in a public company I could not hear them unmoved. I think too that she is herself so sensible of the effect they would have on the mind of a husband, that she would never marry a man who would not pass the greatest part of his time in the country, among a circle of friends that have sense enough to value her for the really noble qualities she possesses, without thinking of the inferior charms in which she is deficient. Next winter she intends making her first visit to London. It will not be unamusing to speculate

---

*   Former.

upon the conflicts she will excite in the bosoms of the beaux of *ton*,* who while calculating on the additional elegances to be acquired by the possession of her fortune, would yet shrink from producing such a woman as a wife.

For in the breasts of those butterflies, such would be the alternative. With me who have "*seen what I have seen, see what I see*,"[12] the question is very different. Setting fortune wholly aside, since, though by no means despising the good things of this world, my own is sufficient to answer all my wishes, the balance in my heart rests entirely between mind and person. Perhaps it were greatly for my advantage could I set person as entirely aside in the question, as fortune, and devote myself to mind alone. Yet habit, inveterate habit, still sways me too powerfully to do this; a devotion to beauty seems a part of my original nature, and reason has no slight task to perform in combating this prejudice. She had for a moment triumphed, but even in the ardour of victory met with a repulse which I can scarcely hope she will ever recover.

Yet I must repeat it, Oh that I could devote myself to mind alone! To that mind which from the purest of motives is constantly seeking no less to establish on an indestructible basis the solid happiness and comforts of all around it, than to contribute to the lighter enjoyments of life, by promoting a varied succession of such pleasures as carry no remorse in their train, but are pleasures equally in the recollection as in the action. To that mind, which full of reflection, full of penetration, loves to contemplate human nature in all its changeful forms and endless varieties, and finds sources for its own instruction and improvement in every character it investigates, even from the exalted genius whose unbounded speculations soar into the sublimest fields of science, whose life is passed in ceaseless efforts to promote the illumination and improvement of mankind, down to the petty pedant who mistaking the passion for becoming an author, for the talents necessary to constitute one, amuses by his follies and extravagances; which can admire the talents of a Ryder, and make him her chosen companion, yet is not too fastidious to be sometimes amused with the ridiculous vanity and conceit of a Percival Altham.

And since, Orlando, the vanity of an Altham may amuse you as well as Olivia, let me bid adieu to this long train of reflection, over which you have perhaps already begun to yawn, and introduce him to your acquaintance.

He is the nephew of Doctor Paul, the *little bit of an author* mentioned in my last. He was introduced here yesterday evening, when we discovered from his conversation that he was not only a *little bit of an author*, but also a *little bit of an actor*. He lately passed some weeks with a strolling company, where he enacted many a hero, many a wit, many a lover, to his own satisfaction at least, if not to that of his audience, till at length grown

---

*   Fashionable society.

too aspiring, he wanted to perform the Widow Warren in the *Road to Ruin*;[13] but this the manager absolutely refused, as he said the young gentleman was far too effeminate for the character.

But though the Doctor with affected humility mentioned his nephew as only a *little bit of an author*, 'tis evident that the nephew does not think so humbly of himself, but on the contrary thinks his productions may be classed with those of the most distinguished writers of any age or nation. Indeed the only respects in which he falls below them, are in style, language, sentiment, interest, arrangement, and a few other such inferior considerations.

The volumes presented by his uncle to Olivia, consist of Poetry without cadence or meaning, Tales devoid of interest or connection, and Plays barren of plot or incident, still they are his own children, and as such 'tis fit he should regard them with parental fondness.

He had not been long in the room when he addressed Olivia, "I understand, Madam, that my uncle has already presented you with my three little volumes. You will excuse the vanity of an old man, Madam, who has always considered me as his child, consequently regards them as his grand-children, and is apt, with a grand-father's partiality, to take all opportunities of exhibiting them."

"Such partialities however," said Olivia, "have surely a claim upon our indulgence, and if we do not think them commendable, they are at least only the effect of an amiable weakness."

The author looked somewhat disconcerted, he was evidently angling for a compliment, and did not expect to have found the fish so shy of the bait. Not altogether discouraged, however, by this one repulse, he resolved to cast his line a second time. "Indeed I am a little angry with my uncle," he said, "for having anticipated my intentions. I had promised myself the honour of laying my humble attempts at courting the Muses in my own proper person, at the feet of such a distinguished patron of literature as Miss Campbell, and had actually begun writing some dedicatory verses to present with them."

But not even the dedicatory verses could draw one word of compliment from the ungrateful Olivia, she still only replied by a gentle inclination of her head, while I inwardly speculated what our poet would try next. He soon resolved my doubts by proceeding: "Pray, Madam, may I ask what progress you have made in reading my volumes? Have you yet perused the Comedy of *The Dasher*, or *Modern Manners?*"

"Indeed, Mr. Altham, I am sorry to say I have not yet had leisure to look into your books. I have been so extremely engaged ever since Doctor Paul was so good as to send them, that I have scarcely had a moment to devote to reading."

"Very unlucky indeed. I wished earnestly, Madam, to have talked over that play with you; the best thing I ever wrote in my life; shameful behaviour of the managers of the London theatres that they would not give the public so high an entertainment; but I suppose they were afraid, for to be sure I am amazingly severe; I lay about me at all rates, I spare neither sex nor age, neither great nor small, but cut, and hack, and slash among 'em all, like any Priam."[14]

"Was Priam so great a *hacker* Sir?" I asked. "I thought hacking had rather been the characteristic of his son Hector."[15]

"Well, well, no matter, father and son you know are one flesh, so it signifies little which name was used."

"Man and wife," said Olivia, "I know are allegorically said to be one flesh, but I never even in allegory heard father and son reckoned so."

"Are not all mankind of the same flesh?" said Beauchamp. "To put Priam for Hector, was therefore no such *prime* blunder."

"At least," said I, "'tis one against which you cannot have much to object, since it has afforded you an opportunity for making such a *first rate* pun."

"You certainly consider it as a pun of *force*," retorted Beauchamp, who is never so much in his element as at a war of puns, "by allowing it to be a *first rate*."

"Of *force* it must be," I replied, "since it seems completely to have silenced Mr. Altham's battery."

"Oh by no means, Sir," said Altham. "I was only waiting till you and Mr. Beauchamp were *silenced*, to observe to Miss Campbell, that the comedy I mentioned is the best thing I ever wrote in my life, full of excellent jokes; I declare I absolutely fell off my chair and rolled upon the ground with laughing, as I wrote one of them."

"Heavens!" thought I, "whither will this man's vanity lead him at last?" Then addressing him, I said, "Pray Mr. Altham, do you understand French?"

"*Un sort peu*," he replied.

I was satisfied. I found by his answer that he could know little enough of it, so I ventured to repeat to Olivia, by whom I was sitting,

> Un sot, en ecrivant fait tout avec plaisir,
> Il n'a point en ses vers l'embarras de choisir;
> Et toujours amoureux de ce qu'il vient d'ecrire,
> Ravi d'etonnement en foi-meme il s'admire.
> Mais un esprit sublime, en vain veut s'elever
> A ce degré parfait qu'il tache de trouver,
> Et toujour mècontent de ce qu'il vient de faire,
> Il plait à tout le monde, et ne fauroit se plaire.[16]

Olivia smiled, and Altham bowed, concluding, I suppose, that I had paid him a compliment, satisfied at least that one was deserved. But Mrs. Harrison, who was on the other side of me, remonstrated against repeating French verses, and said: "Come, Mr. Altham, let's make Mr. Stanhope translate 'em."

"Oh pardon me, Madam," I said, "I can by no means think of making such an attempt. I should be liable to an action from Monsieur Boileau for maiming and defacing his incomparable lines."

Still the good lady insisted that 'twas unfair to repeat what could not be understood by all the company, and again solicited a translation. Altham stared, but did not join in her request, not chusing I suppose to give the company reason to imagine him one of those who did not understand the lines, though the smiles of satisfaction on his countenance shewed very plainly that he understood not a syllable of the whole matter. But Olivia, on purpose to teaze me, insisted with Mrs. Harrison, that the quoting [of] French ought not to be allowed, and nothing but a translation could expiate my rudeness, in having attempted the introduction of a foreign language unintelligible to some of the company. In compliance with her therefore I wrote the following translation, but upon condition that it should go no farther than my neighbours on either hand, since it was written entirely at their solicitation:

> A fool in each sentence he forms will rejoice,
> Nor knows in his writing the torment of choice.
> But contemplates with ever-increasing delight
> Whatever his dull-working brain may indite.
> While a genius who seeks to attain the sublime,
> And aims at perfection in prose or in rhyme,
> Is dissatisfied still, and unlike t'other elf
> Though he charm all the world, yet can ne'er please himself.

I was in hopes that this interruption might have put an end to the author's commentaries upon his own works. But I was mistaken. On such a favourite topic he was not easily to be silenced, and he resumed it once more:

"Excuse me, Madam, but may I ask if you have my volumes near at hand? I would fain read you a few lines which have been extremely admired."

"You shall have them immediately," said Beauchamp, and away he flew to the library, whence he returned with them in a few minutes.

The author turned the leaves over for a while with a look of extreme satisfaction, and complacency, and then exclaimed in transport, "Oh here's the passage! The lines, Madam, are from a poem which I call *Mount Cenis*. I suppose a traveller about to make the tour of Italy; he has crossed this celebrated mountain, and after describing its various charms and wonders in a high strain of poetry, he breaks out into the following apostrophe to Chamberry,[17] where he is resting from the toils and perils of the day:

> And thou, Chamberry, who with vast delight
> Look'st from the vale to yon stupendous height,
> While list'ning to surrounding torrents roar,
> Which echo still reverb'rates o'er and o'er;

> Thee too I hail, since here beneath thy roofs,
> I rest my own and cattle's wearied hoofs.

"Very fine indeed!" exclaimed Beauchamp, as the author looked round for applause, "don't you think so, Mr. Stanhope?"

"Oh truly sublime," said I. "That idea of resting his own and his cattle's hoofs together, makes so pleasing an impression upon the mind, it brings so forcibly to one's ideas those charming pictures of rural innocence, where one parlour serves both the pigs and their masters. Not that I suppose Mr. Altham means to represent the traveller and his nag as literally warming their feet together over the same fire-side."

"Though that would be new," said Beauchamp, "and in an age so thirsty after novelty as the present, an author who can produce one new idea, certainly deserves well of his country."

"Then," said I, "there is something so truly poetical in the word *hoofs*; now an ordinary poet would have use the hacknied term *limbs*, but Mr. Altham's genius is not to be confined to the mere strait road."

"Though," said Beauchamp, "with submission, I think an emendation might be made there. What say you to altering the lines thus?

> Thee too I hail, since here with thee I stop,
> For nag and me to rest each wearied prop.

"Since the *hoof*, though I grant it has novelty to recommend it, describes but a small part of the leg, whereas the whole is very properly described as a *prop*."

"This is somewhat hypercritical, I think," said I. "Surely 'tis no more than a justifiable licence to use the term applied to a part only, for the whole."

"At any rate," said Beauchamp, "Chamberry is from this moment immortalised, don't you think so, Mrs. Harrison?"

"Aye!" said the good lady, putting on one of her very wisest looks, "and I suppose Chamberry gauze comes from Chamberry in France, or Picardy, which is it?"[18] On a vacancy she hopes to be appointed King's Geographer, as well as astronomer.

The author all this time looked first at one, then at the other, as if not absolutely certain what we were about, and whether he was to take our observations as real compliment, or as ridicule. But the Doctor, however well disposed himself to admire his grand-children, seemed satisfied that we thought less favourably of them, and that it was better to check his nephew, lest he should make himself still more ridiculous. "Come Percival," he said, "'tis not good manners to make yourself so much the hero of the company. Miss Campbell will honour your works with a perusal at her leisure." Then turning to Olivia, "I must beg your pardon, Madam," he said, "I am afraid you have already found my nephew troublesome, but he has so long been ambitious of the honour of becoming acquainted with Miss Campbell, that he can scarcely now restrain his transports."

Percival seemed by no means pleased with this apology, and to think that his uncle had no business thus to interfere with him. But as the inflexible heiress still persisted in not giving him any encouragement, he was at length silenced, and an opportunity was afforded for the conversation to advert to other subjects. So let my pen also, to subjects of much greater importance, and which ought to have taken the lead of this, but better late than never.

So altered is Harry within a short time, that I can scarcely now recognise in him the same man who accompanied me hither. Pensive and thoughtful he no longer takes the lead in conversation, rarely even joins in it at all, no longer seeks distinction, but shrinks into himself, and in the midst of a large circle hardly seems to know that there is any body present. I one day noticed this dejection, exhorting him to shake it off, and endeavour to assume, if not the spirits with which he commenced his career here, at least such a degree of composure and cheerfulness as the lenity and kindness shewn us by Olivia demanded.

"Lionel," he answered, solemnly and emphatically, "what composure can I feel? What spirits can I assume? Can the bankrupt prodigal who knows not where to raise a shilling, taste the sweets but of a momentary repose? Can the soul-wounded lover, who feels his former devoted attachment revived even with tenfold ardour, yet without a distant ray of hope, deck his features in chearfulness, while his heart is consumed with corroding anguish. No, Lionel, teach me to retrieve my lost character, my ruined fortune; teach me how to win the affections of Harriot Belgrave, and then, and not till then, expect to see this care-worn countenance illumined with a smile."

I expostulated with him warmly against thus giving way to a despondency, that would only aggravate the evils of his situation, and endeavoured to animate him with courage to face his difficulties with manly firmness. Scarcely could any situation, I urged, be so desperate that it might not be retrieved by resolution and vigorous exertion, and I assured him that no efforts within my power, either in my person or my purse, should be omitted, to assist in procuring his emancipation from his embarrassments. I added besides, that if supplies should be wanted beyond my abilities, ample as they were from my father's unbounded indulgence and liberality, I could engage for him that he would be no less eager than myself in giving all possible assistance to any views that had for their object the reform and restoration of the son of a beloved sister, of a nephew whose lapse had occasioned him so many hours of real heartfelt uneasiness.

After much argument I did at length gain my point so far as to obtain a promise that he would go speedily to Arrenton for the purpose of entering upon a thorough investigation of his affairs, and endeavouring to concert some plan with his steward for putting his debts into a regular train of payment; though, he said, he feared that his estate was already mortgaged to its utmost value. He only entreated me not to urge his departure till after Mrs. Belgrave and Harriot were set out upon their Irish expedition.

Though I thought that this was but to imbibe a slow poison, and irritate the wounds I wished to see healed, I would not oppose his wishes, especially as I felt pretty confident that my compliance would not protract his stay many days. I would fain have persuaded him to let me be the companion of his journey, as I thought the society of a friend would at least be a source of consolation to him, if not of assistance in the arrangement of his affairs. But this he declined, assuring me that without slighting my friendship, he had rather at present remain in perfect solitude, and be left entirely to the pursuit of his own plans, of which he said he had many floating in his mind, though none sufficiently matured to be mentioned at present.

I gently hinted that solitude might only encrease his depression, and endanger its becoming at last a settled melancholy. "No, Lionel," he said, "you need not entertain any such apprehension. I see perfectly well what is now passing in your mind, and I freely confess that there have been moments when self-destruction seemed my only resource for freeing myself from a situation become almost insupportable. But I dare not now rush out of life. No! while existence remains I can still cherish a hope that I may one day be blessed in the possession of Harriot, and how wild soever the idea, while that hope is in view, I could not for worlds, by one rash stroke, dash it from me for ever."

Though I think the hope he thus cherishes a most fallacious one, yet did I rejoice to find that there was any object on this earth which could determine him to live at all hazards. Still I tremble at the thoughts of the investigation in which he is about to engage, since if he should find his affairs as desperate as I apprehend them, in a moment of frantic irritation he may forget both Harriot and his resolution to live for the hope of possessing her, and take the only possible method of releasing himself from the misery of reflection.

Ryder arrived here two days ago.—"*How do you like him?*" methinks I hear you ask.

Orlando, that is a dificult question to answer. Though not much accustomed to feeling awe of my fellow mortals, yet I certainly do feel a degree of something not very unlike awe of him. "*And what occasions this feeling?*"—upon my honour I cannot tell, unless it be that he has the most penetrating eye I ever beheld; nor do I wonder that when cast upon Mr. Bounce with a sarcastic smile, it drove him to a temporary phrenzy.

When this basilisk orb is fixed upon any one, it seems as if exploring the inmost recesses of the heart, nor can the object of its researches hope to preserve a single thought in concealment. His figure too is tall and commanding, and in every look, every action, appears the dignity of concious talent, not justly prized by a misjudging world.

Let me not, however, be understood to insinuate that he is self-conceited and arrogant. I hold this to be widely different from the innate consciousness of superior talents, nay that they are incompatible with each other. The truly great mind is the most sensible of its own insufficiency, and that when it has arrived at the utmost knowledge human powers can obtain, it at last knows comparatively nothing—the little mind alone is vain of its attainments, and seeks to thrust them into notice. This is strikingly illustrated in the contrast between Ryder and Percival Altham. While the latter is incessantly labouring to impress the company with a high idea of his abilities, he only makes his imbecility the more conspicuous, whereas in Ryder, without a single effort of his own, the man of power and intellect is constantly apparent.

One feature in his character I particularly admire. Though deeply sensible of the obligations he is under to Olivia, and behaving to her with the utmost respect and politeness, his attentions never deviate into servility, or flattery; and if on any point he happen not to coincide in opinion with her, he delivers his own sentiments, and controverts hers, with a perfect freedom as he does those of any other person. On the whole, he *must* be respected, he *may* be loved; of this I shall be a better judge on a farther acquaintance. At present believe me
Yours most faithfully,

LIONEL STANHOPE.

LETTER VII.

LIONEL STANHOPE
TO
ORLANDO ST. JOHN.

Campbell-House, September 18.
I said rightly, Orlando, that Harry's waiting for Mrs. Belgrave's and Harriot's departure could not protract his stay here many days. They set off for Ireland yesterday morning.

How did I pity Harry!—He was to be separated from the idol of his soul, perhaps for ever, yet dared not so much as press her hand to his lips, to imprint on it the seal of everlasting fidelity—dared not by a word, or even by a look, express how tenderly he was interested in her welfare— dared not even snatch the momentary gratification of handing her to the carriage that was to bear her from his sight, lest his trembling frame might betray emotions which every tie of honour commanded him to conceal.

Not many hours after her departure he called me into his room, and told me that he should no longer delay fulfilling his engagement to me, but that he was under the most painful and humiliating embarrassment with regard to Arthur. He had for some time, he said, been extremely troublesome, and tormented him with complaints of the dull life he led here, threatening to quit his service if he would not leave the place directly. "And heaven knows," said Harry, "how heartily I wish I were rid of him; but—"

Here the entrance of the valet himself, prevented his master's saying more. "Well, Sir, said the impertinent fellow, I'm come for your final answer, whether or not you mean to leave this damned place, for upon my soul I would not pass another week in it for all the masters in the world."

"Please yourself, Sir. I shall stay as long as I please, or go as soon as I please."

"You are not upon the march, then?"

"I did not say that."

"What, you do begin to think of going?"

"Neither did I say that. You shall know time enough when I mean to go."

"But as you don't seem in a hurry, please to recollect, my dear master, that you gave me warning a full month ago. So if your honour pleases I should be glad of my wages, which are now five quarters in arrears, and then D.I.O."[19]

"I gave you warning, you rascal, what do you mean?"

"The serenade, you know, when all had not gone exactly according to some people's wishes, and they made a very ridiculous figure, and I would have joked with 'em, but they could not bear it, and took huff, and I was treated with a damn or two, and then—"

I thought it was better here to interpose, and stop this torrent of impertinence, so I said—"Yes, yes, Egerton, Arthur is right; if you recollect you did give him warning."

"Well then," said he, "let him go and be damned to him."

"Yes," said the fellow, "but he'll be damned indeed if he goes without the five quarters of arrears. He must handle the cash before he'll budge an inch, and I suppose the yellow boys are not very ready to come forth."

Poor Egerton! it was true that he could at that moment as readily have paid the national debt as the five-and-twenty guineas due to his impertinent valet. As the latter however was contemplating his own beloved person in an opposite mirror, I took an opportunity, unobserved by him, to slip my purse into Harry's hand, which enabled him to pay the sum required. When it was produced, Mr. Arthur seemed all astonishment, but impudent to the last exclaimed,

"Heyday!—how's all this?—what, been on the highway?—or have a pack of coiners got a cave under this fine old castle, and admitted you to a snug birth among em?—and was it one of them that played ghost, and blew out my candle in the cursed long galley?"

"Rascal, begone!—sign me a receipt in full, and get out of my sight directly."

"Boo--oo--oo--oo, how mighty we're grown since we're able to pay our debts! But come, my dear master, let's be *pax*!* I was only joking, and had a mind to try if I could'nt get you away from this muzzy place, where, upon my soul, you'll soon grow as rusty and fusty as the good folks themselves."

"This won't do now. I will no longer submit to being cajoled as I have been, and since you have required your dismission, sign the receipt and begone."

"Well, there's no occasion to make such a fuss about the matter, and to be so mighty, and so huffy—I can get as good a place any day in the week, where my wages will be paid regularly too!"

He signed the receipt; then examining the money—"I was afraid it might be only brass," said he, "but upon my soul I believe it is really pure gold. Farewell, then, my dear master; and I heartily wish you happy with the honest elegant boors of servants belonging to this venerable mansion." Then opening the door, and holding it in his hand, he added, with a significant shake of the head—"Ah, never more will those locks be seen to hang with the graceful negligence in which they have been taught to stray by theirs and their owner's most obedient humble servant to command Arthur Williams"—and with a fine flourish upon his heel, away he marched.

"Oh God, Lionel!" said Egerton, catching my hand, and pressing it eagerly as the valet shut the door, "you know not from what an insupportable torment you have relieved me!—To impertinence like this have I been compelled to submit day after day for the last fortnight, conscious of my inability to satisfy the rascal's just demands."

"And why did you endure it?—Could you doubt my friendship that you concealed your distress?—Oh! Harry, it was unjust."

"No, thou only being on earth to whom I could ever look for consolation in my sufferings, suspect me not of such injustice. Your friendship I did not, could not, for a moment doubt; I only felt that it had been taxed too deeply already. Yet why should I have hesitated to impart this circumstance to one who knows my situation so well as you do? it was perhaps weakness.—But now it is forced from me, nor, after what you have seen, need I add that I am at this moment destitute of even a single guinea—destitute of every means of raising one but by making yet another appeal to that heart the generosity of which knows no bounds—to that heart which has shewn its friendship proof against all that so commonly sunders and dissolves connections of this nature. Yes, Lionel, 'tis to you alone that I can look for such farther assistance as is absolutely necessary for my support, till some permanent plan can be arranged for my future life."

---

*   Latin for *peace*. In schoolboy slang, "Truce" (*OED*).

This morning, at six o'clock, he departed. I accompanied him to Doncaster, where we breakfasted together, nor did we separate without tears on both sides. At his earnest intreaty, his intention of quitting Campbell-House was not previously mentioned, and I undertook to make his apology, and disclose his views to Olivia. She was deeply affected at my relation of his sorrows and remorse, and made the most generous offers of assisting him in any way, or to any extent, that might promote the accomplishment of the arduous and meritorious work he had undertaken. Nor has my good father been less liberal, or less sincere, in his offers of assistance, so that I hope, if Harry can but be prevailed upon to accept their services, all may yet be well.

And here let me make honourable mention of Ryder. His penetration could not fail of being immediately struck with Harry's dejection, and he became instantly anxious to know the occasion of it. Applying therefore to Beauchamp, the Biographer-general of Campbell-House, he received a full and ample detail of Harry's life and misfortunes, which interested him so deeply, that it seemed from that moment the great object of his mind to endeavour to soothe and amuse him; while Harry, finding some relief in the society of one who had not been witness to the shame and disgrace he has incurred under this roof, shewed more readiness to accept his attentions, as feeling them less humiliating to him, than he has ever shewn to accept those of any other of our party.

Many times did Ryder entice him to accompany him in a botanical walk, and initiating him into the elements of botany, while he taught him to feel the powerful fascinations of that science, and to distinguish the different classes, orders, &c. of plants, Harry almost forgot that his heart was a prey to a hopeless passion. Again, when he took him into a laboratory, which he has established here at Olivia's request, to give her some idea of the principles of chemistry, and there exhibited to Harry things which were to him perfect novelties, in the ardour of investigating them our poor friend scarcely recollected that his estate was mortgaged to the utmost extent of its value. Oh that the same courses had been pursued with him years ago! that he had sought in science, instead of dissipation, the Lethe that was to banish the remembrance of his sorrows![20]

Orlando, can you doubt that these indisputable evidences of a truly benevolent and sympathetic heart, have confirmed more strongly my respect and esteem for Ryder's character. I said in my last that he *might* be loved, and I feel now that he *ought* to be, yet I know not how it is, there is still to me a something awful about him. Why I find this I cannot exactly tell. 'Tis not merely that I feel my own inferiority to him, though that I certainly do feel, for I am no less conscious of my inferiority to Olivia, yet I feel no awe of her. I think it must be referred principally to that excessive penetration into character which seems almost intuitive in him, and I am so conscious that mine will not bear this strict scrutiny, that I shrink from the very idea of it. Not that the severity with which he certainly can animadvert upon some persons is ever exercised but upon extraordinary occasions, his extreme indignation is only called forth by complete meanness and littleness of mind. From such strictures as he passes on those who come under this description, good heaven deliver me! But to the petty foibles from which the best characters are not exempt, no one is more candid or forbearing.

He was accused of misanthropy while he was at Gibraltar, and he certainly does possess that measure of what is commonly, though mistakenly, called misanthropy, which is almost the inevitable consequence of so acute a sense of right and wrong as he feels. He cannot but detest the mass of vice and folly in which he sees so large a part of mankind plunged, but he is only the more warmly attracted to any one for whom he can feel a sincere respect, or whom he thinks more an object of compassion than of censure. Yes, in time I think I shall love him.

Let me now return once more to Arthur, who must not be finally dismissed before the anecdotes are detailed which honest Jerry related of him yesterday, as he was attending at my toilette.

"Well, Sir," said he, "so we a got rid of Arthur howsever. Massy on me, well to be sure it frights one for to think that Muster Egerton should a kept un so long, for a sartin as can be a's as big a rogue as iver set foot in an honest man's house. I bid the butler look well to his plate, for I thought 'twere a massy if some did'nt go away in Arthur's box."

"Why you do'n't think he was quite so bad as that surely, Jerry? I know that he was saucy and impertinent, and had several other bad qualities, but I never suspected him of being a downright thief."

"Ah, why I don't know, but its my thought that they as will cheat, won't make many bones a stealing too, and to be sure a was cheat enough to a's master, or else a belies a's own self. 'Twere but t'other day one of the sarvents here had been buying some things at Doncaster, as were wanted in the house, mops and brushes, and such; and so Arthur a sees 'em laying in the kitchen, and a tumbles 'em over and over, '*and what did you gin for this?*' says he, '*and what did you gin for that?*' chucking 'em about as thos he had been as great as any lord. So the sarvent he told un what he gin for 'em, and then says Arthur, says he, '*and what d'ye charge 'em to your mistress?*' says he. So the fellow he stared, for he's a very honest fellow as any that lives, and so to be sure is all the sarvents in this house, which it is quite a pleasure to be among 'em; so the fellow he stared, '*what I gin for 'em to be sure,*' says he. With that Arthur sets up a great horse laugh, '*what a fool,*' says he, '*why I niver in my life bought nothing for my master that I did'n't make interest of the money, threepence in the shilling at least.*' I'm sure I niver was so frightened in all my life, as for to hear un say such a thing, and if I had but had the parts of speech as some folks have, I'd a talked to un, I'd a gin it to un as handsomely as ever a had it in a's life. But your honour knows that I ben't no matters of a talker, only in a simple kind of way like, such as your honour's so good as to let me talk sometimes to you."

"And to be sure, Jerry, he did deserve a hearty trimming—a damned rascal!"

"Rascal enough that's for sartin, your honour, but I beg your honour's pardon, you know your honour were so good as to give me leave to speak, when I heard your honour using them there kind of words."

"What *damned* you mean? 'Tis very true, Jerry, and I think you'll allow that I have nearly left them off."

"Yes, your honour, and I'm main glad on it, and so I hope will Muster Egerton, now a's got rid of that fellow. But as I were going to tell your honour, a did get a dressing, for Madam Jenny she were in the store-room, and the door warn't quite shut, so she heard all, and out she comes, and she did larry un,* massy on me, what a larry she did give un, for Mrs. Jenny to be sure is a mighty good sort of a body, but she can talk at a perdigious rate. But for that matter 'twarn't no more than Arthur deserved, and a fine set to they had, and Arthur telled her she'd better not be so free of her tongue, for a'd go and blow her to all the world, how she and her mistress, and then he called Madam such names as I wouldn't tell your honour again for niver so much, for to be sure it were quite a shame for to hear him, and a said a'd blow how they cooked up cheats together, and wanted to bam her off upon folks for a lady. So with that all the other sarvents sets upon him, for they can't none of 'em bear as nobody should speak a disrespectful word of Madam, and to be sure they've no right, for she's all one as kind to them as if they was her equels; and so massy how they did all scold and jaw, and how Arthur did damn and swear at 'em all for a pack of vulgar stupid country boobies."

"Indeed, Jerry, I think 'tis very well he's gone, if he made such disturbances in the house."

"And, your honour, there's more too I've got for to tell you, if I warn't afeard of being troublesome."

"Oh no, Jerry, you know I always like to hear you talk."

"Ah, your honour, that's all along of your own goodness."

"Why, Jerry, we are old friends, and if they are not kind to each other, I know not who should be."

"God love your honour, you almost makes one cry for joy, and it's all as one the way that Madam talks to her sarvents; there's narrow a better lady its my belief on God's blissed earth. And as I was going to say, last night that fellow truly wanted the butler to give him a bottle of Madam's best Claret, for he swore he was sick of the vulgar stuff they gave him to drink, it was well enough for such fellows as they that knowed nothing of life, but 'twas not fit for a man of fashion's sarvent; though to be sure your honour, there's as good beer and ale in the Sarvents' Hall, as any in all Yorkshire, which your honour knows it is one of the most famousest coun-

---

* Scold.

ties in England for beer and ale. So the butler a telled un as a was surprised at a's impudence. He give him a bottle of Madam's Claret indeed! no, truly, he wouldn't touch a drop of her wine without axing her leave for niver so much, though for that matter she was too good a lady to grutch any sarvent among 'em a glass o wine if they'd a mind to it, which I thought your honour this were a very proper thing for the butler to say. But what does Arthur do, but damns him and his cursed methodestical cant, as he called it, and said there were narrow a sarvent of his acquaintance, as were at all of a gentleman, but what drink'd his master's wine as freely as thos 'twere his own. 'And more shame for 'em,' says the butler, says he, 'for 'tis such rascals as they as makes folks find fault with all sarvents, and damn 'em for rogues, and thieves, and cheats, and 'tis a great shame,' says the butler, says he, 'for God knows there's as many honest sarvents as masters and mistresses' says the butler, which I dare say your honour won't please to be angry as he said so, because your honour knows that there's good and bad among 'em all, which I dare say your honour won't please to deny it."

"Certainly not Jerry. I believe 'tis often as much the fault of the masters and mistresses when servants are not honest, as their own, they set them such bad examples."

"God bless and love your honour, and I humbly thank you. But your honour were always so kind as to speak a good word for poor sarvents."

"It would be a shame if I did not speak well of servants, Jerry, while I have such an one as you."

"And for that matter, your honour is always so kind and so free, and so good-natured, that it quite does one's heart good for to hear your honour talk, and I'm sure I niver would wish no better luck to a sarvent than to have such a master as your honour."

Thus did old honesty and I compliment each other, while from all he had said, I found strong additional reason to rejoice that Harry was well rid of such a scoundrel as Arthur. I never conceived a good opinion of him, though I have sometimes, and I cannot defend the practice, amused myself with his quaint humour; but I did not suppose him such a complete rogue as he now appears.

Adieu, Orlando. If in future you find me a less assiduous correspondent than I have lately been, you will recollect that my leisure must now be principally devoted to Harry, to whom I know you will joyfully resign the pen of

    Yours most truly,

                        LIONEL STANHOPE.

LETTER VIII.

ORLANDO ST. JOHN
TO
LIONEL STANHOPE.

Woodbourne, September 20.

Justly is it observed, Lionel, in one of the finest tragedies modern times has produced, that *"our joys are momentary"*—I hope I shall not find it equally true that *"remorse is eternal."*[21] I cannot say indeed that of this I have much apprehension, since though I certainly do at present labour under a considerable degree of remorse and self-reproach, I hope my offence is not of a nature so heinous as to be wholly inexpiable.

From the date of my letter you will see that the joys I experienced at Scarborough, and truly joyful were the days I passed there, are now no more. I was summoned thence within an hour after I received your last letter, to attend, as from the account brought me I fully expected, the death-bed of my father. I even doubted whether he might at that moment be alive. He had been so severely attacked with the gout in his stomach, that his recovery was considered as impossible. But to my no small astonishment, before my arrival at Woodbourne, he was so much amended as to be out of danger for the present, and as the disorder is settled in his feet, he will probably weather this storm.

And now to my remorse. When I quitted Scarborough, it was with the full impression that my father would never more rise from the sick-bed on which he then lay. I arrived here, and found such an alteration in him, that there is great probability of his continuing not merely months but years. Fain would I experience all the transport a son ought to feel upon such an occasion, and my heart severely reproaches me that I do not; I can only say, that our emotions are not so entirely under our controul as that we can, upon every event, feel the exact measure of joy or sorrow the occasion seems to require.

I know that my father has always been considered by the world as one of the kindest and most affectionate of parents, and indeed I should be guilty of the highest ingratitude did I not acknowledge that he never in his life denied me any reasonable indulgence. One subject of complaint alone can I find against him, but this is one I feel very severely, that being an only son, and heir to a good estate, he has not educated me to any profession. Thus the best years of my life are passed in idleness and dependence; and since I can only be relieved from a situation so irksome by my father's death, whenever he is indisposed, instead of attending upon him with a solicitous and painful anxiety for his recovery, I watch the progress and probable termination of the disorder with a listless and sickly eagerness; and while my filial affection would rejoice at every symptom of amendment, my transports are damped by the cruel reflection that his death alone can put me into possession of that independence for which I sigh.

Oh! had I but been trained to rely on my own industry for my establishment in life, how much more satisfactory had been my sensations. I had then never known the discontents by which I am now assailed, but, placed above the want of my paternal inheritance, my ardent wishes had been offered up to heaven for the prolongation of my father's life. If ever it should be my lot to have a family of my own, I shall avoid with the extremist caution the placing my son in similar circumstances; nor can I be sufficiently astonished that so many fathers as have felt the misery of such a situation themselves, can yet entail the same misery on their children.

And what at last are my prospects, when I shall come into possession of this long and tediously expected fortune?—I must either behold three sisters, accustomed to all the comforts, and many of the luxuries of life, reduced to a state of comparative indigence, or else the income which should maintain a wife and family must be devoted to their support. Had I been turned out into the world to provide for myself, the estate might have been settled upon them, and they would not then have experienced any change in their situations.

One good effect has, however, resulted from my being summoned so hastily away from Scarborough—that I made my escape without offering to surrender my liberty either to Charlotte or Eliza, which possibly might not have been the case had my departure been more deliberate. But thou seest, *mon cher cousin*, that 'tis not with me absolutely, *"out of sight out of mind."* No: I still cherish the fond remembrance of my two charmers, I am still the devoted slave of both; and find no resource for alleviating the regrets of absence, but in living over again in recollection the many pleasant hours passed in their society. In this tender occupation I am greatly assisted by some pieces of poetry which I stole from Charlotte, and a collection of songs presented me by Eliza, chiefly of her own composing. These I turn over for ever and for ever, sighing forth over the poetry,—ah, at such an hour, and on such a spot, was this written;—and then adverting to the songs, and on such another spot, or at such another hour, was this warbled, in strains that might have made the stormy billows themselves mute with attention.

Lionel, I have already sent thee two of Charlotte's poetical effusions—surely they must only have set thee craving for more. Well, then, thou shalt be gratified. In a sea excursion we passed within sight of the rock down which the poor maniac here celebrated, takes his monthly flights—a rock so steep and shaggy that none but a maniac could ascend or descend it—when a gentleman in our party, who had once seen him, told us the story. It made a deep impression upon us all, but most upon the poetical mind of Charlotte, who, before we returned home, had thus versified the tragic tale:

THE LUNATIC.

And dost thou ask why that wild form,
Regardless of the pelting storm,
Down yon' shaggy rock's steep side
Hastes to meet the flowing tide?
Why he now, with hurried steps,
O'er the sandy sea-beach leaps;
And, deep within the whelming waves,
His form with madd'ning gestures laves?
Why his pensive brows around
Are with fantastic sea-wreaths bound;
And, as the briny foam he quaffs,
Why with ideot shout he laughs?
Ah! list to yonder deep-ton'd bell,
Which sounds cold midnight's solemn knell,
And think that tho' surrounding clouds
The vault of heav'n with darkness shrouds,
Veil'd from our sight, the full-orb'd moon
"Is riding at her highest noon."
Then know, that e'en at this chill hour,
Long since, near yonder mould'ring tow'r,
As still the rough rock's brow he pac'd,
And anxious ey'd the watry waste,
To watch the vessel that contain'd
The maid who o'er his bosom reign'd,
He heard, ere yet it reach'd the shore,
The distant storm begin to roar.
He saw—ah! who his pangs can tell!—
The foaming waves begin to swell;
Saw lightnings flash, heard thunders roll,
While wilder tempests shook his soul.

With maddest gestures of despair,
He beat his breast, he tore his hair;
Invok'd the flame-wing'd lightning's dart
To strike, in mercy, to his heart,
Ere in relentless ocean's womb,
His heart's sole joy should meet her doom.
Yet ah! no dart's unerring aim,
In pity, to his suff'rings came:
Still o'er the waste he stretched his sight,
While, through the intervals of light,
He saw the lab'ring vessel drive
Before the raging tempest's reign,

Saw it, with fruitless efforts, strive
    To stem the fury of the main;
Till, to the angry waves a prize,
It sunk ingulph'd, no more to rise.

    With frenzy seiz'd, no fear he knew,
But down the rock as now he flew,
And plung'd amid a dashing wave,
Where too he'd found a watry grave,
But that, by mild compassion led,
One who had mark'd his hasty tread,
And gestures wild, as down this steep
He rush'd impetuous tow'rd the deep,
Undaunted brav'd the billows' roar,
And brought him safely back to shore.

    Yet senseless he—thro' all his veins
Fierce fever rush'd with madd'ning pains,
And held long time his scorching breath
In equipoise, 'twixt life and death.
But youth at last disease o'ercame;
New vigour brac'd his shattered frame;
O'er his pale cheek fresh roses bloom'd;
His limbs their wonted pow'rs resum'd:
Yet, when his fev'rish pulse was slak'd
He not to sense, but madness wak'd.
And now, whene'er the full moon sheds
Its paly lustre o're our heads,
Which faster, while its influence reigns,
Binds the poor maniac's mental chains,
And bids the tossing ocean's tide
Swell higher with encreasing pride,
Soon as the midnight clock he hears
His swift step down the rock he steers,
And plunges, with impetuous haste,
Intrepid 'mid the boundless waste;
To his lost fair there breathes his vows,
And twines sea-garlands round his brows.
But when this mournful duty's o'er,
Again he seeks the rocky shore,
And roves about the neighb'ring plains,
Still warbling sadly-melting strains;
Strains which his anguish'd bosom's woes
In piteous eloquence disclose.
No house e'er shelters his sad head,

Yon' cave's his home, cold earth his bed;
There, inoffensively, he rests,
Nor others, nor himself, molests.

Ah! see where now he leaves the deep,
Again ascends the rocky steep:
Farewell! poor maniac!—may thy woes
Soon in the grave find lost repose!

Monsieur Lionel, thou possibly may'st not be aware of the happiness that awaits thee. Know then that my two enchantresses, with the Tichfields and Peggy Perkins, are to stay a few days at Campbell-House in their way from Scarborough, where they did not propose to remain above three weeks after I quitted it. *Gardez bien votre cœur*, my dearest Li.; for by Jupiter though it has been once offered to the heiress, I suspect its constancy would run a great risk of being shaken by the bright eyes of Eliza de Clairville, or the bewitching dimples of Charlotte O'Brien.

Peggy accompanies the Tichfields to London, where she has now resolved to fix, since, after mature deliberation, she is firmly of opinion that the metropolis is, on the whole, the most advantageous situation for a single unprotected female. Her health, which she flattered herself on her first coming to Scarborough was somewhat amended, is now more deplorable than ever; and nobody, she says, can have an idea of what she does suffer. A few days before I left the place, as I was drinking tea with the Tichfields, Doctor Barford, Peggy's physician, came in, when his patient immediately began to entertain the company with giving him a long detail of her complaints, concluding it with consulting him on the expediency of smoking a pipe every morning in bed, to which, she said, she had been very strongly advised.

The Doctor replied that he really did not suppose it could be of any service to her, and it certainly would be a very unpleasant remedy for a lady to try. Indeed he added, he thought her complaints were principally upon her spirits, and that if she would think less about herself her health would be much better. Such base insinuations roused her just indignation, and she began a violent attack upon the Doctor, who, she said, she was certain had been listening to the malicious stories circulated against her by her *bitter enemies*, which she found had pursued her, even into this northern latitude. After haranguing in the same way for some time, the subject at length grew so extremely affecting that she burst into tears, pathetically lamenting, that go where she would, she could not escape from her persecutors.

When Doctor Barford was gone, Mr. Tichfield began a consolatory address to his fair cousin, exhorting her strenuously not to be influenced by that Tyro,* who really was not worth regarding. He assured her that he

---

* Beginner or novice.

had known many surprising cures effected by a pipe taken fasting, but that the physicians always treated the idea of it with contempt, because if the use of such simple remedies were once fully established, farewell to their fees. Peggy was delighted with this advice, and declared she was determined to make the experiment the very next morning. I even thought she would have embraced Mr. Tichfield, as the dearest of all her *dear friends*. The pipes and tobacco were accordingly prepared, and at the proper time in the morning, the tube was filled and lighted, and the patient began to smoke. She had not however persevered for many minutes before she grew extremely sick, and at length her medicine operated so violently as to make her really ill for the whole day.

From the *dearest of her friends*, Mr. Tichfield instantly became the most *bitter of her enemies*, and she solemnly vowed in the first transports of indignation that she would not, upon any consideration, remain another day under the same roof with him. But afterwards recollecting that, should she put her threat into execution, she did not absolutely know at that moment what to do with herself, she gave herself absolution for breaking her vow, and resolved to shew a bright example of Christian charity, by consenting to remain where she was till she should find it more convenient to depart. *Addio mio caro cugino*, and believe me

Yours most faithfully,
Most devotedly,
Most affectionately,

ORLANDO ST. JOHN.

LETTER IX.

HENRY EGERTON
TO
LIONEL STANHOPE.

Arrenton, September 22.

No time has been lost, Lionel, since my arrival, in commencing the great work which brought me hither; and considering how short a time has elapsed, much has been done towards ascertaining the exact state of my affairs. But 'tis a gloomy prospect indeed that is presented to me. So deeply do I find myself involved, that I was of opinion nothing remained but to make over the estate to the principal mortgagee, and selling all my effects, to let the produce of them be distributed in equal proportions among the rest of my creditors, as an earnest for the remainder's being paid whenever it should be in my power.

But against this plan my steward warmly remonstrated. He says this is so well-conditioned an estate that it would be a great pity to let it pass out of the family; and he offered, if I would surrender my affairs entirely to his management, to allow me a regular annuity of an hundred pounds, and still to put things in such a train as that every incumbrance should be cleared in a course of years. To a proposal so much for my advantage I could not hesitate for a moment to accede, and I have actually invested him with the powers he required. The house is to be let; all the timber that can be spared, without injury to the estate, is immediately to be cut down; and the money arising from this, and the sale of my carriages, horses, plate, pictures, and other useless luxuries, is to form a fund for paying the interest, and reducing the principal of my debts. I cannot say enough of the ardour this worthy man shews in my service; and if at last I shall be extricated from the scene of desolation around me, it must be ascribed almost entirely to his vigilance and judgment.

I am now principally occupied by another subject. I must form some plan for providing a subsistence for myself, not merely that I may leave the annuity he proposes to pay me, for other purposes, but that I may contribute by the fruits of my own industry to the more speedy liquidation of my debts. But what plan to pursue perplexes me exceedingly. I wish to leave the kingdom for a while, as I think a temporary absence affords the best prospect of retrieving my character, in which, alas! I am now as miserable a bankrupt as in fortune.

I have thought both of the East and West Indies, but against either of these ideas my heart deeply revolts. In the fair way of traffick I could expect little advantage from an adventure to the former country; and I will not add to the load of guilt which already oppresses my soul, that of any more seeking relief from my embarrassments by a single step which honour and strict integrity cannot sanction. As to the latter idea, with what horrible images was I not assailed all night, merely from having harboured it for one moment in the day. Every species of barbarity practised against our wretched African brethren seemed present to my eyes, bitter groans and lamentations assailed my ears, and I was forced to start several times from my bed and walk about the room, ere I could shake off the fearfully vivid impressions they made upon my imagination. No, I cannot go to those infernal islands!—my conscience would be lacerated with every stroke under which the back of the wretched negro smarted.

My prevailing idea at present is if possible to purchase a commission in some regiment of our own employed abroad, with the exception that it should not be in either of the countries already rejected. But to this I am sensible there are powerful objections. In the first place, for the purchase of the commission I must draw upon that fund which ought to be considered as sacred to other purposes; and in the second place, there scarcely appears a possibility of saving any thing out of the income of my commission towards assisting in the payment of my debts. I have sometimes thought of entering into the service of some foreign power, but with the nature of such an engagement I am at present too much unacquainted to be able to decide how far the plan might be eligible or not. Would to heaven I could determine on something that would afford a satisfactory prospect of attaining objects I have so much at heart! but 'tis one of the curses of such a life as I have led, that if the mind ever wishes to throw off its shackles, it but wanders about in a maze of perplexity, unable to arrange any plan that requires such a total alteration of its former views and habits.

Oh, Lionel! assist me if you can with your advice. Your mind is less oppressed, and may, perhaps, be more fertile in resources. Yet think not that I lay before you these various projects, or desire your sentiments on the subject, with any view of exciting you to farther offers of pecuniary assistance for carrying my plans into effect. No, no, Lionel; after the repeated experience I have had of your boundless generosity, I should be culpable beyond excuse in thus attempting

"To wind about your love with circumstance."[22]

Of a friendship so ardent and unwearied as you have shewn me, the world can furnish but few examples. A connection of blood led us into an early intimacy, and in the boyish sports we pursued together were sown the seeds of an attachment which I hope will cease but with our existence. For years this friendship, so delightful to both, passed on unobscured by any glaring improprieties of conduct, and though occasionally guilty of youthful follies, to depravity of heart we were equal strangers. One circumstance of deep calamity fatally changed the scene with regard to me, and while I yielded myself up a votary to vice and dissipation, your friendship drew you but too often into similar instances of misconduct, and you incurred opprobrium as a profligate when you ought to have received encomium as a friend. Yet not all the contumely you thus experienced, not all the slight and contempt with which you saw me treated by a world, who, not knowing the fatal cause that drove me into dissipation, could not be expected to shew any lenity towards me, could make any alteration in your affection.

To a friendship such as this I should be unpardonable in making an indirect appeal. But I have resolved to trespass no farther on your generosity. All efforts made in future for my emancipation shall originate in myself alone. Your advice is all I ask—the advice of a mind less distracted than my own.

Has any intelligence yet been received of Harriot?—How my heart aches when I reflect that she is, perhaps, at this moment, traversing the same ocean which proved the grave of my Emily!—'Tis almost needless to say, write the very moment any tidings are heard of her, since you are too well acquainted with the state of my feelings to delay unnecessarily giving me the satisfaction of knowing that she is in safety;—and remember besides, Lionel, what I said to you at parting, that no cordial equal to that of hearing from you very frequently, can be administered to the soul of

Your faithfully affectionate

HENRY EGERTON.

LETTER X.

LIONEL STANHOPE
TO
HENRY EGERTON.

Campbell-House, September 24.

'Tis with heartfelt pleasure, my dear Harry, that I can impart to you the delightful intelligence of Mrs. Belgrave's and Harriot's safe arrival at Dublin. This welcome information Olivia received this morning, in a letter written immediately after their landing. Their voyage was pleasant and expeditious.

Would that it were in my power to write to you as satisfactorily upon another subject! but indeed, Harry, the more I revolve in my mind that upon which you ask my advice, the more deeply do I feel the difficulties of your situation, and how much more easy it is to find a plan that will not answer than one that will. Let me only exhort you not to determine rashly upon any thing, for time may present things to your choice far more eligible than those that suggest themselves at present. I must also enter my protest against your thinking of leaving the kingdom, at least immediately. I own there is much justice in your idea that a temporary absence might be the best means with the world in general, of obliterating the recollection of your past follies; but the few whose good opinions are of the most importance to you, will want nothing but to witness the reformation that has taken place in your conduct, to regard you with the respect you deserve. Suffer your worthy steward, then, to pursue his plan; let him allow you a present subsistence, and thus you will be at liberty to weigh with deliberation any thing hereafter presented to your choice, and probably be ultimately settled in a far more advantageous way than what would be devised by harassing and torturing your mind at this moment.

We have had another most curious scene with Doctor Paul and Percival Altham, of which I cannot forbear giving you a detail.

Olivia, Beauchamp, Ryder, and myself, were taking a walk yesterday after dinner, when we met the illustrious uncle and nephew, accompanied by a Mr. Sewell, a college friend of the latter, and very lately, upon his arriving at the delightful age of twenty and one, become a member of Parliament. Our party would fain have passed on after merely exchanging the customary civilities of "*how do you do,*" and, "*a most delightful afternoon.*" But the Doctor would by no means be thus shaken off. He began prosing in his usual manner, and presently took an opportunity of giving a pretty broad hint, that he and his two companions should like to spend the evening at Campbell-House. Olivia was at first cruel, and disregarded his hint, but after a repetition of it on the Doctor's part, in two or three different shapes, she grew more compliant, and at length made the desired invitation. Accordingly, the three gentlemen joined our company, and walked home with us.

On our return we found Mrs. Harrison extremely impatient for her tea, so that the moment we appeared, she began growling at Olivia, reproaching her that when she got a walking and a talking with Mr. Stanhope, she was so confounded selfish that she never thought about any body else, and they might be starved for what she cared. To this invective Olivia making no answer, the lady's eloquence upon that subject was soon exhausted; but since a certain quantity of spleen had lodged itself in her bosom, of which it was absolutely necessary that it should be disencumbered, she presently selected Doctor Paul as the object on whom it should be vented.

"So Doctor," she began, "why, they tell us that you are agoing to be married to Mrs. Stapleton."

"I, Madam? I going to be married to Mrs. Stapleton? Indeed I—I can't imagine, Madam, where you could hear that."

"Lord, Doctor, why it's the great news of Doncaster. We was over there this morning, and the whole town rung of it."

"The town did me vast honour in interesting itself so much about me, Madam; but indeed I am at a loss to conjecture how such a report ever could come into circulation."

"Lord, why I don't at all wonder that it's reported. Nay, and for my part I believe it's true."

"Surely *Mrs. Harrison* cannot believe it to be true."

"Why, Lord how could any body think any thing else, when you was so very particular to her the other day when we was all there."

"I particular, Madam? Particular to Mrs. Stapleton when *Mrs. Harrison* was in the room?"

"Why you would'n't play at cards with me, but would sit by Mrs. Stapleton and help her pour out the coffee."

"Surely Mrs. Harrison does not mean that as a reflection upon me, when she knows I am no card-player, but rather make it my peculiar province at parties, to walk about and see that all possible attention is paid to the ladies."

"Well, that's all well enough. But you know when I had that dispute with Mrs. Baxter about the odd trick, you was all on my side, till Mrs. Stapleton took Mrs. Baxter's part, and then you was so confounded selfish that you wouldn't say any thing more, and so I was obliged to give up the game, though I'm sure 'twas mine by right."

"My dear Madam, I am quite concerned that you should so much misapprehend the affair. I certainly never expected to be understood as taking Mrs. Baxter's part, but knowing that both she and Mrs. Stapleton were extremely passionate, I thought it best not to irritate them by further opposition."

"So you rather chose to play the hypocrite yourself," said Sir Francis, "than to suffer two old women to pull caps? For my part, I'd have seen all the old women's caps in the kingdom pulled to pieces, aye and their wigs into the bargain, before I'd have acted so sneakingly to save 'em."

"Pardon me, Sir Francis, but I cannot see any thing sneaking or hypo-critical in endeavouring to prevent a quarrel. 'Tis rather performing one of the Christian divine's most sacred duties, by keeping up the '*unity of the spirit in the bond of peace*.'"

"That sounds very fine, to be sure. But I will maintain, that whoever says what he does not think, merely to pacify a couple of sparring old women, is a sneaking fellow, let him varnish over the matter as he pleas-es. I beg pardon, Doctor, but *I* always speak my sentiments, whatever *you* may do."

"Yet with submission, Sir Francis, allow me to observe that you still seem to misapprehend the matter. I did *not* say what I didn't think, but merely withdrew from any farther interference in the dispute, observing, as is really the fact, that Mrs. Stapleton was much better acquainted with the game than myself."

"So insinuated that you thought her right, when you knew very well that she was wrong."

"Oh by no means. The case was simply this. I saw plainly that if I were to support my opinion against Mrs. Baxter and Mrs. Stapleton, it must occasion a long and vehement debate. Fully sensible therefore of the vast superiority of Mrs. Harrison's temper over those of the other ladies, I trust-ed that she would excuse my dropping the subject, rather than suffer such an interruption to the general harmony of the company to be prolonged."

This excuse, and the compliment it contained to her temper, seemed perfectly to satisfy Mrs. Harrison. But Sir Francis was not to be gotten rid of so easily, he was too happy in an opportunity of tormenting his courtly opponent, to let the subject drop, and he proceeded:

"That's no excuse at all; I say, that to insinuate a lie, or to equivocate, is full as bad as to tell a lie flatly. Nay, I think 'tis worse, for, contemptible as a lie is in any shape, there's something more manly in telling one fair-ly and boldly, than in endeavouring to skulk behind the letter of truth, while violating its spirit."

"I am sure, Sir Francis, that nobody can despise a trimming double-dealing mode of conduct more heartily than I do. But I must nevertheless think there is a great difference between saying what you do *not* think, and not saying *all* that you do think."

"Certainly. And I'm far from wishing you to spit your opinions in every body's face. Had you at once declined meddling in the business, I should have had nothing to say against it. But excuse me if I think 'twas damned sneaking when once you had engaged in it, to skulk out of it again in such a paltry manner."

"I own that Mrs. Stapleton drew an inference from what I said, which I by no means expected."

"Then why not set her right?"

"I thought it not worth while in so unimportant a matter."

"But if I see a man dishonest in trifling concerns, I'm damned apt to suspect that he's not over scrupulous in great ones."

"Indeed, Sir Francis, it gives me infinite concern to find you taking up the matter so seriously. Had I conceived that my silence could be so misinterpreted, I would have defended my opinion with all possible warmth. But let me intreat you to drop the subject at present, and if I might hope for the attendance of this company at church next Sunday morning, I have a sermon in my pocket which I shall then deliver, in which the arguments for the generally complying disposition I would recommend, are brought together into a focus, and consequently placed in a more forcible light than they can be in the eagerness of verbal discussion. And I do flatter myself, Sir Francis, that when you come to find that this pacific mode of conduct is enforced so very emphatically by one of the most celebrated teachers of the Christian church, you will view the matter in a very different light."

"I certainly will attend for one," said Sir Francis, "for I shall be damned glad to see where you can find any arguments from Scripture to defend so bad a cause, since I have always been told that they recommend honesty and plain-dealing."

"And may I hope to be honoured with the attendance of the rest of the company," said the Doctor, bowing courteously round.

Mrs. Harrison, over whose countenance the bright sunshine of serenity had been gradually spreading itself ever since the compliment paid her by the Doctor, was by this time so much recovered as to be capable of thinking of a *hoax* again. Perceiving therefore an admirable opportunity for one here presented she whispered [to] me, "*Let's have a little fun with the Doctor.*" Then turning to him she said, "Why, Doctor, I think you mentioned that you had got the sermon in your pocket. I don't see why we should wait for Sunday, ca'n't you read it to us now?"

The Doctor drew himself up with much self-complacency, and as if highly gratified at finding that his compliment to her temper had not been thrown away, but was returned by one to his oratory. As it was necessary however to affect some coyness on the occasion, he replied with a grin of satisfaction, "Oh pardon me, Madam, I could not think of trespassing so far on the patience of the company."

"Pho now, Doctor, don't be so coy, we will have the sermon; I'm sure we shall all like to hear it."

"That's bold, Cousin Becky," said Sir Francis, "to answer for the whole company."

"Lord, why I'm sure you'll like it better than going to church. So come Doctor."

"Oh pray, Madam, excuse me."

"No, no, come begin."

"Well then, if I must not be excused. But we must apply for permission to the mistress of the house; perhaps Miss Campbell had formed some more entertaining plan for the evening."

"Oh no, I'm sure she could not find one more entertaining," said Beauchamp.

"Certainly," said Olivia, "I would wish the company to do whatever will be most agreeable to themselves."

"Nothing will be half so agreeable as the sermon," said Rebecca, "don't you think so, Mr. Stanhope?"

"Most certainly," said I.

"Well, those that are against it hold up hands," said Rebecca.

But of course not a hand could be held up, so the question was considered as carried *nem con*.

"But I say, Doctor," continued Mrs. Harrison, "if you preach you should have a pulpit; a sermon won't sound half so well without a pulpit. So I'll tell you what we'll do; let's go into the library, and then you can get up into them steps that's almost like a pulpit, and preach from there."

"An excellent thought," said Beauchamp, "I second the motion."

"Oh an admirable one," said I, "and as being proposed by a lady, the Doctor certainly can't refuse."

"Excuse me," said the Doctor, "but surely it will be as well read here."

"Oh no," said Mrs. Harrison, "we will have it from the pulpit. Come Miss Campbell."

The Doctor smirked, and smiled; I saw that he was not disinclined to the matter, so flying to the room door I opened it, "Mrs. Harrison is perfectly right," I said, "the sermon would lose half its effect if not delivered from the pulpit."

Mrs. Harrison delighted at my falling thus complacently into her *hoax*, started up, and sallied out of the room, the Doctor rising at the same time and saying, "we'll follow the ladies."

There was now no choice left to the rest of the company, so we all adjourned to the library, where the steps being properly placed, the Doctor ascended them, and we seated ourselves upon chairs around him. Olivia was totally unable to resist a smile, though she seemed to think the scene rather too ridiculous, while Ryder looked somewhat grave and awe-inspiring; Sir Francis was half angry, half diverted; Beauchamp and I enjoyed the *hoax* highly, as did Mrs. Harrison, though in a different way; while Mr. Sewell stared about him, not knowing what to make of the matter; and Percival Altham sat and contemplated his uncle with profound reverence, as if he thought him the greatest man in the kingdom, himself only excepted.

When we were all seated, the Doctor drew out his white handkerchief, hemmed, blew his nose, and then tucking the handkerchief into his waist coat for want of a cassock, the sermon was produced, and he began:

> *In the first Epistle of St. Paul the Apostle to the Corinthians, the ninth chapter, the twentieth, twenty-first, and twenty-second verses, you will find these words. The twentieth, twenty-first, and twenty-second verses, of the ninth chapter of the first Epistle to the Corinthians.*

And unto the Jews I became as a Jew, that I might gain the Jews; to them that are under the law, as under the law, that I might gain them that are under the law;

To them that are without law, as without law, (being not without law to God, but under the law to Christ) that I might gain them that are without law;

To the weak became I as weak, that I might gain the weak; I am made all things to all men—

"To all *women*, I think it rather ought to be in the present instance," interrupted Beauchamp, "since the question arose upon a dispute between two fair ladies."

The Doctor, spite of his usual courtly disposition, was now touched in so tender a part, the interruption of his oratory, that casting a not perfectly complacent look upon Beauchamp, he said, "Would you wish, Sir, to suggest any other emendations before I proceed? they will probably be well received now, since 'tis become so much the fashion to make improvements in the sacred writings."

"I beg pardon for the interruption, Sir," said Beauchamp. "I own it was a breach of good manners; pray proceed."

But before he could proceed, Mrs. Harrison jogged Percival Altham, "Where's the text?" she said, "I didn't rightly hear."

"It was somewhere in Paul, Madam," answered Percival.

"Oh," said the lady, while both giver and receiver seemed perfectly satisfied with the reply.

The preacher, however, overhearing what had passed, said, "With permission, Madam, I will name my text again, as you seem not to have heard it perfectly, and then we shall proceed regularly. But let me be allowed first to premise, for the better understanding that part of my discourse, which is a sort of introduction to the present subject, that I am going through a regular course of explaining St. Paul's Epistles to my congregation, and I therefore take a certain portion in succession for my text every Sunday, which, God willing, I purpose to continue till I shall have gone through the whole."

"An excellent idea," said Sir Francis, "and must save a deal of unnecessary time otherwise spent in selecting texts."

"It was indeed the difficulty of *selecting*, where every part is so beautiful," said the Doctor, "that first suggested this idea to my mind. In this way, ladies and gentlemen, you will be pleased to understand I have gone through the whole Epistle to the Romans, and as much of the first Epistle to the Corinthians as precedes my present text." Then stroaking the frill of his shirt, instead of his band, which he missed on feeling for it, he was about to proceed, but there was yet another point to settle before this could be permitted. Mrs. Harrison, resolved to lose no opportunity of being as *funny* as possible, said, "Doctor, you don't seem comfortable without a band, we'll make you one in a minute," and twitching up a piece of paper she began to rummage her pocket for a pair of scissars. But the Doctor thanking her, begged she would not give herself so much trouble, that there was not the least occasion for a band; she however persisted, so the band was cut and fixed into his shirt collar.

Nor was this grand interruption yet at an end, for now Percival, who had observed his friend Mr. Sewell grinning very much for some minutes, and jealous lest it should imply a sneer at his uncle, asked him rather indignantly what he was laughing at? "I was only thinking," replied the young member of Parliament, "whether St. Paul's Epistles were franked." This was the first word he had been heard to speak since he came into the house, you will easily believe we now earnestly wished that it might not be the last.

At length all was silent, and the Doctor once again began to hem, when, oh more cruel than any of the interruptions he had hitherto met with, a servant came in with a letter, which giving to the Doctor, he said it was brought by the constable of a neighbouring parish, who begged to speak with him directly.

"Pshaw, what can the fellow want?" said the Doctor, "tell him I am engaged, and cannot attend to him now."

"He has brought a woman with him," said the servant, "who is taken up for pilfering things from some of her neighbours, and he hopes you'll be so good as to examine her, that he may carry her to gaol to-night, for she's such an old offender that he's sadly afraid of her giving him the slip."

"Pshaw," again repeated the Doctor. "This is extremely unfortunate. Surely nobody was ever so harassed with business as myself. You see ladies and gentlemen, how impossible it is for me ever to steal a few hours to enjoy the society of my friends. But there's no refusing this man, so I must beg you to excuse me; I will dispatch the business however as quickly as possible, and then I hope we shall not be interrupted any more."

He now descended from the pulpit, read the letter, which he threw down upon the table, and taking Percival with him as his clerk, adjourned to the Servant's Hall to hold his court of justice. Instigated by that curiosity which never deserts me, I took up the letter, and found it so well worth preservation, that I stole it into my pocket, and here, Harry, present you with it. The writer of it, as I afterwards learned, is squire of the neighbouring parish of Watchford. His character may without difficulty be inferred from his style of writing.

Sir,

The woman that's bro^t before you by the officer of my parish, is of a distinguished character for badness and boldness of all kinds; she has broke into several houses by account. one of my houses that was occupied by two young gentlewomen since dead. she traversed the whole house, and broke open a bureau, were she found two purses, one she took and carried off, whi^h in her hurry was that of silver. Mr. W——, my butcher at P——, she gott into his house and took a sum of money, whi^h was found upon her, and

Mr. W—— took from her. the poor people of my parish can't even sett ye smallest triffle out of doors but she conceales it, add to ye she is the loosest of women personally in regard to men, and retains my lower servants half ye night or ye whole night if I was to know the truth. now, Sir, I referr her to your prior judgment.

    I am, Sir,

        Yours most obediently,

B. SPEARE.

The Doctor was so long absent, that by the time he returned all relish for the *fun* of hearing his sermon had subsided among the company, and at his return therefore, when he would have re-ascended the rostrum, Olivia excused us by saying, that she was afraid it was too near supper to think of beginning then, but she hoped they should all have the satisfaction of hearing it on the following Sunday. I suspect it will not be heard in that way, by

    Yours most sincerely,

LIONEL STANHOPE.

LETTER XI.

LIONEL STANHOPE
TO
HENRY EGERTON.

Campbell-House, September 30.

Harry, I must unburthen my heart to you; I have had an altercation with Ryder which gives me the extremest uneasiness, and it will be a relief to my mind to communicate it. That I always thought there was something awful in him you know, though you never were so sensible of it as myself. This insensibility on your part, however, seemed easily accounted for, since the kind attentions he shewed you would of course make impressions upon your mind so much in his favour, that you could not be quick at discerning his imperfections. Yet, perhaps, I am not justifiable in using the term imperfections here, since it may not have been his aim to inspire me with awe though such was the effect—the fault may have been solely in myself. But so often did I meet his eyes fixed steadily upon me, and so dreadfully penetrating are those eyes, that I could not help shrinking from them instinctively.

    I mentioned in my last his looking somewhat grave and formidable when the farce of the sermon was played by Doctor Paul; and that I perceived him several times casting looks of mingled concern and indignation at Olivia, for which I really thought there was no sufficient reason. But till this morning I had not the least conception of the deep impression made upon him by our levity at that time, and on some other occasions when we have amused ourselves at the expence of the uncle and nephew.

Upon my first acquaintance with him, I was disposed to subscribe to the opinion generally received in this house, that he was unjustly charged with misanthropy, and I actually vindicated him from it in a letter to St. John—but I know not how I shall ever be able conscientiously to deny that charge again.

On the very morning after the memorable sermon frolick, I had taken a book with intent to retire to my favourite seclusion, in the wood in which Lucy's cottage stands: when as I approached the spot, my attention was suddenly arrested by beholding Ryder exactly in the position described so poetically by the elegant Gray:

> There, at the foot of yonder nodding beech
>   That writhes its old fantastic root so high,
> His listless length at noon-tide would he stretch,
>   And pore upon the brook that babbles by.[23]

Only that here it was beneath an oak, not a beech, that the moraliser was extended. His head rested upon the end of the root that hangs directly over the water, on which his eyes were fixed, watching the hundreds of little fish that are always scudding there to and fro. And ever and anon he dipped his hand into the stream, as if to catch the sportive navigators, with whom he wished to descant on the comparative happiness of their situation and his own; perhaps to tell them how much he thought their fate worthy of envy, when compared with that of reasoning man, since though placed in a rank so far below him in the scale of creation, yet wanting reason, they were exempted from those sorrows that must inevitably attend on the possession of so proud a distinction. I could have written volumes on the capriciousness of fortune, the instability of human life, the few sources of enjoyment, and the endless ones of misery, it presents, from the ideas with which I was furnished by his looks and actions during five minutes that I stood to contemplate him before he became sensible of my intrusion.

He then started up, and with a quickness in his manner, and an irritation in his eye that rendered it even more than usually piercing, accosted me with a remark on the loveliness of the weather, and the delicious solitude of that spot, which he said he supposed was my favourite resort; then looking at his watch, and catching up his hat which lay on the ground, he walked hastily away, without waiting for any answer from me, taking the path that leads to the cottages.

I was so much struck with all this, that while I stood for some minutes looking after him, lost in astonishment, I did not observe that he had dropped a piece of paper. But when I had somewhat recovered myself, perceiving this, I took up the paper, on which I found the following stanzas. Perhaps I had no business to read them; but my curiosity was at the moment too much awakened to consider whether I were doing right or wrong.

THE SIGH OF HIM WHO IS NOT LOVED.

Oh Nature! since in mutual love
    Thy voice bids all thy creatures join,
Say why that bliss must I not prove;
    For I, too, am a child of thine.

Lives there thro' all thy works so fair,
    In forest wild, or cultur'd plain,
A creature, breathing life and air,
    But loves, and is belov'd again.

Does not each flow'r that charms the sight,
    Do not each plant, each shrub and tree,
In mutual bonds of love unite?—
    Yet ah! still nought loves hapless me!

Dark are to me the sun's bright rays,
    One dreary void seems this vast earth,
Since thus depriv'd, I pass my days
    Of what makes life alone of worth.

I must own however, that by reading this, my curiosity, instead of being gratified, was only the more strongly excited. I speculated much whether the stanzas were his own composition, though if they were, according to Charlotte O'Brien's position, I was not to consider them as a picture of his mind. Yet, spite of her, I suspected that they were his own writing, and the effect of feeling; and on this point I resolved to endeavour to procure satisfaction, by giving the paper to him myself, when I thought his manner of receiving it, would be an index to assist me in discovering the secret. But here I was disappointed. When I saw him at dinner I presented the paper, and said that as I found it at the foot of the tree he had just left, I concluded it to be his. He replied with perfect composure, and indifference, that it was so, thanked me, and took no farther notice of the matter.

I began now almost to think that I had made more of the morning's adventure than it deserved, and to persuade myself that the young cynic was only waiting in the wood till Lucy's school was broken up, and he could go and pay his devoirs to her; a conjecture which his looking at his watch and taking the path to the cottages seemed to render very plausible. I therefore went again the next morning, without hesitation, to the same spot, but on approaching it I found Ryder precisely in the attitude that I had seen him the preceding day. I began now to be vexed with myself, and wished to get away unperceived by him, which at first I flattered myself I had done, but looking back after I had gone a little way, I perceived him walking off so much in the same hurried and agitated manner as the day before, that I could not doubt but that I was the cause of it; and from that instant therefore I resolved to forego my usual visits to the spot during his stay at Campbell-House. To this resolution I strictly adhered till this morning, when accident alone, to my inexpressible mortification, led me to transgress it.

Beauchamp and myself passing together through Maxtead churchyard between eleven and twelve o'clock, where we found a great concourse of people assembled, were induced to enquire what had attracted them thither. It was, as indeed we immediately conjectured, a wedding. The master of the public-house at Watchford was to be united in holy wedlock to the bar-maid of the Campbell-Arms, and the bride folks, as the people told us, were expected every moment. In a sportive mood I proposed stopping to attend the ceremony, to which Beauchamp was by no means reluctant, and accordingly when the bride and her beloved came, in a few minutes after, we followed them into church.

The ceremony was performed, the marriage registered, Doctor Paul received his fee, wished the young couple happy, and was walking away. But the bridegroom stopped him, and said, scratching his head, "I hope your honour'll please to let me have my license again?"

"No, Mr. Welton; I must keep that."

"But please your honour what am I to do, then?"

"It is not any concern of yours, Mr. Welton. The licence always remains in the minister's hands."

"I hope not, your honour, for you knows as I can't sell ale, nor nothing else without it."

"Sell ale?—what do you mean?"

"Why your honour knows, being as you be a justice yourself, that nobody can't sell ale without his licence."

The Doctor now for the first time looked at the licence, for as it was growing late when the parties arrived, and he concluded it to be right, he had not concerned himself about it before. But on examination, he found that the good publican had actually brought his ale licence as a passport to the altar of Hymen.[24]

"Hey?—how's this?" cried the Doctor.—"Why this is a licence to sell ale, not a marriage licence. What did you mean by bringing this, you blockhead?"

"Why I din't know, please your honour. My wife here said as we must have a licence, so I thought this would do as well as another."

"What a stupid ass you must be then, not to know the difference between a marriage licence and this. A pretty piece of work you have made of it truly. And now the canonical hours are just over,* and 'tis impossible to get a proper licence and be married to-day; and to-morrow I go out early in the morning, and I shan't be home for the remainder of the week."

"Lawk, your honour, what does that sinnify. If you'll only please to tell me where to go for such a licence as you'll like, I'll have one ready agin you come back, and then 'twill all be right."

"But you will please to take notice that this is no legal marriage; you are no more man and wife now than when you came into church. Take care therefore not to live together as such, till you have procured a proper licence, and are legally married." He then directed Mr. Welton where to get a licence; and once more strictly enjoining the gentleman and lady not to live together as man and wife, upon pain of eternal damnation, he departed.

"Damn un for a proud parson!" muttered the bridegroom, as the Doctor walked off. "But he don't think, I hope, to fob me off thus'ns. What I suppose, because Madam's so good as to let un come a visiting to hern, that he's so proud nothing but a new licence is good enough for un, and be damned to un!"

He was soon joined in his denunciations by all the company, who declared it was monsus hard—that every thing was prepared for keeping the wedding, and the uncle of one was to come from ten miles off, and the cousin of another was to come seven miles, and the plumb-puddings were boiling in the pot, and then for that there Parson Paul for to go and say that they was'n't married because they had'n't got him a new licence. They wished heartily they'd a gone to Watchfur church to be married.

"Come, come, Patty," said the bridegroom, "never mind; we'll be even with the parson. For sartin as he has said us over once, we are married like in the sight of God, and so who cares for what he says? Come, come, let's us go home and have our merry making, and to-morrow I'll go to Watchfur parson, for he's a mort† better tempered than that there Parson Paul; and if he thinks it ben't right, he can ax us at church, and then say us over again, for damn me if yin old fellow shall have his will on us."

"And quite in the right too," said I. "'Tis very hard indeed that the parson should make people be married over and over again as often as he pleases, and put them to the expence of the Lord knows how many wedding dinners."

"Why that's my thought," replied Mr. Welton; "and I humbly thank your honour for taking our part. I meant to have axed un to dinner if he'd been tolerable civil, and I don't believe as ever he'd a better plumb-pudding at his own table, thos he be so mighty. But damn un if he shall taste it now. But your honour seems so free and so good-natured, that if you and

---

* The time of day within which one can be married (i.e., from 8 a.m. to 6 p.m.).

† Great quantity; much.

Squire Baicham would please to take a bit with us, why your honours should both be heartily welcome, and we should take it main kind, shouldn't us, Patty?"

To this Patty assented with a very gracious smile and curtsey, and both Beauchamp and myself liked the humour of the thing so well, that we did not hesitate a moment to accept the invitation, and promised to be at Watchford by two o'clock, the dining hour.

Full of this scene we turned homewards laughing all the way, and anticipating the jokes we expected to fly about at the ensuing entertainment; nor did I attend to which way we were going, till we burst on a sudden upon Ryder in his misanthropic retirement. I was mortified beyond expression, conscious that this appeared on my part like studiously interrupting him; but Beauchamp, ignorant of what had passed before, consequently not aware how irritating this rencounter was to Ryder, facetiously related our adventure, dwelling much on the amusement we expected from the scene to which we were going.

This was more than our misanthrope could bear. With a countenance expressive of the most superlative contempt, and his awful eyes fixed upon me, he exclaimed, "Good God what trifling and levity! how much beneath men, almost beneath school-boys!"

Beauchamp looked excessively astonished. "Why, how's this, Mr. Ryder," said he, "you were not accustomed to be so unreasonably severe upon a harmless joke?"

"For heaven's sake, Mr. Beauchamp," he replied, "do not remind me of my follies, I have suffered enough for them already. A joke was my ruin, and if you go on thus, your peace of mind may be shattered on the same rock before you are aware of it."

"Pardon me, Mr. Ryder. It was not by any means my intention to recal painful recollections to your mind, nor when I made my observation, did I think of the circumstances to which you allude. I simply meant to remark that I never, till very lately, perceived you backward in joining in the good-humoured hilarity that enlivens Campbell-House."

"Nor should I ever object to good-humoured hilarity. I only regret that this has lately degenerated into a puerile levity which every person of sense must despise."

"I really am unconscious of any thing having passed that deserves so severe a censure."

"The promoters of such things are seldom the first to see their folly."

"This is smart I own, Mr. Ryder, but rather going beyond the *retort courteous*; it approaches pretty nearly to the third degree; you know what that is called."

"The *reply churlish*.[25] Your reproof may be just, but I acknowledge myself irritated when I see a woman with Miss Campbell's superior understanding descend to the encouragement of such buffooneries. For my part I can see no real wit, in drawing forth conceited fools to expose themselves for the entertainment of herself and her company."

"You mean, I suppose, to allude to Doctor Paul and Mr. Altham. But if there was any thing censurable in amusing ourselves with their follies, no part of the blame attaches to Miss Campbell, since she rather discouraged, than encouraged the *hoax*, as Mrs. Harrison would call it."

"Was joining in the general laugh a discouragement of those who excited it?"

"Nay, surely, there is nothing so very censurable in laughing at follies she had not sought to promote."

"Or if she did seem disposed to promote them, it was because she knew her company. But would her conduct have appeared less commendable, had she rather sought to correct, than to encourage, such false taste."

"And allow me to ask," I here interposed, "what prospect of success would attend any endeavour to improve Mrs. Harrison's taste? and you will surely not deny that she has uniformly been the principal promoter of the follies you censure."

"I am not clear that though she took the lead in promoting them, others of the company were less gratified than herself. But perhaps your observation may apply as well to them as to her."

"Take care, Sir, how you push this matter too far, lest I be compelled to demand in a more serious manner than you will perhaps like, to whom you allude in the *other's* mentioned so sarcastically."

"My answer would be *qui capit, ille facit.*"*

"For God's sake, Mr. Ryder," said Beauchamp, "have a care what you say, and do not suffer a momentary irritation, which I, who know you well, feel to be foreign to your nature, to involve you in a quarrel with one who wishes to be your friend."

"The gentleman is extremely kind in his wishes; but when I behold such an alteration between Miss Campbell's late and present mode of behaviour, I cannot feel particularly attracted towards those to whom I think a change so disadvantageous is to be principally ascribed."

"Excuse me, Sir," said Beauchamp, "but I really think the alteration is in yourself, not in Miss Campbell."

"Or if she be altered," said I, "'tis evidently not for the worse, since upon the most minute investigation, I have not been able to find a fault either in her principles or conduct."

"We are not apt to condemn those features in the characters of others, which we are conscious are leading ones in our own."

"For heaven's sake," said Beauchamp, "let us separate before this silly altercation gets to a height that may produce the most fatal consequences. Something has irritated you, Mr. Ryder, I do not pretend to enquire what, but appeal to your own superior understanding, to decide whether you are not acting very unreasonably in thus giving vent to your chagrin? I speak freely, because from the bottom of my soul I wish to avert the mischief I

---

*   Latin proverb: "He who takes it to himself has done it."

see impending. Come, Mr. Stanhope, let us proceed. A moment's reflection, I am satisfied, will convince Mr. Ryder that he is in the wrong."

Here Beauchamp took hold of my arm to draw me away, but I hung back, for I felt my blood boiling, and was about to reply. He however forced me on: "I insist on your coming with me," he said, "you shall both have time to cool before another word be spoken."

Ryder started, he seemed no sooner to have given vent to his gall, than to be vexed at not having had more command of himself. "Yes, yes," said he, "I am wrong, I feel it and I acknowledge it, and ask Mr. Stanhope's pardon; the fiend within me is suppressed, I am sorry that I suffered him for a moment to obtain the mastery. Let us part friends," and he held out a hand to each, which we accepted, and all was reconciled.

Nor did we suffer Ryder's spleen to prevent our going to our dinner, where we were highly amused. We excused ourselves from staying late, and came home through the wood. There we did not find Ryder himself, but we did find another of his compositions, for his I suspect them both to be. This however we only studied till we had made ourselves perfect in it, and then left it where it was. 'Tis a sort of reverse to the picture drawn in the former, as you shall see.

RECIPROCAL LOVE.

Ah could this panting heart, sweet maid,
　　Which oft breathes secret vows to thee,
But hope its feelings were repaid
　　By thine, tho' not in like degree:

That by some kindred warmth inspir'd,
　　Thy gentle wishes mine would meet,
And when a kiss these lips requi'd,
　　Thine would not coldly shun the treat.

Ah then how fiercely would the flame,
　　Now smothering in my bosom blaze,
In bliss e'en fancy scarce could frame,
　　I then might hope to spend my days.

For such is still great nature's course,
　　That love repaid, encreases love,
And what was once of trifling force,
　　It makes, a flame resistless, prove.

If however both be the production of his muse, not much of the real state of his mind is to be inferred from two such opposite pictures, so I have been impertinent without the end being answered. If you should remark that I am rightly served, I will not dispute the point.

I wish much to hear from you again. Remember, I do not admit as an excuse for silence that you have nothing to say. Tell me only that you are well, it will be much more satisfactory to me to have this ascertained under your own hand-writing, than to be left to conclude it.

I should add, that Ryder was perfectly composed when we returned home in the evening, and rather studiously addressed his conversation to me. Still I am tormented with the idea of what passed in the morning, and dread nothing so much now as giving him offence. Adieu Harry, and believe me with the most sincere regard

Your affectionate

LIONEL STANHOPE.

LETTER XII.

LIONEL STANHOPE
TO
HENRY EGERTON.

Campbell-House, October 6.

I cannot imagine what could be the matter with Ryder the other morning. Something must have ruffled his temper, of which I can form no idea, for he has never since shewn the least symptom of a similar disposition, but on the contrary behaved to me with as much politeness and apparent cordiality as to the rest of the company. Yesterday evening only, did I think for a moment that the same fiend was at work within him, and perhaps even then I was deceived. The fact was indeed, that the galled horse winced,[26] for I was playing the fool with Percival Altham, unobserved by him, as I hoped, though I found that this was a mistake, and when detected I felt myself to be in the wrong.

Doctor Paul, as would appear from my last letter, has been absent for some days. He returned two days ago; and yesterday morning as I was wandering among the flowery meads of Maxtead, Ryder having fairly driven me from its shady groves, I met Percival with a book in his hand, on which he affected to be so extremely intent, that he did not see me. I was resolved to mortify his ridiculous affectation by not taking notice of him, so walked on, well assured that ere I had gone many paces I should be called back. I was not mistaken. He soon started as from a reverie, "Oh is it you Mr. Stanhope?" he said, "I beg ten thousand pardons, but I really was so intent upon my studies that I was not at first sensible of my happiness."

"Your attention was probably engaged upon a much more worthy subject than myself."

"Impossible. Yet I own it was not ill employed—I was reading a most admirable romance."

"One of your own writing?"

"Oh, my dear Sir, you cannot suppose that I would have mentioned it in such a way had it been my own. But *à propos*, I have by me a romance of my own writing, which I should think honoured by your perusal and criticisms."

"You could not have applied to a worse person, Mr. Altham; I am no critic."

"Oh pardon me, Sir; this is only your own humility. I have heard remarks from you which convince me that you are a most able and judicious one."

"I certainly will read the work if you wish it, though I am satisfied it will be rather to commend than criticise."

"Dear Sir, you do me too much honour. But I do flatter myself there are things in it of which I have no reason to be ashamed. With your permission, then, I will put it in my pocket this evening, as my uncle and I are to be at Campbell-House."

In the evening it was accordingly produced, and laid upon the table; not, I believe, without a secret hope on the part of the author that he should be requested to read it for the entertainment of the company. And in good truth, Harry, had Ryder not been present I had very probably proposed it.

Percival himself happening to sit by the table, ever and anon drew the darling babe towards him, turned over the leaves for some minutes, yet could not attract the notice of the company, for which, doubtless, he thought them very dull and insensible.

I, sitting on the opposite side of the table, once or twice followed the author's example in turning over the manuscript for a few minutes; and at length, perceiving Ryder earnestly engaged in an argument with Beauchamp, with his back rather turned towards me, I ventured to say slyly to Altham—"This is a romance, I think you said, Sir, not a novel?"

"A romance at your service, Mr. Stanhope. Do allow me to read you a passage or two—you are musical, I think?"

"I am extremely fond of music, though a very humble performer."

"But you undoubtedly understand enough of it to feel the force of this passage; I must read it."

"Excuse me, I fear we shall disturb the company."

"Oh no; you see they are all engaged in different parties, and we are left as it were tête-à-tête. Permit me therefore"—and turning to the passage, he read—"There are moments in which that something which custom has termed sympathy, but which truth must denominate nature, will unfold the genuine affections of the heart, in spite of all our endeavours to conceal them; and if there be a power which is calculated beyond all others to draw forth that graceful weakness, that undescribable charm which shews the human mind in all its softest attractions, it is certainly

MUSIC. The human voice acquires something celestial when tutored to the strains of harmony. All the grosser parts of our natures seem to refine by the vibration of sweet sounds; and the being blessed with that soul seducing power, while it is exercised resembles an immortal."

"Very fine indeed," said I. "Indeed I do not wonder, Mr. Altham, that you pride yourself somewhat upon a passage so far above the comprehension of vulgar minds. The man of common capacity certainly could not immediately see your drift in it; nay might even be led to doubt whether the author, in writing it, had one clear idea in his head—but genius, soaring genius, Mr. Altham—oh how little are its effusions understood by the mass!"

"You really do think it fine, then?—Well, I am vastly happy to have it sanctioned by so good a judge, for I assure you that I have taken more pains with that period than with any other in the whole work."

"And yet there are others, I think, Mr. Altham, which bear no less the stamp of aspiring genius disdaining vulgar trammels. As for instance the making your hero a Creole,[27] the offspring of an Emperor of Morocco, and a Circassian slave whom he purchased at Jamaica, is certainly no common idea;[28]—and your heroine singing airs of Metastasio,[29] though the chronology of your work is three hundred years antecedent to the time when that great poet lived, is an anachronism on which none but a very superior mind would have ventured. I admire too, no less, her singing them as she lay reclined on a bank crowned with *verdure* of a *thousand dies*.[30] One thing only perplexes me, and that is how Sir Hubert could distinguish the track of chariot-wheels in the midst of a thick forest, and in a violent storm of rain and hail, in the middle of one of the darkest nights ever known."

I had now mounted my hobby, and was driving on at a most inconsiderate rate, Percival gaping and staring, as if not understanding me much better than I understood his rhapsodical jargon upon music, when suddenly turning my eyes a little to the left, I beheld Ryder's awful brow contracted into a frown, and for worlds I could not have uttered another syllable. On the contrary, by an almost involuntary impulse, I rose from my seat, and removed to one that was vacant between him and Mrs. Harrison. Why do I feel such awe of this man?—Is it pusillanimity, or merely the irresistible feeling of superior powers? I am willing to excuse myself, by ascribing it to the latter cause. Be this as it may, my forbearance seemed to make a strong impression upon my censor, for his countenance was instantly overspread with a glow of satisfaction that such a countenance alone could have expressed.

Never have I seen him appear to greater advantage than he did for the remainder of the evening—never did I listen to conversation more entertaining or more brilliant. He related a variety of amusing anecdotes of his stay at Gibraltar, as well as of his academical career at Cambridge. But, as if for a judgment upon him, it now became his turn to amuse the company at Doctor Paul's expence, for among other Cambridge anecdotes, he stumbled upon the following story:

"Some years prior to his admission, a Mr. Inglefield, one of the Fellows of his college, was appointed by Mr. Watson, rector of the parish of C——, near Cambridge to his curacy. This was a particularly acceptable addition of income to Mr. Inglefield, as he had a mother and sister in very strait circumstances, whom he wished to assist, but to whom little could be spared out of the mere profits of his fellowship. His happiness however in this promotion was not of long duration; an unfortunate propensity to electioneering in the Bishop of the diocese became the occasion of its speedy overthrow."

I saw Doctor Paul look somewhat confused, and as if he did not greatly relish the commencement of this story. This I attributed to his jealous regard for the honour of the cloth, which led him to be alarmed lest any anecdotes should appear not entirely to the worthy metropolitan's credit. But Ryder, without attending to him, proceeded with his story.

"Not long before Mr. Inglefield's appointment to the curacy, a general election had taken place. In this a clergyman in another county, in which our Bishop had some property, had been of great service in assisting to bring in the candidate espoused by his Lordship, in return for which the spiritual Peer promised to do something for a son of this clergyman's, then resident at Cambridge, and recently ordained to the service of the church."

Doctor Paul drew out his pocket-handkerchief, blew his nose, twisted round on his chair, threw his arm over the back, and fixed his eyes on the window. Still Ryder paid no regard to him, but continued his history.

"How to fulfil the engagement into which he had entered, became the Bishop's next object, and after revolving various schemes in his mind, he at length discovered that the appointment of Mr. Inglefield to the curacy of C—— was irregular, since the rector himself not residing in the parish, it was necessary that the curate should be licensed by the Bishop, otherwise there was no chance of salvation to the souls of the inhabitants,—and this ecclesiastical sanction had never been even asked for Mr. Inglefield. The Bishop accordingly ejected him from his office, and appointed the son of the clergyman to supply his place, licensing him in all due and proper form.

"Poor Mr. Inglefield wrote immediately to the rector of the parish, stating the circumstances of this transaction, and complaining in strong terms of the hardships of his case, deeply regretting the loss of an income which had enabled him to place his mother and sister in a comfortable situation; and he said he felt this the more deeply, from his consciousness that a principal cause of the straitness of their circumstances was, that money had been spent in educating him for the church, which ought to have been saved for their support."

Doctor Paul hemmed two or three times, blew his nose again, and turned to the other side of the chair. Ryder still proceeded:

"But the rector was not of a disposition to submit tamely to an act so arbitrary. His blood could boil as fiercely as that of any Bishop upon the bench, and he was resolved to find some means in foiling his Lordship. To attack him directly was however impossible, since arbitrary as this act appeared, it was no more than was authorised by law. The rector therefore determined to strike the blow through the newly-licensed curate, to whom he immediately wrote as follows:

SIR,

I am apt to believe there has been some damned trick between you and the Bishop of ——, relative to my curacy of C——. I am a stranger to your character but for what your license sets forth, which I will never submit to. The Bishop I well know; his father was a broken merchant at L——, a led Captain, a tool to the late great minister of state, Sir Robert Walpole, who well knew the price of every man. I am descended from a family valuable for achievements for the county, and honesty of mankind, and will never submit to a mitred tool of a Bishop, a state toad-eater. I shall serve my living of C—— myself next Lady-day, therefore quit.

Your humble servant,

Thomas Watson.

P.S. You may exhibit this letter to the Bishop if you please, who I value as little as the dirt under my feet.

"Upon my word," said Sir Francis, "I think his Lordship met with his match—the two divines were well pitted."

"Why lord, uncle," exclaimed Percival, "that's the very letter I have heard my mother talk so much about, which was sent to you when you were at college."

"'Tis very true, nephew," replied the Doctor, "and I am sorry to find that the story has been so grossly misrepresented—I do not mean by Mr. Ryder, but by those from whom he heard it. I wish it were in my power fully to explain the affair, it would then appear in a very different light. But since in doing this I must relate circumstances little to the credit either of Mr. Watson, or Mr. Inglefield, I have always chosen to practise that forbearance my religion teaches, and rather incur odium myself than cast it upon my fellow-creatures."

"A truly Christian spirit indeed," said Sir Francis. "You conceal the truth, and content yourself with throwing out inuendoes which every person interprets according to the way that best suits his malice: thus the characters of both parties are much more effectually stabbed than they could be by direct charges."

"Excuse me, Sir Francis. To you my silence may appear in this light; but he who acts purely from conscientious motives is regardless of the false interpretations that may eventually be put upon his conduct, satisfied with the most grateful of all rewards, the approbation of a higher than human power. Whatever the world therefore may think of the matter, I shall keep the injuries I have received from the two gentlemen in question buried within my own bosom, and only pray that those injuries may never rise up in judgment against them."

"I am extremely apprehensive," replied Sir Francis, "that you will not obtain much credit with the world for being actuated by such pure motives. They will rather suppose your silence arises from a consciousness that the affair will not bear explanation."

"'Tis possible; yet I will never be influenced by such considerations to support my own character at the expence of those of my neighbours."

"Yet, surely, in becoming *"all things to all men,"*[31] this may occasionally be necessary. Supposing you were in company with persons whose constant habit it was to establish their own characters on the ruins of those of others, would you not relax?—would you not then tell how noble had been your own conduct, how unprincipled that of Mr. Inglefield?"

"No, I would still remain silent—for, as I have observed in the sermon I was so unfortunately prevented having the honour of reading to the company, the conformity to our neighbours which I would recommend, consists much more in maintaining silence as to our own opinions than in pretending to adopt theirs."

"Aye, silence is an admirable thing, it leaves so fine a latitude for conjecture, helps a man out so incomparably when he has nothing to the purpose to offer. *Silence* is, next to an *if*, the most able of all peace-makers."

And indeed the Doctor found that he had better take refuge in silence, since the farther he pushed the matter the more he was tormented by his antagonist. He therefore made no answer to the Baronet's last position than by a low bow, and of course the contest ceased.

When he was gone, we all charged Ryder with knowing the Doctor to be a party concerned in this curious transaction; and relating it on purpose to mortify him; an idea in which, to own the truth, I exulted not a little, since I should then have considered myself as at full liberty to *hoax* the Doctor whenever I was so disposed. But he solemnly assured us that he had not the least idea of its touching any of the company present, but merely related the circumstance as one to which the conversation naturally led.

Harry, I must repeat that I am very impatient to hear from you, and shall be seriously uneasy if you delay writing much longer. Surely then you will not refuse to devote half an hour to

Yours most faithfully,

LIONEL STANHOPE.

LETTER XIII.

LIONEL STANHOPE
TO
HENRY EGERTON.

Campbell-House, October 12.

No letter from you yet, Harry? Ah! whence this silence?—'tis most distressing to me. I fear you are not well, or that your mind is too much depressed by your present occupation to permit your writing. But oh, my friend, if this be the case, let me entreat you to employ your steward in the capacity of secretary to tell me so, and I will join you instantly. I blame myself for letting you depart without me. I feel that, however you might desire to be alone, it was a thing to which I ought not to have yielded.

Harry, I have strange things to tell you. That Mrs. Harrison had a taste for discoveries, was evident by the satisfaction she seemed to derive from that she made relative to Chamberry gauze—but a few days ago she made one, or what, at least, she supposed to be one, that gave her infinitely greater pleasure, since it was no less than of an unfortunate lapse made by two of her fellow creatures, one of whom moreover belongs to the class of *clever folks*, the objects of her mortal antipathy.

On the very morning after my last letter was written, when we were all assembled at breakfast excepting Mrs. Harrison and Ryder, the butler delivered an apology from the latter, importing, that in consequence of a letter he had received very early in the morning, he was obliged to set off immediately for Pontefract, nor could he even wait to see Miss Campbell, and make his excuses in person. This message was scarcely repeated, when Mrs. Harrison burst into the room, in a prodigious bustle, and evidently teeming with matters of amazing import. So weighty indeed were they, that she could not even begin her breakfast, though eating is one of the most important of all concerns with her, till she had been delivered of them.

"Well," she said, "so there's been a fine kick up, Nanny's been a telling me, with that Lucy Morgan and Ryder. Well, I always said, my dear, that some day or other you'd get yourself into a confounded scrape about that woman, but you was always so conceited, and would defy the world, and would have a will of your own; but I told you you'd repent, but you never would be for taking of my advice, but you would always be a thinking you was so much wiser than other people, but I hope you'll have enough of your school-mistresses now. Well, I always said, there must be some reason why she would not go to live with that Owen again, but you always would be a despising of my opinion, but I hope you'll be convinced now."

"I beg your pardon, Madam," said Olivia, "I really do not understand you. Has any thing particular happened to Lucy?"

"Lord, my dear, why don't you know that it has just come out that she has had a child by that Ryder, and he's gone away all in a stew and hurry, because he won't perform his promise, and marry her."

"Indeed, Madam, this must be a mistake. Scarcely a day passes that I do not see Lucy, and she could not possibly have had a child lately without my knowledge."

"Lord, my dear, why it is'nt lately. Why the child's two years old, and has been at nurse at the next cottage for a long time, and a hundred pretences have been made about it, but now its all out, and Ryder took it away this morning, and Lucy's been a crying fit to break her heart because he wont marry her."

"Excuse me, Madam, but I can positively assert this to be a mistake, and I hope therefore you will not listen any more to such gossipping stories from your maid."

"Lord, I shall let my maid talk to me if I please, without asking of your leave. Besides I know that this is every word true, for Ryder has paid for the child's nursing ever since it has been there, and Lucy has always been a fondling of it over, and making such a pet of it, that every body said it must be her own."

"That Mr. Ryder has paid for the child's nursing is very true, but that is no proof of its being his own; and with regard to Lucy, 'tis really very hard she could not take notice of a child living at the very next door to her without bringing such an imputation on her own character. I cannot say any thing as to the truth of Mr. Ryder's having taken the child away, but I should think it not very improbable. I shall, however, enquire about it immediately after breakfast."

"Aye, well you may say what you please, and to be sure you'll never own Lucy in the wrong, but I believe it's all true, whether you'll own it or not."

Olivia again remonstrated earnestly with her upon the subject, and endeavoured to make her sensible of the extreme injustice of aspersing a young woman's character upon such very insufficient grounds. But who can reason with so unreasoning a being as Mrs. Harrison?—she only flew into a passion, and used very abusive language to Olivia, to all which the latter made not a syllable of reply, she confined herself to the single point of persisting to vindicate Lucy. But this was crime enough in Mrs. Harrison's eyes; she declared she never in her life was so rudely treated, and she would not stay another minute in the house, unless Olivia would make an apology for her behaviour. To this Olivia replied, that though she should be extremely sorry to see her leave the house in such an abrupt way, and in so much anger, yet she could by no means retract what she had said; she was perfectly assured of Lucy's innocence of this charge, and she must therefore persist in asserting it. This was too much to bear, and ringing the bell violently, while she almost foamed at the mouth, Mrs. Harrison ordered the chariot to be got ready directly, and her maid Nanny to be sent up stairs to pack up her clothes. Then bursting out of the room, with as great eagerness as she had entered it, she desired breakfast to be sent up to her, and in about an hour after, she and her maid drove off, without taking leave of any one.

Had she left the house in a different kind of way, I do not think Olivia would have felt much regret at her departure; but she was very much hurt at seeing her quit it in such a terrible and unjustifiable fit of passion. As soon as she was gone we all took a walk to the cottages, and there found that so much of Mrs. Harrison's story was true as that Ryder had taken his little ward away. He had called for her about seven o'clock that morning, without having given any previous intimation of his intentions, or assigned any reason for departing so hastily.

Nor did we hear more of him till the evening of the third day after this affair, when he made a short stay of about two hours here, and is now, perhaps, gone for ever. Upon his arrival, he first requested a private audience of Olivia, which being granted, he began by expressing a deep sense of his obligations to her, and assuring her that nothing could ever abate his perfect respect and esteem for her character, and then proceeded to say:

"I must entreat, Madam, that however ambiguous my present conduct appears, it may be considered with candour, and not supposed the result of caprice, but of a serious and solemn conviction that I am acting right— though perhaps 'tis needless to ask this of Miss Campbell, whose soul is the seat of candour and liberality itself. I own it, Madam, I did for some time look forward with infinite pleasure to being settled in your neighbourhood in an useful and independent occupation, but circumstances have arisen, I mention the subject with regret, and with the deeper regret, because 'tis impossible they should be explained even to you, which render the execution of this plan impracticable. Nay, how shall I say it? perhaps, Madam, I may never see you more. In what way of life I shall finally settle, is at present wholly undetermined; I only hope, that present or absent I shall still retain your esteem. I am unhappy now, but the loss of that alone could render me completely miserable."

He uttered all this with difficulty, and when he had finished remained silent for a few moments, as if pausing for a reply; but Olivia, lost in astonishment, and deeply affected at a circumstance so unaccountable and unexpected, was unable to utter a syllable. Rising therefore, and with his hand upon his forehead, evidently in great emotion: "You know, Madam," said he, "that I am about to quit England for a short time, may I hope that I carry your esteem with me?"

"Oh that will follow you to the remotest corner of the globe," exclaimed Olivia, too much agitated to say more. Ryder seemed desirous of saying farewell, but unable to pronounce a word so painful, left the room with tears in his eyes.

He went and threw himself down on a bench in the garden, where he remained towards half an hour, and then seeking Beauchamp, they had a short conference, after which he desired a private interview with me. On my appearing he said, "Mr. Stanhope, I have requested this meeting, because I cannot bear to leave the kingdom, which I shall do in a few days, without making a proper apology for the very improper treatment you have more than once, I fear, experienced from me."

"Let what has passed be buried in oblivion I entreat," said I. "If your conduct was not wholly justifiable, I feel that it was not entirely without provocation, since I certainly have indulged too freely in a propensity I acknowledge to be very contemptible, that of amusing myself with the follies of others, and while I fancied I was exposing them, I was in fact exposing myself."

"I shall not deny that I think this has been the case, and believe me I speak solely in friendship, when I advise you to shake off so pernicious a habit; there cannot be a more dangerous one to indulge in, or one more likely to create you numerous and implacable enemies. This species of ridicule is more readily discerned by the objects of it than persons are in general aware, and once seen through, it never can be forgiven. Abuse may be pardoned, but ridicule is of a nature absolutely unpardonable."

"I acknowledge the justice of your admonition, and believe me I shall always bear it in mind, I hope to my future profit."

"Yet, Mr. Stanhope, I am no less sensible that though you might be wrong, I had no authority to assume to myself the office of censor of the company, and consider them as responsible to me for all that passed. In particular I must acknowledge the impropriety of the manner in which my irritated feelings were once expressed. But believe me, my heart was wounded beyond what human nature could support; would to God that it were in my power to expose it undisguised before you! but, circumstanced as I am, that were only to render myself ten times more culpable."

"You have said enough, nor have I any claim to expect such confidence. Of this, however, I am assured, that the man who can so candidly acknowledge a fault, could only be betrayed into its commission by feelings too powerful to be resisted."

"You do me no more than justice. I am placed in no common situation, and my life is now a constant struggle between inclination and principle. But enough of this; my present object is to restore myself to your good opinion, since the forbearance you have opposed to my hasty sallies, has fixed you irrevocably in mine."

"Pray say no more, Mr. Ryder, you shame me. Compliments so undeserved, only make me feel less in my own eyes."

"Were they undeserved I were the last person in the world to bestow them. Believe me I have uttered the genuine sentiments of my heart, and I hope we part in friendship."

"As your friend I always wished to be considered, even before we were personally acquainted; but never did I consider your friendship so valuable as I do at this moment."

"You had then conceived a favourable opinion of me prior to our meeting?"

"Who could pass many days at Campbell-House without conceiving a strong prepossession in Mr. Ryder's favour? Who could hear his story, and not be interested in his fate?"

He started, he paused a moment, his soul seemed deeply agitated; at length he said, "You have then heard my story, and are acquainted with the circumstances which first introduced me to the knowledge of Miss Campbell?"

"I am, and most sincerely wish that all persons who like her possess ample fortunes, would employ them in promoting the happiness of others."

"I am not sure that hers has been employed in promoting my happiness. Yet let me not be understood as meaning to detract from the generosity and benevolence of her conduct; I acknowledge them with gratitude, I admire her character from my soul; but I had perhaps been happier had she never heard of such a being as myself."

"Oh were such an idea suggested to her, how would it wound her benevolent heart!"

"You have a high opinion of the excellence of her heart?"

"Good God! who can know and not admire it?"

"I perfectly agree with you. What pity therefore that her person should be so little attractive."

"Why must that subject be so constantly dwelt upon? She is plain, I acknowledge, but do we think a pearl the less valuable for being encased in an oyster-shell?"

"Do we value the pearl at all till taken out of the shell? And, to speak without metaphor, I fear there are few persons with sense enough to think that Miss Campbell's heart would not be much more valuable if associated with a lovely face."

"Such persons are surely very unreasonable."

"Are not the majority of mankind unreasonable?"

"Some surely might be found who think otherwise."

"We are said commonly to judge of others by ourselves; may I suppose that the case now?"

"Assuredly!—Mr. Ryder, not long after I came hither, from a sudden impulse of admiration at hearing some particular instance of her benevolence, I exclaimed that I did not think the brightest eyes, or the loveliest form, could add one ray of lustre to such a soul as hers; and with my hand here solemnly laid upon my heart I can declare, that every hour I have since passed under her roof, has more and more strongly confirmed me in this opinion."

"Yet you never wished to possess so inestimable a treasure? 'Tis to be regretted; few persons are equally sensible of its value."

"You do not think me unworthy to possess it?"

"Those best deserve a treasure who are most sensible of its value."

"And you would not think it presumption in me to have aspired to its possession?"

"Who could think so? Not a being alive but must acknowledge this no disproportionate match."

"Miss Campbell however might think differently of the matter."

"She *might* undoubtedly, but I cannot suppose she *would*."

"She may not think the match disproportionate, but she certainly has some objection to it."

"How? You astonish me!"

"A man is not in general very ready to acknowledge that his offers have been rejected, but since we have gone thus far, I will confess that 'tis even so."

"My God! This is most unaccountable!"

"Not at all so. I had given her sufficient reason to despise me, and she will not marry a man whom she cannot respect."

"Good God! Good God!" He was silent for some minutes, his countenance was full of emotion, some mighty conflict seemed to agitate his soul. At length he said, "There is yet one thing more I must mention, Mr. Stanhope. You have heard me accused as the seducer of a young woman, whose situation here is of a nature so peculiar, as inconceivably to enhance the criminality of any attempt to delude her into a renewal of her past errors. Of an attempt so atrocious, believe me I am guiltless. The child in question is neither mine nor Lucy Morgan's. Austerity in its grandfather precludes its parents from owning it at present, and in friendship to them I have undertaken to be its guardian. With Miss Campbell's approbation I placed it to nurse in her neighbourhood, and such has been her kind attention to its infancy, that the poor babe has scarcely known the want of a mother. From a situation so advantageous I have, to my regret, been obliged to remove my little charge very hastily, nor know I whether she ever will return to it. And now, Mr. Stanhope, farewell! I am, as I said before, about to quit this kingdom, for how long a time I cannot say. Oh could I hope to find peace of mind in another country, never more would I revisit this!" A tear trembled in his eye, his voice began to falter, he pressed my hand and departed.

And now, Harry, tell me what I am to think of all this? Can it be that he himself loves Olivia, and is assured that she loves me? What else could he mean by the astonishment he expressed at hearing that she had refused me? Yet if she really loves me, and I have sometimes flattered myself, notwithstanding what has passed, that this is the case, how is her conduct to be accounted for? Oh would to heaven I could be satisfied that her heart were mine, and mine alone! Then by the immortal powers above I swear, that without referring to the past, I would instantly defy all senseless sneers and sarcasms, and urge my suit again with an ardour to which she could not choose but yield. Yes, I would not cease the pursuit till I had carried my point, convinced that in her society I should find all that can render life valuable, and that the man who possessed such blessings would be wholly undeserving of his happiness, could he consider for one moment what were the features of a woman with such a heart.

Adieu my dearest, my ever-valued friend, and believe me with the utmost sincerity,

Your affectionate

LIONEL STANHOPE.

LETTER XIV.

LIONEL STANHOPE
TO
ORLANDO ST. JOHN.

Campbell-House, October 12.

Orlando, I am intoxicated! Oh she is beautiful! She must be beautiful! or at least Beauchamp is perfectly right in saving, as he has done repeatedly, that 'tis impossible to be long acquainted with her, without losing all idea of the plainness of her features in admiration of her benevolence and accomplishments.

That I had not attained to the complete knowledge of the former I was very sensible, for extensively as that is diffused, and transcendent as are her virtues, to gain a perfect knowledge of them is no easy matter. But accomplishments are confined within limits so much more circumscribed, that I did not imagine after passing many weeks in the house with her, any one with which she was enriched could remain unknown to me. Yet I have only now discovered a talent which few persons possessing it in the eminence she does, would not have thrust upon my notice long ago.

I have for some time perceived that she possessed a considerable degree of skill in music, both from the taste with which I have heard her accompany singing on the Piano-forte, and from the manner in which I have heard her converse upon the subject, which plainly shewed great knowledge of it as a science. But it still remained for me to learn that she was the finest performer I ever heard upon my favourite instrument, the harp.

This morning as Beauchamp and myself were sitting at our studies under the shade of a noble oak not far from the library windows, my attention was suddenly arrested by strains so enchanting, that I could scarcely believe they came from mortal hands. I instantly started, and dropped my book, exclaiming in transport, "Heavens! whence come those sounds? 'tis nothing less surely than the music of the spheres themselves!"[32]

"As that is a species of music with which I am totally unacquainted," said Beauchamp, "I will not pretend to say how far this may rival it, but she certainly is a very fine performer."

"*She?* Good God! whom do you mean?"

"Miss Campbell."

"Heavens and earth! Is she then so divine a performer on that most enchanting of all instruments, and has it been concealed from me till this moment? Oh why was it kept such a secret?"

"It has not been kept a secret, but the harp was sent to London some time ago to be repaired, and did not return till last night."

"But how extraordinary that I should never have heard this accomplishment mentioned by herself or any one else."

"Miss Campbell never wishes any talent she possesses to be made the subject of conversation. If this will prove a source of entertainment to you it will give her great pleasure, and she will play to you whenever you please."

Away I flew to the library in such mingled astonishment and extasy, that I could not forbear breaking into enthusiastic expressions of admiration, which I afterwards thought bordered too nearly upon some of poor Harry's rhapsodies, though here they were really and truly the *genuine effusions of the heart*. I then apologised for my intrusion, and only begged permission to stay and listen as long as she should continue playing. To this she very obligingly assented, but said I should hear her to great disadvantage, both as she had been long out of practice, and had not yet put the instrument into proper tune. But, oh heavens! if such was her performance under these disadvantages, what must it be when they are removed?

After playing for near two hours, I expressed my astonishment that so long as I had been in the house, I had never heard her mention this talent. "Why should it have been mentioned?" she replied. "It was not from a desire of fame that I sought the acquisition of it, but partly for my own amusement, and still more with a view of contributing to the entertainment of an infirm father, whose confinement I was anxious to alleviate by every means in my power."

"And may I ask how you could procure instruction? You must have had it from a very superior performer to arrive at such proficiency."

"I received my first instructions from a poor Welchman, and after his death for several summers successively I was attended by a very excellent master from London. To the latter I am principally indebted for the progress I have made, yet I must own that the simple unsophisticated child of St. David[33] was always my greatest favourite. There was something in that man's appearance and story uncommonly interesting. Affliction drove him forth a wanderer from his own home and country; his unsettled mind hoped in change of scene to find a charm to soothe its sorrows, but melancholy still preyed upon his mind and brought him at length to the grave. I have his harp still in my possession, and shall always keep it as a memorial of him, though it is too much decayed and out of repair ever to be used."

"Were you long his pupil?"

"Two years. He wandered hither by accident, and was first noticed by the servants, who, charmed with an instrument to which they were till then entire strangers, invited him into their hall to play to them. They soon thought that he might also afford some amusement to my father and myself, and mentioned him to us, when we immediately sent for him. We were both much delighted not only with his harp, but with himself, and entering into conversation we soon learned that he had been in good circumstances, but losing an only daughter just grown up, in whom his whole soul was wrapped, his mind became unsettled, his affairs were neglected, and his harp alone had power for a moment to chase despair from his heart. But after a while he was seized with a sudden fancy to wander, and set out with his harp as his sole source of solace and support."

"Poor fellow! His rugged mountains then proved no barrier against the intrusion of sorrow."

"Alas no! These are afflictions that penetrate even into the remotest seclusions, and 'tis there that they are felt the most severely. Amid the tumult of a capital, where a thousand objects distract the attention, his Winifred had perhaps been forgotten; but in a solitary cottage at the foot of a rugged mountain, she was his all, his world, and every day's experience but made him more and more sensible of his loss. I have a song by me which he wrote to the memory of his child, adapted to one of the most plaintive airs of his country. You shall hear it."

And she gave me the words, Orlando, to read as she played the air. Here they are, and tell me now if you can conceive any thing more affecting than to have heard Llwellin sing this as he sat on the grave of his Winny, which was his constant practice every night, from the time it was composed till he left the country.

THE HARPER'S LAMENTATION.

When the wind rocks the trees, and the sea fiercely roars,
And the big-swelling billows with surge dash the shores,
Oh it soothes my torn heart the storm's fury to brave,
While it waves the long grass that grows o'er my child's grave.

From the clouds when in torrents descend the chill rains,
And the streams from the mountains pour down on the plains,
How I love my parch'd limbs in the waters to lave,
As they wet the cold sods that lie o'er my child's grave.

When the winter's hoar blasts ravage nature around,
And with one whiten'd surface the snow spreads the ground;
From the snow or the blast still no shelter I crave,
For I wish but to rest on my hapless child's grave.

She was once the delight and the pride of the green,
But she's gone, and there's nothing in life's vacant scene

Can her father's gray hairs from distraction now save,
But they'll sorr'wing descend to his only child's grave.

A tear of sympathy stole down Olivia's cheek as she drew from her lyre strains so simple, yet so plaintive and so pathetic, that they could scarcely be heard unmoved even by those least accustomed to the "melting mood."[34] Another drop that trembled in her eye she wiped away. I wished to have said, remove it not, the eye illumined by the tear of compassion cannot fail to be brilliant. "Ah," she said, as she finished, "you hear this but imperfectly, his own feelings alone could give full effect to a melody so mournful."

"And," said I, "from that moment he was received into your house?"

"Not quite so. This indeed was proposed to him, but preferring to live by himself, he was immediately established in the cottage where now live his two countrywomen Lucy Morgan and her mother, which was then just finished. Here in summer evenings his neighbours used to throng around him and listen to his artless strains, nor was any one more known or beloved for several miles round than honest Llwellin. Often was he entreated to play at the country wakes and fairs, but these festive meetings suited not the sadness of his soul, nor could he ever be persuaded to join in them. Placid composure sat on his brow, but sorrow preyed on his vitals, and after two years more put an end to his life. His funeral was attended by all who had been charmed with his strains, and never was mould'ring dust watered with a greater profusion of unfeigned tears."

"Alas! there are wounds so deep that no cares, no kindness, can heal them."

"Too true! Yet one satisfiaction we had, in the hope that his latter days were perhaps less miserable than if we had not known him."

"Oh God! what a blessing is fortune when thus devoted to soothing the miseries and promoting the happiness of all around us!"

"Yes, fortune has blessings peculiarly its own, but is not without its concomitant cares and sorrows. Moments of the purest delight it may impart to the soul in the consciousness that it has been rendered subservient to the happiness of others, yet there are also moments when we cannot but deeply feel how powerless it is to insure our own."

She seemed almost overpowered with the reflections passing in her bosom as she made this observation. An expression of benign sadness overspread her features, which methought, if it did not render them beautiful, gave them at least at the moment an interest that beauty itself could not have increased, and I felt myself so irresistibly affected, that I was obliged to rise and go to the window to conceal my emotion. What could her words import? That she is herself unhappy? And whence can originate this unhappiness? Ryder said he was to quit the kingdom, and he parted from me in emotion similar to those I had now observed in Olivia, while a kind of mystery was thrown over the words of both. Ah! these are assuredly links of the same chain! doubtless they are strongly attached to each other, yet some secret mysterious cause prevents their forming an union equally the wish of both. This, this alone explains the conduct of both, this accounts for the rejection of my offer.

I was in the midst of these reflections when Olivia began again to touch the harp strings. I turned round, her countenance was become serene, and I sat down by her. To what this interesting scene might ultimately have led, had it been suffered to continue, I know not, but at this instant the door opened, and in came Sir Francis and Beauchamp. Heavens! with what a glow of satisfaction was the Baronet's countenance illumined at finding Olivia and me thus alone together. Yet there was a mixture of mortification to alloy his transport, in the idea he had thus unseasonably interrupted a tête-à-tête from which he augured so much good. He would therefore instantly have withdrawn upon some slight pretence, but Olivia detained him, as she said she had gotten some new music which she wished him to hear, for she thought it would suit his taste.

St. John, what a revolution has Campbell-House effected in my sentiments. I entered it fully possessed with the opinion that a woman who was not handsome was an animal just to be tolerated in society, and no more; but I am now much more strongly convinced that beauty is a mere trifle when put in comparison with such superior qualities of the mind as I have long been in the daily habit of contemplating. Yes, Orlando, I do assure you that I reason upon the instability of the one, and the stability of the other, with such true philosophical precision, that were you to hear me you would scarcely think it possible you could be listening to Lionel Stanhope. I entered Campbell-House, besides, little prejudiced in favour of matrimony, and disposed to think it a yoke from which every wise man would shrink; but I would now earnestly recommend it to the wisest, and only regret that I have no immediate prospect of entering into the state myself.

Next week, Orlando, I am to become the object of your confirmed envy, for in the course of it the Scarborough party are expected here. Peggy Perkins, however, does not accompany them. I have already been introduced to her, and admire her as much as you do. Many days have now elapsed since she suddenly appeared at the door of Mrs. Stapleton's house at Doncaster, saying, that if convenient she was come to pass some time with her. With this lady she two or three years since became acquainted at Bath, where they soon grew such *dear friends*, that Mrs. Stapleton, on quitting the place, invited Peggy to come and stay with her whenever it would be agreeable, but the moment when it would be so has only now arrived. Unable any longer to endure being under the same roof with such a *bitter enemy* as Mr. Tichfield, yet scarcely knowing whither to fly, Mrs. Stapleton's invitation suddenly rushed into her mind; a chaise was instantly ordered, and she set off post for Doncaster. Mrs. Stapleton was rejoiced to find herself not entirely forgotten by her young friend; Peggy was rejoiced at having escaped from the persecutions she had endured at Scarborough, and all is at present halcyon days between them—while Mrs. Harrison is a thinking that Miss Perkins is worth a dozen of your Miss Campbells. So does not think

Yours very faithfully,

LIONEL STANHOPE.

LETTER XV.

LIONEL STANHOPE
TO
HENRY EGERTON.

Campbell-House, October 18.

Oh Harry! why do you not write to me?—This suspense is insupportable—'tis agony!—what am I to think of it?—By that sacred friendship which has so long united us, I call on you, I conjure you, to write instantly, though it be no more than to say, "*I am well.*" If I do not hear of you by the return of the post I shall set off immediately for Arrenton, convinced that illness alone can occasion your silence.

Harry, I am myself perplexed and irritated beyond expression. "*What a piece of work is man!*"[35]—Who could have imagined, after what had passed between Ryder and myself at his departure, that he still retained any enmity towards me?—that he could, even at that moment, be brooding over a supposed injury he had received at my hands, and meditating on so contemptible a mode as he has since adopted, of giving vent to his indignation. Fortunate is it perhaps for both that seas now divide us, and that he is placed out of reach of the vengeance he has provoked, for no common satisfaction could atone for such behaviour. Unmanly slander!—first to traduce my character so shamefully, then in mockery to call upon me to answer his charges as a gentleman; yet to shun himself the meeting he had summoned, and, as the climax of all, to shelter himself from my just, just resentment, by skulking meanly out of the kingdom.

Read the following letter, Harry, and then form your own opinion of Ryder's character. To me 'tis now fully developed, and I am only astonished that he has been able so long to impose himself upon people of any discernment as a man of honour and integrity:

SIR,

How artfully soever your illicit intercourse with the deluded woman I had madly intended to make my wife has been carried on, I rejoice to say that your guilt, and her shame, now stand fully detected. My heart, I own, is deeply wounded at finding one I so tenderly loved thus base and false; nor is my pride much less mortified that I could be duped into believing her a sincere penitent, and could consequently think of uniting myself with a woman once so dishonoured. Oh! never can I be sufficiently thankful to that Being who has opened my eyes before my disgrace was inevitably sealed.

But though, from this moment, I cast the faithless Lucy from my heart for ever, I shall take no other method of testifying to her the regret and resentment I feel for her conduct than silent contempt—her sex protects her from my farther indignation. But with you, Mr. Stanhope, 'tis otherwise, and I call upon you to answer as a gentleman for the injury my honour has sustained by your base seduction of this unfortunate creature.—Oh shame! shame!—had she not suffered enough from her former lapse, but must you replunge her into the state of ignominy from which she had just emerged?—This, then, was the errand that attracted you so much to the wood—this it was that occasioned your repeated intrusions on my beloved solitude.

I shall not expect any other answer than your personal attendance to-morrow morning at seven o'clock, at the ruins of St. Martin's monastery, where you will find waiting to receive you,

Sir, your humble servant,

Richard Ryder.

This letter was given to me during dinner two days ago, but, astonished as I was at its contents, I had yet sufficient command of myself not to betray any emotion, but simply to enquire how it came, when I was informed that it was brought by a ragged gypsey-like appearing man, who said he was merely ordered to leave it.

As soon as we rose from table, I took Beauchamp aside, and imparted the letter to him. He was not less astonished than myself, and eagerly enquired whether there was any foundation for the charge. I assured him solemnly that nothing could be more unfounded—that I had never entertained the most distant idea of a dishonourable connection with Lucy, nor could I imagine what had created such a suspicion. During the whole time of my stay at Campbell-House, I said, I had been but twice in her cottage, the first time when I appeared as her champion against Owen, and once afterwards, when he might recollect our calling in to see little Fanny, and Ryder's ward. Upon this assurance Beauchamp promised to accompany me on the next morning to my appointment, when, he said, unless he was extremely mistaken in Ryder's character, he had no doubt of our settling the matter without coming to extremities.

To St. Martin's, therefore, we repaired at seven o'clock, and waited there two hours, without Ryder's appearing, or sending any apology for his absence. I was then, and not without reason, thoroughly incensed against him, and vehemently swore that if he was above ground I would find him out, and both should not quit the field alive.

But Beauchamp, somewhat more calm than myself, had sense enough to prevent my setting out on such a wild-goose chace, and compromised the matter by consenting to accompany me instantly to Pontefract, when, if we did not find the delinquent, I engaged to let the affair rest till his return. We accordingly went to a farmhouse at a short distance from St. Martin's, and there got a pen and ink to write a note of apology for our absence to Olivia, and sending it off to Campbell-House, we proceeded to the place of our destination.

We arrived there, however, too late; Ryder had left Pontefract very early in the morning, so in compliance with my engagement to Beauchamp, I prepared myself to go peaceably home. But I solemnly swore that at whatever distance of time the delinquent might return, he should not find my thirst for vengeance slaked, but that the last drop of my blood should, if necessary, be spilled in obtaining the satisfaction for which my soul so eagerly panted. I entreated Beauchamp, in the mean time, to let the whole transaction remain a profound secret between him and myself, which he faithfully promised. From you only, Harry, I could not withhold it, satisfied that the secrecy I enjoined him will be equally observed by you.

And now tell me, if you can, what I am to think of this affair. It seems altogether of a nature so strange and unaccountable, that Beauchamp has once or twice suggested a doubt whether the challenge really came from Ryder, or whether it was not sent by some other person, either from a mistaken idea of joke, or a diabolical purpose of creating mischief and dissension. I shall certainly take all possible pains to search out the bearer of the letter, and endeavour to learn such farther particulars from him as may throw some light upon the business. Beauchamp, however, while he doubts the authenticity of the letter, yet owns that he believes the handwriting to be Ryder's. But adieu for the present; I am called away.

* * * * *

I resume my pen, Harry, not to elucidate the extraordinary circumstances detailed above, but to give the whole transaction, if possible, a more unaccountable appearance.

It was to Beauchamp I was summoned when I broke off. He said he had been debating strongly with himself whether or not to impart to me some farther particulars respecting Ryder, which he could not help conceiving to be connected with the challenge; and had at length determined that they had better be imparted.

"You may remember," said he, "that on the last day he was here, he had a private conference with me, as well as Miss Campbell and yourself. His business with me, was to put into my hands the following letter, which he had received a few days before, and to request that I would if possible trace out the author of it, since his unavoidable absence from the kingdom precluded the possibility of his making the investigation himself."

Sir,

I am one among a considerable number of persons who have long contemplated with astonishment the extraordinary and eccentric manner in which Miss Campbell conducts herself. That she has uniformly defied all the rules decorum prescribes to her sex, is too notorious to need being dwelt upon, but never has her conduct appeared in a light so truly censurable, as it must now be viewed, both with reference to Mr. Stanhope and yourself. The terms on which you have always been received at her house, naturally led every one to suppose a connection of the nearest and dearest nature, to be a thing determined on, and speedily to be concluded between you and her, nor would any woman but herself have acted as she has done without such views.

But behold it appears that this seeming preference of you, was only an artful plan to make you her tool for bringing Mr. Stanhope, to whom she has been attached from the first moment of their acquaintance, to an explanation of his sentiments. Yet as she never can proceed in the way usual among people of *common* capacities, this marriage is to be concluded with a suddenness and privacy that shall astonish the whole neighbourhood. To-morrow morning at eight o'clock their hands are to be joined by Doctor Paul, in Maxstead church, in the presence only of Mr. Beauchamp and Miss Campbell's favourite Lucy Morgan. Even Sir Francis is to know nothing of the matter till the ceremony is performed, and he is to be surprised at breakfast by being presented with a daughter-in-law.

But as this presentation may probably not be so agreeable a surprise to you, Sir, as to the good Baronet, information of it is sent you by one who compassionates your situation, who feels for such a disappointment of all your hopes, and who thinks that the stroke may be somewhat palliated by not coming upon you entirely unprepared. Anonymous communications, I am sensible, are little entitled to attention, but the accuracy of this intelligence, believe me, Sir, may be depended on, and you will easily see the hazard incurred had it been sent in any other form.

It was to procure the licence and ring that Mr. Stanhope and Mr. Beauchamp were at Doncaster this morning, and to settle the matter with Doctor Paul that they called upon him at their return.

I am, Sir,

Very faithfully yours,

&c. &c.

"This letter," continued Beauchamp, "Mr. Ryder said was given him by a man on horseback whom he met upon the road as he was taking his accustomed walk very early in the morning, and who rode hastily away the moment he had delivered it. He was struck and astonished beyond measure, and his first impulse was to carry the letter immediately to Olivia; but this idea was soon relinquished, as he could not but see that there would be a great degree of indelicacy in it towards her, and he only resolved if possible to trace out its author, in silence, and secrecy. "Nor," he added, "should he have imparted the circumstance even to me, only that being obliged himself to leave the kingdom, his own pursuit of the affair was rendered impossible."

"And did he make no remarks upon the contents of the letter?" said I.

"Not one. Yet he seemed violently agitated as he talked upon the subject, and when he put the letter into my hands, his own trembled to a degree for which I thought the mere circumstance itself no adequate cause."

"And have you," said I, "discovered either the author or the bearer of the letter?"

"I have not yet had time to make such enquiries as were likely to be attended with success; but may we not suspect that the challenge and this letter are in some way connected together, and are the joint offspring of a regular and determined plan for setting you and Mr. Ryder at variance. Who can tell what other insinuations may have reached him, and perhaps almost unknown to himself had some influence in the asperity with which he censured your general conduct."

"Good God! but what motives can any one have for wishing to promote this animosity between us?"

"'Tis impossible to say. Perhaps they may be the intrigues of some rejected lover of Miss Campbell's, who in revenge for his own disappointment, wishes to foil every other suitor who has a better prospect of success. But pass we these speculations, for I have yet more to tell you. I called this morning upon Doctor Paul on a piece of parish business, when he having somebody else with him, I was conducted into the parlour to Percival Altham. The sprightly youth, with his accustomed loquacity, immediately commenced an ample detail of all the news of the neighbourhood collected since he was last at Campbell-House, not any of which was worth attending to, excepting that yesterday morning, at the very time we must have been waiting for Ryder at St. Martin's, he was met by the Doctor's servant in a post-chaise, with a young woman and the mysterious child lately at nurse here, upon the road to London."

"Gracious heavens! still more and more extraordinary!"

"Yes, the whole business is utterly incomprehensible. But since I expect every moment to be summoned to attend Miss Campbell to Lucy's cottage, let me say all that remains."

He then proceeded to make an elaborate apology for not having faithfully adhered to his promise of secrecy on the subject of the challenge, but he said, as Miss Campbell had got some confused notion of our expedition yesterday morning being upon an affair of honour, she had pressed him so closely upon the subject, that he thought it better at once fairly and honestly to tell her the whole story. It was by means of Jerry, the ever-watchful, ever-inquisitive Mr. Jerry, that the suspicion came round to her. When I was about to depart for St. Martin's, I searched for my pistols, but no where could I find them. In a tumult of agitation and vexation I rang for my good valet, and enquired whether he knew any thing about them?

but he had not seen 'em, he said, niver sin he came into the house. At length I recollected that I had never had them since the night of my encounter with the ghost, and that they were therefore probably left in the haunted room.

This recollection by no means helped me out of my difficulty. I dared not ask for admission into that room, lest my motive should be enquired into, and on its being known that I wanted my pistols, an alarm of the occasion for which they were wanted should be excited in the house. I was obliged therefore to depart without them, and borrow Beauchamp's for the encounter. But Jerry, who, good soul, is as communicative as he is inquisitive, could not resist talking to the servants about my loss, and wondering whether the pistols really were left in that room, and wondering still more what I could want with them at that time in the morning, till at length, through the medium of Mrs. Jenny, these speculations reached the ear of Olivia herself.

When she learned the whole story she was not less astonished than we had been before her, and said she had no idea that Ryder ever had entertained any thoughts of marrying Lucy, much less that he was absolutely engaged to her; nay, she thought this impossible, since she knew that Lucy had encouraged the visits of a farmer in the parish, upon terms on which she ought not to have received him, supposing Ryder to be paying his addresses to her. She said however, that she would talk to Lucy upon the subject, and if it should appear that she had been encouraging two lovers at a time, she should reprehend her very severely. Before I close my letter, I may perhaps be able to send you the result of this investigation.

* * * * *

Yes, Harry, the investigation is over, and Lucy declares that Ryder never gave her the least reason to suppose he had any partiality for her. She said that she indeed saw him often when he came to visit his little ward, and he seemed pleased with her taking notice of the child, but she believes he never was in her house above three or four times in his life, and then only came because Maria was there. Lucy owned besides, that she had actually engaged herself to Mr. Boswell, the farmer to whom Olivia alluded, and only waited for a favourable opportunity to mention the affair to her patroness, and express her hopes that the match would meet with her approbation.

When Beauchamp told me this, he added, "I confess I was surprised at what Lucy said with regard to Mr. Ryder, since I always concluded that the visits he made ostensibly to the little Maria, were in reality intended for the school-mistress, and I believe I once said as much to you, Mr. Stanhope."

"You did, and I was not a little astonished at hearing it. But we daily see such very extraordinary matches, that 'tis almost absurd ever to wonder at any."

"True. And though from Mr. Ryder's turn of mind I should have conceived a sensible and rational companion to be the object most likely to gain his affections, yet I know so well the power of a pretty face, that I thought in following that, he had waved the less important subject, as it is generally deemed of intellect."

"But what shall we say now? Do not his partialities appear to lie in a very different direction? This child, the young woman with whom he was seen journeying?"

"Undoubtedly furnish sufficient grounds for conjecturing that he has formed some connection which for private reasons he does not chuse to acknowledge. As to the child itself, I have already told you how much I have frequently suspected it to be his own, and that I even think it like him."

"Yes, all is now solved. In our last conversation he said that austerity on the part of its grand-father precluded the child's being owned by its parents, whence it may justly be inferred that he has married a woman whose friends he is convinced would not approve the match, were it known, and thus 'tis for the present concealed. Or, perhaps, to hazard another ingenious speculation, the marriage is discovered, and he has now taken his wife abroad, to remove her from the persecutions to which she would be subjected here."

"Doubtless you are right, and all his late uneasiness of mind, his emotions at parting with Miss Campbell and yourself, arose from painful reflections upon this subject, from a consciousness perhaps, that he had been the means of enticing a young woman away from a state of ease and affluence, to share his difficulties, his poverty."

Thus have Beauchamp and I, at last, settled the matter to our satisfaction, at least as far as concerns the child, but the affair of the challenge still remains wholly inexplicable. Before, however, I finally take my leave of this babe, who has furnished me so much at sundry times with materials for filling my letters, what has passed with honest Jerry upon the subject must not be forgotten.

The other day, as I was dressing, he was extremely full of Ryder's having taken the child away in such haste, and wondered what could be the reason of it, and wondered whether it really was his own child, with many other wonders and speculations. I plainly saw all this time that there was a something more at bottom on which his mind was extremely occupied, yet which he was doubtful whether he might venture to mention or not, and I therefore charitably gave him the one word of encouragement, which alone was wanting to embolden him to speak without reserve. He then said, "some folks had such odd thoughts about that child."

"What thoughts, Jerry?"

"Why, mayhap your honour would be angry."

"Not with you, Jerry, for hearing them, though perhaps with others for harbouring them."

"Why, to be sure your honour, some folks will have it as its madam's own child, and that Muster Ryder is the father."

"Pshaw!—I hope you don't believe such absurd and scandalous false-hoods, Jerry?"

"Not I to be sure, your honour, and the sarvents is all main angry that any body should dare for to say such a thing of their mistress. But to be sure 'tis somehows or other, main odd about the child, and nobody knows exactly what for to think, so every body's for having of some thought or other."

"And pray who could suspect that the child was Miss Campbell's?"

"Why, it were Parson Paul's sarvent as said it, and he were sartin he said as it were so, and I thought once as Will. Beckford the footman and he would downright a fit about it, for he says he's mortal sartin as the par-son himself has the same thought."

"Well, Jerry, don't let the parson's servant or any other impertinent babbler persuade you to believe such nonsense. The child, I'll lay my life on't, is no more Miss Campbell's than mine."

When I related this conversation to Beauchamp, he said,—"I know this is not the first time that such a suspicion has been hinted. But does it not confute itself?—Supposing Miss Campbell to be attached to Mr. Ryder, what should prevent her marrying him, except his not being him-self inclined to the match, and then 'tis not likely that he should have sought a connection with her in any other way. Besides I think we have already settled the matter very satisfactorily, and without affixing scandal any where."

So here, Harry, I take leave of the infant, for the present at least, and with once more exhorting you not to fail of letting me hear from you by the return of the post, either by yourself or your secretary, I subscribe myself

Your unalterably faithful

LIONEL STANHOPE.

LETTER XVI.

LIONEL STANHOPE
TO
WILLIAM SPENCER,
Steward to Mr. Egerton.

Campbell-House, October 21.

DEAR SIR,

I am under such extreme anxiety at not hearing from Mr. Egerton, that I can no longer delay applying to you for intelligence concerning him. I am apprehensive that he may by ill—perhaps, alas, the unfortunate business in which he has been lately engaged, has proved too much for a mind harassed as his was before it was undertaken. Oh God! this is what I have always feared!

I entreat you then not to delay a moment giving me a line to inform me of his real situation, and if I think my presence necessary, or even that it can in any way be useful, I will fly instantly to the assistance of my poor friend.

I am, Dear Sir,
Your obedient humble servant,

LIONEL STANHOPE.

LETTER XVII.

WILLIAM SPENCER
TO
LIONEL STANHOPE.

Arrenton, October 23.

DEAR SIR,

I am extremely concerned that it is not in my power to give you all the satisfaction I wish, with regard to Mr. Egerton. His presence not being necessary here, about a week ago he left Arrenton, as I supposed to join you. In this, it appears I was mistaken, yet I hope, Sir, that there is no occasion for alarm upon his account, as his mind had been much more composed for several days prior to his departure, than it was on his first coming hither. Indeed I think you may be perfectly easy about him, and may rest assured that before many days are expired you will either see or hear from him. Should any tidings of himself or his route, reach me, Sir, you may depend on my handing you a line immediately from
Dear Sir,
Your most obedient humble servant,

WILLIAM SPENCER.

LETTER XVIII.

LIONEL STANHOPE
TO
ORLANDO ST. JOHN.

Campbell-House, October 28.

St. John, when I tell you that the Tichfields have been here for a week past, will you not envy me?—Will you not be ready to tear out your own eyes, since you cannot reach mine, with very rage at the idea of my enjoying a happiness for which you sigh in vain?—But patience!—I am not altogether as great an object of envy as you may suppose me. The Tichfields are indeed here, but unaccompanied either by your enchanting widow or bewitching spinster. The former, who I understood was to be of the party to this house, is staying at a Mr. Blake's at Doncaster, a family who are rather intimate here; and Charlotte, a few days before the Tichfields left Scarborough, received a summons to meet her father and mother immediately at Bath, who had come over from Ireland a month sooner than they originally intended.

Upon the faith of a true knight, St. John, the widow is an enchanting little creature, and very likely, I fear, to dispute the empire of my heart with the intellectual heiress, spite of the soul-subduing strains she draws from her harp.

We have had routs, balls, concerts, dinners, suppers, and in short gaieties of every kind, under every shape and form that fancy could devise or taste improve. Captain Tichfield paying his court to the lady of the house with such sweet, such tender assiduity, that he has really been almost as attentive to her as to himself.—And alas! must it be owned? Yes it must, for 'tis but too true!—Olivia seems not a little gratified, even with these forced attentions from such a butterfly. Oh woman!—woman;—still woman, whether with a pretty or a plain face, whether with a cultivated or uncultivated mind!—must I then at last rank Olivia only on a level with the rest of her sex?—I could not flatter her, and she rejected me, Captain Tichfield pours a torrent of those unmeaning nothings which the world calls *compliments* into her ears, and to him she listens with evident delight. She will play on the harp at my request, because Captain Tichfield likes it, but in vain did I solicit her hand to dance at a ball, for that would have interfered with the all-elegant, all-accomplished captain.

Yes, Orlando, I came home from a ball at Doncaster, the night before last, full of indignation against the whole sex, and swearing that ugly or handsome they were all flirts and coquettes alike. That the sole object on which the heart of a woman is fixed, is to draw round her a croud of admirers, to receive their flatteries and attentions as long as they continue amusing, and then to buffet them away to make room for another set of butterflies, whose reign is equally transient.

And yet, after I had vented my spleen, I could not forbear asking myself whether this invective did not proceed rather from mortified vanity than from any just cause. Fully convinced, that I Lionel Stanhope, a *fine*, *handsome*, *spirited* young fellow, the heir of a baronetage, of a *very ancient* baronetage, had only to ask the hand of any lady I might wish to select as my partner for the evening, and it would be granted with eagerness and transport—full of these conceited ideas, I never thought of engaging a partner before I went to the ball. I then made my first application to Olivia, but she was engaged for the whole evening alternately to Captain Tichfield and young Blake, a smart student of the law. Next I applied to the gay widow, but she did not choose to dance at all—no, there she sat surrounded by such a croud of officers talking silly frothy nonsense to her, that I not only could not prevail upon her to dance with me, but could scarcely even manage to get in a word of conversation the whole evening. She is an intolerable coquette, St. John, after all.

Yet not absolutely daunted by these two repulses, I did venture farther to make my bow to the two Miss Blakes. But as they are really very genteel girls, and not many of the belles of the Doncaster balls have any claim to be called so, the officers, of whom there are a great many here at present, had taken care to secure them for so many dances, that I had no chance but for a fifteenth or a sixteenth, at the very end of the evening. What then could I do?—I sat myself down in a corner of the room to watch the Captain and Olivia, till at length I was so completely out of humour, that from mere spite, I went and played at cards with the Mrs. Baxters, Mrs. Stapletons, &c. &c. But confound the cards, I could no more attend to them, than to the circle of beauty that surrounded the tables, and I did nothing but make blunders and lose both my own and my partners' money, till I so completely damned my reputation as a disciple of Hoyle,[36] that my partners, poor souls, were ready to swear at me, as heartily as I had railed at the Olivias, the Elizas, and all their tribe.

Yet, one subject of amusement I did find at the card-table in listening to the jokes that flew about. Mr. Baxter, son of the widow of that name, whose fame has been already chronicled in my letters to you, my dear Mr. St. John—yet, hold!—no, not to you, now I recollect myself, it was to Harry that honourable mention was made of her. Mr. Baxter, a dealer in coals, corn, &c. by profession, and a keen wit, by the bye, was the person to whom I was principally indebted for the few moments respite I obtained from devouring ennui.

"What shall I do?" said his fair partner, with her head reclined on her hand in all the agitation of playing for the odd trick.

"Play nothing and take it up again," said the facetious Mr. Baxter.

"Are you for a bet, Mr. Baxter?"

"With all my heart."

"Half a crown on the rubber?"

"Bet you a farthing cake, and I'll have first bite."

"How many are you Mr. Baxter?"

"Want one of half a couple."

But 'twould fill a whole volume were I to retail all the good things he uttered in the short space of two rubbers, and this will suffice as a specimen.

When at length I thought I had disgraced myself sufficiently among the old ladies at the card-table, I returned once more into the dancing-room, and was actually very near being guilty of so great a piece of condescension as to dance two dances with Peggy Perkins. I found her in very great distress in search of Percival Altham, to whom she was engaged for the next two dances, and who was no where to be found. He, as it appeared afterwards, had, like myself, in vain solicited the hands of Olivia, Madame de Clairville, and the two Miss Blakes, but more persevering than I had been, stopped not there, but next proceeded to request the fair hand of Peggy—even that, however, was not to be obtained, till the eleventh and twelfth dances, but these he was faithfully promised.

Content with this trifling success, he solicited no farther, but resolved to wait with philosophical patience the happy moment that was to place him *vis-a-vis* to an object so enchanting. Yet, on mature reflection, he thought that period seemed at so great a distance, that the intervening time could not be better employed than in a nap. When supper therefore was finished, he skipped off to bed, leaving it in charge with one of the fidlers to call him a little before the conclusion of the tenth dance, for which the said fidler was promised a reward of a whole shilling.

But the son of harmony, only in part faithful to his trust, did not summon the pretty youth from his rosy slumbers till the tenth dance was wholly and entirely finished, consequently by the time the eleventh dance was to begin, he was not ready at his post. A strict search for the stray sheep was immediately instituted by Peggy, but all in vain, he was no where to be found, nor could any one tell what was become of him. One advanced that he was gone home, another asserted with equal confidence that he was then drinking in the supper room, and probably by that time totally incapable of dancing, while a third not less confidently than either, affirmed that he was then in the card-room. Peggy was all this time so pathetically lamenting the hardship of her situation, that, at length, in compassion, I offered my services to supply his place. This was joyfully accepted by her, and I was on the point of taking my station among the dancers, when the fidler came in, and said, "the gentleman had been to bed, but was getting up again, and begged his compliments to the lady, and he'd be down in a minute or two."

Yes, Orlando, I returned from this ball railing at Olivia, abjuring de Clairville for ever, and firmly resolved never to suffer any one of the sex again to obtain an interest in my heart. But yesterday we had a little concert here, Eliza sung, Olivia played on the harp—Eliza looked all enchantment, Olivia drew strains from her instrument that might have dissolved the senseless rock itself, and I looked at the one, and listened to the other, till I was in a perfect delirium, and went to bed fully convinced, that if I could but pass the remainder of my days at Campbell-House, in the society of these two enchanting women, the united world could not offer another situation to be put in competition with this.

Thus is tossed about in a tempest of emotions, the bosom of
Yours most faithfully,

LIONEL STANHOPE.

LETTER XIX.

WILLIAM SPENCER
TO
LIONEL STANHOPE.

Arrenton, October 28.

DEAR SIR,

I will not delay a moment to inform you that I have just received a letter from Mr. Egerton, without a date, but the post-mark upon it is Chester. He charges me to assure you that he is well, and that his late silence has been occasioned by very particular circumstances, which shall all be detailed to you at a future period. He cannot absolutely fix the time, he says, of his return to Arrenton, but thinks he shall most likely be absent about a fortnight or three weeks longer. Trusting that you will now be perfectly easy with regard to Mr. Egerton, I remain, dear Sir,

Your most obedient humble servant,

WILLIAM SPENCER.

LETTER XX.

LIONEL STANHOPE,
TO
ORLANDO ST. JOHN.

Kilverton, November 8.

No longer, St. John, am I an inhabitant of Campbell-House. Five days ago I bid adieu to that hospitable mansion, and while I anxiously looked back to catch a last glance at its venerable turrets, as we were about to descend the hill that was to shut it out from our sight, I heaved many a sigh of regret, for the hours of delight I had experienced there, for joys but too rapidly passed away, and which, perhaps, alas! may never return.

Yes, I could not restrain a sigh as I saw the last curl of the smoke that ascended from the chimneys of a house where I have passed three months, certainly the most eventful, I think the most agreeable of my life—a house which I entered full of levity, with a heart, I will not say absolutely devoid of care, but a stranger to all cares except those excited in it by anxious friendship, which I have quitted with a mind full of thought, and oppressed with anxieties concerning my own future destiny, though totally unsettled in its wishes on a subject so important. Which I entered with a heart wholly devoted to beauty—which I have quitted with feelings so much the reverse, that though my rebel senses in the presence of the fascinating de Clairville may dispose me to resign myself to her empire, yet, when that momentary delusion is vanished, which almost impel me to acknowledge the accomplished Olivia alone as the sovereign arbitress of my fate—with feelings that chide my puerile folly, and insensibility to my own happiness, in ever cherishing in my bosom, any other image save that of Olivia.

Any other *image* did I say?—Ah, there's the rub! 'tis that image alone that renders her absolute sway doubtful!—Would to God that her mind were less, or her face more irresistible!—While I hear her converse, while I listen to the strains her magic fingers draw from her lyre, my soul is ravished. When I reflect on the unvarying sweetness of her temper, on her benevolence so unceasing, so unbounded, reason sanctions my raptures, and I ask myself what more the heart of man could wish for? Whether this is not a woman almost to be adored? Yet, even then, Eliza's fairy form will flit across my fancy: I see that a something still is wanting in Olivia, and that something so richly to be found in De Clairville, that I cannot forbear exclaiming, "Oh that the soul of the one, were but enshrined in the form of the other!" Yet no! that were too much—for what heart could resist such collected charms?

Whether it were that the society to which I had been so long accustomed made my bosom revolt against the insipidities of a watering place, or that the season for Scarborough was nearly at an end, or that released from all apprehensions of the good baronet's importunities, I no longer wished to shun his society; to whichever of these causes my determination may be ascribed, I cannot say, yet so it was, that, on quitting Campbell-House, I had no inclination to prosecute the original plan, with which I left Kilverton, but resolved to accompany my dear papa to his beloved home, and good old Dame.

So here I am, Orlando, once more an inhabitant of Kilverton Hall, where my lady received her *dear* spouse, and her *dear* boy, with all that profusion of delight that ladies are wont, after a long absence, to experience at the sight of such *dear* objects, while old Thunder wagged his tail as we descended from the carriage, as though he would fairly have wagged it off, and the servants drew up all in array before the house door, to bid us welcome with each a grin of satisfaction upon their countenances.

And after all, St. John, there is something very grateful to the feelings in finding such a reception as this, these are pure unsophisticated proofs of attachment inspired by nature, and carry in them no disguise, nor should I ever expect much good from a heart insensible to them. I love to see every part of a family, from the highest to the lowest, bound together by ties of affection, not to see the head oppressing the lower members, and the members grumbling at the tyranny and exaction of the head, but all together knowing only one common interest, and such I truly think is the case here. Indeed it must he said for the worthy old baronet and his lady, that they certainly are very good sort of people, with whom 'tis scarcely possible to be long under the same roof and not feel a strong love and respect for them. And if I have occasionally taken the liberty of laughing at their peculiarities myself, you can bear me witness, Orlando, and so could Harry too, that I never allowed this privilege to another, and that the nose of any one who had dared to ridicule them in my presence, would have been in a very perilous situation.

And what will you say, St. John, when you are farther informed, that not only shall I remain here for two months with no other society than that of my dear parents, and the trees, and the birds, and the purling* streams, but that I have even prevailed upon these said parents to pass the winter in London themselves, and to endeavour to persuade Olivia to relinquish her plan of taking a house to herself, and become their guest in South Audley-Street. What a revolution from former times, when I always promoted to the utmost of my power, their remaining in the country all the year, that I might enjoy the world of fashion by myself, in an elegant apartment at an elegant hotel. Oh! I do feel indeed, that my mind has undergone a wonderful transformation.

You will not suppose that this plan met with much opposition from the Baronet and his lady, indeed 'tis not often that they oppose any thing suggested by their Lionel. But this was of a nature so peculiarly accordant with their own wishes, that Sir Francis would scarcely hear it out before he sat down to write and mention it to Olivia. He indeed seems now to consider his favourite point as carried, beyond all apprehension of farther disappointment, since 'tis plain that his dear boy cannot very much dislike the heiress's company; and that she should not admire him is absolutely impossible. 'Tis a fine thing, St. John, to be an only child, especially when heir to a good fortune, we are then considered as beings of so very superior a nature, that sufficient homage can scarcely be paid us, and our humours can scarcely be sufficiently studied.

And yet, gratifying to our self-love as all this may be, heaven knows how gladly I would even yield up privileges so important, could I make Olivia my sister. Oh that this were possible! This would be indeed to form to myself a little paradise upon earth! What a delightful intercourse of fraternal attachment should we then maintain, how affectionately might we participate in each other's joys and sorrows, and administer to each other's happiness, without the tormenting reflection, that if a change of sentiments should arise, we must still be condemned to live together to our mutual torment.

Yet say, is it possible that such a connection as this could be interrupted without pain or remorse? Would the soul experience the less anguish

---

*   Babbling or murmuring.

in the conviction that a separation was necessary, because it was possible to separate? Ah! is there on earth a feeling more painful than the conviction that we must henceforward consider as a stranger to our hearts, and confidence, one with whom we have been accustomed to live on terms of unrestrained friendship and intimacy? There may be circumstances in which the dissolution of such a connection is the wisest plan out of a choice of evils, but what shall we think of the heart that could contemplate such a separation with indifference? No! could I for a moment entertain an apprehension that the time would ever arrive, when as a sister I could no longer love and regard her, all wish that she were my sister would be effectually suppressed! But these are at last mere idle speculations, since my sister she never can be. Heighho!!!

We left Percival Altham in a sad *quandary*; oh no, I am wrong, Beauchamp had just helped him out of one. On the day before our departure from Campbell-House, he made his appearance there, and requested a few minutes private conversation with the privy-counsellor general, Beauchamp. This being granted, he very seriously and solemnly proceeded to say, that as his uncle was absent for a few days, he had taken the liberty to apply to Mr. Beauchamp as a friend, for his advice upon an affair of the utmost importance. An unfortunate misunderstanding, he said, had arisen between himself and young Mr. Blake, from a circumstance that happened at the coffee-house at Doncaster, where they had accidentally met. "And," continued Percival, "I am told, Mr. Beauchamp, that Mr. Blake actually threatens to pull me by the nose the next time he meets me, wherever it may be. Now what would you advise me to do in so difficult a case?"

"Why indeed," said Beauchamp, after a few moments serious and solemn reflection, "I would advise you, Mr. Altham—I would advise you—to soap your nose, and then it will slip through his fingers."

"Egad, and so it will!" exclaimed Percival in a transport; "I never heard a better idea in my life. Then you know it will turn the laugh of the company upon him, he! he! he! I thank you very kindly indeed, Mr. Beauchamp, I never heard a better idea, I should never have thought of it myself,—make an admirable incident for my next comedy." And away he skipped laughing and highly delighted. So no more at present, dear Mr. St. John,

From your very affectionate

LIONEL STANHOPE.

ORLANDO ST. JOHN
TO
LIONEL STANHOPE.

Woodbourne, November 16.

Why, Lionel, never till now, during the whole course of our acquaintance, did I know thee to utter such an exclamation as Heighho!!! How inexpressibly strange was the sensation it gave me when I read it, and how ardently did I long to have seen thee at the moment of writing it. Lionel Stanhope in a thoughtful, nay, almost in a melancholy mood! Upon my soul I shall expect next to become thoughtful and melancholy myself. But would that I could see thee; I should expect to find in thee much curious matter for speculation; and speculation, as thou knowest, Li., is the very delight of my heart.

I dare say thou hast not forgotten the very fine vein of philosophical investigation on the nature of man, his powers, and faculties, into which I was launching on the morning after my last arrival at Kilverton, as we sauntered together through the wood, and which thou didst suddenly cut short, by disclosing the pretty plan just hatched between thee and cousin Harry. I was entering on theory, thou wert all for practice, and while I was speculating on the inventive powers of man, thou, by way of illustration, did'st bring me an example of what extraordinary inventions some minds were capable.

But now, I warrant thee, thou would'st theorise with me as rapidly as the flow of ideas could carry us on; would'st descant on love, its hopes, its joys, its apprehensions, with all the scientific precision of an old votary of the little spiteful deity. For that thou art in love, Mr. Li., I am perfectly satisfied, though faith I can by no means decide whether thy heart be the most devoted to beauty, or to intellect. I hope not to the former, for know, Sir, if this be the case, thou and I must measure swords, or pop bullets upon the matter, since even to thee I cannot tamely resign the incomparable Eliza.

Ha! ha! ha! Lionel Stanhope heartily in love! What canst thou do with thyself, Li.? Fancy pourtrays thee to my mind strolling about with folded arms and eyes fixed on the earth, insensible to every object around thee, unless old Thunder perchance should attend thy wanderings, and then I could fancy thee suddenly starting, clasping him to thy bosom, kissing him with extasy, and calling him thy Eliza, or thy Olivia; and indeed Thunder, to do him justice, has beauty enough for the one, and understanding enough for the other. Or, perhaps, thou art writing woeful ballads to "*thy mistress's eye brow*,"[37] or composing piteous ejaculations to the mighty Cupid, praying the Godhead to compassionate thy sorrows, and render thy fair propitious to thy vows.

Well, gladly would I hasten to Kilverton to contemplate thee in this state, and, as a substitute for Thunder, to let thee woo me as thy Olivia, but hence I cannot stir at this moment, as my father is still unable to move, and I am therefore an important personage in the family.

Looking over the Memorabilia of Scarborough this very morn, I chanced to find the following sonnet, even in the handwriting of the lovely Charlotte herself. It had by some means straggled from my general repository of her productions, and got among some other papers of a very different nature, but the moment I espied it, I clasped it to my bosom, exclaiming,

> Oh learn'd indeed were that Astronomer,
> That knew the stars as I these characters![38]

I read it over with transport, and imprinted on it a tender kiss, for well did I remember the time and spot in which 'twas written, as well as the occasion that called it forth. It was an instance of intolerable selfishness in Peggy Perkins, and the only one for which I will readily pardon her, since it produced such an effusion from Charlotte's pen.

TO SELFISHNESS.

> Oh Selfishness! whene'er thy blasting pow'r
>   Obtains a fatal influence o'er mankind,
>   How does it root each virtue from the mind
> And bid stern desolation round it low'r!
>
> As the great Upas upon Java's shore[39]
>   In solitude, from all the world disjoin'd,
>   With pois'nous vapours fills each passing wind,
> And withers tree and plant, and herb and flow'r,
>
> So, Selfishness, within the human breast
>   In dreary solitude thou reign'st alone,
> Since no innocuous plant can ever rest
>   Within the atmosphere around thy throne?
> Thou fiend, who hast within thyself comprest
> Ten thousand hateful vices all in one.

Match me this if thou can'st, Lionel, with any effusions of thine own. For my own part I am so sensible that every thing produced by my pen must appear poor and insipid after it, that I merely add the only thing I hope you never will find insipid from me, the assurance that I am with the greatest sincerity,

Thy affectionate

ORLANDO ST. JOHN.

LETTER XXII.

LIONEL STANHOPE,
TO
ORLANDO ST. JOHN.

Kilverton, November 20.

No, Orlando, I have not been writing "*woeful ballads to my mistress's eyebrow*,"—neither have I written a sonnet to selfishness, since that is a being unknown at Kilverton, but I have been writing one in a very different strain, as you shall hear.

TO A JACK-ASS.

Poor patient sufferer of life's keenest woes,
 Condemn'd in ceaseless toil to pass thy days,
 While man for all thy drudg'ry nought repays,
But harsh abuse and still severer blows.

Whose life is still a stranger to repose!—
 Be mine to pour to thee the votive lays,
 Since much my pity's mov'd when it surveys
The hardships, which thy wretched life compose.

And oft thou dost remind me too with pain,
 Of those who toil untir'd their whole lives through,
In science' paths, some good for man to gain,
 Yet whom the shafts of malice still pursue,
While the mere *negatively* good obtain,
 The praise to *active* virtue only due.

And think you, Orlando, that ever love-stricken swain before me, when he sought to woo the virgin sisters made choice of such a subject?— and will you now believe that the portrait your fancy has so ingeniously drawn of my solitary wanderings bears any resemblance to the original.

Poor Jacky!—It certainly was, however, during a solitary ramble that thou didst attract my attention!—Whether my arms were folded or not, I really cannot tell, neither can I ascertain with precision the exact direction of my eyes, but thus much will I confess, that I had strolled on perfectly unknowing whither my footsteps were conducting me, when suddenly to my no small surprize, I found my progress arrested by the gate at the extremity of my dear father's territories, which opens from the wood upon Kilverton common, and is not less than three miles from the house.

And do you ask me on what subject my thoughts were occupied all this time?—Orlando, I protest upon the faith of a gentleman, I do not know myself.

But at the gate I halted, for over the upper bar the poor long-eared drudge had raised his head at my approach, as if desirous of pouring out the sorrows of his full heart into my sympathetic bosom. And methought he complained that his brute of a master, after working him hard all day, had sent him with a heavy clog* on his foot, to pass the night in that barren spot, where no mortal ass could find herbage sufficient to satisfy the cravings of his hunger. "Ah, poor wretch!" said I, stroaking his long ears, and patting his shaggy coat, but upon my honour, without the least idea that he was either Eliza or Olivia, "thou art not the only hapless being in the kingdom, who, after twelve hours of painful drudgery, neither can obtain a comfortable meal to recruit his exhausted strength, nor a decent bed whereon to rest his wearied limbs! But thy hardships shall be alleviated as far as lies in my power!—Would to God it were equally within my ability to relieve all thy fellow-sufferers!"

I immediately drew a bundle of hay from a rick† belonging to Sir Francis, not far from the gate, and gave him to eat, till he appeared satisfied, and expressed his gratitude by a loud and sonorous bray. "Ah!" thought I, "'tis an uncouth way of uttering thy feelings, but thou hast done thy best, and the most exquisite warbler could do no more." I then threw him over more hay for a breakfast the next morning, on which, as if to secure it from marauders, he lay down to repose. Seeing him thus cheered, I turned homewards, and by the way invoked the sisters nine[40] to aid me in immortalising his sorrows. Perhaps they ought rather to have been made the subject of an epic poem, than of a mere sonnet, since there certainly was a beginning, a middle, and an end, in his adventures, well adapted to the Epipœa.‡ His being thrown on the barren common after a variety of toils and adventures, his recounting his tale of woe to me, and lastly the relief of his woes by my athletic arm, and his resting in peace and composure, would have furnished the proper divisions to compose a sublime whole.

Now, tell me, Orlando, could any thing be more truly sentimental, than this transaction?—But who can have passed three months at Campbell-House, without learning to consider every thing possessing life and animation as a brother. Yet, though I now feel my soul more expanded than formerly towards all nature, I hope there never was a moment of my existence, when I should not have shewn the same kindness to this poor animal.

Nor did my muse stop at this one sonnet. Having once obtained the company of the maids of Helicon,[41] I would not let them off so easily, but perceiving the sun all at once burst forth in meridian splendour, after having for many days been totally hidden from our sight by a mass of envious clouds, I gave my pencil a second flourish and wrote:

---

*   Block attached to impede motion.
†   Haystack.
‡   Epic.

TO THE SUN.

Fountain of light, and heat, resplendent Sun,
    With joyful heart thy glad return I hail!
I seek not now thy noon-tide beams to shun,
    Nor woo, to check their force, the passing gale.

Thy long concealment's taught me how to prize,
    More fully prize, the splendour of thy reign;
I see thee now with more admiring eyes,
    Than when thy constant smiles illum'd the plain.

So when th' enamour'd youth, who from his fair
    Has long been absent, once again beholds
Those sparkling beauties which his heart ensnare,
    And to his breast her charms once more enfolds,
He owns he ne'er before like raptures prov'd,
Nor, till her absence, knew how much he lov'd.

And I know not how many more sonnets I might have written, had I not perceived that I had already deviated from the legitimate to the illegitimate, and I thought that if the maidens were in this capricious humour, and had a mind to play tricks with me, their next frolick might be to make me produce one after the still more illegitimate fashions of modern days, in blank verse perhaps, or in five or six stanzas of ballad measure—so telling them that I would not be made their sport in that way, I put up my pencil and bade 'em begone.

In my last effusion, however, as you will see, Orlando, some traces of the lover do appear, and such will be my feelings when—yes, that must be when I see Eliza de Clairville again, for since *sparkling beauties* are the question, it can have no reference to Olivia. And if, Mr. St. John, in consequence of this declaration, you think it absolutely necessary that we should measure swords upon the matter, behold me ready for the meeting at any time and place you will appoint, and old Jerry shall be my second.

Our invitation is accepted by Olivia, with expressions of very great pleasure in the idea of passing her winter in South Audley Street. I wonder whether any part of that pleasure is to be attributed to the idea of being in my company. Be that as it may, I expect this visit to be decisive of my future destiny. Heavens! should I at last be united to a woman whom I so long resolutely refused even to see!—Will any thing that can happen to me afterwards, appear extraordinary?—I protest I should hardly believe my own ears, were I to hear myself repeating, "*I Lionel, take thee Olivia.*"

I forgot to mention in my last, that Peggy Perkins, who was to have accompanied the Tichfield's to London, a few days before they left

Campbell-House, took a sudden freak into her head that she never enjoyed her health in that region of smoke and noise, so decamped in a great hurry to a *dear friend* at Leeds, with whom, as she says, she intends to pass the winter. The true occasion of this hasty movement is, however, suspected to be, that she learned lately by a letter from this *dear friend*, that Mr. Peters, who has long been endeavouring to get an engagement in some theatrical corps, has lately succeeded, and is now actually in a course of performing at Leeds. Till Peggy learned this, she was always talking with delight of passing the winter in London, and recounting with a sort of triumphant exultation over the young ladies at Doncaster, who are strangers, alas, to the delights of the metropolis, the constant round of gaieties in which she should be engaged.

As soon as Christmas is over, and the festivities with which the mansion of Kilverton always abounds at that season, are closed, we shall adjourn to London. A period expected with some impatience, by

Yours most truly,

LIONEL STANHOPE.

END OF VOLUME SECOND.

1 *Chancery.* One of the three divisions of the High Court of Justice and notorious for long and exhausting suits. The most famous description of Chancery is in the first chapter of Dickens's *Bleak House.*

2 *Shakespeare's Francis.* See *Henry IV, Part 1* 2.4. Francis is a waiter in a tavern who responds to all calls with the same answer: "Anon, anon, Sir."

3 *Guthrie's Introduction to Geography.* Most likely William Guthrie's very popular *A New Geographical, Historical, and Commercial Grammar* already in its 18th edition by 1800. It has a chapter entitled "Problems performed by the globe."

4 *"She meant to live there all her days, / She felt she could not live there long."* Source unidentified.

5 *"more was meant than met the ear."* Milton. *Il Penseroso*: "In sage and solemn tunes have sung, / Of Tourneys and of Trophies hung, / Of Forests, and enchantments drear, / Where more is meant than meets the ear" (117-120).

6 *the daughters of Parnassus.* The Muses. Parnassus is a mountain in Greece which was regarded as the seat of poetry and music. See note 44 Volume I.

7 *Saint Ursula* and *her eleven thousand virgins.* According to legend, Ursula was a fifth-century British princess who led eleven thousand virgins on a pilgrimage to Rome. All were massacred by the Huns at Cologne. One explanation of the story is that the name of one of Ursula's companions, *Undecimilla,* was mistaken for *undecim milla* or "eleven thousand" (Brewer's).

8 *the achievements of a Marlborough in the fields of Blenheim and Ramilies.* The duke of Marlborough, John Churchill (1650-1722), British statesman and soldier, was famous for his brilliant military career. His victories included the Battle of Blenheim (1704) and Ramilies (1709), both part of the War of the Spanish Succession. The Battle of Blenheim was the first great battle won by an English general on the continent since Agincourt.

9 *the glorious campaigns of an Uncle Toby, and a Corporal Trim in the bowling-green.* Characters in Laurence Sterne's *Tristram Shandy* (1759-67). Uncle Toby is a retired army captain who enthusiastically follows the military campaigns of Marlborough using a complicated set of miniature fortifications set up on the bowling green. He is assisted by his servant Corporal Trim.

10 *all my "perfections on my head"* See *Hamlet* 1.5.74: "No reckoning made, but sent to my account / With all my imperfections on my head."

11 *you are left in the state of Tantalus, upon the shore indeed, yet deprived of all enjoyment of its delights.* Tantalus, a son of Zeus, was condemned to spend eternity in frustration. He was placed up to his chin in water, but every time he went to drink, the water receded. In a similar fashion, fruit was suspended just above his reach. His name has given us the word *tantalize.*

12 *"seen what I have seen, see what I see"* *Hamlet* 3.1.169.

13 *the Widow Warren in the Road to Ruin.* A character in Thomas Holcroft's play *The*

Road to Ruin (1792). Holcroft describes Widow Warren as "A girlish, old coquette, who would rob her daughter, and leave her husband's son to rot in a dungeon, that she might marry the first fool she could find."

14 *... but cut, and hack, and slash among 'em all, like any Priam.* Priam was ancient Troy's last king. He is presented in the *Iliad* as a gentle old man who begs his son Hector's body from Achilles.

15 *Hector.* The son of Priam and Hecuba and Troy's greatest warrior.

16 *"Un sot, en ecrivant fait tout avec plaiser, ..." Satires II* (1666, 87-94) by Nicolas Boileau-Despréaux (1636-1711), literary critic and poet.

17 *Chamberry.* Chambéry is a town in the former duchy of Savoy (annexed by France in the 1790s). Mt. Cenis is on the border between present day France and Italy. Percival has his traveller going in the wrong direction; on his way to Italy, he comes down the mountain and back into France.

18 *I suppose Chamberry gauze comes from Chamberry in France, or Picardy, which is it?* Although there is a lightweight fabric known as *Chambery* that is woven with a silk warp and a goat's hair filling, Mrs. Harrison probably refers to *Chambray*, a cotton fabric originating in Cambrai, France. Picardy is a region in northern France.

19 *and then D.I.O.* "Damme!, I'm Off." A men's catch phrase of late eighteenth-early nineteenth centuries, satiric of initials on cards of invitation, etc. (Partridge's *Dictionary of Slang*). Thanks to Ron Lieberman for the reference.

20 *the Lethe that was to banish the remembrance of his sorrows!* See note 3, Volume I.

21 *"our joys are momentary" ... "remorse is eternal"* Source unknown.

22 *To wind about your love with circumstance" Merchant of Venice* 1.1.154. Slightly misquoted ("To wind about my love with circumstance").

23 *"There, at the foot of yonder nodding beech / That writhes its old fantastic root so high"* Thomas Gray, "Elegy Written in a Country Churchyard," 101-104. Slightly misquoted ("That wreathes its old fantastic roots so high").

24 *Hymen.* Greek god of marriage.

25 *the retort courteous / the reply churlish.* Terms from a book entitled *Of Honour and Honourable Quarrels* by Vincentio Saviolo (1594). See *As You Like It* 5.4.85-95: "O, sir, we quarrel in print by the book, as you have books for good manners. I will name you the degrees. The first, the Retort Courteous; the second, the Quip Modest; the third, the Reply Churlish; the fourth, the Reproof Valiant; the fifth, the Countercheck Quarrelsome; the sixth, the Lie with Circumstance; the seventh, the Lie Direct." (Arthur E. Baker, *A Shakespeare Commentary*, 1957).

26 *the galled horse winced.* English proverbial expression: "Touch (or rub) a galled horse on the back, and he'll wince (or kick)." See *Hamlet* 3.2.253: "Let the galled jade wince, our withers are unwrung."

27 *Creole.* Originally referred to a native of Spanish America or the West Indies of European parentage. The term has sometimes been used to indicate mixed race.

28 *a Circassian slave.* Circassia is a region of the North-West Caucasus.

29 *singing airs of Metastasio.* Italian poet Pietro Trapassi (1698-1782).

30 *with verdure of a thousand dies.* Percival probably means to allude to "verdure of

a thousand dyes" (i.e., colours). Of course, even with the spelling corrected, there are serious problems with the phrase.

31 *"all things to all men."* Corinthians 9:22:"I am made all things to all men, that I might by all means save some."

32 *the music of the spheres.* According to Pythagorus, the music produced by the movements of the heavenly bodies. This music was imperceptible to human hearing and could be heard only by the gods.

33 *the simple unsophisticated child of St. David.* The "poor Welchman." St. David is the patron saint of Wales.

34 the *"melting mood."* *Othello* 5.2.349.

35 *"What a piece of work is man!"* *Hamlet* 2.2.316.

36 *a disciple of Hoyle.* Edmond Hoyle (1672-1769), English writer on games. A professional teacher of fashionable games, Hoyle's books established him as the supreme authority on a number of games, particularly those played with cards.

37 *"thy mistress's eye brow"* *As You Like It* 2.7.149.

38 *"Oh learn'd indeed were that Astronomer, | That knew the stars as I these characters!"* *Cymbeline* 3.2.27.

39 *As the great Upas upon Java's shore.* According to the *London Magazine* of 1783 and Erasmus Darwin, the Upas was a great Javanese tree so poisonous it killed all life within fifteen or sixteen miles. It was fatal even to birds flying over it. The source of this fiction, supposedly from a true account by a Dutch surgeon serving in Samarang in 1773, was apparently an invented story by George Steevens.

40 *the sisters nine.* The Muses. See above note 44, Volume I.

41 *the maids of Helicon.* The Muses. Helicon is the home of the Muses, a part of Parnassus. See note 44 Volume I and note 6 Volume II.

VOLUME III

HENRY EGERTON
TO
LIONEL STANHOPE.

Dublin, November 24.

Forgive, Lionel, the moments of anxiety and painful suspense which I well know my silence must have occasioned you. I feel, and acknowledge that my conduct has been extremely reprehensible, and the more so, as I am conscious I have no sufficient excuse to make for my weakness. I can only say that I am urged on by an awful impulse which I have no power to resist, yet, ashamed of my folly, I have not dared to impart my purpose to any one; I would, if possible, have concealed it even from myself.

Oh why do I think thus of Harriot? why have I come hither in pursuit of one whom I dare not attempt seeing, except by stealing a transient glimpse of her in public when she may be seen by thousands as well as myself, by thousands of senseless beings who will contemplate even charms like hers with coldness and apathy, while to me a single glance at them will be a new existence. No, she must not, shall not know that I am here! I will not add to my folly in coming hither, the guilt of attempting to thrust myself on her observation. Secretly will I watch her footsteps, content to know that I can kiss the earth whereon she treads, that I breathe the same air she breathes; that I may, oh transport inexpressible! sometimes be gratified with beholding her.

And am I then in Dublin? Am I on the very spot that should only recal agonizing recollections of a deceased object, and yet do I find myself thus absorbed in a living one? Oh God! when I recur for a moment to the idea of my lost, lost saint, I can scarcely pardon my soul its present infidelity! Yet 'tis not infidelity! No, 'tis still the same passion! Were Harriot not the living image of my long-loved departed Emily, she had never obtained this interest in my heart. I endeavour farther too, to excuse myself in the persuasion that 'tis impossible for ever to retain a passion for an object irrecoverably lost, and that 'tis rather a subject of regret that I had not sooner fixed my strong affections on another, than of censure that I have done so now. Oh had I earlier known the object of my present pursuit, I then perhaps had not fallen into those errors which I must now for ever deplore! Let me not think of them, lest I grow hateful to myself for daring, such as I am, to raise my eyes to purity like hers. But no! since the idea of a departed angel has been the cause of all my guilt, of all my sufferings, that of a living one shall be the charm to recal me to virtue and peace of mind, even though she herself never must be mine.

If you would ask, Lionel, what are my intentions in coming hither, I can plead no other motives than what I have already stated, that I exist but in knowing myself to be in the same place with Harriot, and that I am inspired with a restless eagerness unaccountable even to my own heart, to possess myself of the particulars of her story, which I thought I should certainly learn here. But how, alas, have I found myself mistaken! I arrived at Dublin two days ago, and immediately began making enquiries of my landlord at the inn, into the state of Mrs. Belgrave's cause, concluding that it must now form a principal subject of attention and conversation among all ranks of people. But strange to say, though otherwise a true innkeeper in curiosity and garrulity, he is totally unacquainted even with the name of Belgrave. At the coffee-house 'twas the same, I heard many topics discussed as I sat listening for several hours together, but the name of Belgrave was never once mentioned.

Is not this most extraordinary? Do then the worthy inhabitants of this place differ so widely from their fellow-creatures in all other towns in the known world, that they never concern themselves about their neighbours' affairs? That surely is impossible. I am however by all this but the more fully assured that there must be something very peculiar relative to the transaction, since, as I often observed to you, all was mystery on the subject at Campbell-House, nor could we ever learn more than that Mrs. Belgrave's journey to Ireland was in the hope of recovering an estate long litigated. Oh that I were better informed on this matter! Yet how, alas, is the desired information to be obtained, since, ignorant as I am as to the particulars of the story, I cannot by the mention of them learn what else I want to know; I can only enquire about it by the name of one of the parties concerned, and that seems so little known, that it will not serve as a clue to assist in making any discoveries. The pursuit however shall not be hastily relinquished.

Lionel, I know that I deserve reproof for thus yielding to the weakness of my feelings, at a time when my whole attention ought to be devoted to other subjects. But perhaps the many difficulties I found in forming a plan for my future establishment, contributed in no slight degree to keeping my mind in that unsettled state which impelled me at last to follow the *ignis fatuus** that now misleads me. Yet I was willing to flatter myself that I might here find some situation suited to my purpose. I flattered myself so, because I felt a diseased eagerness to come hither, though had not Harriot been here, an establishment in this kingdom had probably never entered my idea.

Write to me, Lionel, tell me that you compassionate rather than censure me, and that assurance will be a soothing balsam to the soul of
      Your truly affectionate

HENRY EGERTON.

---

*   Will-o'-the-wisp. A misleading or delusive aim or object. Literally *foolish fire*, so called for the phosphorescent light sometimes seen flitting over marshy ground at night and misleading those who follow it.

LETTER II.

HARRIOT BELGRAVE
TO
OLIVIA CAMPBELL.

Dublin, November 30.

Accept, dearest Olivia, my very sincere thanks for your repeated kind and welcome communications on the subject of Mr. Egerton; they give me earnest hopes that all will be right with him at last, though how far this may influence my future fate time only can determine. I must be thoroughly convinced that his heart is still capable of feeling all its former affection, before I can think of being any other to him than I am present. I am perhaps unreasonable in making a doubt of this, but such, alas! is the inveteracy of habit, and so dreadful the effect of passing a course of years immersed in dissipation, that I know well, nothing can be more difficult than for the mind to break loose from its shackles and regain its proper tone. The hand of correction has lately fallen upon him in various ways, and still smarting under its effects, his present feelings lead entirely to penitence and remorse, but when the pain arising from the chastisement is past, I dread a relapse into his former courses.

Our business will, I hope, be finished in six weeks or two months, when we propose returning to England. To that period I shall look forward with no common degree of anxiety, as my fate will then probably be finally decided. I was once apprehensive that the impression made upon Mr. Egerton, by his idea of my resemblance to Emily had been transient, and was now thought of no more, but I hear with the greatest pleasure that it has taken permanent possession of his mind.

I rejoice extremely, my dear Olivia, to find that you are to pass the winter in South Audley-Street. I told you before we parted, that I believed Mr. Stanhope to be really and firmly attached to you, and all your subsequent communications have confirmed me strongly in that belief. Your objections to accepting his offer at the time it was made, were unanswerable and worthy of yourself, but as they can exist no longer, supposing that offer to be repeated, it would surely not be doing justice either to him, or yourself, to let them have farther influence with you.

Shall I not confess that you appear in my opinion to conceive erroneous ideas on the subject of wedded happiness, when you express a doubt whether you ought ever to think of changing your situation. Can you suppose, my beloved friend, that the most exquisite personal attractions will retain their original ascendancy over the heart of one, to whom, by the frequent contemplation of them, they are become entirely familiar? The most perfect features, or the loveliest form, *may*, nay almost of necessity *must* cease to be impressive when no longer recommended by novelty. Mere external charms, from never varying, seem constantly to diminish, and with them too declines the passion that rested on so frail a foundation; but Mr. Stanhope's attachment rests upon a basis so much more solid, that to doubt its permanence seems alike injurious to him and to yourself.

Oh let me then, as one to whom your happiness is dearer, far, far dearer, than her own, conjure you not by an over-cautious, I might almost say, romantic refinement, to raise up imaginary obstacles to your mutual happiness, but to bestow yourself upon a man, who I am convinced will prove himself worthy of you, by shewing that he is capable of justly estimating the value of the treasure he possesses; though, believe me, my friend, I think it no easy matter justly to appreciate its worth.

I shall be very impatient to learn the event of your stay in London. Ah, dearest Olivia, indissolubly united as our hearts have long been, how deeply must each participate in the present crisis of the other's fate! Let me then, I entreat, hear from you very frequently. To be assured that every thing is settled to your entire satisfaction, will confer the highest possible pleasure upon the heart of
Your faithfully affectionate

E. H. BELGRAVE.

LETTER III.

LIONEL STANHOPE
TO
HENRY EGERTON.

Kilverton, December 6.

No, Harry, though I was much concerned at seeing the date of your letter, far be it from me to reprove you. I am not insensible to the nature of those feelings by which you were urged, I can perfectly conceive and sympathize with them. I only regret most sincerely that your intentions were concealed from me, since if they had been imparted, I had undoubtedly solicited permission to be your companion. I disapprove nothing in the whole affair but your going alone on an expedition, in which you will probably find so many things to harass and torment you. It was a very great relief to my mind to hear that you were well, and to learn the cause of your late silence, as it had occasioned me many hours of the most anxious and tormenting apprehension.

I quitted Campbell-House without obtaining any satisfaction upon the subject of Ryder or either of the letters. In spite of all our efforts we could not trace out the bearers of them, we could only suspect that the gypsey-like appearance of the man who brought the challenge was an assumed disguise, as we cannot learn that any groupe of gypsies has been lately in the neighbourhood. I had once begun to entertain a suspicion that the writer of the letter might himself be also the bearer, but upon enquiry the latter was rather below the middle size, so that this conjecture, however ingenious, must fall to the ground—Ryder might give his complexion the gypsey hue, but it is not so easy a matter to cut a stature of full six feet, down to so low a standard.

One thing, however, I have learned, that the Ensign's object in going abroad, is to visit his old friend George Barry, who had been travelling about the continent for more than a year, and is now settled at Lausanne[1] for the winter. Removed to such a distance from his father, the young squire thinks he may safely venture to solicit the company of this cherished companion of his youth, and Ryder, as Beauchamp thinks, is glad on any terms to quit England, in hopes of finding in another country, that peace of mind to which 'tis evident he is a stranger here. He has written to no one since his departure—this silence I am disposed to attribute to conscious shame on the subject of the challenge; yet, why then did he send it?—his conduct is altogether perfectly unaccountable.

I am surprised at Mrs. Belgrave's affair not being a matter of greater publicity, but I know that every thing relative to it is in a very prosperous train, and that she and her lovely daughter propose returning to England as soon as it shall be decided, but how soon that may be is at present totally uncertain. The law does not travel with the expedition of a mail coach.

Adieu my dear Harry, believe me now, as ever,

Most unalterably yours,

LIONEL STANHOPE.

LETTER IV.

LIONEL STANHOPE
TO
ORLANDO ST. JOHN.

South Audley Street, January 8.

Orlando, the accomplished Olivia and myself are, to my inexpressible satisfaction, once more inhabitants of the same house. She is our guest in South Audley Street, easy, unaffected, and enchanting as ever. Oh, with what eager impatience do I look forward to her introduction into the gay world!—yet, while I wish, I more than half dread it. How if some of my former dashing acquaintance should enquire who that beautiful creature is that seems to belong to my party?—I must put on a very consequential look and answer—"That lady? oh, she is the celebrated Miss Campbell, the great Yorkshire heiress, the daughter of General Campbell who distinguished himself so much in the war of fifty-six[2]—one of the most cultivated and accomplished women in England."

"God! what, that's Miss Campbell!—the *celebrated* Miss Campbell!—Faith, Stanhope, she is not celebrated without reason. She may be very amiable, very accomplished, but curse me if I ever saw any thing in a female form half so ugly. But I beg pardon, I ought not to be so free in my remarks, for since every body gives her to you as a wife, we are to suppose she is handsome in your eyes."

I shall look foolish, wonder how I could think of offering my handsome person to a woman who could be made the subject of such remarks—persuade myself I must have been mad at the moment, and thank heaven that she was not mad enough to accept me—then go home, hear her talk or play on the harp for the rest of the evening, forget her face entirely, go to bed, think about her, dream about her, rise in the morning convinced that she is as much superior to the rest of her sex in one description of charms as I am to mine in another, and determine to renew my offer the very first opportunity.

St. John, what revolutions cannot female power accomplish!—such is the revolution this admirable woman has wrought in me, but her power by no means stops here. Would you believe it, on the day that she was expected in town, I went down to dinner and there found Sir Francis so transformed, that I protest, as his back was turned to me at my entrance, I had no idea whom it was I beheld. His bushy wig was thrown aside, and a venerable head of grey hair, which had been suffered to grow slily and unknown to any one was displayed—the gold-laced suit was exchanged for a neat plain coat, with a black satin waistcoat and remainders, and the little stiff-plated stock for a cambrick cravat. And all this to compliment his expected guest, who has long waged a most determined warfare against those precious reliques of ancient days, which no one but herself could have made the worthy Baronet resign. But oh, the ingratitude of woman!—still the saucy heiress was not content, and wickedly asked why he had not pantaloons.

Indeed should she ever become my wife, I shall be intolerably jealous of my dear papa, for upon my soul I believe he is a much greater favourite than myself. I wonder sometimes how Lady Stanhope can take all her husband's gallantries to another woman so patiently, but she always was a quiet, mild, enduring soul. And to be sure if the Baronet had the good fortune to find favour in the sight of the heiress before, I do not wonder that she is much more charmed with him now, for with these alterations in his dress, he is become one of the handsomest old men I know, altogether as handsome, Orlando, for an old man, as his accomplished son is for a young one.

Charlotte is perfectly correct in her idea, 'tis impossible, I am convinced, to write upon a subject that one feels very deeply. Ambitious of being particularly gallant on occasion of the heiress's arrival in London, I thought I would receive her with a copy of verses expressive of my transports at being again blessed with her society, and giving an oblique hint by the way, that the attachment I had once professed to her was by no means diminished, but on the contrary, still continued to burn with ever-increasing force. So down I sat, took pen in hand, and invoked every muse by turns, and all the nine collectively, but I could make nothing of it at last; not a line that I wrote was at all suited to my purpose, beauty was constantly thrusting itself in the way, and that I knew I must not celebrate. Curse the poets, I could almost say, since Jerry is not at my elbow to reprove me for using such words, why have they been such egregious dunces through all this long succession of ages, as to make beauty their sole theme, the one object to which their tender lays have been devoted?—This abominable principle has rendered it so extremely difficult for a bard now-a-days to break loose from their shackles, that I could scarcely find any appropriate language in poetry to express my admiration of the charms Olivia really does possess.

In short, after sitting three full hours threshing my poor brains at a most unmerciful rate, I had worried them at last to so little effect, that instead of what I wished, I only produced the following stanzas, which though, perhaps, not wholly irrevelant to the state of my mind at the moment, are yet far removed from the impassioned tone in which I intended to write. There is indeed a philosophical turn of reflection in them, which appears no unnatural result of Olivia's occupying my thoughts so entirely at the time they were written, and presenting perhaps a more faithful portrait of the calm transports I feel when I revolve in my mind her numberless virtues and accomplishments, than if they had been written with more passion.

ON LOVE AND FRIENDSHIP.

No more, ye mortals, to the sighing shades,
    In strains of piteous eloquence complain
That love where'er he comes your peace invades,
    And disappointment lurks in Friendship's train.

Alike unjustly ye describe the first
    Beneath the semblance of a guileful boy,
Who, when the heart is by his influence curs'd,
    "Robs virtue of content, and youth of joy."

"Or, as from Etna's burning entrails torn,[3]
    More fierce than tygers on the Lybian plain,
Begot in tempests and in thunders born,
    And wildly raging like the roaring main."

To him who bows to reason's potent sway,
    Love ne'er in such forbidding forms appears;
'Tis when we passion's voice alone obey,
    That the mild God this awful aspect wears.

If reason in the bosom holds her throne
    The heart will ne'er for worthless objects burn,
And 'tis misplac'd affection which alone
    Can love's soft raptures into poison turn.

'Tis thus with friendship too, she only leads
    The erring heart thro' sorrow's mazy dance,
If reason foster not the bursting seeds
    First scatter'd by the careless hand of chance.

But ne'er will Disappointment's "stealing pace"
    Be sadly tow'rd the throbbing bosom steer'd
If virtuous sympathy still forms the base
    On which the sacred dome of Friendship's rear'd.

Can we then justly Love or Friendship blame,
    If erring paths we take to seek those pow'rs,
Or 'gainst their joys as springs of woe exclaim,
    When 'tis ourselves plant thorns amid their flow'rs.

If with cool judgment, not with headstrong haste,
    We yield our bosoms to those sacred ties,
Our hearts no sorrow from their springs shall taste,
    But still new raptures shall on raptures rise.

For nought on earth can equal bliss impart
    As when in virtuous love or friendship join'd
Soul twines with soul, and heart unites with heart,
    From the soul dross of selfishness refin'd.

Thus sweetly link'd, by petty jars and strife,
    We ne'er should find our wedded transports cross'd,
Nor would, as now too oft, the hapless wife
    Lament the lover in the husband lost.

Then friendship too would be no more esteem'd
    An empty name, more fragile e'en than love;
But the exhaustless source would still be deem'd
    Of all the purest joys our hearts can prove.

For love, tho' teeming with ten thousand charms,
    Must still to one sole object be confin'd;
While friendship wider opes her outstretch'd arms,
    And to her throbbing breast clasps all mankind.

Yes, Orlando, I do find that I daily grow more and more sentimental and philosophical, and should I wed my monitress at last, ye Gods! 'tis by no means improbable that I may become a second Socrates, or Seneca,[4] and that the wise saws of Lionel Stanhope may be in as great repute some thousands of years hence, as are at this moment those of the two above-named philosophers.

Heigho!!! Orlando, I must repeat again and again Heigho!!!

Yet believe me not the less

Your truly affectionate

LIONEL STANHOPE.

LETTER V.

LIONEL STANHOPE
TO
HENRY EGERTON.

South Audley Street, January 9.

What a happy place is London, Harry! It now contains the most amiable woman existing in the known world. Olivia entered it for the first time in her life two days ago, to my inexpressible satisfaction. So rejoiced was I to see her again, so many hours of true delight did I look forward to enjoying in her company, that I had well nigh flown up to her, and clasped her in my arms as she entered the drawing-room; but I know not how it is, I don't think after all that is a mode of expressing transport suited to Olivia, she however held out her hand to me, which I took with the utmost cordiality, and if I could read aright the expression of her countenance, she was well pleased that I did so.

She brings intelligence of Ryder's return to England, and by himself, so that it should seem the ingenious plan Beauchamp and I settled, that he had married privately, and was gone to live abroad with his wife, has no foundation in fact. As soon as his arrival was known at Campbell-House, Beauchamp wrote to him upon the subject of the challenge, and the day before Olivia set out, his answer came, solemnly disavowing any knowledge of it, and regretting extremely the light in which his character must all this time have appeared to me. Thus is the affair involved in greater perplexity than ever. That the thing is a forgery, is now evident; yet it appears even more strange that such a paper should have been sent me without any apparent motive, than that Ryder should have fallen into an error, and, inconsistent as man is, in consequence of it have acted for once in a manner unworthy of his character.

For what satisfactory motive can be found for any one having forged

Ryder's name to such a paper? Could it originate in malice, in an odious wish to create an irreparable breach between him and me? Yet who can have been actuated by such a wish? Who can be interested to set us at variance, or hope to receive advantage or gratification from it? Is it intended as a joke? Who can have been such an egregious blockhead as to sport with such edge-tools? What if Ryder had not been out of my reach, I know not whether Beauchamp's explanations might have proved of any avail, incensed as I was at that moment. Neither is it easier to conjecture who can have devised such a joke. The letter came from Doncaster, so far the messenger said, and as there was no post mark upon it, must have been sent by somebody there. Besides, none but a person in the neighbourhood could have been sufficiently acquainted with the circumstances of the several parties to whom it related, to have composed it. I cannot form any satisfactory conjecture about the matter, so I will neither teaze you or myself with farther speculations upon it.

Harry, I am very impatient to hear from you again. My mind is ill at ease while I know you to be in Dublin: I wish I were with you, I seem to myself almost wanting in friendship not [to] have set out for Ireland the moment that I knew of your being there; but with all our boasted disinterestedness, man is at last a merely selfish animal, and since I knew that by going to town I should soon see Olivia, I could hardly resolve to take any other route. Strange, that Olivia Campbell should now be an object of greater consideration than Henry Egerton, in the bosom of

His faithfully affectionate

LIONEL STANHOPE.

LETTER VI.

OLIVIA CAMPBELL
TO
HARRIOT BELGRAVE.

South Audley Street, January 15.
To you, my dear Harriot, who know so well the high esteem in which I hold our good friends in South Audley Street, and the gratification I always feel from their kind attentions to me, it would be needless to expatiate on the pleasure I feel at being now their guest; a pleasure which receives no small addition from reflecting that the unpleasant obstacle which has hitherto subsisted to my being so, is removed.

My journey was rendered extremely agreeable by having Madam de Clairville as my companion. Instead of passing a fortnight with the Blakes, which she declared at coming to them was the utmost possible limits of her stay, she has been there more than two months, and so reciprocally pleased with each other were the hosts and their visitor, that they scarcely knew at last how to separate. Sorry am I to add, that her two daughters and the governess have remained all this time at Scarborough, without her appearing to concern herself about them, and they are now ordered down to their grand-father's in Berkshire, while the fair widow herself is mingling in all the gaieties of the metropolis. Alas! in what a degraded point of view does this fascinating woman's conduct appear, when she is considered as a mother, yet so enchanting is her company, that 'tis impossible in her presence to recollect she is in any respect an object of censure.

As she was no less inclined than myself to see the celebrated University of Cambridge, we agreed to stop for two days at that seminary of sound learning and religious education. On our arrival I immediately dispatched a note to my relation, Mr. Campbell of Trinity College, informing him that I was then at the Rose Inn, where I should be very happy to see him; while Madame de Clairville sent one of the like import to a Mr. Macklin of St. John's, with whom she had a slight acquaintance, a *queer* mortal, she said, but as we should want two beaux to walk about with us, he would be better than nobody. The gentlemen, who fortunately are rather dear friends, came immediately to pay their respects to us, were extremely happy to see us, and thought Cambridge much honoured by our presence, only regretted that we had come at a time of the year very unfavourable for seeing any place to advantage. Mr. Campbell then gave us a very pressing invitation to adjourn to his rooms for the evening, but this we declined, and begged that he and Mr. Macklin would rather be our guests. To this, however, they would by no means consent, till we had promised to dine with the former on the next day, and the latter on the day after.

The mornings of both these days were passed in seeing the lions,[5] but I have neither time nor inclination now, my dear Harriot, to enter upon a detail of all that we saw. Besides, I am far from being perfectly assured I could make such a description as amusing as I wish, and nothing is more wearying than a mere dull narrative of the dimensions of buildings, and a catalogue of the books, manuscripts, and other curiosities that each library contains. Suffice it therefore to say in general, that I have been so much pleased with the place, even under the disadvantage of seeing it in the winter, that I shall certainly take some future opportunity of visiting it at a more favourable season.

One of the curiosities we saw, I cannot however forbear honouring with particular notice. This was a painter who is so great an adept in his profession, that he cannot paint an arm, and to supersede the necessity of his gentlemen and ladies being accommodated with those useful members of the human frame, he puts them all indiscriminately into long cloaks. Once indeed, when grown more aspiring than usual, he had thrown aside the cloak for a little way, just to discover the hand, and add a variety to the groupe, he made an unfortunate mistake, and gave the lady, for it was no less a personage than one of the Graces themselves, five fingers besides the thumb. He possesses indeed an excellence not common to all artists, that of bending *nature* and *custom*, those two great masters whom gentlemen of his profession are usually emulous of imitating with fidelity and accuracy, entirely to his own abilities and convenience.

When we went into the room, we found a large canvas upon his easel, on which he seemed very earnestly employed. "What are you doing there, Mr. Barnes?" enquired Mr. Campbell.

"Painting those two famous rocks, Scylla and Charybdis,"[6] replied the artist.

"Rocks, Mr. Barnes? I thought Charybdis had been a whirlpool?"

"Right, Sir. But I avail myself of the poetical licence, and make them both rocks."

When we were satisfied with contemplating the artist and his works, we were taking leave with thanks for our entertainment; but he with a very profound bow, and an air of great importance, stepped up to us, and begged to know when we intended him the honour of sitting?

"Oh, Sir," said Mr. Campbell, "the ladies did not come with that view, they merely wished to see your paintings."

"Possibly, Sir. But when they had seen them, I flattered myself that with whatever intention they came into the room, there was but one with which they could leave it."

To this modest conclusion I made no reply, but the more eloquent Madame de Clairville assured him that nothing but the necessity she was under of being in Town in the course of two days, prevented her sitting. But, she added, he might rest satisfied, that should she ever wish to have her portrait taken, at whatever distance she might be from Cambridge, she should certainly never think of applying to any one but himself, and should regard a journey of three or four hundred miles as nothing, for the sake of being painted by so admirable an artist. With this assurance Mr. Barnes seemed tolerably contented, and suffered us to depart.

At dinner at Mr. Campbell's, there were, besides ourselves, a Mr. Walters, and a Mr. Servan, both, as well as Mr. Campbell and Mr. Macklin, Masters of Arts and Fellows of their respective societies. I sat down to table full of expectation of the delight and instruction to be received at an academic dinner, which I concluded I should find truly and literally,

"The feast of reason, and the flow of soul."[7]

At the top of the table was a large Mock Turtle Soup. This I soon found to be a dish held in high respect in the University, from the eagerness with which the four gentlemen emulously strove to pay it honour due. When it was demolished, they all began to be eloquent in its praises, and unanimously agreed that it was scarcely inferior to one of which they had partaken a few days before at St. John's feast. Upon this Mr. Campbell observed, it was not surprising that the merits of Trinity and St.

John's cooks should be so much upon an equality, since they were apprentices together at one of the first shops in London, and their master had often been heard to declare that he never sent two fellows out of his house who understood their business better.

"Aye indeed?" said Walters. "Well, I never knew before that they were brother apprentices, but I always said they were indisputably the best cooks in the University."

"And I don't recollect," said Servan, "that St. John's cook exerted himself with better effect, than at the last feast there. Far the best dinner we've had all this Christmas."

"And well it might be," said Walters, "for no other college had such luck in presents. The Bishop of —— sent them a whole doe, and the Dean of —— one of the finest salmons that ever was seen, and Doctor —— a noble north country pye and they had besides a profusion of game from different noblemen and dignitaries of the church formerly of the college."

"Yes," said Mr. Macklin, "our old pupils seldom forget us, and they know that they cannot testify their recollection of us so acceptably as in this way."

"'Tis true," said Mr. Campbell, "the salmon was uncommonly fine, and the lobster sauce, as far as it went, exquisite; but the greatest fault to be found with the dinner was, that this same sauce was terribly *morish*. I unfortunately sat by one of the boats, and was obliged to help others till there was scarcely any left for myself."

"And I was in a similar situation unluckily with regard to the venison," said Mr. Walters. "I had to carve one of the haunches, consequently, by the time I had helped every body else, there was nothing but the pickings of the bone left for myself, without any fat to help them down, though faith it was the fattest doe venison I ever saw."

"Indeed," said Mr. Servan, "I should say the greatest defect in the dinner was, that the cook had not shewn his usual judgment with respect to the venison. The necks should have been roasted with the haunches for the sake of the fat, whereas he had put them into the pasty,* where they were not near so much wanted."

Harriot, would you wish for any more of our instructive academical conversation? Surely this specimen is sufficient, and during the whole day it consisted but of two subjects, eating and card-playing. In short, I found that at this jovial season of the year, at least, when there is a continued round of feasts in the halls of all the colleges, the minds of the gentlemen were too much absorbed by them to think of any thing else.

Yet I cannot take my leave of Cambridge without a few words more to Mr. Macklin. Once in indigent circumstances, and supported at the University principally by charity, he was humble and modest in his demeanour, and thought only of rendering himself worthy of the favour

---

*   Meat pie, usually of venison (*OED*).

shewn him, by the regularity of his conduct and a diligent attention to his studies. He sought not be any thing but what he really was, and he was respectable and respected. But truly does the poet say:

> When the soul is steel'd
> By meditation to encounter sorrow,
> The foe of man shifts his artillery
> And drowns in luxury and careless softness
> The breast he could not storm.[8]

Such was the case with George Macklin. Adversity he could support with dignity and propriety; he could not stand the harder trial of prosperity. By the unexpected patronage of one to whom his humble merit was his recommendation, now placed in a state of comparative affluence, he cannot be sufficiently elevated with his good fortune. His great ambition is to be considered as a complete man of the world, and he is continually expatiating on the qualifications necessary for forming that character. One of the most essential, he says, is to understand Spanish, and he is therefore studying that language with such unwearied assiduity that he hopes soon to have made sufficient progress in it to be properly qualified for admission into the gay circles of London, where he ardently longs to exhibit himself. His deficiency in this most essential ingredient for forming the man of fashion, has alone withheld him hitherto from making his début in that centre of taste.

When he learned that I was on my way to making my first visit there, he threw himself back in his chair, not in the style of a person of the very highest breeding, and opening wide an enormous mouth, burst into an immoderate *horse-laugh*. Yes Harriot, I must be allowed to use that expression, since no other can describe the horrible noise he made, and the strange convulsive agitation of his whole frame. Alas! that a fine gentleman should be extremely subject, as I understand he is, to similar fits! Three times did this convulsion subside, and three times again break forth before we could comprehend what had occasioned it, when at length the whole terminated in his wishing earnestly that he could accompany me to London, he should like so much to witness my astonishment on entering it, and to see how I should stare about me at the novelty of the scene. This was not altogether unamusing in one who had never been there himself.

As we had the same party at dinner on both occasions, Mr. Walters and Mr. Servan, now in their turns, pressed us earnestly to prolong our stay for another two days, that they also might have the honour of our company at their rooms. Indeed I thought the fair widow seemed to have made a little impression upon Mr. Servan's heart, for he was absolutely on the second day of their meeting more attentive to her than to the dinner. We however declined the gentlemen's invitation, and pursued our route to London at the time we had originally fixed.

And now, Harriot, allow me a few words on the subject of Mr. Stanhope. His manner of receiving me was much more than merely polite, it was with a degree of interest and satisfaction which precluded all possibility of doubt that he really was happy at seeing me again. Indeed I find the invitation to fix my residence in town at Sir Francis's house, was entirely his suggestion. To this he could only be induced by feeling a pleasure in my company, if by no stronger motives. Indeed that he has farther views I can scarcely doubt from his whole manner. Sir Francis seems so well assured of this, as to entertain no more fears upon the subject, but to consider his favourite point absolutely and irrevocably carried. Ah, perhaps he still flatters himself too far!

For though thus satisfied that I am far from being considered with indifference by Mr. Stanhope, nay more, that I possess his perfect esteem, I yet feel as irresolute as ever what to do in case of his former offers being renewed. Devoted as he has been all his life to beauty, nay so much as he still continues its slave, dare I hope that his heart can ever experience that unbounded attachment to me which I must be assured of in a husband, or I should be miserable? Though you have so often reproved what you call my romantic ideas of wedded happiness, and gave me a friendly hint upon the subject in your last letter; yet, my dear Harriot, I still cannot conquer my doubts, not can I even allow the justice of the term you employ, or that my ideas are romantic according to the general acceptation of the word. For would any woman capable of using her reason, marry under the cruel apprehension that in a few short years, or perhaps months, she may no longer enjoy the entire affection of the man on whom the chief happiness or misery of her life must depend. And could I marry Mr. Stanhope without such a latent apprehension? Ah! there, there is the cruel question!

'Tis true that while his eyes wander after other objects, his understanding may condemn them; but should I act wisely to stake my whole happiness upon such a chance as this? Can a man who through the mistaken indulgence of over-fond parents, has been permitted to waste the most important years of his life in the pursuit of pleasure, be expected in one moment to shake off habits so pernicious, without occasionally feeling a restless desire to return into this path of mingled roses and thorns? Ah! Harriot, your own judgment will best determine this point.

The mighty power of mind I am willing to allow; with circumstance it perhaps divides the empire of the world, nay, may occasionally controul even circumstance itself. But a mind not trained from its earliest infancy to the exertion of its powers, scarcely ever attains the full possession of them, and my fears are that Mr. Stanhope is too recently awakened to the exertion of his energies, and to a sense of the value of such exertion in others, to afford sufficient security against his relapsing into his old propensities.

Of one thing I shall always rest assured, that my fortune never can have any share in influencing such a mind as his. If his offer should be renewed, I shall be satisfied that 'tis entirely from motives of preference for me, and with a firm resolution to do all in his power to make me happy. What I dread is self-deception in him, and that not feeling at present any attachment more powerful, he may be deluded into the idea that this never will be the case, nor be awakened from his error till he too late finds himself fatally mistaken.

Yet thus far I must confess, that a principal cause of the doubts which harassed my mind when last I wrote to you is removed. I then thought that Madame de Clairville had made a deep impression upon his heart, and in that idea felt many an uneasy moment. But I am now convinced he considers her only as a lively coquette, with whom 'tis pleasant to trifle away an idle hour, but who is ill-suited to becoming the object of a serious passion. Yet though convinced of this, I cannot forbear asking myself, whether all that I have witnessed in his conduct with regard to her, ought not the more fully to confirm my general apprehensions, since his imagination at least, if not his heart, was for a while so much influenced by her attentions.

Before I quitted Yorkshire, we heard, though merely by accident, of Mr. Ryder's return to England. Mr. Beauchamp immediately wrote to him, mentioning the affair of the challenge, and requesting an explanation of it. In answer, he made a solemn disavowal of any knowledge of the circumstance, accompanied by expressions of strong indignation against the author of so malignant a forgery, but not a word transpired respecting himself or his future plans. This persevering silence upon these subjects, distresses me so much, that I have requested Mr. Beauchamp to see him, and endeavour, if possible, to procure some explanation of his late conduct, which, at present, appears wholly inexplicable. With this view, Mr. Beauchamp was to go to Pontefract, whence Mr. Ryder's letter was dated, as soon as he could conveniently spare the time, and I wait with no small impatience to hear the result of their interview. What can have occasioned this sudden reverse in his behaviour to me, is far beyond my conception. I am sometimes fearful lest he should be under pecuniary embarrassments, and while this preys upon his mind, he is yet unwilling to acknowledge it. But such an idea I ought, perhaps, at once to reject, as 'tis inconsistent with his principles to have involved himself in expences his means would not answer; and if he had been imprudent in this way, I think he would hardly have suffered his temper to be so changed by it, rather than candidly and fairly confess his fault.

Peggy Perkins, unfortunate as she is, after staying only two months at Leeds, finds herself under the disagreeable necessity of quitting a place where she has been happier than ever she was in her life, not from the malice of her persecutors, for I have not heard that the tongue of calumny has yet pursued her into this retreat, but from the too extensive influence of her charms. They have had so powerful an effect upon the heart of a grocer's son in the town, that in the frenzy of his passion, unmindful of the great distance between himself and the object of his adoration, he even dared to make formal proposals of marriage to her. She has taken care, however, to shew all proper indignation at his unparalleled assurance, but still she thinks that it is not right to remain in the same place with him, lest that should be considered as a tacit encouragement not to drop the pursuit.

It may, notwithstanding, be made a question, whether the young grocer would have driven his adored mistress from the town, had not Mr. Peters too quitted it, oh, cruel to say, without confessing a tender passion for her. Had he made such a confession, though only an actor, 'tis probable his suit would not have been rejected with the same disdain as the unfortunate grocer's.

Adieu, my dear Harriot. I have already written so long a letter, that I will not now enter upon a detail of where I have been, and what I have seen; I will only say, that though I acknowledge London to be a fine city, the first sight of it did not excite in me the strong emotions of astonishment expected by Mr. Macklin. Present my kindest remembrances to Mrs. Belgrave, and believe me

Your truly affectionate

OLIVIA CAMPBELL.

LETTER VII.

REGINALD BEAUCHAMP
TO
OLIVIA CAMPBELL.

Maxtead, January 20.

I returned yesterday evening, my dear madam, from passing a week at Pontefract, but am sorry to say, that the result of my visit will afford you little satisfaction.

Mr. Ryder received me with the utmost friendship and cordiality, and at first endeavoured to assume his accustomed cheerfulness, yet the mask was too thin to conceal the evident uneasiness that preys upon his mind. I was weak enough to believe that his secret might be drawn from him by dexterous management, and therefore attempted by circuitous means to accomplish the important discovery. This might have succeeded with a common mind, but could not with one so acute as Richard Ryder's. Nothing less than penetration equal to his own can extract it, and to that I make no pretensions.

"Mr. Beauchamp," he said, when he found me thus playing Rosencrantz and Guildenstern,[9] "I see your drift, and only ask you whether this be acting like a man? You think me unhappy, and I shall not hesitate to acknowledge that my soul is a prey to a secret sorrow which all my fortitude cannot shake off. But have you known me thus long, and can you suppose, that if there were not insuperable objections to the cause of my unhappiness being revealed, it would be concealed from you? Is it generous, then, to attempt discovering by some unguarded word or look, what 'tis evident I wish should remain unknown?"

"Mr. Ryder," I replied, "I stand corrected, and intreat your pardon. I acknowledge that I was wrong, but believe me I was actuated solely by motives of friendship and delicacy. I will now, however, speak plainly, and without circumlocution. Miss Campbell was apprehensive you might be under pecuniary embarrassments, which dwelt on your mind, yet which you were reluctant to impart to her, and she flattered herself if this should be the case, that you would not mortify her so far as to refuse her assistance."

"I am no stranger, Mr. Beauchamp, to the generosity of Miss Campbell's soul, and she is almost the only person on earth from whom I could condescend to receive obligations of this nature. But determined as I am to preserve my independence, my means, not my wishes, have always regulated, and shall continue to regulate my expences; and when I accepted from her the commission which furnishes my present income, I was resolved to look to my own industry alone for all future advancement. My purpose is now to dispose of this commission and settle at Lausanne in the practice of physic, to the study of which, as you well know, all my leisure hours have long been devoted."

"You mean then to quit this kingdom for ever?"

"Assuredly."

"And may I ask how soon?"

"As soon as I can settle my affairs, which may possibly detain me three or four months."

"You returned to England then solely for this purpose."

"Solely."

I thought immediately of the young woman seen with him in the post-chaise, and the conversation soon after furnishing me with an opportunity of mentioning her, I began to rally him upon the subject.

"Good God!" he exclaimed, "is it then impossible to perform even the slightest act of friendship, without being made an object of curiosity to all the country round, and the subject of their contemptible observations and conjectures. What if that woman had been my wife, it was no concern of any one except her and myself. However, sir, I can assure you she is not so, and that I only accompanied her abroad as a friend, who thought it highly unadvisable for her to undertake a long journey in a foreign country by herself. This you are authorised to say from me, since, though I do not hold myself accountable to a gossiping world for my actions, I by no means wish that young woman to be supposed my wife."

He uttered the last words with an emphasis and emotion which methought seemed to indicate that they imparted more than actually appeared upon their surface, and I interpreted them, that he was thus anxious to contradict the report of this woman's being his wife, lest it should reach one whom he wished to make so, and create uneasiness between her and himself. This contributed strongly to confirm an idea I had before entertained, that love, that delightful, and tormenting passion, was the secret cause of the late change in his temper and manners—that having fixed his affections unfortunately, he was condemned to drag on a life of vain and fruitless wishes, and his philosophy was not proof against such a state of ever-increasing anguish. And that this idea was not unfounded was still farther confirmed, by a subsequent conversation.

We were discussing the comparative happiness of a single and wedded life, when I said that though I had once earnestly wished to exchange my present freedom for rosy fetters, yet, I was now, upon the whole, better satisfied that my attempt had not been crowned with success, since I was not certain that the increased happiness acquired by matrimony was proportionate to the increased anxieties inevitably attached to the state.

"Good God!" he answered hastily and eagerly, "that a man can harbour such an opinion!"—Then seeming to recollect himself, "and yet," he added, "you may be right!—I believe, indeed, generally speaking, that you are right—I was, perhaps, about to have controverted your position too hastily."

He paused, he sunk for a few moments into a deep abstraction, and then proceeded.—"Yet no, a wedded life must be far happier than a single one, provided the husband and wife be the decided objects of each other's preference. But, alas, how rarely is this the case!—at least, how seldom is it that this preference is formed upon such rational grounds, that a constant intercourse is likely to strengthen, and render it more permanent. This, this, is the principal reason why so few, even of what are apparently marriages of real attachment on both sides, answer the expectation formed. Struck with a beautiful face, or an enchanting form, the lover annexes to these external charms, all those qualities of the mind and heart which alone can render a lovely person valuable, and sighs for the possession of the perfect being his fancy has thus formed. He endeavours to recommend himself to her favour—he succeeds—those charms, once possessed, are charms no longer—he finds this model of perfection insipid as a companion—capricious in her temper—the slave of her own beauty, but a tyrant to all around her—he wonders at his infatuation in ever loving her—he grows negligent of the object he so lately worshipped, and seeks abroad for that peace and comfort he cannot find at home. The fair one loved nothing in him but his attentions and assiduities—a cessation of these alienates her heart from him for ever—if they meet 'tis but to vent their mutual reproaches, and to harmony and confidence they bid an eternal farewell."

"A melancholy picture, indeed!—yet, surely a brighter might be drawn. Even I, though not the professed advocate of a wedded life, should scarcely have given so gloomy a sketch as this."

"Oh yes!—a brighter may indeed be drawn. When a long acquaintance has made the respective parties thoroughly conversant with each other's virtues, each other's failings, so that they have learned properly to value the one, and to feel indulgence towards the other—when their minds are united in the firmest friendship, and reason sanctions the choice of passion, then, indeed, may they look forward to the enjoyment of the highest possible earthly happiness. Yet, alas! such is the perverseness of our fates, that rare indeed are the instances of such an union. Too often does it happen, where an attachment of this nature is formed on one side, that the object of it cannot be inspired with reciprocal feelings, but perhaps sighs after some other object, either unattainable, or in an union with which it would be miserable."

As he spoke, his eyes sparkled with more than common animation, till towards the conclusion, when his countenance changed to an expression, I could almost call it of sublime sadness, while, in his voice, spite of his efforts to speak with firmness, a faultering was perceptible, which seemed to indicate that he felt but too sensibly the force of his own observations. Indeed, from that moment, he studiously dropped the conversation, as if distrusting his own self-command, should it be carried further.

On all this, my dear madam, I leave you to make your own reflections. I can only wish I had been able to obtain a more ample elucidation of the mystery. Since that, however, was impossible, I have nothing more to add, but that I am with the sincerest regard,

Your faithfully affectionate

REGINALD BEAUCHAMP.

LETTER VIII.

HENRY EGERTON
TO
LIONEL STANHOPE.

Dublin, January 20.

Oh, Lionel! what have I not endured since last I wrote to you!—Though my enquiries respecting the Belgraves have been pursued with unwearied assiduity, I have not been able to learn any thing satisfactory upon the subject. Yet, perhaps, it was folly, madness, to expect to procure information in the way in which only it was in my power to seek it. Unknown, unrecommended, in public coffee-houses, I have sat for hours together in perfect solitude, amid a surrounding croud, listening, if possible, to catch some sounds that might satisfy my anxious soul. But alas in vain!—still I have sat on, till wearied, exhausted with not being able to catch a sound which could convey the remotest gleam of satisfaction to my bursting heart, I have returned home half frantic, scarcely knowing where I was, or what I did.

Once only did I think I had obtained some information, when some scattered fragments I caught of a conversation between two gentlemen of the law, led me to imagine that the estate was actually awarded to Mrs. Belgrave, and that she and Harriot were gone down to Limerick to take possession of it. With the swiftness of an arrow did I post to that town, there did I linger for three long weeks, still hoping that each successive day would prove more fortunate than the preceding, yet still disappointed—no trace of any such persons could I find, no mention ever reached my ears even of such a circumstance, as the expected termination of a suit of long standing respecting an estate in the neighbourhood, and I at last returned to Dublin, with the mortifying conviction that I had trusted too eagerly to vague and uncertain sounds.

But oh, what tidings awaited my return hither!—tidings that have driven me almost to frenzy, and on the confirmation, or refutation, of which, hangs my life or death!—Lionel, 'tis rumoured that the widow and daughter of Captain Trelawney, after having lived for many years in the utmost obscurity, uncertain of the event of the claim made to the Trelawney estate, are now at Dublin, expecting every day that the suit will be determined in their favour.

Oh God! Oh God!—can this be!—Can it be that Emily and her mother yet live, and have concealed themselves for so many years, not only from the rest of the world, but even from me!—No, no, I torture myself in vain!—what but a doubt of my faith could induce them to suffer me to believe them dead?—And that they should doubt my faith is impossible. Too well did they know my heart—too well did they know it was Emily herself alone whom I loved, to entertain even a momentary idea that any change in her fortune could alter my sentiments towards her. No, from the very commencement of our acquaintance, her situation was well known to me, and sensible that she was even then, perhaps, poor as she was lovely, my whole heart was nevertheless devoted to her. They saw me ready to brave my father's utmost anger, and resist his wishes rather than not possess her—they saw that fortune was nothing in my eye, else might I at any moment have become the husband of a wealthy wife—but so far was I from seeking riches by the sacrifice of my Emily, that it was evident I never could enjoy even my own fortune unless shared with her.

Away then with the idea!—it cannot be my Emily and her mother who are now in Dublin. The present claimants of the estate must be of another branch of the family. My heart assures me that this is so, my reason says the same, yet I cannot be satisfied till I arrive at a greater certainty upon the subject, nor will I rest till I have obtained it. Life could not be supported many days in my present state of agony.

And should I at last be assured that my Emily still lives, in what a situation am I placed!—I have survived the assurance of her death, oh, how survived it!—dragged on a wretched existence, a burthen to myself, injurious to the world—a creature that ranked in the class of rational beings, yet unable to reason—but to find that she is alive is a stroke that must crush me at once. For,—oh, heavens, I cannot bear the idea!—if this be she, 'tis plain that she lives not for me!—Some strange caprice must have alienated her heart from me, or could she, by concealing herself from my knowledge, have inflicted such torture upon me?—on me, conscious as she must be that she was my all, my world, the sole object for which I wished to live?

Oh, Lionel! though I own that it was an unpardonable weakness in me to come hither, yet regard with compassion your agonised,

Your distracted

HENRY EGERTON.

LETTER IX.

LIONEL STANHOPE
TO
REGINALD BEAUCHAMP.

Kilverton, January 30.

Forgive, forgive, the importunate strain in which I must now address you, Mr. Beauchamp, but my anxiety is too great to be longer suppressed. The peace of mind, perhaps the very existence, of a friend dear to me as my own soul, is at stake, and silence would be criminal.

You cannot have forgotten the extreme eagerness with which, soon after the commencement of our acquaintance, I sought to learn Miss Belgrave's story, or the powerful impression it made upon me when I heard it. Shall I say that the particulars you then imparted, far from satisfying the impatient thirst of my soul, only increased tenfold, that feverish, restless curiosity which burned within me incessantly. Too plainly I saw that though much was revealed, much more was still withheld from me— ah, I was not even then without a suspicion what the remainder might be—and other circumstances have now encreased that suspicion, till 'tis almost converted into a certainty.

Miss Belgrave's *story* might be imparted to me, but the *name* of the wretch who could so basely trifle with artless beauty and innocence, must be cautiously concealed. Ah, why was this? Surely, the knowledge of it was only refused, because it was one with which I was so nearly connected, both by blood and friendship!—Tell me! oh tell me, I conjure you by all that's sacred,—by the sensibility and philanthropy that warms your own bosom, tell me, I conjure you, that I am right!—that by some wonderous means indiscernable at present to my half-informed mind, Emily Trelawney and Harriot Belgrave are the same person!—tell me but this, and eternally will I bless the hand that communicates intelligence so miraculous, so transporting.

Oh read the enclosed, Mr. Beauchamp, 'tis a letter I have just received from Harry at Dublin,—see the tortured state of his mind, and surely if it be in your power to elucidate this mystery you will not withhold the elucidation for a moment.

Has Miss Belgrave laboured under some cruel deception with regard to her lover?—has she believed him false, when, alas! he was only a martyr to his too eager constancy?—Undeceived in so fatal an error, surely she will not refuse her pardon to his frailties—will not refuse to receive again into her heart the reformed penitent—the man whose very failings are the most incontestible proof that his attachment to her has continued no less ardent than hers to him.

The particulars you imparted to me, dear Sir, relative to Miss Belgrave, I never dared communicate to Harry. He knows nothing farther therefore concerning Mrs. and Miss Belgrave's journey to Ireland, then that it is taken in the hope of recovering a long contested estate, else had he probably been struck, like myself, with the coincidence between the story of the latter and that of Emily Trelawney. Thus, while he thinks there is a possibility of Emily's being alive, he has no idea that she lives in Harriot, nor shall he have a hint of this from me, till I am myself better informed upon the subject.

As I cannot bear the idea of Harry's remaining any longer by himself, I mean to join him as soon as possible. I will therefore request of you, my dear Sir, to direct to me at the Post-Office Dublin, and I trust that to intreat an immediate answer would be superfluous. In a case like the present, your own feelings must urge you to write without a moment's delay. Had I been in London, I had instantly flown to Miss Campbell to seek the information I wish, but at present, as you will see, I am at Kilverton. I came hither two days ago upon business for Sir Francis, and had intended setting out on my return to-morrow, but instead of that I shall now proceed with the utmost expedition to Ireland.

Trusting that apologies for the urgent manner in which I have written will be no less superfluous than entreaties for a speedy answer, I shall only beg to be believed,

Very faithfully yours,

LIONEL STANHOPE.

REGINALD BEAUCHAMP

TO

LIONEL STANHOPE.

Maxstead, Feb. 1.

No, my dear Sir, the important secret shall be withheld no longer. In Harriot Belgrave you have indeed beheld the same Emily Trelawney to whom Mr. Egerton's faith was plighted so many years ago. From all that has passed in the various conversations you have had upon the subject, both with Miss Campbell and myself, it seems evident that the unfortunate separation of these lovers originated on Mr. Egerton's part from a fatal error, in supposing Emily and her mother to be on board the Cornwall Packet when she went to the bottom; and on Emily's, from a no less fatal belief that she was abandoned through caprice, by the man to whom she had so entirely devoted herself.

And indeed it was their intention to have gone in that packet, and their passage was taken accordingly. But from some cause, I do not now recollect what, people were at that time flocking in great numbers from this country to Ireland, in consequence of which so many more passengers applied for places on board the Cornwall, than she could possibly accommodate, that several of them, and among others Mrs. and Miss Trelawney, as they were then called, were turned over to a merchant vessel, which was to sail about the same time. Thus, though they were in imminent peril from the same storm in which the Cornwall was lost, they finally escaped.

But certain that the news of the ship's disastrous fate would be instantly spread in England, and occasion the most agonizing apprehensions to all who supposed they had friends on board her, Emily dispatched letters immediately on her landing, both to Mrs. Egerton and Harry, acquainting them with her's and her mother's fortunate escape. I have already told you, my dear Sir, that neither to this, nor to several other letters she wrote, did she ever receive any answer, and the effect these repeated disappointments at length wrought upon her. By what means the letters failed of reaching Mr. Egerton, since it appears from you that they never were received, can scarcely be ascertained at this distance of time.

That our lovely friend has borne two such different names, has arisen from the circumstances of the estate. On Captain Belgrave's succeeding to it, which was in right of his mother, he took the family name of Trelawney, and thus his widow and daughter were known only by that, at the time of Mr. Egerton's becoming acquainted with them. But since Mrs. Belgrave thought it ridiculous to call herself by the family name, while her claim to the estate was doubtful, on her return to England she resumed the name of Belgrave. Ah, little could she foresee to what unhappy consequences a circumstance apparently so trifling might lead, since 'tis probable that if the name of Trelawney had been retained, it might long ago have reached Mr. Egerton's ears, and all might have been explained. Still more unfortunate was it perhaps, that the Christian name by which Miss Belgrave was usually called should be changed; but as she has both the names of Emily and Harriot, Miss Campbell liking the latter best, used to call her by it, at first rather from playfulness, till at length it became a habit among the family to call her by the name of Harriot only, and that of Emily was entirely dropped.

You will perhaps ask whether at Miss Belgrave's return to England, she felt no anxiety to procure intelligence of her lover, how false soever she might conceive him? Indeed this was the first, great object of her solicitude, and she spared no pains consistent with the privacy she thought necessary to be observed upon the subject, to obtain the information she wished. She fully expected to hear, that wanting resolution to resist his father's wishes, he had at length yielded to them, and married the lady selected for him, and equally wanting courage to inform her of his infidelity, had left to chance the means by which the intelligence should reach her.

But far from finding these suspicions confirmed, she soon obtained the heart-rending information that the unfortunate Mr. Edgerton was under confinement in a state of raving madness, nor could any reasonable conjecture be formed respecting the origin of so dreadful a calamity. Fain would she have flown to the sequestered abode whither she was informed the hapless sufferer had been conveyed, there to have watched over him as a ministering angel, and to have caught the first lucid internal, to renew the tender vows they had so often exchanged; but circumstanced as she was with regard to his parents, this was impossible. Nothing therefore remained but to wait the event with anxious uncertainty, and to rely on the solacing hope that the moment of his restoration to reason would be equally that of the revival of his former attachment.

Yet alas! she found that this was but to rest on a broken reed. She learned afterwards, to her soul's deep and lasting anguish, that he recovered from distraction but to devote himself to a life of licentious dissipation, and was at length reduced to the painful necessity of rejoicing that he had never sought the renewal of a connection, which under such circumstances she must have rejected. Yet though forced to condemn him, she never could listen to the addresses of another, or cease to feel the most poignant regret that the conduct of his maturer years should have deviated so lamentably from his youthful promise.

You will now see clearly, my dear Sir, by what means your's and Mr. Egerton's imposture was so immediately detected. An impulse of anxious curiosity, surely not unnatural, induced a wish in Miss Belgrave, when she learned that the object of her former ardent attachment was coming hither, to see him, and prove whether he had absolutely forgotten her, or whether a meeting so unexpected might not suddenly strike him with shame and remorse, and produce effects that might ultimately lead to his repentance and reformation. Yet it will easily be imagined, that after she knew him to be in the house, some little time was requisite to compose her mind, and enable her to assume sufficient fortitude for making the experiment; nay, even at last she could not appear before him without a considerable degree of painful agitation. Conceive then what must have been her feelings at seeing this object of her fond anxiety presented to her as Mr. Stanhope, and his companion, the striking resemblance of Sir Francis, as Mr. Egerton. Was it surprising that she started, and appeared confused? Or could she fail of being anxious immediately to impart the important secret to her friend, and put her on her guard against such an imposture?

Indeed, without her information the imposture had probably not proved very successful, since how well soever you might flatter yourselves that you performed your parts, Miss Campbell plainly perceived, almost from the first moment of seeing you, that all was not right. I leave to her hereafter to describe her feelings upon hearing her suspicions confirmed by Harriot, as well as to explain her motives for retracting a resolution made in the first impulse of indignation, to turn you both out of the house with contempt and disgrace.

But Harriot, though willing to deceive herself into the belief that she had no other feelings towards her former lover except indignation at his treachery, and that she felt this even more forcibly from his behaviour to her best and firmest friend than to herself, yet could not bear to remain in the house with him, and fled the trial she wanted fortitude to face. Olivia on the contrary, however incensed against him for the fallacy he was then practising, was yet more anxious to punish and expose him for his falsehood to Harriot, and had probably never treated him with so much asperity but on her friend's account. These feelings were first softened, on Miss Campbell's learning from you, Mr. Stanhope, the fatal error under which Mr. Egerton laboured with regard to Emily, and the cruel consequences with which it had been attended. The supposed culprit was instantly transformed into the wretched martyr of a hopeless passion, and the benevolent soul of Miss Campbell became no less anxious to soothe, than before this discovery, she had been to expose him.

She immediately wrote her friend an account of what had passed, which induced the latter's return to Campbell-House. It was however agreed that Mr. Egerton should not then be undeceived with regard to Emily's supposed death, but that time should first be given to see whether the dawning hopes of his reformation would be realised. Indeed this discovery would not have been made, even to you, Sir, till Miss Belgrave's return to England, had not your letter rendered it almost indispensable. But as things are now situated, I have no doubt of Miss Campbell's and Miss Belgrave's perfect concurrence with me in saying that you are at full liberty to act entirely according to your own discretion in communicating the affair to Mr. Egerton.

Whenever, or in whatever way it shall be disclosed, by informing me of the result you will much oblige,

>Dear Sir,
>>Yours with great regard,

REGINALD BEAUCHAMP.

LETTER XI.

OLIVIA CAMPBELL
TO
REGINALD BEAUCHAMP.

South Audley Street, February 6.

Your last letter, my much-esteemed friend, was so very unsatisfactory, that I have written to Mr. Ryder myself, to try whether I cannot obtain the confidence you have sought in vain. As I am acquainted with some circumstances relative to him, which I believe have never been confided to any other person, possibly he may be less reluctant to trust the farther secrets of his soul to me, than to you. I cannot bear to know that such a man is unhappy, without endeavouring to find out and remove, if it be in my power, the cause of his unhappiness.

That a secret attachment preys upon his mind I have sometimes been myself apprehensive, and have always regretted that I did not question him farther on the subject of our last meeting, when he parted from me in such extreme emotion. Yet, at the moment, I found this perfectly impossible. Agitation in the common run of mankind we may endeavour to soothe and compose, but in such a man as Mr. Ryder, all enquiry into its origin, or observation upon it, seems precluded. Thus I felt at the time, and perhaps the same reflection ought now to prevent my taking any notice of what has passed, yet I know not how to forbear enquiring whether I am right in a suspicion lately awakened in my mind, since, if so, his intention of settling at Lausanne, will encrease instead of allaying the evil.

Indeed, the only way in which I can solve his conduct ever since the beginning of his last visit to Campbell-House, is by the conjecture to which I allude. This will account for his general abstraction while he was with me, for his silence during his absence, and for his sudden determination to leave England entirely.

Adieu, my dear Sir, I have not now time to enter upon any other subject, else the present eventful period—eventful both to myself and to all nearly connected with me, would furnish materials to fill many sheets of paper. Of these things more at another time—at present I remain with great regard,

Your very affectionate

OLIVIA CAMPBELL.

LETTER XII.

OLIVIA CAMPBELL
TO
RICHARD RYDER.

South Audley Street, February 6.

Were I not well assured, dear Sir, that your heart is too candid and ingenuous to mistake the motives by which I am actuated, and to suspect me of being influenced only by idle curiosity, I might, perhaps, hesitate in addressing you upon a subject of so delicate a nature, as that which now induces me to write. Highly as I respect and esteem your character, and interested as I must always feel for your happiness, could I see with indifference the agitation of mind in which you last parted from me?—No, Mr. Ryder, my heart felt then, and has continued to feel ever since, the most painful anxiety to know the cause of your uneasiness, from a hope that it might be in the power of friendship to contribute towards its removal.

Think not that I am presuming too far on that confidence which has now for some length of time, subsisted between us, I hope with still encreasing esteem on both sides, when I thus seek to penetrate into those sacred recesses of the soul, the veil of which scarcely any one is justified in attempting to draw aside, save only its own high priest. Yet I cannot forbear to say that a letter lately received from Mr. Beauchamp, has strongly confirmed a suspicion first awakened in my bosom, during your last visit at Campbell-House, that your heart was the victim of an unfortunate attachment. Dare I presume to say more?—presume to hazard a conjecture at the beloved object?—to hint a painful apprehension that 'tis one never to be obtained?—one to whom every tie of honour and principle forbids your giving the remotest hint of your sentiments?—Yes, I must speak, my pen cannot be restrained.

Oh, tell me then, I conjure you! am I right in fearing that the same attractions which captivated the heart of your friend have made an equal impression upon yours?—Alas! you were placed in a dangerous situation!—The sacred nature of the marriage tie may withhold the tongue from uttering the feelings of the heart, but it cannot always teach the heart not to feel. Gracious heaven! if this be the case, to what conflicts have you not been exposed, and how nobly have you supported yourself through them!—but oh, let me then, as a friend, conjure you to abandon your present intention of settling at Lausanne, at least as long as your friend shall remain there. 'Tis not that I doubt your continued adherence to that honourable integrity you have hitherto maintained, yet 'tis cruel to think of your living in a constant struggle between honour and passion, and I shudder for the consequences to your life perhaps, or even more fatally, to your reason.

That Mr. Barry should wish for the society of such a friend, for the council of such a guide, is not surprising—but some consideration is still due to yourself. All that friendship can reasonably expect you have performed, I fear to your own injury. To go through the journey you lately undertook, under such circumstances, without one word, one action, escaping to which your heart could not afterwards give its decided sanction, was an effort that required no common degree of fortitude. Ah, Mr. Ryder, I cannot but apprehend that it was a reluctance to own this fatal passion, yet an almost equal reluctance to write without confiding to me the cause of your unhappiness, that occasioned your silence while you were absent. Oh, how was my heart wounded by that silence, for I felt that it could arise from no trivial cause.

I think I scarcely need add, my dear Sir, that I shall expect your answer with very great impatience—and that I ardently wish you may be induced to place full confidence in

Yours with the highest esteem,

OLIVIA CAMPBELL.

LETTER XIII.

RICHARD RYDER
TO
OLIVIA CAMPBELL.

Pontefract, February 18.

Ten days have now elapsed, my dear madam, since I received a letter so full of kindness, written in a strain so accordant to all the former friendship I have received from you, that it undoubtedly called for my immediate and most grateful acknowledgement. Ten days successively have I taken up my pen to answer it, but ineffectually endeavoured to write in a style that could satisfy myself, or prove in any way satisfactory to you.

You ask my perfect confidence, dear madam,—you ask it with such frankness, such ingenuousness, such solicitude for my happiness, that I cannot reject your kindness without the greatest reluctance; nor should the confidence you solicit be withheld, but that it would be the height of criminality in me to grant it. On one point, however, I can give you perfect satisfaction, and so far satisfy myself in being explicit with you.

That my heart is oppressed by a secret sorrow is but too true, yet I can safely assure you, that this does not in any way originate from an unfortunate attachment to Maria. She is a very sweet and amiable young woman, and I have been highly interested by her situation, yet were she perfectly at liberty, I think she never could win my affections in any farther degree than as a friend. In resolving to become an alien from my native country I shun, not court, temptation, and if I do not find perfect happiness, I trust, I shall at least find a great degree of tranquillity at Lausanne. The charms of nature in the delicious country to which I am going, are enough to fill a mind open to the reception of such pure and simple delights, while the unsophisticated hospitality of the independent rustics, inspires the heart with more worthy views of its fellow-creatures, than the factitious refinements of what are called more civilized nations.

No, madam, believe me, that in chusing Switzerland as the place of my future residence, I am guided by the dictates of mature reflection, not led by a blind and fatal impulse. England, though my native country, has been to me more like an unkind step-mother than a fostering parent, and while I wander among the peaceful vales and mountains that border the Leman Lake, there will be only one spot in this island towards which I shall ever heave the sigh of regret.

I am at present under considerable anxiety respecting my friend and Maria. I never approved her going to Lausanne, and should have pointed out to Barry the strong objections that appeared against his scheme, had time been allowed for it; but the whole business was arranged in too much haste to admit of my writing to him. Sorry am I to say, that I fear she must now be left alone, as Barry is himself sent for home with all possible expedition to attend the death-bed of his father, who is in the last stage of a dropsy.* I can scarcely conceive a more awkward situation for a pretty young woman inexperienced in the world, than to be left by herself in a foreign country, where she is a stranger even to the language—yet, considering the haste in which Barry must travel, it seems hardly possible she should accompany him.

It only now remains for me once more to intreat, dear madam, that my withholding the confidence you so kindly solicit, may not be considered as arising from any diminution of that perfect esteem and respect, with which I shall always be,
     Your most faithful humble servant,

RICHARD RYDER.

---

*   Disease in which watery fluid collects in the body.

LETTER XIV.

LIONEL STANHOPE
TO
REGINALD BEAUCHAMP.

Dublin, February 16.

Your very kind communication, my dear Sir, is not the less entitled to my grateful acknowledgement for coming only to confirm the story I had heard but a few hours before. I arrived at this place in the fortunate moment when the presence of a friend was peculiarly wanted to support Harry through the most trying scene he ever can experience.

I landed at Dublin about four o'clock on Tuesday last, and went immediately to the inn whither my letters to Harry had been directed. There I was informed that he was dining with a Mr. Tryon who lived in the next street, and to his house I accordingly proceeded in search of him. I sent in a note informing my friend of my arrival, and requesting to speak with him. He was with me in a moment, and seemed truly rejoiced at seeing me. By desire of Mr. Tryon I was invited to join the party, which invitation I gladly accepted, after half an hour's private conference with Harry. In this he told me that he had heard no more of the Mrs. and Miss Trelawney mentioned in his last letter, and he believed the whole report originated in mistake. That this had been confounded with Mrs. Belgrave's cause, which from all he could learn, was of a similar nature, and which he understood had been actually decided in her favour two days before, so that she and Harriot were now really going down into the neighbourhood of Limerick to take possession of the estate, after which they were to return immediately to England. Satisfied on this point he said, he had resolved to return home himself without delay, and apply himself very seriously to his own establishment.

Happy to find him thus composed and contented, I joined the company, and amid much pleasant conversation so lost the idea of my presence being of importance to Harry, who was really cheerful, that I began at last to blame my own precipitation in coming over, and heartily to wish myself again in London. After a while we went upstairs to the ladies, where we found some other company arrived for an evening party, and learned that more were expected. We took our chairs, but had not been seated above five minutes, when the door opened, the names of Mrs. and Miss Trelawney were announced, and Mrs. Belgrave and Harriot appeared. I started and flew to Harry just in time to catch him as he was falling senseless from his seat.

Astonishment seized the whole company at my hasty rising, and a violent scream from a lady who sat next to Harry, drew all eyes towards him. Among others those of Harriot were attracted that way. In the pale and senseless form before her, the well-known features of Egerton were at once recognized; with an involuntary emotion she sprang forwards, and clasping his hand, sunk herself almost equally senseless into the arms of those that surrounded us.

Terrified at the consequences of such a scene to both, I entreated some of the gentlemen to assist me in carrying Harry out of the room, while the attention of the female part of the company was directed to Harriot. It was long before Harry in any degree recovered, and he then seemed totally to have lost all idea of what had passed. I was left alone with him, and he asked me how he came there? I told him that he had not been well, and asked whether he did not remember being seized with faintness or giddiness in the head? No, he said, it was merely fancy in me, and he desired me to go back with him to the company immediately, and not give way to whims that only exposed him and myself. Then starting up, he seized hold of my hand and said, "come along, Lionel."

"Stop a few moments I entreat," said I. "You have not been well, indeed you have not, and had better remain here a little longer to compose yourself."

"I understand you," said he, "I had drank too much wine and fell asleep, and you are afraid that I am not yet recovered. But upon my soul I am, Lionel; indeed you may believe me; so let us rejoin the company."

"No, no, you look flushed and hurried even now."

"Pshaw! nonsense!"

"Had you no odd dreams while you were asleep?"

"What makes you ask that question? Did I start or scream?"

"I thought indeed that something seemed to distress and disturb you."

He started.—"O God!" he cried "'tis true. Why did you remind me of it? I had otherwise never thought of it more. I dreamed that I was fishing in the Bay of Dublin, and I found the net very heavy, so that it was dragged into the boat with difficulty, when on examining it, Lionel, think of my agony, it contained the lifeless body of my Emily. Half wild with horror I clasped the pallid corse to my bosom, it seemed to revive—when I saw standing before me—Oh still more strange!—Harriot Belgrave."

"Good heavens! Your agitation then was not surprising."

"Did I appear much agitated?"

"Extremely so."

"Yet the recollection is very faint; but absorbed as are all my thoughts by Emily and Harriot, it was not surprising that I should dream of them. Scarcely a night passes, but in idea I behold them alternately, alternately clasp them to my bosom, and fancy myself alternately the wedded husband of the one and the other. But come, let us rejoin the company."

"Harry, I know not how it is, but your dream troubles and perplexes me."

"Why should it trouble you? I have more reason to be disturbed at it. Lionel[,] what's the matter? Why do you look at me with such a countenance of mingled compassion and anxiety? Do you think that this dream was fancy, and that my reason is disturbed? No, on my soul my head is calm and clear, I truly dreamed what I have related."

"I do not doubt your accuracy, yet I am troubled. Said you not that Mrs. Belgrave's cause was determined in her favour?"

"Lionel what do you mean?"—He struck his hand upon his forehead, a sudden recollection seemed to cross him, he seized my arm eagerly, and fixing his eyes wildly upon me, "Tell me," he cried, "tell me instantly, I conjure you, what you mean, and how I came here?"

"I told you before, you have not been well."

"A fit—is'n't it so?"

"Too true."

"And by what occasioned?"

"Do you recollect nothing?"

"No—nothing—and yet—methinks—methinks.—Say was it not a dream?—have I really seen her?"

"Seen whom?"

"Harriot.—No, no, Emily."

"I believe you have."

"Oh God then where, where is she?"

"Can you be calm?"

"As yourself."

"Dare I leave you alone?"

"Oh no! I would not for worlds be left alone! let us go together."

"I am afraid of your coming too suddenly on Emily."

"On Emily?—No, no, mock me not! mock me not!—'twas only Harriot."

"Be it which it will you must not see her yet Harry, your mind is still too much agitated for such an interview. Let me go to her, let me speak in your behalf; do you meanwhile stay here and endeavour to compose yourself."

He threw his arms round me, a sudden gush of tears seemed to awaken in him a clear and full recollection of all that had passed, and after some minutes he said, "Lead me instantly to her I conjure you, I am now myself again, and cannot rest a moment without an explanation of this strange mystery! Yes, I saw in the same form both Harriot and Emily."

At this moment our host entered, and said that after a very severe conflict Miss Trelawney was become tolerably composed, and begged to see Mr. Egerton. I supported Harry into the room, his steps tottered, but the moment he beheld the long lost object of his adoration, with one spring he was at her feet. He lay there for some minutes like one entranced; he took her hand, which he pressed to his lips, and bathed with his tears, but not a word was spoken. Then suddenly starting up, he ran to me, and throwing himself upon my neck, "Take me, take me away," he said, "how can I have been such a wretch!" and he rushed out of the room in a tumult of passion.

I followed him, "What means this?" I said.

"Ask me not," he exclaimed with agony. "You must understand me. Only accompany me home."

I paused not a moment, but followed him to the inn. He walked up and down the room for some time violently agitated, and at length sitting down by me and clasping my hand in agony, "How could you let me see her?" he exclaimed.

"What do you mean?"

"Oh God can you ask that!—I had forgotten myself.—In my transports I did not recollect that I was not the same Henry Egerton on whom the pure and artless affections of Emily Trelawney were placed. I, a prodigal, a bankrupt, have dared to contaminate that angel form with my touch! Oh Lionel[,] you ought to have prevented it."

"Did she not desire to see you?"

"Did she not desire it?—and is that an excuse for me!—Her sweetness, her gentleness, might pardon me, but never, never can I forgive myself!—No, heavens be my witness while here I swear—"

"No rash oaths, Harry!"

"No, I will not swear, yet I am not the less unalterably determined never to allow myself to see her, no not even to think of her more. Too sensible I am of what is due to purity like hers, not to perceive the difference between what I was and what I am, and that the eye which I might once raise in confidence to such exalted worth and charms, must never presume to look upon her again. What phrenzy could possess me to indulge but for a moment in the idea that to see, was to be re-united to her? But 'tis past, my senses are restored, and my offence shall be severely expiated. Lionel, speak not another word, I am resolved."

A mind torn by such a conflict of passions as then agitated Harry's, is not in a state to listen to reason, and I forebore to make any reply, trusting that after the present paroxysm had somewhat subsided, he would not prove so much his own enemy as to reject a pardon if offered him.

He continued violently agitated during the whole evening, sometimes walking hastily up and down the room, then throwing himself into a chair, and sitting with his face buried in his hands, then starting up again, falling upon my neck, and bursting into tears. Once only did he speak, and then it was to exclaim, "Oh Lionel, this is too much!—I cannot support it!—my heart must break!"

At length, with some difficulty, I persuaded him to go to bed and take a composing draught, when nature being perfectly exhausted, he soon sunk into a state of composure rather than of sleep. As I sat watching by him, a note was brought me from Miss Belgrave, desiring to see me immediately, if possible, if not, on the following morning. Fearful of leaving Harry, I excused myself from seeing her then, but promised to wait upon her the next day as she desired.

Watching a favourable opportunity therefore, I left Harry under the care of my servant, and attended my appointment, when I found Harriot scarcely less agitated than my poor friend. "Mr. Stanhope," she said, "all must now be explained, since after what has passed 'tis impossible for you any longer to doubt that in me you behold that Emily Trelawney, whose death Mr. Egerton has so long and so deeply deplored. Alas! how fatal has been this error both to his repose and to my own! and how much is it to be regretted that he has been undeceived in a way so unfortunate and premature. While I was revolving in my mind how this discovery could be accomplished with the least possible agony both to him and myself, I have been suddenly thrust upon his notice, in a manner peculiarly painful to us both. Tell me, how does Mr. Egerton support this conflict?—and why did he break away from me so suddenly, and in such a tumult of emotion?"

I told her all that had passed, that a deep sense of his own unworthiness had driven Harry again from her presence, nor did I believe this was a feeling hastily to be conquered. Yet, I added, if she were disposed to pardon his failings and restore him to that place in her heart which he once possessed, I did not despair of subduing at last his high, perhaps over-strained principles of honour. After much more conversation, and receiving from her an explanation of all the mysterious parts of her story, we parted, she giving me the strongest assurances that she was satisfied with regard to Harry's conduct, and that I had full authority to manage her re-union with him according to my own discretion.

Thus empowered, I returned to the inn, where, finding Harry tolerably composed, I imparted to him the particulars I had just heard, assuring him that it now rested entirely with himself to possess the treasure an unhappy error alone had for so many years withheld from him, and exhorting him not from excess of honour to protract further the misery which both himself and Harriot had already too long endured.

"No Lionel," he answered solemnly, yet resolutely, "to possess that treasure is now impossible!—Ask your own heart whether this would not be to incur even greater guilt than I have incurred by all my past errors united. Bankrupt alike in fortune and character, shall I solicit that angel, shall I even permit her, to become a sharer in my disgrace and ruin? Oh, in a moment of passion she may have resolved to forget all, and from the strong impulse of ardent affection she may hope that in the possession of each other, our mutual sorrows will be soothed, and the past buried in oblivion. But a short interval of reflection must teach her how fallacious is such a hope. Every look of hers would reproach me as a monster, for suffering her to share in my degradation and infamy, and those mutual endearments which I could once have considered as transports that angels themselves might envy, could now only fill me with agony and remorse. Oh God!—Oh God!—why was a shadow of reason ever given back to me, only to plunge myself into everlasting shame and misery, and to store up for myself tortures far, far more severe than any inflicted on the condemned in another world!—Come phrenzy!—oh come once more, and release my soul from such a state of agony!"

He rolled his eyes, he beat his breast, he clung round me—I thought the phrenzy he invoked was indeed coming to his rescue. I entreated him only to see Harriot, but that he peremptorily refused.—"No," he said, "honour has now the ascendancy, I feel that I am acting right, but one glance from her might overturn all my virtuous resolutions. Could I behold that form, nor involuntarily clasp it to my bosom?—Could I see those lips, those cheeks; nor imprint on them a thousand tender kisses?—No, no, no, I must not, will not see her,—I will fly her and my country for ever."

I would still have reasoned the matter with him, but as he absolutely prohibited all farther endeavours to pervert his present virtuous principles, as he styled them, I was obliged to relinquish the attempt, secretly resolving however, as my last resource, to try the effect of his seeing her once more. That the motives on which he acted were generous, I felt to be undeniable, yet I could not bear the idea of their mutual happiness being sacrificed to what seemed a too refined delicacy, and I thought it but acting the part of a friend to both, to leave no effort unessayed for their re-union. I therefore dropped the subject for that time, and soon after, Harry rose and dressed himself. We then talked about our return to England, which seemed now the object on which his mind was the most steadily fixed, and he urged me so forcibly upon the subject, that I promised to accompany him thither without delay, nor would he let me rest till I engaged to go immediately, and secure our passage in the next packet. Glad of this pretence for absenting myself awhile, I departed, leaving him reading with tolerable composure. Satisfied that he was following the dictates of strict honour, he seemed in that consideration to lose all ideas of superior happiness.

I repaired immediately to Harriot, and told her what had passed, asking whether she would accompany me to the inn, and try the effect of another interview. To this she consented without hesitation, and returned with me instantly to the apartment where we had left Harry. On hearing the door open he started and turned his eyes towards it, when, beholding Harriot, his book on which he appeared to have been earnestly intent, dropped instantly from his hand, and he became motionless as a statue with his eyes fixed wildly upon her.

Trembling and agitated she caught hold of me, I supported her with difficulty, and thought she would have fainted in my arms. "Harry," I said, "can you still resolutely refuse to make both yourself and this lovely creature happy?"—Alas! he did not seem to heed me. His eyes remained fixed upon her with the same senseless stare, but he spoke not, he moved not, and such a ghastly paleness spread over his whole countenance, that I expected every moment to see him fall senseless to the ground. Oh, how did I then repent my rashness in making this experiment!—I saw, but too plainly, that neither was able to bear the presence of the other with tolerable composure, and while I wanted to fly to the support of my friend, it was impossible to quit the trembling Harriot. The only thing that remained to be done, was to remove her, and I did, with some difficulty, lead her into another room, all the time in agony with the terrors I felt on Harry's account. There, summoning assistance, I left her for a few minutes to the care of the landlady, and returned to Harry.

I found him still in the same situation, with his eyes fixed on the spot Harriot had quitted, yet senseless, motionless—he breathed indeed, else was to all appearance a mere lifeless corse. Driven myself almost to distraction at my own imprudence, I sent off instantly for medical assistance, and leaving the servant with Harry, hastened back to Harriot. It was some consolation to me to find her sufficiently recovered to be able to return home, and after accompanying her thither, I flew again to the inn, under the most dreadful apprehensions, lest by this fatal step I had overturned my poor friend's reason for ever.

But happily these terrors were unfounded. After some time he gradually recovered from this state of insensibility, to a perfect recollection of all that had passed, when he reproved me very severely for what I had done, and said that it had rather been the part of a friend to keep him out of the way of such temptations, than rashly to plunge him into them. In short, after a long and tolerably unimpassioned conversation, I became so thoroughly convinced that his resolution was not to be shaken, that I resolved to abandon the attempt, and leave the event to time.

When I imparted this determination to Harriot she assented to it, and said she must confide every thing entirely to my friendship, on which she knew the firmest reliance might be placed. Thus, therefore, the matter rests at present, but I do still flatter myself, that when the violent agitation this sudden and unexpected event has occasioned in poor Harry's mind, has so far subsided, as that he can consider it with calmness and composure, all will yet be well.

His great anxiety being now to return to England, I have consented to accompany him thither immediately. The same packet therefore which conveys this letter, will also convey him and
  Dear Sir,
   Your affectionate humble servant,

LIONEL STANHOPE.

LETTER XV.

OLIVIA CAMPBELL
TO
REGINALD BEAUCHAMP.

South Audley Street, February 23.

I have received an answer from Mr. Ryder, my dear Sir, but a very unsatisfactory one. He assures me that I am mistaken in the cause from which I suspected his unhappiness might have originated, yet he gives no hint of what it really is. He writes with an appearance of studied coldness, yet, while in his expressions, he endeavours to be as phlegmatic as possible, there were evident traces of tears having dropped upon the paper as he wrote. Alas! Mr. Beauchamp, this could not proceed from any trivial cause!—tears in some men might be the effect of mere feminine weakness, of a morbid sensibility, but in Mr. Ryder they could only proceed from real heart-felt misery. Oh would to heaven I knew more of this unaccountable affair!—What can the important secret be, which he says, "*it would be the height of criminality in him to impart to me?*"

I know not whether I should have written to you again so soon, but that I strongly suspect I have made a discovery, which you have for some time been pursuing in vain. That if I have not actually detected the author of Mr. Ryder's challenge to Mr. Stanhope, I have at least found a clue that will lead to his or *her* detection.

Chequered as are the scenes of life, so chequered must be our relations of the adventures we meet with in passing through it, I cannot, therefore, forbear to introduce here two ludicrous scenes, as a contrast to the serious manner in which I began my letter, and as a prelude to the discovery I have to impart.

A few days ago, I went over to make a morning visit to Mrs. Harrison at Twickenham, when on entering the house I perceived that she was at a violent altercation with some one, for as I approached the dressing room, I could hear her say in a very loud and angry tone, "Lord, what does the fellow mean?—don't talk to me of your *providential* cavalry, I tell you I won't go, and I'm sure you had no business to put me in."

"I beg your pardon, Madam," replied another voice, "but you don't seem to apprehend the thing rightly; give me leave to explain it to you."

"Lord, I don't want your explanations, —d'ye think I don't know as well as you, and I tell you there never was such a thing heard of as a woman going for a cavalry man. Why, pray did you ever hear of their being drawn for militia men?"

"Certainly not, Madam, but this is quite another thing."

"Aye, but 'tis ten times more absurd to talk of a woman's going for a cavalry man, than for a militia man, for didn't you say yourself that the cavalry was all to be horse?"

By this time I had arrived in the room, and was so irresistibly amused with the debate, that I could not forbear smiling, which so grievously offended the good lady, that looking at me very fiercely, "Well," she said, "I see no such mighty reason to laugh—it's no laughing matter I'm sure— but I suppose, Miss Campbell, you'd like to see me a horseback a going among the cavalry."

"Indeed, Madam, no such thing was passing in my mind. But surely you mistake when you suppose you are expected to go yourself. You are only to furnish a man and horse." [10]

"But I don't see that they've any right to be a making me do that, and I can assure you I shall take the advice of a lawyer before I consent."

"Certainly, Madam," replied the assessor, "you have a right to take the opinion of counsel if you please, but I don't think you will gain much by that. You will be so good as to observe, however, that if you do not appear at the meeting on Thursday, either by yourself or substitute, you may have more to do with lawyers than you will find perfectly agreeable, and so, Madam, good morning."

So saying he took his hat and walked off, Mrs. Harrison calling after him as he went down stairs, "I certainly shall go to the meeting, not as a cavalry man however, but to complain to the gentlemen of your impertinence." Then returning into the room, "and for you Miss Campbell," she said, "I think it would have been quite as proper if you had taken your relation's part instead of laughing at her, and encouraging that fellow in his insolence."

"I beg your pardon, Madam, I really did not mean to give any particular encouragement to the assessor, though he was only acting according to his duty, but I could not forbear smiling at the unfortunate mistake you made. Surely however you will excuse that, we are all liable to make mistakes, and must expect, when they are made, that others will be diverted with them."

"Well, but I don't see that I said any thing ridiculous; but you think yourself so clever that you're always a finding fault with every body else."

"Surely, my dear Madam, there was something laughable in the idea of a woman drawn for a *cavalry man?*"

"Well, but that was what the fellow told me."

"I should rather suppose you must have misunderstood him, that he only said your name was drawn to furnish a man for the new provisional cavalry."

"Well, but I don't know that they had any business to draw me."

"Why you know, Madam, that you keep horses for your chariot."

"Then they might just as well put you in, for you keep horses."

"I am put in, in Yorkshire."

"But I think it's monstrous hard to put women in, for they can never expect that they'll go and fight."

"Some women perhaps might advance to the charge with greater courage than some men. Not that I think fighting by any means a feminine occupation, yet surely it is very proper that our sex should contribute amply towards this new levy, since one of the primary objects of the corps is to be the preservation of our chastity."

"Lord I don't care about my chastity, but I'm determined they shan't have one of my horses."

"I am afraid that determination will be of no avail."

"But I'm determined it shall. I've no notion of their clapper-clawing* in this way. Besides, I'm engaged every day for a month, and what am I to do if one of my coach-horses is to be a learning his exercise all that time."

---

*   Abusing or reviling.

Here we were interrupted by the servant coming in to say that Miss Perkins was just come ashore, and she wished Mrs. Harrison would go down the garden to her, as she had met with an adventure which had hurried her extremely, and she was so nervous that she did not know how she should ever be able to walk to the house.

Away went Mrs. Harrison, as fast as the weight she carries would allow, when the servant staying behind to make up the fire, I asked whether Miss Peggy had met with any accident. To which the man replied, "no, only a fellow had been *sarcy* to her." He then proceeded to relate that Miss Peggy "had heard say as rowing was a good thing for ladies with weakly health, so she had persuaded his mistress to buy a little boat, that she might row herself upon the Thames for an hour every morning. Most commonly, he added, his mistress went with her to teach her how to row, but she couldn't go this morning, so Miss Peggy had taken her maid with her, and some how or other they'd run a ground, and they did not know how to get the boat off, and a waterman had laughed at 'em, and offered to help 'em off for a kiss of their pretty faces. But however another man was civiler, and came and helped 'em without saying any thing; but Miss Peggy was so frighted by what the first fellow said, that she was hardly able to row herself home."

I am afraid I was more disposed to be entertained with, than duly to commiserate poor Peggy's misfortunes, and wished extremely that I had been aware of this new medicine she was trying, time enough to have gone and seen her exhibit. But as I was too late for this, I sat myself down contentedly, and took up a book that lay upon the table, which I found to be the *Complete Letter Writer*, and the property of Margaret Perkins, whose name was inscribed on the blank page at the beginning. I began turning over the leaves, and soon came to a challenge sent by a gentleman to his friend, whom he suspected of intriguing with his mistress. Of this I had read a few lines, when I was interrupted by the entrance of the two ladies; but the little I had seen, almost convinces me that the challenge Mr. Stanhope received was copied from this, only with such variations as to suit it to the occasion. You, my dear Sir, I think have the challenge in your possession, and I wish therefore you would compare the two together, and tell me whether I am right or not.

Poor Peggy came into the room, *"like Niobe all tears,"*[11] grievously lamenting the hardship of her fate, that her *bitter enemies* would not let her quietly pursue an exercise she had taken up solely on account of her health, and from which she had found greater benefit than her most sanguine hopes could have conceived for the short time she had tried it, but that they must still be lying in ambush for her, to mar every prospect of peace and comfort the moment it began to dawn upon her. For confident she was, she said, that the impertinent fellow never would have dared to crack his vulgar jokes upon one whom he must see immediately was a person of consequence, had he not been set on by those who were resolved to leave no stone unturned for effecting their wicked purposes with regard to her. They wanted to persecute her into her grave, she knew that was what they were aiming at, and they were likely to succeed but too well, for her health was already in such a state that it could not much longer stand these repeated trials. They had better stab her to the heart at once, than keep her thus on the rack dying by inches.

In this way did she continue running on, till wearied with listening to it I took my leave. So will I now of you, my dear Sir, but not without an assurance that I am with great regard,

Your affectionate

OLIVIA CAMPBELL.

LETTER XVI.

OLIVIA CAMPBELL
TO
HARRIOT BELGRAVE.

South Audley Street, February 28.

I have received your long and interesting letter, my dear Harriot, by the hands of Mr. Stanhope, who arrived in town two days ago. To say how much I participate in all you have gone through were unnecessary; professions of this kind are much better waved between those who know each other's hearts as well as we do. The manner in which you were discovered to Mr. Egerton I truly regret; had opportunity been afforded for managing the discovery with more circumspection, how different might have been the effect. As matters rest at present, I fear it will be difficult to shake his resolution, powerful and over-whelming as are his feelings, and founded as they are upon a deep and strong sense of honour.

He was by no means to be prevailed upon to accompany Mr. Stanhope to London, but is left by himself at Arrenton, still wholly undetermined what course to pursue, and though resolute not to see you, yet I suspect upon your account unable to fix on any plan that would carry him out of England. Harriot, I asked Mr. Stanhope how he could leave Mr. Egerton by himself in such a state of mind? "Rather ask, Madam," he replied, "how I could go over to him at all when you were in town.—Ah, he knows not the sacrifice I have made."—He paused, he looked at me earnestly. "Yet, Madam," he added, "I would not for worlds that you should think I have acted with unkindness or insensibility towards Harry. His steward will pay him every attention the harassed state of his mind requires, and knowing, as my friend does, the motives I have now to wish myself in London, he would not be easy for a moment under the idea that he was the occasion of my absence from it being prolonged."

Ah Harriot, was it possible to mistake the meaning of these words? Oh no! they are still but a commentary upon his whole behaviour to me ever since my arrival here; they assure me but too plainly that I have a severe conflict to sustain. I sometimes think I was wrong in accepting Sir Francis's invitation to South Audley Street, that I had done better in suffering matters to remain as they were, and averting all farther explanation between us, yet at other times I think differently, and am convinced that whatever may be the final issue of this affair, 'tis very desirable for both that we should speedily come to a thorough understanding upon it.

And oh, should I at length be satisfied that we had better not think more of entering into a nearer connection than the friendship by which we are now united, I trust I shall have sufficient fortitude to put my feelings, whether founded on my partiality for him, or on the anxiety of my heart to comply with the wishes of my father, entirely out of the question, and to be guided by the dictates of reason alone. How much do I wish, Harriot, that you were now with me!—Never did I feel so deeply the want of a friend with whom I could converse freely upon all subjects.

But no more of this. 'Tis time enough to face the evil courageously at the moment, if it must come, 'tis idle to encrease it by anticipation.

You cannot have forgotten George Macklin, to whom I introduced you as one of the beaux that attended Madame de Clairville and myself about Cambridge. His thorough knowledge of the world led him, upon the strength of that acquaintance, to seek me out immediately upon his arrival in London, as his guide and protector on entering such a theatre of temptations; although, from the extreme entertainment he expressed at the idea of my awkward astonishment at scenes so new, it could scarcely have been supposed that he would consider me as properly qualified to be the guardian of another.

He came up to town by the mail, on alighting from which, at the Post-Office, he enquired whether he could not have somebody to walk with him, and shew him the way to South Audley Street? A porter immediately offered his services, and took charge of the portmanteau, which George said might as well be left at Sir Francis Stanhope's, till he had determined where he should fix his residence during his stay in London.

Yesterday morning as I was talking with Sir Francis at the parlour window, I was surprised by the sight of George with his attendant ascending the steps to the house. He enquired whether Miss Campbell was at home, and being answered in the affirmative, he told the porter to leave the portmanteau, and that he should not want him any longer. "And here, friend," said he, "is something for your trouble," offering him sixpence.

The porter eyed the diminitive piece of coin not with a look of much complacency, and swearing a hearty oath, asked if he supposed he had come all that way for no more than sixpence? No, damn it, he was not to be caught so! and resolving to be proportionably exorbitant in his demands, as George seemed disposed to be economical in his payment, he stoutly required five shillings, which he said he was sure the job was well worth. A warm altercation ensued, in which George extended his offer to a shilling, protesting that was all he would give, and calling the man an impudent scoundrel for asking more. The latter however persisting in his demand, which he strenuously contended was a perfectly just one, Jerry, who had opened the door, was at length referred to as umpire of the difference.

This office however honest Jerry declined, alleging "that he wasn't no matters of a schollard, and he didn't like for to pretend for to speak his humble thoughts in a quarrel betwixt gentlefolks and poor folks, because it was always his fancy like, that gentlefolks who had so much more larning than he, think'd differently about the matter from his simple notions. And thos to be sure it were a great way to carry a heavy portmanteau from Lombard Street up to this here end of the town, which for sartin it must be three or four miles, yet he know'd it wasn't for sarvents to say as a shilling wasn't enough to pay for it. Howsever he'd ax his master to come down, and whatever he said, to be sure he should be sartin as it were right, being that he, God love him, were always just as much for seeing poor folks righted, as rich."

Away therefore he went, and Mr. Stanhope coming down at his request, he soon arranged the matter, by awarding to the porter his exact due, which the latter, perceiving he was now dealing with one who knew what he was about, took very contentedly, and walked away. George then making known his name and errand, requested permission to leave his portmanteau in the hall, till he had fixed upon some place of residence, when perhaps Sir Francis would be so good as to let one of his servants carry it to the lodging, that he might not be imposed upon any more by such impertinent fellows as the porter.

Mr. Stanhope was somewhat surprised at this perfect freedom in an entire stranger, but too good tempered to be offended at it, he made no other reply than by a slight bow, and then introduced this singular visitor into the parlour, where I had been extremely amused with all that had passed, not a word of which I had lost, as the altercation was not carried on in a very gentle key, and the door had been accidentally left a jar.

George now addressing me, said he had taken the liberty of waiting upon me, as he had no other acquaintance in London but myself and Madame de Clairville, of whose address he was unfortunately ignorant; and he thought I might possibly be able to recommend him to a lodging, as he had been informed it was not safe for a person of character to take one by chance, lest he might unknowingly get into a house of ill-fame.

How laughable soever was this instance of George's knowledge of the manners of polished life, yet we listened to it with perfect composure of features, and Mr. Stanhope very gravely suggested that as a single gentleman, he thought he would find a coffee-house, or hotel, much more convenient than a private lodging, and he mentioned two or three where he might be accommodated upon reasonable terms, and be sure of civil treatment. For this information George made many acknowledgments, and at length, after sitting for more than an hour, rose to depart, but after he had got to the room door, he turned round again: "Perhaps, Sir," said he to Mr. Stanhope, "you will be so good as to accompany me to the coffee-house and assist me in settling about a lodging, otherwise I may very likely be imposed upon again, since, to judge by that fellow who shewed me the way hither, people in London don't make much bones of putting tricks upon travellers."

Whether this very cool request were intended as the easy manners of the perfect gentleman, I will not pretend to determine, but Mr. Stanhope certainly seemed to think it was ease rather carried to excess. Plainly perceiving, however, that poor George was not fit to be trusted about London without leading-strings, he with very great good-nature complied with his request, and they departed together, while Sir Francis, actuated by a like spirit of benevolence, asked the forlorn youth to dinner, an invitation the latter was by no means reluctant to accept.

In the evening Mr. Stanhope proposed going to the play, as Mrs. Siddons, whom George had never seen, was to play Calista.[12] Had I not been engaged out to dinner we had probably made a party to go, but as it was, the two gentlemen set off together in a hackney coach. Whether George's heart was somewhat exhilarated by the good Baronet's wine, and so was become very generous, or that after the specimen he had already seen, he began to think there was no bounds to the impositions of people in London, I cannot pretend to determine, but in their way to the play he asked his companion whether half-a-crown would be enough to give the coachman, and seemed not a little surprised at hearing that it was only an eighteen-penny fare.

Arrived at the theatre, they were surrounded as usual by the daughters of Pomona[13] presenting their oranges for sale, accompanied with offers of a bill of the play gratis, in case of purchase. George, too much lost in astonishment at the novelty of the scene to attend minutely to the conditions on which the oranges were to be had, concluded them a part of the evening's entertainment, and taking two, quietly continued to follow Mr. Stanhope. But the lady of whom he took them perceiving him walking away without an idea of paying, immediately began to vociferate most unmercifully, with all the force of language commonly used by such ladies, whenever the wonted serenity of their tempers receives a momentary interruption. This was no sooner heard by her sister nymphs, and the cause explained, than true to the alliance offensive and defensive established among them, they all united their voices to her's, and surrounding their devoted victim, the powers above only know what might have been his fate, had not Mr. Stanhope interposed as his guardian genius, and hearing the cause of the tumult, appeased the incensed goddesses, and led off the rescued sufferer quietly to a box.

There however they had not long been seated, when another lady of the same tribe came in and demanded payment for her book.

Mr. Stanhope denied having taken one, and bid her go away, but she said it was not him, it was the other gentleman, and he told her to follow him to the box for the money.

Mr. Stanhope immediately concluding this to be the second act of the orange farce, enquired whether he had taken a book, which he positively denying, Mr. Stanhope bid the woman begone in a very authoritative tone. She however still insisted that the gentleman had taken a book, and begged he would feel in his pocket, for he certainly had forgotten it. George immediately felt, and actually did find a book which the lady had probably sufficient reason for believing to be there, since she had doubtless deposited it herself with her own fair hands.

In what manner George might have acted in an affair of so delicate and embarrassing a nature, had he been left to himself, 'tis difficult to determine, but Mr. Stanhope here again helped him out, and insisted upon the good lady's taking the book back, which she did very reluctantly, muttering, as she departed, probably not a blessing upon the two gentlemen.

I am only afraid that Mr. Stanhope by his good-nature will find he has drawn a terrible incumbrance upon himself, as this man of the world, whose ease and freedom know no bounds, seems extremely disposed to fasten himself upon us for the whole time of his stay here. He called this morning immediately after breakfast to say how very comfortable he found his apartments, and to make his acknowledgments to Mr. Stanhope for having recommended him to so eligible a situation, and then proposed their taking a walk together, since, he said, as he was a total stranger in London, it would be much more agreeable to have a companion who could direct him to what was best worth seeing, than to walk about by himself. He was certainly right in this, but he never seemed for a moment to consider whether the office of *cicerone** might be altogether agreeable to Mr. Stanhope. The latter, however, extended his kindness even to this. I asked George how he liked Mrs. Siddons, to which he replied, that he never saw her so great as the evening before. You will recollect it was the only time he ever had seen her.

Adieu, my dear Harriot, and believe me ever

Your truly affectionate

OLIVIA CAMPBELL.

---

* Tourist or sight-seeing guide.

LETTER XVII.

LIONEL STANHOPE
TO
HENRY EGERTON.

South Audley Street, March 6.

After all that passed between us, Harry, upon the subject of my affairs, at such intervals as we could attend to any thing besides your own, you will not be surprised to hear that I have broken my vow not to hazard another refusal from Olivia, and have absolutely renewed my proposals to her. Oh that I could say I had received such encouragement to this step, as that I opened my heart with full confidence of my proposals being joyfully accepted!—but alas, it was too evident, that while I undoubtedly was not indifferent to her, she shrunk from the explanation I so eagerly sought. Yet, I was not the less resolved that all should finally be settled between us—the state of suspense in which I have passed some months, is no longer to be supported, and though heaven can be my witness, how ardently I wish a favourable termination of the affair, yet I had much rather know at once decidedly that I must think no more of this truly admirable woman, than be kept on the rack between hopes and fears.

And, if at last, I am to undergo the mortification of a second refusal, of one thing I shall be assured, that her conduct is not the result of pique or caprice, but proceeds from the purest motives, and is dictated by such an enlarged and extensive view of the probable happiness or unhappiness that would result to us both from this union, as only a mind like hers is capable of taking.

To this conclusion I am fairly led, from the detail she has given me of the motives by which her conduct was influenced in her former rejection of my proposals—motives which do equal honour to her head and heart, and which I admire too much to conceal. But, to explain them effectually, I must give you a sketch of all that has passed between us upon the subject, in which, I doubt not, you will feel too deeply interested, to find the narrative dull or tedious.

On my return from Ireland, Sir Francis told me that, during my absence, some conversation had passed between himself and Olivia, which convinced him of what he always suspected, that my rejection at Campbell-House was entirely owing to the ill opinion the heiress had conceived of me from the manner in which I first appeared there; but that my subsequent conduct, having, in great measure, effaced this impression, if my offer should now be renewed, he had little doubt of its meeting with a more favourable reception. He assured me, nevertheless, that he by no means desired the experiment made, unless I were fully satisfied the union would promote my happiness—for the good old Baronet, all the time he has been endeavouring to conquer my very evident reluctance to his wishes, has uniformly assured me that my happiness was all he sought.

274   ANNE PLUMPTRE

What the nature of the conversation was, that led him to this conviction, I could not learn—he said it was difficult to give the particulars, but he was sure that the inference drawn was just. I was not, however, equally sanguine upon the subject—I was sensible that great allowances must be made for his ardour in the cause, and that the conviction with which he was impressed, probably arose in great measure from his ardent wishes that he might be right. But as I was no less desirous of the explanation than himself, I resolved to enter upon it the first favourable opportunity.

Nor was I kept long waiting for one. Yesterday morning Olivia and I being accidentally left alone together, I began to consider in what way I could best introduce the subject. I paused, I took some moments to prepare myself, I studied a speech I thought suited to the occasion, and attempted to begin—but alas! the words, though quivering on my tongue, died away unuttered, for methought there was [something] repulsive[14] in her manner which seemed to indicate that she rather dreaded than wished to hear what I was about to say. Again I attempted to speak, again I was repulsed, and we separated at last without the subject being mentioned. I was heartily vexed with myself, nor less mortified with her coldness. This I suspect she perceived, and reluctant to wound me, shewed me particular attention at dinner, appearing anxious to convince me that I was not indifferent* to her. But since her conduct was only thus rendered the more ambiguous, I became but the more desirous of arriving at the real sentiments of her heart.

Nor did I wait long for a second opportunity suited to my purpose. Sir Francis, whose observation I believe not a single look of mine escapes, seeming to suspect this morning that I really was so far influenced by what he had urged, as to wish for a private conference with Olivia, the moment breakfast was finished, called Lady Stanhope out of the room upon some trifling pretence, and left us together with a countenance sufficiently expressive of what was passing in his mind.

I did not now waste my time in studying a speech, but hastened to the point at once, and in unstudied phrases, laid open my whole heart to its mistress. She listened to me with profound attention, she sat for some minutes with her eyes fixed on the fire, as if lost in thought, and at length turning to me began:

"Yes, Mr. Stanhope, I must, I will, express my obligation to you for thus compelling me to come to a speedy and final decision upon a subject that has so long dwelt on my mind, whether with sensations more painful or pleasurable I can scarcely determine. Suffer me to be somewhat diffuse in my reply, since 'tis of the utmost importance to the happiness of both, that all possibility of misunderstanding between us should now be precluded, and I hope and trust you will be as frank and explicit upon the subject as myself."

---

* An object of indifference.

"Ah! dearest Olivia, assure yourself I am now incapable of being otherwise. To tell you that sincerity has always been a leading feature in my character, may appear almost like an insult to your understanding, since my first introduction to you was under the most base and contemptible disguise. Yet surely, even the circumstances of that imposture, may be adduced as an argument that I am no hacknied deceiver, since never was a project of deception formed, or carried on, with less probability of success. One, more practised in deceit, would not have embarked in an undertaking of the kind, in such a rash and headlong manner without a single precaution for averting detection. Oh heavens!—would that you could read my heart!—could see with what horror and remorse I look back to that transaction, and how ardently I wish the disgraceful period could be blotted for ever from the annals of my life! Nay, I could almost consent to relinquish the happiness I have experienced from my acquaintance with you, dearest Olivia, and the infinitely greater happiness I hope from our still nearer connection, could I thus erase from the calendar of events, a period that reflects such everlasting shame upon me."

"No more on this subject I entreat, Mr. Stanhope. If at the time I passed the matter over with levity, be assured it was only to disguise the feelings of a heart wounded past expression, at beholding the son of my father's most esteemed friend stoop to conduct so degrading—at reflecting that this man was one whom I had always been taught to consider as a person of strict honour and moral principle, though occasionally misled into youthful irregularities. Bear with me, Mr. Stanhope, if I am tedious and seem to preach, but 'tis impossible to come to that full explanation I wish, without taking a retrospect of the origin and progress of all that has passed between us.

"Our fathers were intimate friends. Accident brought them acquainted in youth, and similarity of dispositions united their hearts in bonds which remained unshaken, till the death of my father dissolved the connection. To continue this friendship, even beyond their own lives, soon became the favourite object of both, and each having an only child, though of different sexes, an union between them seemed the natural means of eternizing their bonds. They accordingly agreed mutually to use every possible means not inconsistent with their integrity as men, or their affection as parents, to accomplish this alliance, as soon as their respective children should arrive at years of maturity.

"But in the prosecution of this favourite object, they pursued a different course from that commonly taken under such circumstances. Experience had taught them that educating children very much together often operated against their forming the attachment their parents wished, and it was therefore resolved that we should not meet till we were of an age, when the union might be completed at once. In the mean time, every possible advantage of education was to be given us, that nothing might be omitted within the compass of human foresight, to secure our attracting the future notice and admiration of each other, and the period fixed for our first meeting, was the time of your coming of age, when I should be just seventeen."

"Good heavens!—and how, dearest Olivia, did you arrive at the knowledge of all this?—I knew long ago that an union between us was the mutual wish of our parents, but, till this moment, I never had an idea that a plan for effecting it had been so early formed, or so systematically pursued."

"Nor had it probably been revealed to me, but, in consequence of a severe illness of my father's, when he thought himself dying. Oh, never shall I forget that moment!—it was when I was about fifteen years of age, and before that time I scarcely recollect ever having reflected at all upon the subject of matrimony, although 'tis one to which the attention of our sex is commonly directed, even from our earliest infancy. I had been watching for some time by my father's bed-side, while he had been in a sort of disturbed sleep. Opening his languid eyes, and seeing me, he said, 'Olivia, my dearest child, are we alone?'—With a sigh, I answered yes, when, taking my hand and pressing it affectionately—'Olivia,' he said, 'I feel that my distemper must be mortal, from this bed I shall probably never rise more, let me then, while my senses are yet spared, unfold to you my whole heart.

'You have ever been,' he continued, 'one of the best of children—far be it from me, to repay your filial affection with any attempt to controul your heart on a subject on which the great happiness or misery of your life must depend; yet I know not how to take my leave of you for ever, without disclosing the secret wishes on your account, which I have so long and so eagerly cherished.' Then imparting to me the agreement he had entered into with Sir Francis, he added,—'And now my beloved child, I have only this request to make. I do not ask of you a promise never to marry any other than Mr. Stanhope, but I do my dearest girl, I do most earnestly wish you not to engage your hand to another till you have seen him. Yet, observe me, I even then would not have you think of uniting yourself to him unless you can give him your whole heart. My child's happiness is what I seek, I know that is not to be obtained in an union with one who is not the decided object of her choice. Olivia, can you make me this promise?'

"I threw myself on my knees by him, and pressing his pale hand with my lips, 'Oh yes, my father!' I exclaimed, 'I promise it most faithfully.'—'Bless thee! bless thee!' he cried, with his eyes raised to heaven, 'thou art good to the last!—now I shall die in peace!'—Oh God! to the last moments of my life, never shall I forget the expression of his countenance at that instant—after beholding the smile of satisfaction with which his features were then illumined, pale and expiring as he appeared, for worlds I could never have engaged my hand to another till I had seen the man of his choice!

"From this illness 'tis true, he very unexpectedly to himself and to all about him, did at length recover, but the impression made upon my mind by the scene, lost not, by this means, the smallest particle of its force. My heart was at once devoted to the object of his wishes, though to the object itself I was a perfect stranger. Every other man was viewed by me with indifference, I delighted only in contemplating the picture of him whom I hoped one day would be my husband, which my father immediately gave me, and every new accomplishment I acquired, obtained a double value in my eyes, from the hope that it would render me more amiable in his. From the promise I had made, my father would, indeed, afterwards have released me, but my fate was fixed; he had awakened this attachment in my bosom, and it was for ever closed to any other."

"Oh God Olivia!" I exclaimed here, "why was not this sooner made known to me!—Could I have conceived an idea of the circumstances in which you were placed, I had instantly flown to Campbell-House, either to have convinced your heart that it was deceived in the favourable sentiments it entertained of me, or to have secured to myself the highest possible earthly bliss in possessing such a pattern of faith and affection!"

"No, Mr. Stanhope, the more firmly I became devoted to this romantic attachment, as it must doubtless be considered, the more firmly was I resolved that your heart never should be biassed by any knowledge of the state of mine. I would be the object of your decided choice, or I never would be yours at all—yet, I was no less resolved, that if I should be so fortunate as to attract your affections, I would never be united to you till I had told you the whole story."

"Oh excellent woman!—how, at every word you utter, do I feel my own inferiority!—But is it not most extraordinary that Sir Francis, who cannot, in general, keep the most trifling circumstance concealed, should on this single subject, have been so wary as that amidst all his importunities not a hint of these particulars, no not even of the agreement, made between him and General Campbell, should ever have escaped him."

"The most unguarded can always be sufficiently reserved when a favourite object is in question, and Sir Francis probably was apprehensive that your gaining any idea of the scheme would prove an insurmountable barrier to its accomplishment. Indeed he does not himself know all that I have related to you. I entreated my father never to mention what had passed between him and myself, and I believe that Sir Francis even now, supposes the secret of this projected union to be wholly confined to his own bosom. But to proceed with my story.

"You arrived at the age of twenty-one—by that time I began to be somewhat known in the world, and as the heiress of a large fortune, to become an object of general attention. But, notwithstanding the pains that had been taken in the formation of my person, as well as in the cultivation of my mind, where nature had done so little, art could do nothing, and I was soon no less celebrated for the plainness of my person, than for the fortune I was to inherit. What could have given rise to the report, that I was little removed from idiocy, I cannot positively decide, as I am not conscious that any part of my conduct could ever authorize it. I can only suppose it was circulated by an officer of my father's regiment, whose hand I had rejected, but who, still wishing to possess himself of my fortune, hoped by thus endeavouring to keep other men at a distance that he might be accepted at last.

"You, Mr. Stanhope, at the time of which I am speaking, a gay and volatile young man, could feel little inclined to join the dull society you expected to meet at Campbell-House, and as the devoted admirer of beauty, could still less be disposed to make one of a circle from which that was totally excluded. When, therefore, it was proposed to you to accompany Sir Francis hither, it was not surprising that you should wish to excuse yourself from a visit, the prospect of which appeared so little inviting. Your first refusal of what Sir Francis so ardently wished, was little pleasing to him—your second still less so. He grew importunate, this only strengthened your reluctance to seeing me, and finally transformed distaste into a settled and rooted aversion, and a pertinacious resolution of resistance. Thus, at length, your coming hither, became a matter of regular contest between Sir Francis and yourself, in which the spirits of both were too mighty to give way, while I breathed many a secret sigh of regret at the insuperable obstacle which seemed raised to our ever meeting.

"You will easily imagine then, when, after having long relinquished all hope of seeing you, I at last was informed of your intended visit at Campbell-House, in your way to Scarborough, with what transport the intelligence was received. But, in proportion to the delight I had felt in the prospect of seeing you, was my chagrin and mortification at the manner in which your visit was made. Had you and Mr. Egerton been persons indifferent to me, I had doubtless, in the first paroxysm of indignation, turned you both out of the house with reproach and disgrace. Oh God! I scarcely know how I retained any command of myself, when those suspicions of the truth, which I entertained almost from the first moment I saw you, were fully confirmed by Harriot. Yes, in the agony of my soul I wished that the grave had first received that heart which had been so fondly devoted to you, ere it beheld the object of its attachment so fallen, so degraded.

"But it was no time to give way to unavailing sorrow. Short was the space allowed me for determining how to act; I must instantly either shew you that you were exposed, or resolve for a while to impose upon you the belief that your imposture was successful. Dreading the consequences that might attend your suddenly finding yourselves in a situation so degraded, supposing I should act on the former principle; anxious for my own sake if possible to reclaim one of the parties, and for Harriot's to reclaim the other, I at length determined to humour the deception, till I hoped such impressions might be made as would favour my purpose, and I summoned together all my resolution to enable me to go through the task I had undertaken. Well aware that ridicule was often a more powerful weapon in awakening a sense of misconduct than reason, I resolved to try its effects, and as you know, Mr. Stanhope, practised many tricks, which to my infinite satisfaction I saw were not unattended with the consequences I wished.

"At length the match was put to the long train of combustibles I had laid, and all was discovered, while the torture before inflicted upon you lessened in no small degree the horror of that moment, and from your behaviour on that occasion I thought I had abundant reason to congratulate myself upon having chosen to pursue the path of lenience rather than of severity. Yes, Mr. Stanhope, all that I observed convinced me more and more strongly of the truth of what you asserted, that this was a plan hastily and inconsiderately formed, for the double purpose of procuring a release from paternal importunity, and assisting a friend in distress. Ah, too deeply had I always regretted that importunity, not to feel the utmost indulgence towards any steps taken to procure a release from it!—Too warmly had I felt myself for the distresses of a friend, not to make the greatest allowances for any faults committed in assisting one."

Oh Harry! will you not suppose that here I burst forth into transports of admiration and gratitude, at conduct so generous, so noble? But no, I could not utter a syllable, I could only listen with silent astonishment, for it seemed to be the soul of eloquence herself that spake.—I could only contemplate with a sort of reverential homage the sublime emotions by which her whole frame was agitated.—They appeared to overpower her for a moment—she paused—she reclined her head upon one hand—I involuntarily drew my chair close to her, and taking the other, pressed it to my heart, when starting from her temporary abstraction she proceeded:

"Yet though convinced that my preconceived good opinion of you was not unfounded, I hesitated not a moment to decline accepting the proposals you soon after made me. How strongly soever inclination pleaded in your favour, I had other scruples not to be overcome. I could scarcely doubt that Sir Francis's persuasions had, perhaps almost unknowingly to yourself, considerably influenced this offer; if so, my refusal absolved you entirely to him, while I was well assured that if it were perfectly voluntary on your part, time would bring us to a right understanding, provided only I could retain you with me."

Here she looked at me earnestly—"Was I not right?" she said. "Had not Sir Francis urged you strongly to this step?"

"I acknowledge it madam. He saw that on becoming acquainted with you my sentiments had undergone a total revolution—he saw what must inevitably be the case with all who know you, that I was charmed almost to intoxication with your manners, your conversation, your elegant accomplishments. On these points he urged me strongly, while I, well-disposed to what he wished, readily yielded to him, nor did my vanity suffer me to harbour a doubt of my success."

"Yet confess, though you say you yielded readily, that you were not eager to make the offer? You felt rather a wish that you could be wholly devoted to me, than a conviction that you were so."

"Ah, dearest Olivia, you probe my heart very deeply; but I will not attempt to dissemble, I will frankly own that nothing escapes your penetration."

"I thank you sincerely for a confession so candid. I am almost afraid of fatiguing you with this tedious detail, yet I would fain leave nothing unexplained."

"Oh, proceed, I entreat, and let my admiration of your heart and understanding be raised to its utmost height, since every word you have hitherto uttered has increased it immeasureably."

"Perhaps what I have now to add, may produce an opposite effect, yet I think no part of my confession shall be withheld, since, when all my motives are exposed, you can better decide on their merits. Smile then, if you please, when I tell you, that conscious of the unpleasant impression my first appearance must make wherever I am seen, I have long resolved never to marry, till, by passing a winter in London, I should be somewhat known in the gay world. Various causes have combined to detain me in the country till this year, perhaps a degree of reluctance to shewing myself, has not been among the least powerful, but even that objection is now overruled by superior motives. I have always been sensible that the remarks likely to be made upon me in the circles of fashion, must be mortifying in the extreme to a husband, and might create a degree of disgust never to be recovered. But since such things cease to strike when the novelty is over, so after I became well known, a husband would not be equally subject to these petty mortifications, nor have his irritable feelings put to so dangerous a trial. You will think, possibly, that I pay no compliment to the understandings of mankind, but without meaning any reflection upon them, I well know that the jokes a man has to encounter under such circumstances, are often greater trials of the temper, than objections of a nature much more serious and important."

"And could Olivia suppose that this was a confession to depreciate her in my eyes?—Oh no, it only teaches me to regard her with a tenfold degree of admiration!—Dearest Olivia, what a mind is yours!—there is not a single point in which any subject can be viewed that it does not encompass at the very first glance. Yes, it is but too true, that a childish dread of these contemptible remarks had a powerful influence in reconciling me to my former disappointment, and though I deeply feel the folly of giving them a moment's attention, 'tis not to be denied that nothing is more mortifying to the feelings of our sex in general, than nonsensical reflections cast upon the object of our choice. But, thank heaven, you have taught me to rise superior to this weakness. Come then," I added, pressing her hand more eagerly than before, "have you no farther confession to make? I am impatient to hear all, though I question whether it be possible for my admiration to be encreased?"

"No," she replied, "you are now fully acquainted with the motives by which I have hitherto been actuated. But one question still remains to be asked. Is your present offer perfectly voluntary, or are you not still influenced in a considerable degree by the known wishes of Sir Francis?"

"Believe me I am not. The satisfaction he would receive from the success of my suit would add indeed in no small degree to my happiness; but if I am acquainted with my heart, I think I should have acted precisely the same had his wishes been out of the question."

"Then, since none of my former objections subsist, it should seem that I ought not to hesitate now in giving you an immediate and decisive answer. Yet, Mr. Stanhope, my mind is still so torn with a thousand harassing doubts, that I know not what to say. Shall you think me unreasonable in requesting a few days deliberation before I come to a final decision?— I trust you will give me credit for not making this request from caprice, or a wish to trifle."

"Oh no! of such littleness I believe you wholly incapable, or my suit had never been renewed, and anxious as my heart is to know its fate, yet on no account would I urge a hasty answer on a point of such importance. Take your own time then dearest, best of women, only remember that my happiness is wholly in your hands."

"And should I at last decline your proposals, you will not, I hope, consider me as acting unhandsomely by you, or as having encouraged this repetition of your offer for the paltry triumph of repeating my refusal. Believe me, oh Mr. Stanhope! that strongly as I am prepossessed in your favour, this offer was by no means my wish at the present moment."

"Would to heaven that I had not heard such a doubt!—Yet, dearest Olivia, assure yourself, whatever may be your decision, I shall always consider you as having acted towards me according to the truest, most exalted dictates of honour. Too much do I feel my own unworthiness, not to be sensible that many things are to be overcome on your part before you can resolve to become my wife; and if at last I am to be denied that happiness to which my soul so eagerly aspires, though you should decline giving your reasons for rejecting my suit, I shall be satisfied, that however I may deplore the effect, I must admire the motives, were they known."

Such is my present situation, Harry. When I reflect upon it, I am almost tempted to question whether I am still Lionel Stanhope. That same myself who have so often vowed that in the choice of a wife beauty should be my principal object, and that a woman who had once rejected me never should have a second refusal in her power. Yet now has one singularly the reverse of handsome, acquired such an ascendancy over me, that after having been once refused by her, I am patiently abiding her determination upon my fate amid a thousand anxious doubts and fears. There must be an omnipotence in mind, of which we have no idea till we are led in some extraordinary way to feel its force, otherwise this could not be.

But surely after the affection she has avowed for me I have nothing to dread. She did speak doubtfully on the matter 'tis true, yet a passion so powerful as that which influences her, will not yield to trifling objections. Oh! if at last I am forbidden to think more of her, I shall think there is indeed some resistless operation of fate which invariably overrules all marriages agreed upon between parents in the infancy of their children. Yet perhaps 'tis unnecessary to conjure up such a fate, the natural course of things is sufficient to solve the whole matter. In the present case I am sure it is so, since the situation in which I am now placed, originates entirely in the well meant, but mistaken, endeavours of Sir Francis to accomplish the point on which his heart was fixed. The idea of having a wife forced upon me was so revolting to my soul, that I long loathed the object he wished me to love, merely because she was his choice, not my own, and this has led by progressive steps to the present crisis. Had all things been left to their natural course, I had probably not long retained my reluctance to see Olivia, and from the commencement of our acquaintance she might have been the object of my decided preference.

When my fate is determined, Harry, you may depend upon the earliest information of it, as I know you will feel a sympathetic anxiety upon the subject. Of this however be assured, that whatever it may be, no alteration can be made in the firm regard with which I shall always subscribe myself

Your faithful

LIONEL STANHOPE.

LETTER XVIII.

OLIVIA CAMPBELL
TO
HARRIOT BELGRAVE.

South Audley Street, March 19.
I was not mistaken, Harriot, Mr. Stanhope a few days ago renewed his proposals to me, but for very important reasons I could not then give him a positive answer. I however fully explained the motives of my former refusal, and requested time to deliberate upon this renewed offer. He readily assented to my request, and in this state of suspense we remain at present, a suspense which probably even to-morrow will be terminated by my decided negative.

Ah, my dear Harriot, 'tis needless here to recapitulate the doubts I have so often expressed, whether it could be possible for me to fix the affections of such a man as Mr. Stanhope. The whole tendency of his life has been adverse to forming a character that could be devoted to mind alone. He may own its supremacy, but habit, inveterate habit, will ever lead him to refute by practice what he allows in theory. These *were* speculations, they are now converted into assurances.

In requesting a few days deliberation upon this affair, I was influenced principally by a wish, that before my final answer was given, Mr. Stanhope should see Charlotte O'Brien, who was then expected in town every day. For, ah my friend! notwithstanding all his professions to me, in which I have no doubt he was sincere at the moment, I could not repel an apprehension that the moment he beheld this fascinating girl, his heart would teach him a different story, that he would find he had been cherishing a fatal error, and rejoice in a delay which had placed it not beyond the power of remedy. Do not, Harriot, do not ascribe this apprehension to a mean and capricious jealousy; to a passion so contemptible I hope my heart is a stranger, but it was irresistibly obtruded upon me from all I had observed of Mr. Stanhope's disposition, particularly from the impression made upon his imagination, at least, if not upon his heart, by the lively but coquettish Madame de Clairville.

Ah, if she could obtain a momentary ascendancy over him, was there not sufficient reason to apprehend that Charlotte might obtain a permanent one? Though he might at first be caught with the ease and vivacity of Madame de Clairville's manners, for who can fail of being attracted by them, yet since he could not respect, he could never really love her. Besides, Mr. Stanhope has too much intellect himself to be long pleased with a woman who has none, and most certainly all Madame de Clairville's vivacity is mere surface, without any thing solid beneath. But Charlotte unites to equal vivacity, and superior charms of person, an understanding that qualifies her to shine no less as the bosom friend of a husband, and the chosen companion of his serious hours, than her unaffected gaiety does to be the ornament and admiration of a public company. In short, I do not know any one within the circle of my acquaintance so calculated at once to charm the senses and captivate the understanding. Could I then reasonably expect that she would be regarded with indifference by such a man as Mr. Stanhope? Oh no, I could not expect it, nor have I found it.

On the day following that upon which Mr. Stanhope explained his sentiments to me, this lovely girl arrived in town with her father and mother. I called upon them the same evening, and at the request of my kind host and hostess, invited them to dine the next day in South Audley Street. They came accordingly, and were met by the Tichfields and Madame de Clairville.

At the very first glance Mr. Stanhope was uncommonly struck with Charlotte, nor could he withdraw his attention from her a single moment during the whole day. In the evening, after the company were gone, he became thoughtful and abstracted to a degree that I never observed in him before. Ah! could I wonder at this? I could not, I did not. I was sensible that there was sufficient reason for it, nor did it come upon me unexpectedly, and if my heart was for a moment disposed to give way to a pang of jealousy, the emotion was involuntary, and repressed as soon as felt.

Yet harassed as my mind has long been, the moment when doubt first yielded to certainty, was more than I could support, and finding myself unable wholly to suppress the anguish of my soul, I excused myself by saying that I had a bad headache, and rose to leave the room. Mr. Stanhope was struck, he saw the uneasiness I could not dissemble, his heart accused him as the cause of it, and following me, he caught my hand eagerly, and said with affectionate anxiety, "*dearest Olivia!*" but had not power to utter more. Totally overcome, I withdrew my hand from him hastily, but I trust not angrily, and hurried up to my room, where I burst into a flood of tears, not less from dissatisfaction with myself, than at the cruel idea of relinquishing for ever the hand of a man whom I had for so many years considered as the sole arbiter of my fate, the only man for whom my heart ever has sighed, or can sigh.

The next morning at going down into the breakfast room, I found him, contrary to his usual practice, already there. He looked pale and haggard, as if he had passed a disturbed night, and though I believe he had come down early for the express purpose of meeting me, he had not courage to say more than anxiously to enquire after my health. Indeed so much did I myself dread rather than wish his entering upon any explanation relative to the preceding day, that I began to talk eagerly upon indifferent subjects, till Sir Francis and Lady Stanhope entered to the infinite relief of us both.

In the evening we were to go to the play according to an engagement made the day before, and I was to call Charlotte in my carriage accompanied by Mr. Stanhope. At dinner the latter appeared very uneasy and embarrassed, as if there was something on his mind which he wished to say, yet knew not how to give it utterance. At length, making a great effort, he began a long apology, but hoped I would excuse his attending me to the theatre, as he wished to call upon a particular friend, who was unexpectedly going out of town early the next morning, and whom he should therefore have no other opportunity of seeing. He owned that this was a shabby apology to make for such rudeness, but he must trust to my goodness to excuse it.

All this was said with a confusion and hesitation which left me no room to doubt of its real meaning—that Charlotte was to be with us, and he dared not trust himself again in her company. But this was to me the strongest reason possible for urging his going, since if he felt absence his only security against her power, it was obvious that even in this one interview she had gained an ascendancy over him, on the transitoriness or durability of which my answer must be finally regulated. If this were only a fleeting admiration of a new object, the novelty being at an end, the effect would of course cease; but if on the contrary it was the commencement of a serious and lasting attachment, by frequent intercourse it would be the more fully confirmed, and, in either case, by promoting their meeting I should learn the lesson requisite for determining my future conduct.

Yes, Harriot, I felt all this deeply, and why should I attempt to disguise my feelings?—I felt it painfully. The path of duty was plain to me, but I beheld it strewed with thorns, yet I suffered not the prospect to subdue my fortitude, but entered it courageously, convinced that whatever might be my sufferings in passing through it, they would be repaid by my reflections when the conflict was past. I therefore pressed Mr. Stanhope upon the subject, and enquired whether his friend was to go so early on the following day that it would be impossible to see him then, or if so, whether he could not call upon him immediately, and return in time to accompany us to the theatre.

For this suggestion he seemed wholly unprepared. He hesitated, he wavered, he knew not what to answer. I urged him farther till at length he agreed to attend us, and said he would see his friend directly as I had proposed. He accordingly left the room, but sought not the company of a friend, rather that of a foe, since it was evident, when he rejoined me at the appointed hour, that his own disturbed thoughts had been his sole companions. He trembled in every limb as he handed me to the carriage, nor had power to utter a single word.

At the sight of Charlotte his face was instantly covered with a deep scarlet; he did not get out to hand her into the carriage, he did not even offer her his hand at all, but remained in the corner motionless as a statue. At the play he sat between Charlotte and myself, with his back almost turned to her, and while to me he endeavoured to be extremely talkative, to her he addressed not a syllable of conversation, but affected scarcely to heed her when she spoke to him. Ah! could the most devoted attentions have explained what was passing in his mind in terms half so forcible.

Since that evening they have met three times. Twice did Mr. Stanhope behave in the same cautious and reserved manner, but the third time at supper he was unfortunately seated next to her, after taking the utmost pains to avoid it. She was even more than commonly animated, and addressing herself particularly to him as her neighbour, he was at last entirely thrown off his guard, and yielded up his whole soul to the intoxication of the moment. But never shall I forget his looks, his manner, when we returned home. Conscience seemed to reproach him far more than I thought he deserved, and in hopes to soothe his mind, I took my harp and began to play. Yet alas, instead of soothing, I only encreased his tortures, he cast on me a look of mingled agony and admiration, and rushed out of the room.

At that moment I resolved that another day should not pass over our heads without my putting an end to a situation so tormenting to us both. Yet without shrinking from my resolution to prove no obstacle to his happiness, I have not felt my heart sufficiently strong to sustain with due fortitude the conflict it must go through in taking my last farewell of the object on earth most dear to me. This evening they will meet again, as we are engaged to cards and supper at Mr. O'Brien's. This then shall be their last trial, to-morrow my answer, my final, my positive answer shall be given.

Harriot, if in writing thus of myself alone, nor once adverting to your situation, critical and interesting as it is, I might appear to others selfish and insensible, you I know will never judge so harshly of

Your truly affectionate

OLIVIA CAMPBELL.

LETTER XIX.

REGINALD BEAUCHAMP
TO
LIONEL STANHOPE.

Maxtead, March 20.

Not unmindful of an engagement made to you long ago, my dear Sir, instantly to communicate any discoveries I might make relative to Mr. Ryder's mysterious child, I hasten to impart the following information which I have just received. In the silence observed towards you with regard to her, you could patiently acquiesce, but that the same secrecy should be observed towards me, the general confident of Campbell-House, the man who first introduced Mr. Ryder to Miss Campbell, was to you matter of the deepest offence. Indeed I believe, had you been in my place, you would peremptorily have demanded a participation in the secret, under pain of renouncing for ever the society of beings so incommunicative, so regardless of the sufferings of ungratified curiosity, as obstinately to preserve a mystery, the developement of which would have diffused such infinite satisfaction all around them.

But all reserve, all mystery, is now at an end. Attend then to the explanation so long, so anxiously wished.

You are not now to learn that Mr. Barry, the original patron of Mr. Ryder, though generous in pecuniary matters, was stern and haughty in his manners, and entertained very high notions of parental authority, and if he did sometimes relax and shew indulgence to his son, as in the instance of allowing him to invite Dick Ryder to the hall as his play fellow, yet in general he exacted the most unlimited obedience to his arbitrary will. Unfortunately too for George Barry, this habit continued to encrease with encreasing years, till by the time the young man arrived at the age when parental authority ought to cease, and the tie of parent and child be lost in that of friends, the old gentleman held the reins even with a tighter hand than ever. In fact, such was the sternness of his disposition, that never did Turkish slave feel greater awe in the presence of his despotic Bashaw,* than did George Barry in that of the author of his existence.

---

* An honorary title denoting high civil or military rank in Turkey. It is an earlier form of Pasha.

Among a long list of offences this affectionate parent one day enumerated, by the commission of any one of which his son would inevitably incur the penalty of being disinherited, first and foremost stood that most heinous of all misdemeanours in the eyes of parents, the consulting his own inclinations in the choice of a wife, rather than referring the matter entirely to the prudence and experience of his father. "In short," Mr. Barry said, "you know my temper, George; you know that I am ready to grant you every indulgence a child can expect, provided you shew me the obedience due to my situation, but depend upon it that if you marry without my consent, whatever may be the merits of your wife, no prayers or intercessions shall move me to forgiveness."

Till this denunciation George had manifested a considerable degree of indifference towards the fair sex, but no sooner was he led to consider them as prohibited goods, than, according to the general propensity of human nature, they acquired an inconceivable charm in his eyes. Impressed with a strong conviction that he must not fall in love, in his restless anxiety to guard his heart against the inroads of that fatal passion, his imagination dwelt with a sickly tremor on every pretty face he beheld, and while dreading the effects of mingling in female society, he was yet craving for it incessantly.

About that time the rector of the parish, who had for above fifty years paid the most unremitting attention to the duties of his office, became from age and infirmities unable to perform them any longer, and leaving his flock to the care of a substitute, he retired himself to pass the remainder of his days with an only daughter who had been married many years. It so happened that among many candidates for his curacy, his choice fell upon the very Mr. Deacon who had married one of Richard Ryder's aunts, and who was now become the father of a very large family. Mr. Barry however was ignorant of the relationship between the former object of his patronage and the new curate, or this circumstance might not have proved a strong recommendation of the latter to his favour.

The eldest of Mr. Deacon's children was a daughter about seventeen years of age, a perfect model of rural beauty. The white rose was not fairer than her complexion, nor did the delicate bloom of the red rose exceed that on her cheek. Her soft blue eyes seemed formed for conquest, yet were so unconscious of their power that they never wandered in search of admiration, but rather seemed to shrink abashed within themselves, if perchance they encountered the roving glances they had irresistibly attracted.

This dangerous creature was first seen by George at church; his heart was instantly in a flame, nor could he restrain his eyes from occasionally wandering towards the pew to which they were so magnetically drawn, though often as he caught them at these dangerous excursions, he recollected his father's denunciations, and instantly recalled them. But spite of all his caution the impression he had received did not wholly escape observation. The lovely Maria had no less attracted the attention of the old Squire, than of the young one, and beautiful as he saw her, he could not be insensible to the danger of such a temptation being placed within the reach of his son. Thus alarmed, during the whole time of service he watched the young man's looks with the most tormenting anxiety, so that not a glance was stolen by George but it was faithfully registered in the bosom of the attentive parent.

No sooner was the service over, and George, as his father thought, safely lodged at home, than the latter repaired to the parsonage to pay a gracious visit to its newly arrived inhabitants. He expressed very great satisfaction in the rector's judicious choice of a substitute, and wished the curate much health and happiness in his new situation, hoped that they should be good neighbours, and begged he would drop in and take a family dinner at the Hall whenever it would be agreeable. He offered him besides the free use of his library, which he said was a pretty good one, and should he find his own garden insufficient for the supply of his large family, entreated him at any time to send to his for whatever he might want.

Mr. Deacon, perfectly overwhelmed with this excess of politeness, scarcely knew what to reply. He bowed, and bowed again and again, expressed his high sense of the honour and favour shewn him, which he said so much exceeded any thing he had ever experienced in former situations, that he was at a loss how sufficiently to acknowledge it. He assured Mr. Barry that he should think himself extremely fortunate in being received at the Hall upon such sociable terms, since a good neighbour in the country was a thing rarely to be found; he only hoped that he should not abuse his kindness by growing too intrusive. Of this Mr. Barry said he had not the least apprehension, and to shew that he was sincere in his invitation, insisted upon Mr. Deacon's immediately accompanying him home to dinner.

A request so flattering the transported curate was no way disposed to decline, and accordingly he and the squire set off together to the Hall, which was about half a mile distant from the Parsonage, while in the course of the walk the patron's views in this superabundant condescension began to unfold themselves.

"Mr. Deacon," he said, "as the father of a family yourself, you must be well aware of the many tender anxieties, hopes, and fears, by which the breast of every parent is agitated. Nor can you be less sensible that if these be painfully acute where the family is obscure, the fortune small, and the children numerous, they must encrease in proportion as the stake grows greater, and in such a case as mine, where I have an only son, the representative of an ancient and illustrious house, and the heir to a large fortune, that they must rise almost to agony. You cannot wonder therefore, that my son's settlement in life should be the subject of my constant anxiety, that my day dreams and my nightly visions should centre primarily in this most important concern, that to see him happily wedded should be the object of my incessant wishes, in short, that this great affair should be the pole to which every thought of my heart and soul invariably points."

"Oh I can enter with perfect sympathy into these feelings. My parental anxieties indeed cannot be so entirely centered in one object, but though my affections must necessarily be divided, I do not believe that I am therefore the less fearfully anxious for the welfare of my children [or] less eagerly desirous of seeing them advantageously settled in life as virtuous and happy members of the community."

"Indeed, Mr. Deacon, had I not been well assured that I was addressing myself to a man who from his own feelings could truly participate in mine, I had not, perhaps, on so short an acquaintance ventured to touch upon a subject so delicate as what I am about to mention. Oh, Mr. Deacon, you know how easily the youthful heart is led astray from the path of duty, particularly in all matters that concern the senses or imagination. You know how many fathers have been rendered miserable by not paying a strict attention to avert temptation from their children, and you will therefore sympathise with my anxiety to preserve my son from finding his filial obedience put too severely to the hazard."

"Nothing surely can be more natural or meritorious than such an anxiety, nor can it be doubted, Sir, but that under the direction of such a parent your son will prove an honour to his family."

"I believe indeed his propensities are at present good, can I then pay too much attention to keeping them so? Mr. Deacon, forgive my freedom, but you have a daughter, one of the loveliest young creatures I ever beheld; she seems artless and innocent, and I doubt not her disposition is truly amiable. But young men, Mr. Deacon, in the ardour of passion will not always reflect upon the sufferings they bring on others by seducing the affections of youth and innocence, and I could wish therefore to suggest—excuse me, Mr. Deacon—I do not mean to wound you—but surely it were desirable, very desirable that she were kept as much as possible out of the way of my son.—Have you no friend, my dear Sir, no relation under whose protection she might be placed?"

Astonishment for a few minutes held poor Mr. Deacon mute. What could he suppose, but that notwithstanding Mr. Barry's profession of his belief in his son's virtuous propensities, the young man was really a libertine, within whose reach no pretty woman could remain in safety, and that the father had thus put him upon his guard in the softest and most varnished terms he could devise. When his first emotions therefore subsided, he poured forth a profusion of gratitude for this fresh instance of Mr. Barry's kindness, and assured him that without giving a hint of the subject of their conversation, he would send his daughter as speedily as possible to a widowed sister of his wife's who lived at Pontefract, and with whom she was accustomed to pass a great deal of time. Meanwhile he would be very cautious to keep her at home, so that she might be in no danger of meeting the young man. The old gentleman delighted to find his project succeed so well, paid some fine compliments to the curate's discretion, which were returned by the latter with fresh expressions of gratitude, till in short the two gentlemen grew so ardent in the business, that before they sat down to dinner every thing was arranged for Maria's departure in the course of the week.

In the mean time George, whose whole soul was engrossed with the idea of the lovely object he had so transiently beheld, did not remain long at home when he returned thither after church, but went out to take a walk, and almost involuntarily directed his course towards the parsonage, though by a different route from that which his father had taken. He did not indeed, when he set out, think of calling there, but finding himself in a field adjoining to the very garden, he thought it would be very ill manners to return without paying his respects to the new curate, and he approached the garden-gate for this purpose. But behold, as he had nearly reached one gate, who should he espy entering at the other but Mr. Barry himself. He started back, well assured that he had not been noticed, and retreated behind a hedge whence he could distinctly see every entrance and exit to and from the parsonage, without any risk of being discovered himself, and after waiting there about half an hour, had the satisfaction of seeing his father and Mr. Deacon depart together, taking the way directly to the Hall.

When they were out of sight he ventured from his hiding-place, and knocking at the curate's door, boldly enquired if Mr. Deacon were within. He was answered in the negative, that he was gone home with the squire to dinner. He then enquired for the ladies, to whom he was immediately introduced, when he said that he had come with the intention of paying his compliments to Mr. Deacon, but finding that he was unluckily not at home, he had taken the liberty of asking for them. They were extremely flattered by his polite attention, and informed him that Mr. Barry too had done them the honour of calling, and most obligingly insisted on Mr. Deacon's accompanying him home to dinner, a circumstance at which George rejoiced exceedingly, since he should thus have the pleasure of being introduced to him, though he had failed of seeing him at his own house.

The poor wounded deer extended his visit to the utmost limits he thought it could be extended with safety, all the time drinking in large draughts of luscious poison from the bright eyes of Maria, and then scampering home as fast as possible, fortunately arrived there just as the roast beef was carrying into the parlour. But even in this short time never was faithful Corydon more devoted to his Phillis[15] than he to his new charmer; never did Arcadian shepherd breathe firmer vows of unalterable fidelity to his beauteous shepherdess than he inwardly vowed to the object of his adoration.

Little did he then suspect the plot which during this interval had been contrived against him by the two fathers, but it was not long before it was made known by the effect. The young lady, according to the plan concerted, was sent to her aunt, the very exciseman's widow who in the moment of Mr. Ryder's distress had so kindly offered him protection and assistance, and Mr. Barry still remained ignorant that his son had ever seen Miss Deacon excepting at church, congratulating himself on his own dexterity in having thus removed so great a temptation out of his way.

But love, ever vigilant, soon discovered the retreat of the beloved, and the enamoured youth suspecting the motive that occasioned his Maria's removal, was only stimulated the more forcibly to pursue his inclinations. Under some trifling pretence therefore, he made an excursion from home for a few days, when he repaired to Pontefract, to the house which contained all that was dear to him on earth. Here, by dexterous management, he so far insinuated himself into the aunt's favour, to whom, as the friend of her nephew Ryder, he was already not unknown, that he easily obtained permission to renew his visits as often as he could find opportunity. Thus while the unsuspecting father was pleasing himself with reflecting upon the happy effects of his own prudence and foresight, he had in fact facilitated the intercourse he was so anxious entirely to prevent.

But lulled in security, and unapprehensive of danger, he never thought of watching his son in the frequent excursions he was now making from home, for which the young man always contrived to frame some specious reason. This intercourse, rendered the more sweet by being stolen, at length so encreased the attachment of the lovers, that to exist any longer without the possession of each other became impossible, and George ventured to propose a private marriage as the only practicable means of their being united, since to obtain his father's sanction to their wishes was absolutely hopeless. The aunt's consent was however necessary, but this was obtained without difficulty, and the hands of the young people were accordingly joined, Maria being by agreement still to remain in her former situation.

This marriage, far from diminishing George's passion, seemed rather to strengthen it, and his stolen visits to his fair Gabrielle[16] were if possible now carried on with greater assiduity than ever, while to complete his transports, but a short time elapsed before he found himself likely to become a father. Yet alas, even in the midst of this intoxication of delight, a stroke intervened to dash the cup of sweets with a cruel mixture of the bitter, in the death of the aunt, who was carried off in a moment by an apoplectic fit.

Fortunately for Maria, this event happened when her husband was with her, or it might have been attended with very alarming consequences, since she thus not only lost a kind and affectionate friend, but was reduced to a terrible dilemma with regard to her own situation. The marriage had been hitherto concealed even from Mr. Deacon, though that gentleman was not altogether without suspicion that in some, at least, of the young squire's frequent absences from the mansion at Blakeney, he had made visits to his daughter. This however he had taken no particular pains to ascertain, since he had so firm a reliance upon his sister-in-law's prudence and discretion, that he was convinced she would guard against any illicit connection between the young people, and he probably was not quite as anxious as Mr. Barry to prevent the formation of a legal one.

But Maria's situation rendered it absolutely necessary that some immediate steps should be taken, and as her father was of course sent for upon her aunt's death, the obvious way of proceeding was to confess to him what had passed, which indeed it would have been impossible to conceal, and then consult with him upon their future plans. Mr. Deacon was in the first place anxious to assure himself that his daughter was really married, but this done he did not display any very strong symptoms of displeasure at her having disposed of herself without consulting him, and as George did not fail to paint to him in very forcible colours the dreadful denunciations under which his father had prohibited his marrying without his approbation, Mr. Deacon consented with little reluctance to the marriage being still kept secret.

The principal difficulty now was, how to dispose of Maria. The house and furniture at Pontefract, the sole property left by the deceased aunt, were bequeathed to Mr. Ryder, but he being then absent from the kingdom, it was resolved that Mrs. Barry should remain there at least till after her confinement, by which time Mr. Ryder's pleasure with regard to the disposal of his bequest might be known. Mrs. Deacon was accordingly sent for to be with her daughter while she remained at Pontefract, and in this situation Maria was brought to bed of a daughter, to the inexpressible delight of herself and her husband.

It was only a few days after this event that Mr. Ryder returned to England, when he was immediately informed of all the circumstances of this affair. He instantly requested that Mrs. Barry would not think of removing, but would remain where she was as long as it would be any kind of convenience to herself and her husband. And there she did remain about half a year longer, when another blow, which at first wore a very alarming aspect, came upon them, and rendered a different arrangement inevitable.

Though it was long before Mr. Barry began to entertain any suspicion of the motive that occasioned his son's frequent excursions from home, yet at length, from some obscure hints he had collected, he grew less easy than formerly on the subject of Miss Deacon, nor was altogether free from apprehension that the young man's first sight of her had not been the only one. Still he was far from suspecting the real truth, he was only sufficiently alarmed to be desirous of removing him more effectually out of her way, and he accordingly began again to advert to a plan he had long ago formed, but had suffered to lie dormant in his mind, of sending his son to finish his education by travel. The first mention of this scheme was like a thunder-stroke to poor George. He had however so much presence of mind as not to start any strong objection to it, but answered by a sort of evasion, which was neither a positive consent, nor opposition to the plan, and thus the matter for a time passed off.

But in proportion as the squire's suspicions of his son's secret attachment encreased, his importunities for the adoption of the scheme encreased also, till at length finding the young man still putting him off with evasive anwers, he fairly told him he was sure there must be private reasons for this ambiguous conduct, and even hinted suspicions that it originated in some concealed amour. The remotest idea of such a suspicion was enough to alarm George; he saw that the peril was imminent, and that any farther opposition on his part might endanger the ruin not only of himself, but what was an infinitely greater consideration with him, that also of a wife and child in whom his whole soul was absorbed, and he could not hesitate to prefer a temporary separation from them, to the hazard of having them torn from him for ever. He told his father therefore, that though he had no wish himself to visit foreign countries, yet since it was his desire, he would not say another word against it, but would cheerfully and without delay prepare for his departure.

With tears did he impart these afflictive tidings to Maria, and with the tenderest caresses and assurances, that no absence or change of place could alter his affection for her, did he endeavour to soothe her anguish, and reconcile her to their inevitable fate. She clung round him and wept in his bosom, yet promised to exert all her resolution to support herself under this stroke, and to seek consolation in the hope of their future reunion under more propitious circumstances. On his departure it was judged best for Maria to return to her father's house, while Ryder was requested to find a proper situation for the child, since by this arrangement they thought all suspicion would be the most effectually removed from the squire's bosom.

With the situation in which the infant was placed you are not unacquainted, but since there were so many mysterious circumstances attending the child, Mr. Ryder judged very rightly that there would be a great impropriety in placing her so immediately under Miss Campbell's observation without acquainting her with the story. Her benevolence naturally led her to take a deep interest in it, and she was happy by her attentions to the little Maria, to alleviate some of the anxiety felt by her parents at being thus obliged to estrange themselves from her.

These arrangements happily deceived Mr. Barry so completely, that every trace of his former suspicions speedily vanished. He even encreased in his kindness and attention to Mr. Deacon and his family, as if to atone for such suspicions ever having been entertained, the only circumstance in the whole affair that gave real and lasting pain to the family themselves, or to George.

This latter, after travelling about for some time, at length by his father's consent determined to settle for a while at Lausanne. He had grown so extremely anxious to have his wife and child with him that life was scarcely supportable longer without them, and he thought that at such a distance from England they might join him with perfect safety.

The difficulty was, how to get them over. But here again recourse was had to Mr. Ryder, who, though not in his heart approving of the plan, kindly undertook the charge, and conducted them in safety to the borders of the Genevan Lake. He indeed saw reasons against their undertaking this journey, of which George himself could not be aware, that the declining state of Mr. Barry's health rendered his son's stay abroad very uncertain, nay, made it probable that it could not be of much longer duration.

In fact Mr. Ryder had not been returned to England many days before Mr. Barry, who had long been insensible to his danger, began to think his end approaching, and anxious to see his son again before his death, sent off an express to Lausanne desiring him to return with all possible expedition. George was now embarrassed* in the extreme about his wife and child, but unable to endure the idea of leaving them friendless and unprotected in a foreign country, he resolved rather to chuse the lesser evil of making them his companions, and risking the inconvenience they might eventually experience from so hasty a journey.

The event has not afforded him any reason to repent this determination. They all arrived safely in England, nor have Maria or the child suffered the least inconvenience from the rapidity with which they travelled. Mr. Barry just lived to see his son, but died within a week after his arrival, leaving him sole heir to a very ample fortune. Thus, all motives to secrecy on the subject of his marriage being at an end, Maria is publicly acknowledged as his wife, and has taken possession of a station in which there is little reason to doubt that her conduct will justify her husband's choice.

Such, my dear Sir, is the history of the mysterious child who has alternately been given by the world to Olivia, to Lucy Morgan, and to half a dozen other women, without any suspicion of the real truth ever having transpired; and since she appears at last to be Mr. Ryder's cousin, the resemblance so often discovered to him may not be wholly imaginary. One thing however still remains to be cleared up, and that is, why she was taken away from Maxtead in so great a hurry. But on this subject Mr. Ryder, who himself sent me the above detail, is perfectly silent.

May I trouble you, Sir, to inform Miss Campbell that the challenge sent to you is undoubtedly taken from the book to which she referred me. The only difference between the two, is such as must necessarily be made, to adapt the printed challenge to the circumstances in which it was to be used. I will also say to you in confidence, that the letter to Mr. Ryder respecting Miss Campbell's intended hasty union with you, was most undoubtedly taken from the same book. As I wish to have some conversation with Mr. Ryder upon this subject, I shall not mention it to him by letter, but defer the communication till I see him at Blakeney, where he is now staying, and whither I am going very shortly for a few days. Adieu, my dear Sir, and believe me

Your obliged and affectionate

REGINALD BEAUCHAMP.

---

*   Distressed or perplexed.

LETTER XX.

LIONEL STANHOPE
TO
HENRY EGERTON.

South Audley Street, March 21.

Harry 'tis past—the same woman has actually refused me twice—I am forbidden ever to think more of becoming the husband of Olivia—I am commanded to abandon the pursuit of her, even at the moment when I am first made fully sensible of her value.

Oh read, Harry, and then tell me whether you really can think her a mortal? 'Tis true that the mortality of a woman is seldom questioned unless she be transcendently beautiful, yet why is this? Is then symmetry of form and features so much the distinguishing characteristic of superior beings, whether they be real or imaginary, that this alone constitutes their superiority, and shall the soul be entirely set aside in the comparison? No, Olivia's soul is so exalted above that of all other mortals, that I never can suppose her to belong to the tribe of petty beings that crawl about this globe! A mere woman could not, as she has done, while with one breath she owned a partiality for a man, with the next have resigned him undauntedly to the arms of a rival, without betraying the least emotion of pique or resentment either to her faithless lover, or to the woman who had superseded her in his affections.

Yes, she has with a magnanimity to which no parallel can be found resigned me to a rival! O Harry! Harry! what reliance can ever be placed upon a heart so accustomed to rove as mine! It was but two days after I had assured Olivia of my perfect and entire devotion to her, that I first beheld the lovely Charlotte O'Brien. Intoxicated with her charms, I could see, could hear, no other object, while she was present, nor was I roused to a recollection of my criminality till we were separated, when my heart instantly began to reproach me with having acted like a monster towards Olivia,—towards the woman who was then sole arbitress of my fate.

I now only wished to confess my fault and solicit pardon of her against whom I had sinned so deeply, firmly resolving to see Charlotte no more, at least till all should be settled between me and Olivia. This I thought I owed both to her and myself, but to my utter astonishment she proved the obstacle to my carrying this resolution into effect. She studiously avoided giving me an opportunity for explanation, and when I would have excused myself from attending her to the play, because I knew Charlotte was to be of the party, she urged my going so earnestly, that no alternative remained but to comply, or confess my reasons for breaking my engagement.

Unfortunately for me, scarcely a day now passed but I was thrown in Charlotte's way, and though I made every possible effort to command myself, I was constantly baffled, the sorceress would engross my attention, nor permit me to act according to my own sense of propriety.

Yet all this time the moment I lost sight of her, my soul was seized with the deepest remorse, and I became pensive, gloomy, wretched. One evening when Olivia beheld me thus agitated, she took her harp, and in hopes of composing my spirits—yes, she sought to compose my spirits, she whose bosom I could only expect would glow with indignation at my perfidy, but she thought not of her own wrongs, she thought only of calming the agitations of my soul—she took her harp, and drew forth strains so soft, so ravishingly sweet, yet so solemn, so sublime, that my senses were overpowered, the conflict was more than I could sustain, and I rushed out of the room. Every note she struck seemed a reproach for some attention paid to Charlotte, every string as it vibrated seemed mournfully to ask me in what was Charlotte so much her superior? why was she to be deserted for Charlotte?

But this was only a prelude to the severer trial I was afterwards to undergo. Yesterday, being left alone with her, she began: "At our last private conversation, Mr. Stanhope, I requested a short time to deliberate upon the subject on which we were then occupied. I have deliberated upon it, and my decision is now finally made. You will recollect then giving me a promise that whatever it should be, you would not consider it as the effect of caprice, but as the result of cool and dispassionate judgment. I now demand farther of your candour that it shall not be attributed to pique or mean jealousy, to both of which, unless I mistake my own heart, I am a perfect stranger."

"Oh do not proceed! I can hear no more!"

"Yes, it must be, Mr. Stanhope! Let us still consider each other as friends—'tis all we ever can be."

Oh God! never can I forget the tone and manner in which these few words were spoken! Her voice did not falter, yet the evident effort it cost her to pronounce them with firmness, was far more affecting than any tears, any hesitation. I started from my seat, I walked several times up and down the room, then throwing myself beside her upon the sopha, I eagerly took her hand, and pressing it to my bosom, "Olivia," I said, "I acknowledge my guilt, I acknowledge that I have deserved this, but recal those words, unless you would drive me to distraction."

"No," she replied, "my resolution is irrevocably fixed. I blame you not, believe me; what you call your guilt I consider rather as a subject for rejoicing, since it has instructed me how to decide upon a matter on which I was before too much inclined to hesitate."

"And affixed a stigma upon my character, which no time, or remorse, can ever efface."

"Oh say not so! Say rather that we were both acting under an error, which but for a fortunate combination of circumstances might have proved fatal to the peace and happiness of both."

"No, no, Olivia, I cannot bear to hear you talk thus! Such forbearance on your part only forces me to take a more severe retrospect of what has lately passed, and makes me appear a greater monster in my own eyes.

Never, never, can I forgive myself unless your sentence be revoked! Yet how dare I think of this! My conduct ever since we became acquainted, has been a tissue of folly and meanness which you cannot but heartily despise."

"Judge not yourself so harshly, my much-esteemed friend."

"Oh for heaven's sake insult me not with that appellation! Call me wretch, villain, I shall feel that I deserve such epithets; but I am too much humbled at hearing myself addressed by a title which I am conscious I so little merit."

"Yet I must again give you that appellation, and entreat, as my much esteemed friend, that you will not suppose yourself become an object of contempt, or entertain so ill an opinion of my candour, as to think me capable of condemning you for feelings which I well know reason has so little power to controul."

"And what reliance can henceforward be placed on any declaration I shall make? how can any stability of sentiment ever be expected from me? when, notwithstanding the sacred nature of the professions I had made, notwithstanding the powerful reasons I had to be devoted wholly to you, my heart could so easily be drawn aside by the false glare that has seduced it."

"You do not state the question fairly; I must be your counsel, and I trust you will find me a more able advocate."

"You torture me, Olivia! Indeed you torture me! But allow me only a few days in which to recal my scattered senses, and I trust I shall never again give you occasion to condemn me. And if your candour can draw a veil over the past, and take a repentant sinner once more into your confidence, believe me you never shall have cause to repent such generosity."

"No, Mr. Stanhope, this is the only proof of my still continued friendship, and esteem, that I never can or will grant. I only entreat you thoroughly to probe your own heart, and enquire whether, if we had become acquainted in the common course of occurrences? if you had never known that our union was the earnest wish of our parents? never considered yourself as having violated the principles of honour and morality in your conduct towards me, and that I had therefore reason to expect some atonement from you? whether, if all these things had been out of the question, you really think I should have been the object of your choice?"

"But supposing I should ask myself these questions, how, most admirable Olivia, can I be sure that my answers are sincere?"

"Well then, if you think these questions not easy to be answered, let me put another, which you can surely find no difficulty in resolving. Before you became acquainted with me, had you ever seen a woman with whom you had formed a serious wish to unite your fate?"

"Never! Passionately admiring and following every pretty woman I beheld, I never seriously attached myself to any one, but all were regarded with like indifference after having been seen half a dozen times."

"And at the commencement of our acquaintance this propensity was somewhat on the decline?"

"Most true! Beauty then could not interest me even for a second time, unless united with the more powerful charms of a cultivated mind and refined manners."

"And you began to find the latter so attractive, that you could even think beauty might be dispensed with, where they eminently existed."

"Could I be a single day in your company and think otherwise?"

"Yet when introduced to Madame de Clairville, you found that the charms of polished manners and conversation received a considerable addition from charms of person. Believe me, Mr. Stanhope, I mean not this remark as a sarcasm, or reproach, but I wish to make you thoroughly acquainted with your own heart."

"Oh forbear, lest in displaying it thus before me without varnish or disguise, you make me think it truly detestable."

"That you shall not do. On the contrary, before we separate you shall think it as amiable as I do."

"Then say no more of Madame de Clairville."

"I must indeed. I must observe that while you saw her charming, you found her so deficient in the qualities most estimable in the female character, that you could not respect, therefore were in no danger of loving her."

"Indeed you do me no more than justice."

"You felt disappointed in her; you began to think that beauty was but a source of folly and vanity, and at length reasoned yourself into a persuasion that you were grown indifferent to it, and could devote yourself to me entirely."

"Of which I am still convinced."

"No, 'tis here you are in an error, nor would you ever have imagined this, but that a singular combination of circumstances have led you ardently to wish it. But cherish such a delusion no longer. You have now seen a woman formed in the very mould to fix your affections, be hers then, and be happy. Her personal charms are truly worthy of your admiration, her worth and accomplishments no less merit your perfect esteem. She has a refinement of taste and manners that will embelish any station in life, and even your rank and fortune will receive additional lustre from such an alliance; while Sir Francis, though he may experience a momentary disappointment, will soon lose the recollection of it, in beholding a son on whom his affections are fixed so unboundedly, settled happily in life, and the family name and title likely to be handed down to distant posterity. For me, rest assured I shall truly rejoice in the idea, that though I have lost a lover I have confirmed a friend, and shall ever feel no common degree of self-approbation, in reflecting that I have had sufficient resolution to persuade that friend to pursue the path of real happiness, rather than that of false honour."

"Olivia!" I cried, passionately kissing her hand, "you have conquered, you have indeed taught me thoroughly to know my own heart; you have unfolded to me truths which I could not have dared to unfold to myself! Yes, I do love Charlotte O'Brien! ardently, devotedly love her! Olivia, I can say no more!"

Egerton, was it a time to speak? were feelings like mine to be expressed by words? Oh no! Fain would I have told Olivia that I thought her more than mortal, but such a silly unmeaning compliment, which is paid a hundred times in a day to a hundred silly women, was not language to use to Olivia. Fain would I have assured her of my unbounded respect and esteem, but a hundred women have been esteemed and respected, and they were cold terms to express my feelings towards her. Besides, I do much more than esteem and respect her, I love her ardently, but 'tis with the affection of a brother, not with the passion I feel for Charlotte.

I still continued eagerly to clasp her hand; she withdrew it gently; could she have uttered words half so expressive? I started up, and again paced the room several times with hurried and perturbed steps, while she sat with her head reclined upon her hand, wrapt in thought, satisfied with what she had done, yet I feared not without a mixture of regret that she was no more to think of becoming my wife. Was it vanity that induced this suspicion; or was it simply the perception of a fact? Oh would to heaven I could satisfy myself that it was the mere effect of vanity.

Her generous purpose however now fulfilled, she seemed to think the trying scene had better be closed, and rising up she held out her hand to me and said, "We part friends, Mr. Stanhope?" I took the hand she offered, but to make any answer was impossible. I pressed it to my lips, I dropped a tear upon it, the seal of unalterable, unalienable friendship. Oh must it be no more than friendship? No, no, she has the first, the strongest claim to my heart, and I will yet school it to be hers alone.

I have not seen her since. After this conversation she went to her friend Mr. Villars's at Camberwell, to dine and stay all night, and I suspect she had purposely chosen the morning of that day for our explanation, when a temporary separation would give us time to compose ourselves.

I passed the remainder of the day principally in my own apartment, dissatisfied with myself, inclined to detest Charlotte, yet unable to resist loving her; one moment resolving never to see her more, trusting that Olivia might then at last be prevailed upon to revoke her decision, the next recalling to mind the generous exhortation she had given me to pursue the path of real happiness, rather than that of false honour, and persuading myself that to reject her counsel would be making a very ungenerous return for conduct so noble and disinterested.

In the evening I did summon up sufficient courage to impart what had passed to Sir Francis, though it occasioned me no small struggle. But I believe it did not come upon him unexpectedly; his own observation, I suspect, had anticipated my story. He took my hand affectionately and said, "Well, heaven bless thee and make thee happy, my dear boy, in whatever connection thou mayest form, and mayest thou never live to repent that such a treasure was suffered to escape thee." Less than this he could not say, and considering the severity of his disappointment, he could scarcely be expected to say so little.

To-day at dinner I shall see Olivia again. Oh what a meeting to me! Bowed down with shame and confusion, how shall I ever dare to raise my eyes to her. Egerton! Egerton! she must, she shall still be mine! Never could I be happy in the possession of Charlotte, while haunted by the recollection that I had acted basely towards Olivia! Oh God what will become at last of

Your truly affectionate

LIONEL STANHOPE?

LETTER XXI.

OLIVIA CAMPBELL
TO
HARRIOT BELGRAVE.

South Audley Street, March 25.

Harriot, the conflict is over, and nothing now remains but to reconcile my mind in the best manner I am able to my irrevocable determination. The meeting between Mr. Stanhope and Charlotte on the day that I wrote last, added so strongly to my conviction of the sentiments each entertained for the other, that I could not hesitate any longer what to do, and the next morning therefore I imparted my final resolution to Mr. Stanhope.

But excuse, Harriot, my not giving you a detail of the scene, my mind really at present is not sufficiently composed to enter upon it. Were I suffered quietly to abide by my resolution, I think my satisfaction in what I have done, would soon overcome the pangs it has cost me to relinquish for ever the man whom the peculiar circumstances of my fate has long taught me to consider as the only one on earth to whom my hand could be given. But his conduct distresses me beyond measure. So much is he the creature of feeling, that he would even now involve both himself and me in a situation which we must expect would end in a long and fearful futurity of repentance to both, because he is apprehensive that otherwise his conduct towards me must appear to the world dishonourable and culpable.

Upon this subject we have had several contests; for though he allows I have sufficient reason for the decision I have made, yet he says he is satisfied that if I would but concede to him, and recant it, his behaviour for the future would be such as should give me no reason to repent my candour and generosity. Ah he knows not how he harasses my soul by this conduct. I have armed myself with resolution to resist an inclination which reason does not sanction, but such repeated conflicts almost wear me out, till sometimes from a relaxation of my physical, rather than mental powers, I have scarcely firmness sufficient left to adhere to my purpose. I believe indeed the only way to put an end to a situation so painful, is to separate myself from him entirely, and I shall probably therefore leave London very soon, instead of staying till the end of May, as I originally intended.

'Tis an additional vexation to me that Mr. Stanhope, in consequence of what has passed, now resolutely refuses to see Charlotte, and has lately declined several parties solely on her account. His absenting himself thus from our society evidently gives her no slight degree of uneasiness, and last night she asked, as if in joke and raillery to me, what was become of him, expressing apprehensions that I had treated him with cruelty. How deeply I was wounded by this raillery you will easily imagine, yet I was not so entirely occupied by my own feelings, but that I could observe her sufficiently, to see how poorly this assumed jocularity veiled real mortification.

I am sorry I cannot send you any very satisfactory intelligence with regard to Mr. Egerton. Mr. Stanhope has heard from him several times, and always in the same strain, that he never can think of becoming your husband under his present circumstances, yet he seems unable to apply himself to any thing that might improve his situation. Mr. Stanhope talks sometimes of going down to Arrenton to see him, and I earnestly wish he would do so, as I could then continue in town without being harassed any longer by the conflicts I now experience. I suspect indeed that the only thing which prevents his going to Arrenton is, that though he obstinately refuses to see Charlotte, he knows not how to quit the place where she resides.

I was last night at a masquerade, with the Tichfields, Madame de Clairville, Charlotte, Peggy Perkins, and George Macklin. When Peggy was first invited to join the party, she hesitated much about going. She had heard so many terrific* stories of masquerades, that she expected nothing less than to be carried off by some wretch, whom charms like hers, even though shrouded beneath an envious mask, would inspire with a passion so tumultuous, that it would not stop even at the most desperate attempts for obtaining possession of them. Nor would she at last, I believe, have resolved upon encountering perils so imminent, had not the gallant George Macklin, who has appointed himself her beau in ordinary and extraordinary,[17] employed all his powers of persuasion to prevail upon her to make one of the company, promising as an inducement to it, that

---

*   Terrifying.

he would take all possible care of her, and never quit her side the whole evening. After what you already know of his character, you will easily judge how well qualified he, who is so little capable of taking care of himself, is to be guardian to another. But Peggy was satisfied, and yielded to his wishes. We recommended to her to go in the character of Amphitrite,[18] as being emblematic of the occupation to which she has lately taken, and proposed George as her guardian; going as Neptune, when we would all be Tritons.[19] But she was not quite pleased at the proposal, as she said we might have known that in consequence of the persecutions of her *bitter enemies* she had been obliged totally to give up her aquatic excursions.

Indeed, Harriot, a masquerade may be a very fine subject of terror to a Peggy Perkins; but I can only say, that of all the dull modes of killing time invented by mankind under the idea of amusement, I think this by far the dullest. We went as a company of strolling players, and intending to be highly amusing, as well as amused, had studied several scenes from different plays, which we thought might be introduced with good effect in the course of the evening. But as we found the company all too much occupied with themselves, and the refreshments, to attend to any thing else, we were compelled to abandon our intentions, and remain silent.

As to the other characters, they consisted of modest shepherdesses, with the manners of courtesans; and Italian peasants, with those of English clowns and milk-maids. Of Quakers, who seemed to consider Quakerism as consisting only in making rude speeches to every body about them; ballad-singers quavering the Children in the Wood, Barbara Allen,[20] and the like simple melodies, with Italian airs and graces; gallant admirals, who did not know the main from the mizen-mast; generals crowned with laurel, who could not distinguish between a sabre and a broad sword; Turks drinking wine like English squires; and many more equally absurd, too numerous to detail.

We were not induced to stay very late in a scene that afforded so little amusement, therefore returned home by two o'clock. But not one of the company was so completely disappointed as Peggy Perkins, for she had not met with a single adventure, notwithstanding that she lost her protector very early in the evening. He was hunted for in vain by the gentlemen of our party for a long time; but at length, just as we were coming away, was found without his mask, with two ladies of not the highest reputation, who were disputing about him, and pulling him different ways, he all the time expostulating with them, and assuring them that he was a clergyman of respectable character, and not a gentleman of the description they supposed him.

Adieu, my dearest Harriot, and believe me under all circumstances, and in all situations,

Your truly affectionate

OLIVIA CAMPBELL.

LETTER XXII.

OLIVIA CAMPBELL
TO
REGINALD BEAUCHAMP.

South Audley Street, March 31.

So much have I been occupied on other subjects, my dear Sir, that I could not till the day before yesterday pursue my researches with regard to the challenge. But on the morning of that day I went to Twickenham, determined to let Mrs. Harrison and Peggy Perkins know that they were discovered, as I suspected the whole scheme was their joint concern, since they were together at Mrs. Stapleton's at the time the challenge was sent.

In my way I amused myself extremely with the idea of the confusion and contrition of the two ladies when they should find themselves detected, and meditated much upon the best way of introducing the subject. At length I resolved upon telling the story of the challenge, to see what effect it would have upon them. I accordingly soon took an opportunity of beginning my narration, which I interspersed with some pretty severe animadversions upon sending such letters, whether it were done through malice, to set friends at variance, or from a mistaken idea of humour. But I had not proceeded far, before Mrs. Harrison burst into an exclamation of extasy: "Oh then Mr. Stanhope did receive it! Well, Miss Perkins and I was always afraid that neither Mr. Stanhope nor Mr. Ryder received their letters, because we never heard any talking about 'em."

I stared, affecting great astonishment and replied: "It should seem then, Madam, that you and Miss Perkins know something about this affair?"

"Lord, my dear, why it was we as sent the challenge for a hoax."

"How, Madam, did you endanger the lives of two people for a hoax?"

"Lord no, my dear, we knew there was no danger of their fighting, because Mr. Ryder was out of the way."

"What will you say then, Madam, when you hear that though Mr. Ryder was not immediately on the spot, this was no security against Mr. Stanhope's apparently just indignation, who on not finding him at the place of appointment, set off instantly to Pontefract in search of him, where, if he had found him, the loss of one, or both of their lives, had been the probable consequence."

"Lord, why then Mr. Stanhope's a mighty peppery gentleman, and one must take care how one has any fun with him. Lord, why I could have sent such a challenge to twenty people, and when they didn't find any body there, they'd never have thought any thing more about it. But I declare I'll never attempt having any fun with him again."

"Probably, Madam, you could not make a resolution more consonant to his wishes. But if I understood you rightly, a letter of the same kind was sent to Mr. Ryder."

"No, that was a different letter. That was to hoax him about you, because he was always a saying that he was very sure Miss Campbell would never do any thing but what was right and proper. So we wrote a letter pretending to be from a person that thought he was in love with you, and would be mortified to hear that you was a going to be married all in a hurry to Mr. Stanhope, and that the wedding was to be the next morning, and nobody was to know any thing about it till it was over; and we knew he was so formal and precise, that he wouldn't think this right, and would be in a stew and fuss. And mayhap I might have told you all about it, if it hadn't a been what you was so confounded angry at what Nanny had been a telling of me about Mr. Ryder, and Lucy Morgan, and the child, and so I was obliged to go away in such a confounded hurry."

"And you wrote a letter to Mr. Ryder, as if from a person who supposed him to be in love with me?"

"Aye, my dear, but we was always afraid Mr. Ryder didn't receive it, because he went away in such a stew that morning."

I felt at first so extremely indignant at the idea of such a letter having been sent to Mr. Ryder, that I with difficulty restrained myself from entering upon a warm remonstrance with the two ladies against this species of fun, as it is called, and from representing in strong colours the particular indelicacy of what had been done, considering how Mr. Ryder was circumstanced with regard to me. But a moment's reflection convinced me, that persons capable of acting in such a manner could have so little sense of delicacy, that to reason with them upon the subject must be vain, and I therefore contented myself with requesting of Mrs. Harrison and Peggy, that when next they should find themselves in a funny humour, they would select some other subjects on whom to exercise their mirth, who would have more taste for it, than myself and my friends.

Mrs. Harrison hummed, and stared, and hesitated, and looked vastly wise, as if desirous of saying something uncommonly severe in reply; but as nothing occurred, the matter dropped. As for Peggy, she coloured extremely the moment that I began upon the subject, yet said not a word, only snatching up her work she sat twitch, twitch, twitch, as hard as her needle could go, nor once lifted up her eyes during my stay. But the door of the room was no sooner closed upon me at my departure, than I heard a grand burst of laughter, which sufficently explained to me the conversation that ensued.

What I thus learned, however, with regard to Mr. Ryder, has given me very serious uneasiness. Tell me, Mr. Beauchamp, do you know whether he ever received such a letter as Mrs. Harrison mentioned? 'Tis strange and hard, that a young woman in my situation cannot receive men as visitors at her house upon sociable terms, without being subject to such idle nonsensical gossip. Alas! perhaps 'tis the silly reports which have been circulated respecting Mr. Ryder and me that have driven him into the resolution of declining my farm, and have made him absent himself so entirely from Campbell-House, while from a sense of delicacy he has chosen to conceal the motives by which his conduct is influenced.

What passed about the challenge I imparted to my friends here, but did not mention the letter to Mr. Ryder. Sir Francis, on hearing the story, declared he would roast Peggy about it the first opportunity. Accordingly, the next day when she, with Mrs. Harrison, the Tichfields, Madame de Clairville, and George Macklin, dined here, a novel lately published being mentioned by one of the company, as we were sitting after dinner, and its merits being discussed, Sir Francis at length asked Peggy's opinion of it?

"*I* never read novels, Sir," she replied, laying a particular emphasis upon that favourite little pronoun.

"You think them much beneath your notice?"

"Very much indeed."

"Then I suppose history is your favourite study?"

"I am no pedant, Sir. I hate female pedants."

"And you think it pedantic in a woman to read history?"

"I certainly do."

"You prefer biography, or theology, perhaps?"

"Biography is as pedantic as history, and I'm sure theology is no proper study for a woman."

"Voyages and travels then perhaps suit your taste?"

"No, indeed! I love old England too well to trouble my head about other countries."

"You confine yourself entirely to Mother Goose's Tales, and such light kind of reading?"

"No Sir, I read my Bible, and I consider that as the only book a woman has any business to read."

"Nay, surely you don't confine yourself entirely to the Bible: you do sometimes relax and indulge in a little innocent variety? A magazine, perhaps, or some of the fashionable periodical publications? One is scarcely fit to live in the world without some knowledge of them."

"And I am sure by reading them we should be rendered unfit to live in another."

"How do you know that, unless by perusing them? Ah! Miss Peggy, indeed I'm afraid you've been poaching and found something naughty."

"There are other ways of knowing that things are not fit to be read."

"Well, then, if these publications are so pernicious, there is the *Complete Letter Writer*, that surely is a very innocent one?"

Peggy's face was in a moment of a deep scarlet. "Ha!" said her tormentor, "What is there something naughty in that too? I am very unfortunate in my recommendations."

Peggy snatched up a glass of wine, and swallowed it in a vehement hurry and flutter. "Nay, don't be so alarmed, young lady," said Sir Francis, "I'm not going to investigate the matter too nicely. But since you do not seem wholly unacquainted with the work, you can perhaps tell me whether there are any specimens of challenges in it? if not, I think I have one here which would come very well into a new edition. Do read it, and give me your opinion," and he handed a copy of the challenge to her.

She snatched it up, tore it into scraps, and bursting into tears, hastily left the room, Mrs. Harrison calling after her, "Lord, my dear, never mind Sir Francis. Lord, I dare say he has *hoaxed* people enough himself before now;" but she called in vain, Peggy's bosom was too much overcharged to listen to the consolation offered.

I began to be seriously vexed, and followed her up stairs, but she bounced into the drawing-room, and flung the door in my face, saying, "I insist upon being left alone." Indeed I saw so plainly that she was in a temper of mind better left to itself, that I relinquished my pursuit and returned to the company. Nor was I at last very sorry that she had received such a correction, since it was one well suited to her offence; and I heartily wish it may prove a warning to her against such practices in future. I only wish that a like impression could have been made upon Mrs. Harrison; but to make her feel is, I believe, impossible.

George Macklin, however, who left the room almost immediately after her, was permitted to interupt her privacy; for when we went up after dinner, we found them sitting together in a very loving manner. On our appearance he retired, when Peggy began to give free vent to the overflowings of her heart, by arraigning the whole party as in a conspiracy against her. "But I will bear this treatment no longer," she said. "I was under the necessity of quitting Leeds, where I hoped to have passed a peaceable and happy winter, for reasons which you all well know, and I then hoped that beneath the hospitable roof of Mrs. Harrison I should be free from persecution. But I see that not even being her guest can secure me from the shafts of malice; and though from her individually I may receive all imaginable kindness, I am destined to be the butt and sport of her acquaintance. These indignities, however, I am resolved to bear no longer, and I shall once more endeavour, by change of place, to escape the storms which here assail me on all sides. Mr. Macklin alone, of the whole set among whom my time has been chiefly passed, has behaved to me with the humanity of a Christian, and the respect of a gentleman. Under his protection I have therefore placed myself, and he is now gone to secure a chaise to convey us away together to-morrow morning. Whither I shall go is as yet undecided, though I am strongly inclined once more to try Bath; but wheresoever my adverse fate may place me, Mr. Macklin kindly promises not to abandon me till he sees me comfortably and happily settled. Ah! how many, like myself, have thus found that protection and kindness from a stranger, which was vainly expected from friends!"

"Lord," said Mrs. Harrison, "why, Miss Perkins, I hope you don't mean to go away in such a stew because you was a little hoaxed. That's being as bad as Mr. Stanhope himself."

"Indeed but I do, Madam. If you can submit patiently to being made the jest of others, 'tis more than I can, I assure you."

This spirit, though not in itself censurable, but far otherwise, I thought however came with a very ill grace from one to whom the *hoax* she had received was only retaliation. Mrs. Harrison took great offence at it, and began warmly to combat Peggy's resolution of departure, till at length the two ladies got into so violent an altercation, that they are likely henceforward to be as *bitter enemies* as ever they were *dear friends*.

But what shall we say to Peggy the prude, who has so long made it her pride and her boast that she never was alone in a room with a man, yet is now about setting out upon a journey she knows not whither, accompanied by one with whom she has been so short a time acquainted. How irresistible must be the man who has effected this change.

I am, my dear Sir,
Yours with great regard,

OLIVIA CAMPBELL.

LETTER XXIII.

REGINALD BEAUCHAMP
TO
OLIVIA CAMPBELL.

Maxtead, April 10.
Yes, my dear Madam, 'tis indeed true that Mr. Ryder received such a letter as Mrs. Harrison mentioned, and that motives of delicacy alone restrained his imparting the circumstance to any one but myself. How much he was distressed when he learned that you had been informed of it at all, and how much more so at the manner in which you heard it, I cannot easily describe. I must confess, however, that I do not feel the same degree of regret upon the subject, since it has ultimately led to my discovering, what we have long wished in vain to know, the cause of that secret sorrow by which our friend's mind has been long harassed.

I have had considerable debates with myself whether or not I should impart this discovery to you, Madam, but at length I have determined on revealing all. Only let me premise that Mr. Ryder himself knows nothing of my present purpose, and I have no doubt would have laid strict injunctions of secrecy upon me, had he suspected it. Perhaps indeed I am wrong, but I am actuated by the purest motives, nor should I have mentioned the subject, had not all idea of an union between you and Mr. Stanhope been at an end.

That this affair has terminated thus, allow me to remark, my dear Madam, before I proceed further, appears to me far the happiest thing for you both, and I think your judgement and resolution in what you have done are equally worthy of admiration. Though Mr. Stanhope possesses many amiable and estimable qualities, I do not think him a man altogether calculated to make you as happy as you deserve. Without being able to urge any strong objection against him, I feel that a number of trivial ones may be found, and trivial causes often lead to great unhappiness in the marriage state. Mr. Stanhope is undoubtedly a very pleasant companion, but he is a spoiled-child, and though I readily allow that little of the waywardness arising from over-indulgence is perceptible in him, yet it does sometimes break out in a manner which I should be sorry to see in your husband.

Now then to my story. I returned home only yesterday from passing a few days at Blakeney with Mr. Barry and Mr. Ryder. In the course of conversation one day, as the latter and I were sitting alone together, I happened to mention your having finally rejected Mr. Stanhope, with some expressions of satisfaction at your determination, mingled with admiration of your conduct. Mr. Ryder gave an involuntary start at hearing this, the colour rushed with violence into his face, his eyes flashed fire, his whole frame was as if struck with an electric shock. In a moment, however, he recovered himself, and said with calmness and composure, "You surprise me, Mr. Beauchamp, can this really be true?"

But the emotion I had witnessed was sufficient to confirm me in a suspicion I have for some time entertained, though I have forborne to mention it; and resolved to try him farther, I said, "Why should this excite your astonishment so much? Are you then one of those who think Mr. Stanhope so absolutely irresistible, that no woman could refuse him. I know this is a very prevalent opinion."

"No, not so. I allow there is much in Mr. Stanhope's character to admire and esteem, but I will freely own that I do not think him altogether worthy of Miss Campbell. I thought, however, she had been too strongly attached to him to reject his hand if offered to her."

"He certainly was not indifferent to her. Yet convinced that she did not possess the first place in his affections, she resolutely declined a hand unaccompanied by a heart."

"How?—not possess the first place in his affections?—Good God! and could he really find a woman to prefer to her!"

"You speak with enthusiasm, Mr. Ryder."

"True, Sir."

"Mr. Ryder, forgive me. In our last private conversation you refused any explanation of that sorrow which has evidently corroded your bosom for some months past, perhaps therefore I am not justified in mentioning the subject again. Yet while I think that if I could obtain your confidence, your unhappiness might eventually be alleviated; I know not how to maintain silence."

Never did I behold him so overcome. His self-command was gone, he turned round upon his chair, threw his arm over the back, and fixed his eyes upon the window, while a thousand conflicting passions seemed to agitate his bosom, and he was unable to make any reply. Resolved to take advantage of the impression thus made, I proceeded: "Yet have I no right to enquire farther? Surely I have a right, and one that will always be upheld by every feeling heart, of claiming a participation in sorrows which it may be in my power to alleviate. Excuse me then, Mr. Ryder, if I confess a suspicion that—"

"Forbear! forbear!" he cried, "I can hear no more!"

"No, I will not, cannot, forbear. I have embarked in this affair, and I will not shrink from pursuing it to the end. Oh Mr. Ryder pardon the enthusiasm of a friend anxious for the happiness of one whom he has even from her infancy regarded with the purest fraternal affection! You but this moment expressed the utmost astonishment that Mr. Stanhope could prefer any other woman to Miss Campbell. What is to be inferred from this? You were wont to be lavish in Miss Campbell's praises, on that subject you are become uncommonly reserved; not a note of admiration when she was mentioned, have I heard escape your lips for some time past except this so recently uttered. What is to be inferred from this? Ah, not that your admiration of her has decreased, not that her virtues and accomplishments, from being familiarised with them have ceased to charm, but that the subject is become far too interesting to be mentioned?"

He turned round again to me, his countenance was pale and ghastly, his eyes no longer flashed fire, but beamed with a sublime and affecting sadness, while they seemed to reprove my unwarranted intrusion into the secrets of that soul of which they were the index. "Well then," he said, "since you will intrude thus into the weakness of my heart, I will not deny that I do love her; yes, ardently, devotedly love her; not with the common passion that mortal feels for mortal, but with the homage due to a superior being. Listen to me, Mr. Beauchamp.

"You who were the person that introduced me to this admirable woman, well know the circumstances under which that introduction took place. Till I had seen her, I hesitated to receive an obligation from her; once known, all hesitation vanished. I saw her so far superior to all the littleness of soul in which her sex is generally educated, saw her mind, though polished to a degree that would ornament the highest circles of genius and intellect, yet retaining all the simplicity of unsophisticated nature; saw her dealing blessings and happiness around her, yet unconscious that she was herself the source whence that happiness flowed; saw her, in one word, so richly endowed with all that is charming in the female character, unalloyed with the weakness which too often throws a shade over its brightest tints, that I scarcely thought I was in the society of a mortal. All this I saw, nor could refuse the homage due to a character so rare and exalted.

"I soon after quitted the kingdom, nor had any farther intercourse with her, but by correspondence, for four years, yet each letter I received from her, more firmly fixed my admiration of her heart and mind. Every sentiment she uttered breathed the purest and most unaffected philanthropy, and while she never talked of her sensibility, her whole soul seemed to overflow with the genuine feeling. I returned to England, and our personal intercourse was renewed. Every interview unfolded to me some new charm, that continually encreased my devotion to her, yet I felt the difference of our situations too strongly to think of aspiring to the possession of her. I never even ventured to ask myself whether I wished it, but had perhaps been for ever content with being admitted into her society, and secretly paying her that homage her perfections attracted, had not jealousy of another awakened me too keenly to a sense of the feelings of my own heart.

"Some vague rumours had occasionally reached me of an intended union between Miss Campbell and Sir Francis Stanhope's son, but as I never heard such a thing hinted at in my visits at Campbell-House, and had frequently seen Sir Francis there himself without his son, I paid them no attention. I had besides often heard Mr. Stanhope mentioned as a gay dissipated young man, and such a character I was assured never could gain the affections of Miss Campbell.

"But when at length I saw them together, and that appearances indicated, if not an absolute engagement between them, at least that this was a thing not foreign to the ideas of either, then it was that I first became sensible of my own situation, then it was that the dæmon of jealousy took possession of my soul. I saw Mr. Stanhope in his person almost a model of manly beauty, polished and engaging in his manners, and in endowments of the mind far above the common level of mankind. Thus accomplished, I could not but own that he was more worthy of possessing such a woman as Miss Campbell, than the generality of his sex, and the idea of his worthiness but added to my torments.

"Yet while I was irresistibly compelled to acknowledge his merits, the man himself became obnoxious to me. I was angry with my heart for harbouring an aversion so unreasonable, and dissatisfied with myself, became consequently dissatisfied with all around me. I wished to tear myself from a scene of such agony, yet found myself spell-bound within the magic circle, and that to escape was impossible. Thus I became restless, cynical, wretched, nor could forbear sometimes venting upon others the ill-humours excited by my own weak conduct, and I was the more inclined to cavil at follies scarcely worthy of observation, because I was mortified that I could not find more serious matter for objection in a character I was resolved not to approve.

"It was these feelings that occasioned my abstraction in company, and frequent absences from it, to brood in solitude over my secret discontents, nor is it possible to conceive the torments I endured at those hours, between my impotence to conquer my feelings, and my consciousness of their culpability. You, Mr. Beauchamp, may in some measure conceive the state of my mind, by the manner in which my spleen* once burst forth to

---

*   Ill temper. The spleen was once regarded as the seat of various emotions.

yourself and Mr. Stanhope. I was then for a short interval really in a state of little less than distraction, but the mild expostulations you opposed to my intemperance, happily awakened me to reflection, and taught me to shudder at the precipice from which I had escaped.

"From that instant I felt my soul as it were re-invigorated, and convinced how unreasonable my conduct had been, I firmly resolved to keep a stricter guard upon myself in future. I sought to divest myself of all prejudice, and weigh Mr. Stanhope's merits and demerits in an equal scale; but in my anxiety to allow their proper preponderance to the former, I gave him credit for qualities which my cooler judgment has since convinced me he does not possess. I endeavoured to school my heart to endure with patience and composure the severe trial of beholding my idol in the possession of another, and at length persuaded myself that I had gained so complete a victory, as earnestly to wish for the match against which my feelings had once so powerfully revolted.

"Yet while I had conquered myself thus far, I felt not sufficient confidence in the permanent effects of such a victory, as to trust myself with living on the very spot where I must constantly witness a rival's happiness. I resolved therefore to decline a situation in the idea of which my soul had once so fondly delighted, and as I had undertaken, at George Barry's request, the charge of conducting his wife and child to Lausanne, I thought this a convenient opportunity for imparting to Miss Campbell the alteration in my intended plan of life.

"On this subject I was ruminating when the letter was brought me announcing that Miss Campbell and Mr. Stanhope were to be united on that very morning. The fiend was again roused for a moment within me; I could not endure to face the rejoicing this event would occasion in the house, and leaving an apology for my absence, I went immediately for my little charge, as I thought the taking her with me would effectually throw a veil over the real cause of my hasty departure.

"All this passed so rapidly that no time was allowed for reflection, and 'tis impossible to describe from what an oppressive burden my mind seemed relieved, when I found myself clear of Maxtead parish before the clock had struck eight. So entirely indeed was I occupied with this idea, that I had gone several miles before I thought of taking a retrospect of what had passed; but then recurring to the letter, I gave it a second and more attentive perusal. The first idea that struck me upon receiving it was, that you, Mr. Beauchamp, suspecting the situation of my heart, had sent it to soften the stroke to me, but when I came to reconsider it more dispassionately, it appeared so unworthy of having received a moment's attention, that I condemned myself extremely for having acted with so much precipitation upon such insufficient grounds. To recal what had passed was however impossible, and to return would have been worse than to proceed, so that I had no alternative but to pursue my journey. I hastened therefore to Pontefract, where Mrs. Barry met me the next day, and every thing was arranged for our immediate departure for the continent.

"But resolved not to leave England without once more seeing Miss Campbell, I returned, as you will recollect, to Campbell-House, for a few hours, when I imparted to her my resignation of her farm, and the probability of my never seeing her more. Oh God! no mortal power can have an idea of the agony I endured at that moment! I thought my mind was fortified to go through the scene with becoming firmness, but I found this vain flattery; my emotions were but too evident, and I left the room in dreadful apprehension lest they had betrayed my secret. I afterwards consigned the letter to you, Sir, and then sought Mr. Stanhope to make my apology for many things in my conduct towards him which I was conscious demanded explanation. How much was I astonished to learn in the course of our conversation, that he had recently been refused by Miss Campbell—for a moment I wished I had not been so hasty in relinquishing the farm, but a very little reflection convinced me this made no real alteration in my situation, that the same distance still subsisted between myself and the object of my idolatry, and that no hope of regaining any peace of mind remained for me, but in tearing myself from her for ever.

"This, Sir, is the great secret of my heart, which remember is not imparted voluntarily, but extorted from me, and I throw myself upon your honour not to make an improper use of the knowledge you have thus acquired. You cannot be insensible to the extreme delicacy of my situation, and must allow the propriety of my resolution to settle in a foreign country far from the temptations to which I am exposed here. This all-subduing passion has for a while kept the powers of my soul under its subjection; but in another clime I trust they will be roused again to active exertion, and in prosecuting my scientific researches I shall expect to bury in oblivion all recollections but those on which memory must ever dwell with transport."

I listened with astonishment and admiration to a relation so interesting and affecting, and was about to express the emotions it had excited in my bosom, but he stopped me—"No commentaries, Sir," he said. "You have wrung from me a secret which I hoped would have remained for ever buried in my own bosom. The consciousness that it is known to another will hasten my departure from this country."

After such a prohibition it was impossible either then to talk farther upon the subject, or ever to introduce it again, and accordingly I left Blakeney without our having any more private conversation. Mr. Ryder talks of quitting England in a fortnight or three weeks, and indeed but for Mr. Barry's earnest entreaties, his departure had not been delayed so long.

And now, my dear Madam, nothing remains but once more to solicit your pardon for this communication, and to subscribe myself
      Your very affectionate friend,

REGINALD BEAUCHAMP.

LETTER XXIV.

LIONEL STANHOPE
TO
HENRY EGERTON.

South Audley Street, April 12.

Harry, I have adhered to my resolution, and not seen Charlotte since the day of my explanation with Olivia. I am still so dissatisfied with myself, that I cannot bear the thoughts of an interview, though I acknowledge that this very feeling is one of the strongest proofs I can give of her power over me, and of the absurdity, perhaps it deserves a harsher name, of my conduct, in attempting to prevail upon Olivia to revoke her sentence.

But alas, she is not to be moved!—Firm as a rock of adamant* she adheres to her purpose, nay, brings such arguments to support her determination, that 'tis impossible to refute, though I am very unwilling to yield to them. Overcome by the conflicts that rack my bosom, yesterday in a conversation with her, I even went so far as to say, that I was confident there must be a rival in the way, else solicitations so ardently preferred, and so frequently repeated as mine could not be thus pertinaciously rejected.

The dignity of offended generosity instantly rose within her, and with somewhat more of severity in her manner than I ever before witnessed,—"Away with so ungenerous and unmanly a suspicion, Mr. Stanhope," she said. "Is it not enough that I endure these conflicts for your sake, that I have set aside all my own feelings and endeavoured to promote your happiness rather than my own, but must I be suspected of having acted with duplicity instead of disinterestedness? of having assumed the mask of generosity only to serve base and sinister purposes of my own? No, Sir!—If my heart had become devoted to another object, I would frankly have told you so, convinced that in so doing I should act more honourably towards you, than in giving you the title of husband, while my heart was a stranger to the affection which should accompany it."

"Oh forgive! forgive me, Olivia!" I cried "—I scarcely know what I say!—Why will you persist in making me such a wretch in my own eyes?"

"Can I consider you as a wretch, when I only exhort you to act as under similar circumstances I solemnly assure you I would act myself?"

"Ah, why will you persist in believing that my heart is alienated from you?—No, no, be assured it is still devotedly yours!—How can it be otherwise while I daily listen to the charms of your conversation—daily contemplate those virtues and accomplishments that first taught me accurately to distinguish between what constitutes the real excellence of the female character, and the trappings which, while they are considered as ornaments, too often disguise and disgrace it."

---

*　A very hard imaginary mineral.

"Why then in Charlotte's company is she the sole object of your attention?—Why do you now shun her society, but because you feel it dangerous to your repose, since you think honour forbids her ever being yours?—Mr. Stanhope, do not suppose that what I say arises from mortification and disappointment, or that I have any intention to reproach you; I hope whatever may be my feelings I am above expressing them in a way so degrading to myself, but I wish earnestly to chase from your bosom some Quixotic notions you cherish there, to the injury both of my repose and your own. Why will you not be satisfied with my reiterated assurances that I freely and entirely acquit you of all dishonourable conduct towards me, and wish most earnestly to see you pursue, what I daily feel more and more forcibly to be the strong bias of your inclinations—what you would be yourself convinced is so, were not your mind perverted by certain false principles which you have suffered to gain possession of it under the idea of honour, and which endeavour to persuade you that your inclinations are directed as you think they ought to be, rather than as they really are."

We argued this point long and eagerly, she all the time pleading Charlotte's cause with such ardour and eloquence, and developing with such extraordinary acuteness and discrimination the secret workings of my heart, that while she made me feel irresistibly that Charlotte is the dearest thing to me on earth, she no less strongly convinced me that she herself ought to be so. Thus by endeavouring to make me more decided, and to convince me in what way I ought to decide, she has left me in a state of greater indecision than ever.

Harry, I have thought several times of joining you at Arrenton, for, restless and uneasy as my mind is at present, and discontented as I am with myself, I think it possible that I might find some relief in change of place—yet, I know not how it is, a magic spell confines me here, and I find it impossible to pass the circle drawn around me. Perhaps, when separated from my tormentor, I may regain some degree of composure—and separated we shall be very shortly, as Olivia quits us in a few days to go for a short time to her friends at Camberwell, whence she returns into Yorkshire.

Ah, Harry, how much do I wish you would come up to town, for no consolation could I find in my distresses equal to that of having you to share them with me. I could almost swear to renounce love for ever, and devote myself to friendship only, as a sentiment much more congenial to the bosom of a rational being. Come then, Harry, Oh come, and in the reciprocity of affection which is to be found only where hearts have been long connected like yours and mine, let us once more experience that calm delight to which of late we have both been strangers, and which is the only thing that can now soothe the bosom of

Your faithfully affectionate

LIONEL STANHOPE.

LIONEL STANHOPE
TO
HENRY EGERTON.

South Audley Street, April 14.

Never surely was such a woman as Olivia!—Harry, she seems determined to make me the husband of Charlotte in spite of myself. When she found me obstinately persist in refusing to see the lovely Hibernian, she contrived an interview between us wholly unexpected by either. Oh yes! Charlotte is an angel, but Olivia is an archangel!—I know not how to have either, since I cannot have both!

But though I have been compelled to see this syren[21] once, my resolution is no less firmly fixed than before, never to see her voluntarily. The more Olivia seeks to press Charlotte upon me as a wife, the more am I convinced that she ought to be my wife herself, and here I swear solemnly and irrevocably never to give my hand to another while she remains unmarried!—In our last conversation, I told her that such was my unalterable resolution—she remonstrated against the folly of it; she convinced me that my conduct was foolish, almost that it was contemptible, yet she did not shake my purpose.

Harry, I had intended to be with you before this time, but am detained in town by particular business. Oh, come then to me!—You know not how much I long for your company, and surely there is nothing of consequence at present to detain you at home: do not think that I want to entice you into dissipation; I am a perfect recluse myself, for I have not now even the temptation of attending Olivia into company to seduce me from my solitude. She left us this very morning.

I have been frequently bantered during her stay, upon the beauty of the lady to whom my attentions were devoted. This mirth I have uniformly answered, by inviting the facetious gentleman to a family dinner— I have made him listen to the charms of Olivia's conversation, to the dulcet strains she draws from her lyre, and his jokes have never been repeated a second time. Oh yes, Harry! she must, she shall, at last bless with her hand,

Yours very affectionately,

LIONEL STANHOPE.

LETTER XXVI.

OLIVIA CAMPBELL
TO
REGINALD BEAUCHAMP.

Camberwell, April 24.

It is not because I blame you, my dear Sir, for communicating to me the information contained in your last letter, that I have suffered it to remain so long unanswered, but because my heart has been ill at ease, and my mind so much occupied upon other subjects that I have scarcely known how to write.

I forbear at present to make any commentary upon the particulars you mentioned—I can only say, that they surprised me much, and that I wish they did not exist. Among the numerous causes which had at various times occurred to me as the probable occasion of Mr. Ryder's unhappiness, this never entered my mind. Good Heavens!—with reason do the poets fable the God of Love as blind, and shooting his arrows at random, for how rarely do we find in any union, that the persons united are the objects each would decidedly prefer to all others. Few indeed I fear are the instances in which this is the case with either—the object on which the heart is fixed is not to be obtained, and that to which other circumstances lead it to unite itself, though perhaps highly esteemed, is one to which reason, more powerfully than inclination, first turned its attention. And after all, I know not whether such an alliance may not be productive of a larger portion of tranquil happiness than those founded on the strongest passion. Moments of far more exquisite transport are doubtless experienced where passion takes the lead, but I believe the aggregate of happiness to be greater from the constant uninterrupted friendship that reigns in the other case.

If so rare then the instances in which a decided preference is reciprocal, how guilty should I feel myself in proving an obstacle to these reciprocal wishes being gratified where they do exist. No, that guilt never shall be mine!—difficult as is the task to resist Mr. Stanhope's arguments and importunities, they shall be combated to the last. For my own satisfaction I have contrived, in spite of his resolution not to see Miss O'Brien any more, that they should meet again three different times, for there really have been moments when I was half persuaded that his passion for her was fleeting and transient like many of his former ones, and that I was perhaps wrong in adhering so pertinaciously to my purpose. But his manner of meeting her convinced me that his affections were at last firmly rivetted, and nothing now can shake my resolution. To put an end therefore to all farther controversy between us, I have already left London, and shall return into Yorkshire as soon as possible. I am only now detained from setting out on account of my dear Harriot and Mr. Egerton.

'Tis needless here to recapitulate what passed between them in Ireland, and the hasty manner in which Mr. Egerton quitted that kingdom. I own I thought at the time that the whole affair had been ill managed, and that this alone prevented Mr. Stanhope's accomplishing their reunion. I therefore wished them to meet again immediately on Harriot's return to England in the full confidence that a second interview under more auspicious circumstances, would be productive of much happier effects. I was the more inclined to hope this from the length of time that has now elapsed since Mr. Egerton first knew of the former object of his heart's fond attachment being alive, which has given him sufficient time to reflect calmly upon the subject, and convinced as I was of his entire reformation, I was extremely anxious that his virtuous propensities should receive every possible encouragement. It was therefore agreed between Mr. Stanhope and myself, that he should endeavour to draw Mr. Egerton to town so as to meet Harriot upon her arrival, though without her being mentioned.

And I have now reason to rejoice that the experiment was made. On Mr. Egerton's coming to town, he was informed of Harriot's return; nor was much entreaty requisite to induce him to see her. To accomplish an interview was to gain every thing, and all was soon settled between them. The state of Mr. Egerton's circumstances was the only thing that occasioned any hesitation in him, since he thought it dishonourable to depend on Harriot for his support; but even this scruple was at last conquered. Mrs. Belgrave and Harriot, now placed in affluence, would fain have given up to me again the one her annuity, the other the fortune presented to her by my father, but I have prevailed so far as to get the consent of all parties that they shall be appropriated to the disencumbering Mr. Egerton's estate, and as soon as that is cleared, I have agreed to resume the annuity.

These things were not finally arranged till yesterday, and now I trust no other obstacle will arise to the conclusion of an engagement contracted so many years ago, and suspended by circumstances so unfortunate. I once hoped that Mrs. Belgrave and Harriot, with Mr. Egerton, would accompany me in my return to Campbell-House, but their business will not permit this. They will however follow me as soon as possible, since the hands of our friends are to be joined at Maxtead church.

In the hope that not many days will elapse before we shall meet again,
  I remain, dear Sir,
   Your very affectionate

OLIVIA CAMPBELL.

OLIVIA CAMPBELL
TO
HARRIOT BELGRAVE.

Campbell-House, May 3.

When I last parted from you, my dearest Harriot, I hoped that the few remaining hours of my stay at Camberwell would be passed in peace and composure. I thought I had managed admirably in making my farewell visit in South Audley Street while Mr. Stanhope was absent, and that I had effectually guarded against his knowing that the time of my departure for this place was fixed. But alas! I found myself cruelly mistaken! and that I had if possible a more severe conflict to sustain than any I had previously endured.

I had not been returned to Camberwell, after my morning's excursion to London, above ten minutes, when as I was sitting alone in the parlour, neither Mr. or Mrs. Villars being at home, to my astonishment I beheld Mr. Stanhope enter the room. He looked hurried and agitated, and was almost breathless. Poor old Jerry had learned from my servants that we were to set out for Yorkshire the next day, and had communicated this intelligence to his master, in the way of regret at our departure. Mr. Stanhope instantly ordered his horse, and rode to Camberwell in the utmost haste. I felt so overpowered at seeing him thus unexpectedly, that I lost all command of myself and burst into tears. He walked up and down the room several times before he was able to speak, and at length throwing himself into a chair by me, "Olivia," he said, "can you, can you leave me thus?"

I had no power to reply—a silence of several minutes ensued, when again making a mighty effort to utter all the emotions of his heart, he proceeded:

"Olivia, 'tis in vain longer to attempt disguising the real motives of your conduct towards me. Some days ago I hinted a suspicion of a rival, I am now assured that I was not deceived. Yes, Madam, had Mr. Ryder been out of the question, I had never been reduced to this humiliating situation, never been compelled to this fruitless pursuit. You had not been so ready to suspect me of another attachment, had not your own heart sighed in secret to find such a reason for evading the wishes both of your parents and mine."

I felt my spirit roused by the injustice of these reproaches, and casting off the feminine weakness by which I had been for a moment subdued, "Mr. Stanhope," I said, "I have hitherto esteemed and respected you, and while I have steadily resisted your solicitations, I have only regretted the mistaken notions that led you to pursue them to such lengths. Do not teach me to despise you!"

"Ha! despise me, did you say? God of Heaven! is it not enough then that I must be condemned to endure the torture of conflicts like those I have long sustained, but must I be told that they render me contemptible?"

"No, it is not these conflicts that render you contemptible; from my soul I regret and compassionate your sufferings; 'tis your ungenerous suspicions of the motives by which I am actuated that excite my contempt."

"Tell me then that your hand is not promised to Mr. Ryder?"

"On my soul it is not."

"And that you do not think of becoming his wife?"

"By what authority do you interrogate me thus?"

"Nay then I am satisfied. I see plainly how it is."

"Mr. Stanhope, what has occasioned this mean jealousy?"

"Have you not received proposals of marriage from Mr. Ryder?"

"No, upon my honour."

"Olivia, you are not dealing sincerely with me. Some deep reserve lurks beneath this apparently open disavowal of any connection with him."

"Mr. Stanhope, though your ungenerous conduct little deserves such candour, yet I will tell you truly and fairly all that has passed upon this subject. Would to God I had still remained ignorant of what I have so recently learned! or rather, would to God the circumstances that have been communicated to me had not had existence! But first tell me whence originated your suspicions?"

"Yes I will confess it sincerely. Very early in my acquaintance with Mr. Ryder I began to suspect that he was strongly attached to you, and was surprised to find that others, and yourself in particular, did not appear impressed with the same idea. I know that some correspondence had passed between him and you immediately before your last refusal of me, and this, united with your present hasty determination to return into Yorkshire, has led me to suspect that but for him my offers had not been rejected. When I made them you requested a few days to consider of your answer. Would a moment's hesitation have been requisite had you really loved me? But your heart was then divided. Oh God! perhaps not even divided, perhaps it was wholly my rival's, and you only waited to know the state of his affections before my fate was decided."

"If you really believe this, how can you think farther of a woman who could act so basely? If you do not believe it, how can you be so mean and base yourself as to accuse me of such treachery?"

"Oh yes, yes, they are base and vile suspicions! Forgive me! Forgive me, Olivia! I scarcely know what I say or do! But tell me sincerely, am I not right in believing that Mr. Ryder has confessed a strong attachment to you?"

"If you mean that any professions of this kind have been directly from him to me, you are mistaken. That he loves me is but too true, yet the confession of this passion was not made to myself, but to another, by whom it was communicated to me, and even to him it was not made voluntarily, it was extorted by importunity."

"You have however encouraged him to hope that his passion may be returned?"

"Never. Yet if I had, by what claim, Mr. Stanhope, am I to be considered as responsible to you for my actions?"

"Oh no, no, no! I do not claim such a responsibility, I am even conscious that I only add to my former faults in questioning you thus; in thus repeating my importunities. Yet such are the tumultuous feelings which now agitate my breast, that I find I can bear all things save the idea of beholding you in the possession of a rival."

"Mr. Stanhope, this is the excess of weakness and folly. When your own heart is devoted to another, why should the idea that mine also may be fixed on a new object, occasion you a moment's uneasiness. Supposing you were right, ought you not rather to rejoice in the hope that our separation may prove no less the means of promoting my happiness than your own?"

"Would to heaven, Olivia, that I could reason thus coolly upon the matter! But I cannot reason, I can only think of your perfections, and then curse my own folly which has deprived me of all hopes of possessing them. I can only deplore the fatal concurrence of circumstances which has prevented my securing a heart that once regarded me with such distinguished partiality."

"Mr. Stanhope, this phrenzy, this infatuation, is torture both to me and to yourself. Did I believe that our union would afford a reasonable prospect of permanent happiness to either of us, this hand should be your's to-morrow. But convinced as I am that while for a moment you might feel satisfied and transported with the idea that you had acted rightly, and pursuant to the dictates of strict honour, yet that when the intoxication of that moment was over, you would daily feel more and more how fatally you had sacrificed the strong affections of your soul to follow a delusive phantom. Convinced as I am of this truth, I am firmly resolved that you shall rather endure the anguish of your present feelings, which can be only transitory, than store up both for yourself and me lasting years of unhappiness and remorse. Farewell, Sir, I can hear no more. Act reasonably, no longer madly shun the only woman who can make you happy; remember the sacrifice I have made, that I have resolutely subdued my own inclinations because they interfered with yours, and that 'tis acting ungratefully by me thus obstinately to persist in rejecting that happiness which I have thought no sacrifice too great to establish."

So saying I rose to leave the room, when starting from his seat he eagerly caught hold of my hand, "Olivia!" he said, in a tone of inexpressible passion.

"Oh attempt not to stop me!" I replied, withdrawing my hand. He looked wildly at me, and throwing himself down upon a sopha, buried his face in his hands. For a moment I hesitated, I could scarcely endure to behold him in such agony, yet from an apprehension of future and distant consequences refuse what I knew would instantly calm his bosom, and I had almost flown to him to revoke all I had been saying. But fortunately, to strengthen my wavering resolution, Mr. Villars now came in, and as he knew how I was circumstanced with regard to Mr. Stanhope, I scrupled not to leave him to his care, and hastening up to my own apartment, there gave free vent to all the emotions, which till then I had been compelled to suppress.

Mr. Villars himself kindly accompanied Mr. Stanhope home, and assured me that before they parted he was tolerably composed. This afforded me some satisfaction, yet even now my mind is ill at ease upon the subject. I have asked myself several times whether such behaviour could be induced by any other feeling than strong affection, and whether the errors I impute to him are not really my own. Yet when I recal to mind how evident it appeared whenever he was in Charlotte's company, that his heart was wholly hers, I dare not allow myself to think of wavering in the resolution I have taken. Oh Harriot! it was by mine and Mr. Stanhope's united efforts that Mr. Egerton was restored to his senses, let yours and Mr. Egerton's now be exerted to restore Mr. Stanhope to his.

Of my journey I have nothing to say but that it was truly delightful, and as I only arrived here last night, nothing has yet occurred worth relating. I can scarcely express how much I rejoice at finding myself again in this beloved place. Though I have found much to admire in London, I still feel that this is my home, and the tranquillity that reigns around me here is more congenial to my habits and feelings than the bustling scenes of a busy capital. Adieu my dearest Harriot, and believe me always

Most affectionately yours,

OLIVIA CAMPBELL.

LETTER XXVIII.

LIONEL STANHOPE
TO
OLIVIA CAMPBELL.

South Audley Street, May 3.

Olivia, how could you leave not only London, but even its neighbourhood, so hastily, so abruptly! Ah worse, how could you leave me on the morning of our last meeting, without hearing half what I wished to say? Is it possible that the bosom which feels so deeply for the sufferings of every other fellow-creature, can be callous towards mine alone? I thought if I could not prevail upon you to relent in your refusal of what your heart must tell you I so earnestly wish, that I might at least have offered some arguments against your immediate departure, which you would have found conclusive, but even the trifling satisfaction of urging them was denied me.

How is it that you who have ever been influenced yourself by the nicest sense of honour, can be insensible to those feelings in the breast of another? How is it that you can readily believe others sincere in the professions they make to you, yet obstinately doubt the sincerity of similar professions from me? Olivia! dearest Olivia! believe me you are refining away both your own happiness and mine! You have heretofore given me reasons, 'tis true, the justice of which I could not but acknowledge, for not hastily believing in the permanence of those impressions your excellence, your accomplishments, had made upon my heart. Tell me now, do those reasons still exist with equal force? Can the permanence of my attachment to you still be doubted? While I confess with shame that my eyes have sometimes wandered after other objects, have not my heart, my reason, my understanding, uniformly led them back immediately to yourself? Has not every transient lapse but encreased the ardour with which I returned to you the moment that the first intoxication of the new impression began to subside? Can you think that I would have taken all the trouble I have done in controverting the arguments you have at various times urged to prove your own conduct right, had I not been sincere in the professions I have made you? Nay, can you think that I would have flown in such haste to throw myself at your feet and solicit your stay, the moment I learned your intended departure, had I not really felt all that ardour of affection for you which I have so often professed?

No, Olivia, you cannot doubt my faith, my love! Attend then while here I solemnly swear once more, that as long as a possibility remains of obtaining the hand of Olivia, I never, no never, will accept that of any other woman. I will not swear not to see her who has been the innocent cause of my disgrace; I will see her, but it shall be to convince every unprejudiced mind, that I can meet her with perfect indifference. Olivia, will you not accept the testimony of others, friends equally to you and to myself, when they shall assure you that I behold Charlotte without emotion? Yes, you shall be convinced that her empire is at an end; you shall hear, that when we met no colour tinted my cheek, no passion sparkled in my eyes, that my heart remained motionless in my bosom, that my pulse beat firmly and evenly; all this shall be well attested by those in whom you can confide, and then surely you cannot any longer doubt my sincerity.

I blame myself for so frequently refusing to see Charlotte while you were in town. I feel that it bore too much the appearance of confessing her power. I wished to satisfy you that my heart was indifferent to her, and that I could exist without the smallest regret out of her presence; but I ought rather to have endeavoured to prove to you that I could behold her with indifference. Nay, believe me, Olivia, what you mistook in me for embarrassment from my passion for her, was merely confusion arising from the consciousness that you entertained such ideas.

Our beloved friends Harry and Emily are shortly to be united under your hospitable roof. Oh let me accompany them to be present at a ceremony which will convey transports to my soul only to be exceeded by one other event. Ah you cannot doubt to what I allude. Let Charlotte too be of the party, and you will then be convinced by your own observation that her power over me is at an end. Do not, I conjure you, do not refuse this request. You cannot in justice refuse it; you owe me such a probation. Let not then the generosity you practise towards all others be denied to
    Your faithfully devoted

                        LIONEL STANHOPE.

LETTER XXIX.

OLIVIA CAMPBELL
TO
HENRY EGERTON.

Campbell-House, May 8.

To you alone can I apply, my dear Sir, in the dilemma to which I am reduced, and I hope I need not exhort you to answer my enquiries with perfect sincerity. Do you in your heart believe that I am the real object of Mr. Stanhope's preference, not Charlotte O'Brien. From my own observation I was decidedly of opinion that his continued pursuit of me was mere delusion on his part, and that in fact his affections were wholly and entirely Charlotte's. Yet the interview I had with him on the day before I left Camberwell, and a letter I have received since my return hither, have almost staggered my former conviction.

He says he is resolved to see Charlotte, that he may convince my friends he can meet her with indifference, and earnestly solicits permission to accompany you and Harriot hither, to be present at your marriage. I know not how either to grant or refuse this request. What had I best do? These doubts, these anxieties, these uncertainties whether I am acting right or wrong, almost distract me.

I still cannot but incline to my former opinion, that Charlotte is the real magnet to which his heart adheres. He had not seen her when he wrote to me. Ah, my dear Sir, when an interview has taken place, do let me know immediately what effect it had upon him. I would too that Charlotte's sentiments with regard to him could be ascertained, though I have scarcely more doubt of her attachment to him, than of his to her. Oh if he would but let me quietly resign my claims upon him, the pang would be trifling, but I cannot bear these incessant altercations, this perpetual renewal of a subject that I still feel but too deeply.

Believe me, my dear Sir,

Yours with great regard,

OLIVIA CAMPBELL.

LETTER XXX.

HENRY EGERTON
TO
OLIVIA CAMPBELL.

South Audley Street, May 12.

I hasten, my dear Madam, to reply to your obliging favour, and should esteem myself culpable indeed could I hesitate a moment to answer your question with perfect sincerity. However then I may regret what I must communicate, yet it is not to be denied that Lionel's heart does seem devotedly fixed on Miss O'Brien. In pursuance of the resolution he declared in his letter to you, he never refuses now to see her, nay seeks all possible opportunities of being in her company; but so far is he from beholding her with indifference, that each interview convinces me more and more strongly of the correctness of your judgment upon the subject.

Their first meeting was unexpected. I was rejoiced that my friend was taken without preparation, as it gave me an opportunity of observing the workings of his heart with the greater accuracy. Yes, not a word, not a look escaped me, and I could not but see that his whole behaviour betrayed a devotion to her, of which I really believe he is himself scarcely sensible. Eager to convince me that she had no power over him, he attached himself to her the whole evening; and yet while every body present regarded his attentions to her as too palpable to be misapprehended, he could so far delude himself as to say at our return home, "Well now, Harry, are you not convinced? Have I not talked to her, have I not contemplated her, as if she were no more to me than any other woman?"

In vain did I withhold my assent to this proposition, in vain did I urge to him that my observations led me to a very different conclusion; he only said he had conceived a better opinion of my penetration, and that though I had been thus mistaken once, the next interview, he was confident, must convince me. But after the next I still retained my former opinion, and again endeavoured to represent to him the excess of folly in which he was bewildering himself. Still I could make no impression. I afterwards tried to place his conduct in another point of view, by painting the ingratitude of tormenting himself as well as you upon a subject on which you had behaved so nobly, and which but for him would be immediately settled to the satisfaction of all parties. He still insists that I am mistaken, that I cannot know his heart as well as he knows it himself, but that however sceptical I am now, in a short time I shall be no longer able to resist conviction. Ah, could I believe that he speaks truly, how ungenerous must I think his behaviour not only to you, Madam, but to Miss O'Brien, whose affections 'tis evident he has irrevocably engaged.

Our business in London being nearly finished, I am desired by my dearest Harriot to say that we hope to be at Campbell-House very shortly. I am, Madam, with the highest regard and esteem,

Most faithfully yours,

HENRY EGERTON.

LETTER XXXI.

OLIVIA CAMPBELL
TO
LIONEL STANHOPE.

Campbell-House, May 15.

Why will you thus torment both yourself and me, Mr. Stanhope? Was your behaviour at our last interview, or is the letter I have since received from you, the act of a reasonable being? I have hitherto delayed answering that letter, because I wished first to be fully assured of the truth or falshood of the belief with which you endeavoured to impress me, that you could see Charlotte with indifference. I am now well assured that this fancied indifference was mere self-delusion, and that I have acted perfectly right in not hastily giving it credence. Torture me then no more, I conjure you. My conduct has been the result of reason and principle, let them too be the guides of yours, nor seek thus madly to make me swerve from their dictates.

This is the last exhortation I shall give you. Any farther communication between us cannot but be painful to both, and here therefore all intercourse must cease, till you can resolve to act more reasonably. Do not think me unkind; if I seem severe now, believe me the moment will come when you will regard my present resolution in a very different light.

It grieves me to the soul to refuse your request of being present at Mr. Egerton's marriage. I know 'tis almost barbarous to forbid your being witness to the happiness of such a cherished friend; yet I dare not trust you. A month must however elapse before that event can take place; if within that time you can assure me that you are acting reasonably, that you have addressed the offer of your hand where it is due, then will I not hesitate a moment to say, "Oh hasten hither! Come and be present at the consummation of your friend's happiness! Come, and let the same hour see you both united to the women of your hearts!"

But till you can give me an assurance which will authorise my saying this I must bid you farewell; yet do not think me the less

Your most sincere friend,

OLIVIA CAMPBELL.

LETTER XXXII.

REGINALD BEAUCHAMP
TO
OLIVIA CAMPBELL.

Blakeney, May 23.

What shall I say, Madam? May I address you on a subject of so very delicate a nature as the present? May I venture freely to lay before you all the sentiments and wishes of my heart? Yes, to Miss Campbell I may speak freely; if her own sentiments do not coincide with mine, she will at least pardon the freedom with which mine are given.

At the commencement of your acquaintance with Mr. Ryder, my dear Madam, however a secret wish might sometimes steal across my bosom that a man with so many valuable qualities, so rich in all gifts, save those of fortune, might one day be admitted to a more intimate connection with you than merely that of a friend, yet I knew enough of your situation with regard to Mr. Stanhope, to be morally certain that no other man had any chance of gaining your affections while he remained unknown to you. Whatever therefore were my wishes, they were confined to my own bosom, while no prospect appeared of their being accomplished.

But your situation is now so altered, that the hopes I then dared not cherish, have of late ventured to obtrude themselves upon me. You have acted nobly by Mr. Stanhope, oh that the same generosity which has made so great a sacrifice to promote one man's happiness, might be extended to another! Mr. Ryder still lingers in this country; his friend Mr. Barry is very unwilling to part with him, and has persuaded him to protract his departure from week to week for some time past, but he positively declares that next week shall be the very utmost limit of his stay. I ventured to suggest, since a principal reason for his relinquishing your farm was now at an end, his resuming that idea, as I felt confident that this would be a thing, my dear Madam, perfectly agreeable to you. "No, Mr. Beauchamp," he replied, "circumstances are totally altered since I could think with delight of being placed in that situation. Had you suffered me to retain the great secret of my heart, I might perhaps have resumed with transport the idea of continuing to pay my distant homage to Miss Campbell's exalted virtues, since I was to be spared the mortification of seeing her united to a man I think not altogether worthy of her. But my fatal passion known, I am determined never to see her more."

And yet, my dearest Madam, 'tis surely in your power even now to command his stay. Oh that you would but give him the little encouragement necessary to impress his bosom with a hope that his passion may at last be returned! That you would authorise me to give him a hint that time may efface past trials from your remembrance, and open your heart to the reception of other objects than the single one by which it has hitherto been occupied! Ah could you act more meritoriously than in retaining so valuable a subject in the kingdom? than in rewarding the sufferings of a mind whose misfortune it has been to be raised so far above its situation in life?

Tell me then, I conjure you, that I may speak consolation to his soul. Tell me I have authority to bid him hope that an attachment so pure, so refined, may at last be returned. And remember, my dear Madam, 'tis only by bestowing yourself upon another, that you can put the final consummation to your noble conduct with regard to Mr. Stanhope, since 'tis this alone can release him from the rash vow he has taken, and enable him to offer his hand to the woman in whom his affections are centered.

But I will say no more. Perhaps I am wrong in having said so much, since your heart and understanding are much better judges of the conduct proper to be observed on this occasion, than are those of
Your truly sincere friend,

REGINALD BEAUCHAMP.

LETTER XXXIII.

OLIVIA CAMPBELL
TO
REGINALD BEAUCHAMP.

Campbell-House, May 26.

No, Mr. Beauchamp, I do not blame your zeal in seeking to promote the happiness of a man, who, if happiness were dealt only according to moral desert, would be one of the most blest of mankind, but I sincerely regret that from a chain of untoward circumstances, all your zeal must be fruitless. 'Tis not in your power, 'tis not in mine now, to make Mr. Ryder happy. That I should have been the involuntary occasion of creating him a moment's uneasiness, that I should have been the innocent cause of palsying* for a time the vigour and energy of such a mind, from my soul I deplore, but reflect what it is you require of me, and then ask yourself whether it be possible for me to yield to your wishes, or if it were so, whether the evil you lament would be remedied.

You ask permission to hint to Mr. Ryder that time may wear away the present impressions from my mind, and others may succeed to them; but it would only be to deceive both you and him were I to consent to your giving such a hint. My heart is above disguise, I shall not attempt to conceal any of its feelings.—It was wholly and solely Mr. Stanhope's even before I became personally acquainted with him, it remained his no less entirely after his introduction to me, spite of my judgement, spite of the disadvantageous light in which he then appeared. Yes, I have loved him with perfect devotion, and had probably continued to love him no less devotedly, had he not pursued the only course that could have shaken an affection so ardent, so unbounded.

I have shewn that my heart was capable of making the greatest sacrifices to promote his happiness, and had he yielded at once to his passion for Charlotte O'Brien, I might perhaps have felt moments of deep regret at our separation. But while he has daily convinced me more and more strongly that I had formed an erroneous opinion of his character; while he has convinced me that when reason and feeling are in opposition, he cannot listen to the voice of the one, he can act only upon the impulse of the other; while he has persecuted and tormented both himself and me, merely to save appearances to the world, and to satisfy his own mistaken notions of honour, he has taught me to rejoice that this disposition was fully developed before we had gone too far to recede, before the indissoluble bond of marriage had united me to a man who, acting under such impulses, would have given me perpetual cause of regret and uneasiness.

Yet while I have these feelings towards him, I feel no less sensibly that every avenue to my heart is closed against any other passion. This has become, as it were, a part of my nature; I have lived for many years but in the hope that my father's earnest wish might one day be accomplished. It is a feeling which has been so long interwoven with every habit of my life, every step I have taken, that I have considered Mr. Stanhope as the only man with whom it was possible for me to unite myself. This may be considered as a weakness, yet when I consider to what it owes its origin, 'tis one with which I can scarcely reproach myself.

A strong friendship for Mr. Ryder I have felt from the very commencement of our acquaintance; nay, I feel for him something more than the mere partiality of a friend, I regard him as I have ever done you, my dear Sir, with a sisterly affection, and feel no less anxiously interested about him than if he were really my brother. But Mr. Stanhope is the only man I ever did think of for a husband, the only man I believe I ever can think of.

---

* Paralyzing.

Yet I have shewn this to be no selfish feeling, I have shewn that my passion was no less disinterested than ardent, and heaven be my witness that I would still do any thing more within my power, not inconsistent with honour and principle, to bring him to reason, and promote his happiness.

But I can go no farther. I have no right to sacrifice Mr. Ryder, or any other man, to his infatuation; and if he will obstinately adhere to a vow, it was the height of folly to make, and which 'tis almost criminal to keep, unless released in the manner you propose, he must abide by the consequences, and may go down to the grave with the reflection that he ruined his own peace of mind, and that of an amiable woman, whose affections I am convinced he has engaged, by his mistaken notions of religion and honour.

No longer think then of the hint you suggested ever being given to Mr. Ryder. In a moment of infatuation he might be tempted to embrace it, and make proposals to which I never could accede, or if I did yield to them, which would place us in a situation that could not add to the happiness of either. Could he ever forget that he was not the decided object of my choice? Could I ever forget that I had betrayed such a man, by marrying him with a divided heart?

Mr. Beauchamp, tell him all this; I do not wish a syllable of what has passed between us to be concealed from his knowledge; he cannot esteem me the less for candidly owning all the feelings of my heart. Tell him, that from my soul I wish no obstacles existed to our being as happy together as the chequered scenes of life will permit, but I am convinced that he, no less than myself, will see how little desirable is an union with me under the present circumstances; tell him how ardently I wish to hear that his lost peace of mind is regained, and what transport it would give me, could I in any way contribute to its restoration. Much, very much, do I wish that I could see him before he leaves England, yet I would not ask a thing which might inflict on him one unnecessary pang. I hope however, that if he cannot resolve upon seeing me, he will at least indulge me with sometimes hearing from him. With what delight shall I read descriptions of the enchanting scenery in Switzerland drawn by so able a pen; how will my heart glow with transport at details of the industry and happiness of its simple inhabitants, given by a heart that will feel them so warmly.

Yet there is one thing more I would fain say. Mr. Ryder and I have now lived on terms of intimacy and reciprocal esteem for some years, and notwithstanding what has lately passed, I trust we shall ever continue to do so. He knows my heart, he paid me the compliment of not refusing a trifling present when he knew less of me than he does now, then surely he will not deny to a tried friendship the acceptance of the enclosed note. I would not ask this, but that I feel the necessary expences he must be at in removing and settling in a foreign country, and I wish him to allow me the satisfaction of thinking that I have contributed towards his being more speedily established with those comforts and conveniences around him, the absence of which is always severely felt by those accustomed to them.

I wish indeed he could be prevailed with to make more ample use of my fortune. He is desirous of becoming as useful as possible to his fellow-creatures; he has made a considerable progress in the study of those sciences which most enlarge the mind, and are the most beneficial to society, how much then is it to be wished that he should prosecute these studies to the utmost extent allowed by mortal powers. This end can in no way be so effectually obtained as by travelling from clime to clime, and communicating with the men of science and literature in all countries, nor could he gratify me so highly as in suffering me to enable him to do this, while in pursuing such a plan I trust he would find the most effacious* of all medicines for healing the wounds of his heart. Then, after a course of years, he might return to his native country, with a mind at ease, and so richly fraught with knowledge that he would become one of its brightest ornaments, while at every tribute paid him by a grateful people for the benefit derived from his toils, my heart would exult in the recollection that a small portion of their praise and gratitude is ultimately due to me.

Adieu, my good friend; let all that I have said be communicated to Mr. Ryder, and impart the result as soon as possible to

Yours very sincerely,

OLIVIA CAMPBELL.

LETTER XXXIV.

REGINALD BEAUCHAMP
TO
OLIVIA CAMPBELL.

Blakeney, May 28.

Yes, Madam, I have shewn your letter, and explained your whole conduct to Mr. Ryder. He clasped his hands together as I finished my story, and raising his eyes to heaven exclaimed: "Was ever such a woman! Oh God, that a heart like this should be so thrown away!"

Then musing for a few moments, he continued: "But she is right, Mr. Beauchamp. Yes, though I acknowledge the kindness of your intentions, and shall ever feel grateful for the interest you have taken in my sufferings, yet I must repeat it, Miss Campbell is right, nor, however ardently I love her, could I accept her hand were it now offered me. Ah Sir! can you suppose a passion like mine could be satisfied with the idea that it was not fully returned? Could the husband of Olivia endure the thought that

---

*   Probably *efficacious* is meant.

he not only did not possess her undivided affections, but that he did not even enjoy the first place in them? Oh no, the more devotedly a man loves himself, the more fearfully will his soul recoil from the idea of possessing even the object of his adoration, under the impression that the hand which ought to be the seal of his happiness, is given from compassion, not from preference. To have been assured that I was the decided object of Miss Campbell's choice, would have been a transport with which no other mortality can offer, could be put in comparison; but he would be unworthy of her who could think of being her husband on any other terms."

Thus are my hopes, my wishes, at an end; yet while I regret the effect, be assured, my dear Madam, that I feel the warmest admiration no less of this than of every other part of your conduct. Ah, I said rightly, that your judgment was much more competent to decide upon this matter than mine.

One thing however I have great pleasure in communicating, that your letter has entirely overcome Mr. Ryder's reluctance to seeing you, and he promises to pass some days at Campbell-House before he leaves the kingdom. He will then talk over with you the plan you proposed, which he does not seem disinclined to adopt.

  I am, my dear Madam,
    Most affectionately yours,

REGINALD BEAUCHAMP.

LETTER XXXV.

HENRY EGERTON
TO
ORLANDO ST. JOHN.

Campbell-House, June 8.

I told you in my last, Orlando, how much Lionel was impressed with hearing of what had lately passed between Miss Campbell and Mr. Ryder, and that I was in hopes he was at last becoming more reasonable. But the day before I left London I was heartily mortified at finding that he was yet wide of this mark, and had even raised up another phantom to torment himself. I hope and trust however that this may be combated without difficulty, but its removal must rest with you alone.

When at the conclusion of nearly two hours' conversation on the subject of Charlotte he seemed unable any longer to refute my answers to his old objections against yielding to his passion for her, he at length took refuge in urging, that besides the difficulties in which he was involved with regard to Miss Campbell, there was another, which if it had not equal weight in his mind, was yet by no means to be slightly passed over. You had often, he said, in your letters written of Charlotte as if you were very far from considering her with indifference, and if you really had that partiality for her he suspected, your claim was undoubtedly prior to his, and he would by no means interfere with it.

Write to him then, I intreat you, and satisfy him upon this point. Let us try whether this will have any influence with him, or if he will persist in his present unaccountable infatuation he shall be left wholly without excuse.

Mr. Ryder is now here, and has consented to the plan marked out for him by Miss Campbell, in consequence of which his route is changed, and instead of going immediately into Switzerland, he goes first to Paris. The disclosure of his secret, into which he was drawn so reluctantly, has proved a great relief to his mind, and if not so happy as he might have been had all things been propitious to his becoming the husband of the woman he adores, he appears now perfectly contented and composed.

For myself, I can only say, that in the intoxication of delight at the idea that in little more than three weeks I shall call my long lost Emily mine, I scarcely recollect the dreadful scenes I have passed through since our separation. Oh God! he only be truly sensible of the value of a mind at ease, who has experienced the sufferings that long harassed
 Your truly affectionate

            HENRY EGERTON.

LETTER XXXVI.

ORLANDO ST. JOHN
TO
LIONEL STANHOPE.

Woodbourne, June 6.

No, Lionel, believe me my inclinations interfere not in the least with yours, nor will prove any obstacle to your pursuing the course to which, not your affections alone, but I will say your honour and duty equally urge you.

That my heart was for a moment slightly wounded by the charms of the fascinating Charlotte is true, but it was a mere scratch. Had I ever been seriously and deeply smitten, think you I could have prattled of the passion, and made it the subject of my mirth as I did. Ah, no, he little knows what love really is who can think this. Make yourself easy then, and believe me I shall feel nothing but transport in the idea of your being united to a woman every way suited to you. Did I not from the first moment of my acquaintance with her, tell you that she was the girl of all others to set your heart in a flame? Nay, did I not even arraign you for insensibility in not being over head and ears in love with the bare description of her.

Let not then any considerations with regard to me prevent your pursuing the happiness now within your reach. Olivia is a noble minded woman, and you owe her the satisfaction of knowing that her generous efforts in your favour have not been thrown away. I shall expect therefore soon to hear that you are the husband of the lovely, the amiable Charlotte; and believe me that to hear this will convey inexpressible pleasure to the heart of

Your faithfully affectionate,

ORLANDO ST. JOHN.

LETTER XXXVII.

LIONEL STANHOPE
TO
HENRY EGERTON.

South Audley Street, June 12.

Harry, I am awakened. Various causes have combined to disperse the mist which lately obscured my senses, to restore me to a proper sense of my own interest, and to impress my soul with the deepest and most unbounded gratitude for the kindness I have received. Yes, Harry, tell Olivia that I think of her no more but as the guardian of my honour and happiness, as the angel who has vouchsafed to guide me through a dark and dangerous road, which but under her protection I had never passed in safety. Tell her I speak the pure effusions of my soul when I declare that I consider her as something superior to mortality, and assure her it will ever be my first and most ardent wish that I may hereafter have it in my power to make her some atonement for the many hours of uneasiness I have so long and so fatally occasioned her.

This revolution you will perhaps suppose has been effected solely by reason and reflection. Alas! no, Harry, still true to my nature feeling has achieved what reason attempted in vain—Yet thus much I may say, that reason, in this instance, sanctions my following the impulse of feeling— Ah, 'tis but seldom that even this trifling boast can be mine. Charlotte's life has been in imminent danger from an overturn in a curricle,* and till

---

*   A two-wheeled, two-horse carriage.

I saw her likely to be torn from me for ever, till I myself rescued her from the jaws of destruction, I had no idea of the excess of my passion.

Satisfied that I was only convincing the world of the perfect indifference with which I could behold her, I have scarcely ever been absent from her side since you left London, and while giving both herself and her friends every possible reason to suppose that my visits had particular views with regard to her, I meant them only to satisfy others that she was indifferent to me. Yes, I have been acting no less dishonourably to her than ungratefully to Olivia, and was gaining her affections with the sole intention of making this intimacy subservient to my views upon another.

But, thank heaven, the delusion is over!—Oh never can I forget the agony I experienced when I saw her life in danger, or my transports at finding that I had been so blessed as to save her from injury. When I clasped her unhurt to my bosom, then was my heart fully awakened to the force of that passion I had long vainly endeavoured to persuade myself had no existence!—And while unable to command myself, I kissed her cheek pale with terror, I secretly breathed a blessing upon Olivia, that I could do this without a reproach from my conscience.—From that moment I resolved no longer to trifle as I had done.

This accident happened as we were going on a party of pleasure to Richmond, Mr. O'Brien and Charlotte in the curricle, and myself on horseback. But such an event untuned our minds for all enjoyment of the scheme, and instead of proceeding we returned to town. To quit Charlotte was however impossible. So strongly was my mind impressed with the danger in which I had beheld her, that scarcely even in her presence could I believe her in safety, and absent, she had been constantly pictured to my alarmed imagination as in some peril, by which she must be demolished, since I was not at hand to rescue her.

Yes, Harry, I remained at Mr. O'Brien's all day, and in the course of it a favourable opportunity being presented, I laid open my whole heart to Charlotte, told her all that had passed with Olivia, and asked whether she could accept the hand of a man so circumstanced? And she did accept it, and I am blessed. Well then, my long loved, long cherished friend, no longer need Olivia prohibit my coming to witness your happiness. She has declared that she will not refuse to see me as the betrothed husband of Charlotte O'Brien. Tell her then, Harry, that our faith is solemnly pledged to each other, and that I earnestly solicit permission, no less to pour forth in person my unbounded gratitude to her for the happiness to which I look forward, than to see your love and constancy crowned with its just reward.

Oh, Harry! though it will occasion me a temporary separation from Charlotte, yet I cannot express with what transport I shall revisit Campbell-House—that seat of pure unsophisticated delights, where first I learned to distinguish solid happiness from the tinsel joys of what is commonly called a life of pleasure.

Farewell, Harry till we meet, and believe that no change of circumstances or situation can abate the sincerity with which I shall always be
Your faithfully affectionate

LIONEL STANHOPE.

LETTER XXXVIII.

LIONEL STANHOPE
TO
ORLANDO ST. JOHN.

Campbell-House, July 2.

Not a moment will I delay, Orlando, to make you a sharer in the happiness I now experience—to tell you that the hands of Harry and Emily were joined this morning. Good God!—after a separation of so many years, after having so long believed one of the parties dead, to have witnessed this event at last, appears almost like a dream. Yet if a dream, 'tis one of so much delight to myself, through the transport I see it communicate to my friend, that I should be little inclined to thank any one for awakening me from it.

The ceremony was of course performed by Doctor Paul, and was honoured by him with a new wig, and the surplice clean washed; while Percival Altham, not to be behind-hand with his uncle in paying due respect to the bride and bridegroom, presented them, as they came out of church with a congratulatory ode, which will doubtless find a place in his next three volumes of miscellanies. Indeed his muse can seldom be furnished with so copious a subject for the display of its powers, upon so many sublime and interesting topics did it give him an opportunity of descanting. There was the storm from which Emily so narrowly escaped, Harry's phrenzy, the law-suit, and the distress in which it involved Emily and her mother, with the late General's and Olivia's kindness to them, the recovery of the estate, the consequent meeting and re-union of the long separated lovers, and lastly prophetic visions of the happiness they are now to experience. On all these subjects he touched most sublimely, most eloquently, and concluded with pathetically contrasting their transports thus arrived at the summit of their wishes, with his own forlorn state doomed to languish out his days the victim of hopeless love, of bitter disappointment.

Yes, Orlando, the victim of disappointment—for know he has been an unsuccessful suitor to a heroine who has often been honoured with a place in the pages I have written thee from hence—to the pretty Lucy Morgan. She, oh lamentable deficiency in taste! could actually prefer a farmer to a poet, and about three weeks ago was united to Mr. Boswell, long since chronicled as her lover.

And while I am upon the subject of matches, let me not omit to mention another, in which you will also feel deeply interested. Peggy Perkins has rewarded the gallantry of her knight-errant, George Macklin, with the possession of those charms he so generously took under his protection. Well, peace be with him!—As a man of the world I doubt not his doing honour to the fortune he has thus acquired, and should his domestic felicity be occasionally interrupted by the unfortunate temper of his wife, a page or two of Spanish never can fail to recompose his ruffled spirits.

And now, having seen the friend of my heart put into possession of his treasure, I hasten to take possession of mine. Of Olivia I can say with some degree of satisfaction that she seems to lose the recollection of her situation in endeavouring to promote the happiness of all around her— her mind appears serene, even cheerful—I hope this is not mere appearance. Yet alas! it will always be an allay to my transports even in Charlotte's arms, when I reflect on all that has passed with regard to Olivia, and that but for me she might have been happy as the wife of a man more worthy of her than myself. But in this respect how much has she the advantage over me. She has no recollections wherewith to reproach herself, but wedded, or unwedded, may look back on all the transactions of her life with a self-approbation that must essentially contribute towards calming and tranquilizing her soul, while my reflections are adverse to the attainment of this state of tranquillity, which is the highest source of mortal enjoyment.

One other source of consolation do I also find with regard to her, in the hope that when Mr. Ryder returns from four years of travel, on which he set out a few days before I reached Campbell-House, the impressions that at present occupy both his mind and Olivia's, may be so worn away, that they may be able to enjoy in the possession of each other, that happiness to which I have hitherto proved so cruel an obstacle. Then, and then only can remorse be entirely banished from the bosom of
Yours ever most faithfully,

LIONEL STANHOPE.

THE END.

1 *Lausanne.* A city in Switzerland situated on the northern shore of the Lake of Geneva.

2 *the war of fifty-six.* The Seven Years' War began in 1756.

3 *"Or, as from Etna's burning entrails torn"* Etna is a volcano in eastern Sicily.

4 *a second Socrates, or Seneca.* Socrates (?469-399 BC) was a Greek philosopher whose teaching methods are exemplified in the Dialogues of Plato. Accused of impiety and corrupting the young, Socrates was sentenced to death and forced to take hemlock. Lucius Annaeus Seneca (3 BC-AD 65) was a Roman Stoic philosopher, statesman, and author.

5 *seeing the lions.* The *lions* of a place are those sights and celebrities worth seeing. Until 1834 the lions kept at the Tower of London were a popular tourist attraction.

6 *Scylla and Charybdis.* Charybdis was a dangerous whirlpool off the coast of Sicily. Scylla was a rock opposite the whirlpool on which was thought to live a six-headed sea monster fond of snatching crewmen off passing ships.

7 *"The feast of reason, and the flow of soul."* Alexander Pope (1688-1744). *The First Satire of the Second Book of Horace*, 128.

8 *"When the soul is steel'd . . ."* Source unidentified.

9 *playing Rosencrantz and Guildenstern.* Hamlet's schoolfellows who spy on him for Claudius. They are no match for Hamlet, however, and their attempt to betray him results in their own deaths.

10 *You are only to furnish a man and horse.* In 1796 the government decided to raise a "Supplementary Militia" in an effort to augment home defenses and free the regular forces for offensive action. This militia included a new corps of cavalrymen called the *Provisional Cavalry.* Owners of horses were grouped in tens and a ballot determined which of the ten would provide the force with a trooper, horse, and accoutrements. The entire force was disbanded in March, 1799. See J.R. Western, *The English Militia in the Eighteenth Century* (London: Routledge & Kegan Paul, 1965. 221-22).

11 *"like Niobe all tears" Hamlet* 1.2.149. According to Greek legend, when Niobe taunted Latona with the number of her children (Niobe had fourteen and Latona only two), Latona had all of Niobe's children killed in revenge. Zeus turned the grieving Niobe into a stone which continued to shed tears.

12 *as Mrs. Siddons . . . was to play Calista.* Sarah Siddons (1755-1831) was a famous tragic actress, particularly known for her portrayal of Lady Macbeth. Siddons played Calista in Nathaniel Rowe's *The Fair Penitent* presented in Drury Lane in 1782. The role remained in Siddons' repertoire until at least 1805.

13 *the daughters of Pomona.* Young women who sold oranges at the theatre. Pomona is the Roman goddess of fruits and fruit trees.

14 *was [something] repulsive.* Original text reads *there was a somewhat repulsive in her manner.*

15 *never was faithful Corydon more devoted to his faithful Phillis. Corydon* is a conventional name for a shepherd or lovesick swain. It occurs in Theocritus' *Idylls*, Virgil's *Eclogues*, and Spencer's *Faërie Queene*. Phillis is a pastoral name for maiden. See, for example, Milton's *L'Allegro*.

16 *his fair Gabrielle.* "La Belle Gabrielle" (1573-1599). Henri IV fell in love with the nineteen-year-old Gabrielle when he chanced to stay a night at the Château de Cœuvres. Although Gabrielle married, she went to court as the king's mistress. She was made Duchess of Beaufort in 1597.

17 *beau in ordinary and extraordinary.* See Volume I, page 10.

18 *in the character of Amphitrite.* In Greek mythology Amphitrite is the goddess of the sea.

19 *going as Neptune, when we would all be Tritons.* See note 8, Vol I.

20 *Children in the Wood, [and] Barbara Allen. Barbara Allen* is a Scottish ballad about a man dying of unrequited love and the woman's subsequent remorse. *Children in the Wood* is a ballad which has as its subject the story generally known as "The Babes in the Wood." In it a wicked uncle hires two ruffians to murder his nephew and niece. One of the men relents, kills his companion instead, and leaves the two children alone in the forest where they die of cold and hunger. Both ballads were included in Percy's *Reliques of Ancient Poetry* (1765).

21 *this syren.* A syren is a mythical monster, half-woman and half-bird, whose sweet singing lured seamen to destruction on the rocks.

APPENDIX: Eighteenth-Century Views of Beauty and Ugliness

The material in this section is meant to assist the general reader in setting *Something New* in the context of the period. While a short section on wit and behaviour has been included, the bulk of the material deals with the importance of female beauty as reflected in the fiction and non-fiction of the period. In early eighteenth-century popular novels authors often merely indicate that the heroine is beautiful and leave the particulars to the reader's imagination. I have included a number of more detailed descriptions, some from well-known works of the period such as *The Italian*, others from less-known novels such as Mary Ann Hanway's *Ellinor*, and one from a contemporary satire, Barrett's *The Heroine*. The material on contemporary views of beauty and ugliness is taken for the most part from the periodical literature of the period. These selections touch upon a range of topics such as definitions of beauty, ugliness, and deformity; beauty as a source of power and danger; and how various understandings of beauty work to inscribe notions of class, race, and gender.

ја   ја   ја

Consulting a sensible friend upon my intended work, I read to her, as a specimen, the character of my heroine.

After a pause, "You say nothing," said Mentoria, "about her beauty and accomplishments."

"I did not think," replied I, "that a particular description of her personal attractions was necessary for those, who only read her life."

"You may put your manuscript in the fire," said my friend, "not a soul will read it; who do you think will be interested in the fate of a girl, whom they do not know to be handsome and elegant?"

I answered, "she shall be simple in her manners, gentle in her disposition, possessed of an improved mind, and a benevolent heart. Her fortitude shall be tried, her patience exercised, her humility,"—

"My dear Prudentia," interrupted Mentoria, laughing, "... Does any one care for the distresses of merely good sort of people? Every body says, we are sorry for them, but the nerves of pity can never be affected, unless beauty, elegance, and refinement, constitute the character of the sufferers. Do not all novels turn upon this hinge?"

"I detest imitation," said I, "and besides ... by delineating human life in false colours, expectations are formed which can never be realized; the consequence of which is, that life is begun in error, and ended in disappointment."

"Do not you intend then," said Mentoria, "to conduct your heroine through the severest trials, to wealth and felicity, and to reward her patience and humility by a faultless husband, and an immense fortune?"

"No," said I, pettishly, glowing with the spirit of female pride, "I do not chuse to hold up matrimony as the great desideratum of our sex; I wish them to look to the general esteem of worthy people, and the approbation of their own hearts, for the recompense of their merit, rather than to the particular addresses of a lover...."

"Your intentions," replied my friend, "are as romantic as those which you design to eradicate; at least, if improbability of success constitutes the romantic. Your work will, I foresee, rest peacably on the shelves of your bookseller ..."

"Cannot then," said I, "nature and simplicity please beyond the age of twelve years; will no one be interested about Polly Williams, because," my friend at the name of Polly, laughed so immoderately, that in compliance to her taste (for she is a woman of the world) I have adopted the name of Maria, and have even consented to allow her beauty and elegance, lest I should not have one reader in her teens.

[Source: Jane West, *The Advantages of Education, or, The History of Maria Williams, A tale for Misses and their Mammas.* London, 1793. Volume 1: 1-5.]

ɩ ɩ ɩ

But though thus largely indebted to fortune, to nature she had yet greater obligations: her form was elegant, her heart was liberal; her countenance announced the intelligence of her mind, her complexion varied with every emotion of her soul, and her eyes, the heralds of her speech, now beamed with understanding and now glistened with sensibility.

[Source: Frances Burney, *Cecilia, or Memoirs of an Heiress*, 1782. Edited by Peter Sabor and Margaret Anne Doody. Oxford: Oxford UP, 1988, 6.]

ɩ ɩ ɩ

Ellen was lovely as Hebe, fair as Venus, pure as an Angel; lively, sensible, and of the sweetest disposition. She was gentle as the dove, harmless as the lamb, and modest, without being reserved.

[Source: Elizabeth Bonhote, *Ellen Woodley*. 1790. Volume 1: 7.]

ɩ ɩ ɩ

Monimia, though dressed like a parish girl, or in a way very little superior, was observed ... to be so very pretty, that nothing could conceal or diminish her beauty. Her dark stuff gown gave new lustre to her lovely complexion; and her thick muslin cap could not confine her luxuriant dark hair. Her shape was symmetry itself, and her motions so graceful, that it was impossible to behold her even attached to her humble employment at the wheel, without acknowledging that no art could give what nature had bestowed upon her.

[Source: Charlotte Smith, *The Old Manor House*, 1793. Edited by Anne Henry Ehrepreis. Oxford: Oxford UP, 1989, 14-15.]

ɩ ɩ ɩ

It was a slim elegant female, dressed in a callico jacket and coat, short enough to discover a beautiful turned ancle, open at the neck, and arms as white as snow, a profusion of light brown hair in natural ringlets, shaded her alabaster forehead, a pair of lovely brows and lashes, two shades darker, gave her clear blue eyes a hazle cast, her features were more beautiful than regular, her lips of the deepest rose pink, half open, displayed a set of small white teeth, her complexion pure and elegant, and her form a model of symmetry; she tript along the gallery, tying on a straw hat, and was followed by a short thick black eyed girl, carrying a white dimity cloak and a pair of mittens.
[Source: Anna Maria Bennett, *Ellen, Countess of Castle Howel*. London, 1794. Volume 1: 31-32.]

ta   ta   ta

... the breeze from the water caught the veil ... and ... disclosed ... a countenance more touchingly beautiful than he had dared to image. Her features were of the Grecian outline, and, though they expressed the tranquillity of an elegant mind, her dark blue eyes sparkled with intelligence.
[Source: Anne Radcliffe, *The Italian, or The Confessional of the Black Penitents*, 1797. Edited by Frederick Garber. Oxford: Oxford UP, 1968, 6.]

ta   ta   ta

Ellinor Harcourt was rather above the middle size, of the most light and Sylph-like figure, appearing as if she could bound over "new-fallen snow, nor leave a track behind;" her face a little inclined to the oval, her eyes were of the darkest hazle, her nose small and aquiline, her teeth white and even, her cheek, in which the lily and rose were most beautifully blended, was shaded by a profusion of auburn hair; her round arms and taper fingers appeared to be modelled from those of the Grecian Venus.
[Source: Mary Ann Hanway, *Ellinor; or, The World As It Is*. London, 1798. Volume 1: 12.]

ta   ta   ta

That I am not deficient in the qualities requisite for a heroine is indisputable. I know nothing of the world, or of human nature; I have lived in utter seclusion, and every one says I am handsome. My form is tall and aerial, my face Grecian, my tresses flaxen, my eyes blue and sleepy. Then not only peaches, roses, and Aurora, but snow, lilies, and alabaster, may, with perfect propriety, be applied to a description of my skin. I confess I differ from other heroines in one point. They, you may remark, are always unconscious of their charms; whereas, I am, I fear, convinced of mine, beyond all hopes of retraction.
[Source: Eaton Stannard Barrett, *The Heroine, or Adventures of Cherubina*. Philadelphia, 1815. Volume 1: 16.]

ta   ta   ta

Beauty is doubtless a desirable possession; and when blended with modesty, and tempered by refinement, acts as a charm upon the senses. We are endowed by Nature with a kind of sympathetic feeling for whatever is gentle, lovely, and attractive; and a beautiful woman, labouring under affliction, is allowed to be the most interesting object in creation.

If Beauty possesses such an attractive charm, and is capable of producing such soft sensations, how necessary is it that those who enjoy the gift should prove themselves deserving of the interest they inspire. Yet how often do we find that this magnetic boon is bestowed on those unworthy of the possession; and, instead of merit being joined to loveliness, we find it stripped of that attractive grace.

If Imperfection were necessarily the companion of Beauty or Virtue and Attraction were absolutely incompatible,—Deformity would be preferable to the most transcendent charms, and a plain face be considered as a general passport to approbation. But as Merit is frequently attached to personal Attraction, and Error often the concomitant of Plainness, that mind must be illiberal, indeed, which could be weak enough to suppose, that, because a girl was by nature lovely, she must consequently be unamiable.

The failings which are generally ascribed to Beauty, are vanity, caprice, and ill-humour; and these are more frequently engendered by the folly of parents, or the adulation of dependants, than by any natural defect either in the heart or the understanding. A young female who promises to be strikingly attractive, is accustomed from its infancy to hear little else but panegyrics upon its charms, and taught to regard Beauty as the choicest gift bestowed by Heaven.

Thus early initiated into the path of Folly, and taught to prefer personal to mental attractions, can we be astonished if a girl displays a fondness for that which seems a mother's pride, or values herself upon a possession which she hears admired as greatly superior both to worth and merit?

[Source: *The Lady's Monthly Museum*, February, 1800. Volume 9: 118-120.]

ঽৡ ঽৡ ঽৡ

... there is ... a kind of beauty which lives even to old age; a beauty that is not *in* the features, but ... *shines through them*. As it is not merely *corporeal*, it is not the object of mere sense; nor is it to be discovered, but by persons of true taste, and refined sentiment. There are strokes of sensibility, nice touches of delicacy, sense, and even virtue, which, like the master traits in a fine picture, are not to be discerned by vulgar eyes, that are captivated with vivid colours, and gaudy decorations. There are emanations of the mind, which, like the vital spark of celestial fire, animate the *form* of beauty with a *living soul*. Without this the most perfect symmetry in the bloom of youth is but a "kneaded clod;" and with this, the features that time itself has defaced, have a spirit, a sensibility, and inexpressible charm, which those only do not admire who want faculties to perceive.

[Source: *The Lady's Monthly Museum*. June, 1803. Volume 10: 361.]

૨ઢ ૨ઢ ૨ઢ

We seem to have implicitly adopted Grecian ideas.... But from whence did the Greeks take their straight profile? Not from nature, for it has every appearance of artifice.... Professor Camper, in his book upon the different forms of the human cranium, seems to have traced this style of face to its source.

The projection of the mouth and flat nose marks that kind of face which is nearest allied to brutality. There is but one degree between a dog, monkey, ape, orang-outang, calmuc, and negro. From the last to the European's face are many degrees, which might be supplied by a general acquaintance with the human species; between the best modern faces and the antique are still many gradations.

It is highly probable, that the Greeks observed the near resemblance between the lowest class of human faces and monkeys; and, in consequence, conceived beauty to be far removed from it. As the lower part of the brutal face projected, the human face sublime should be depressed in that part; and as in the former there was a descent from the forehead to the nose, in the latter it should be perpendicular. As a small space between the eyes gives the appearance of an ape, they made the distance wide in man. As a great breadth of cranium at the eyes, ending above in a narrow forehead, and below in a peaked chin, marked the face of a savage, the Greeks gave a squareness of forehead, and breadth of face below to express dignity of character.

These principles clearly account for the Grecian face; but as all extravagance is bad, the antique cast of features, to impartial eyes, is not the most beautiful, because it is beyond nature.

[Source: "*On* BEAUTY," *The Lady's Magazine; or Entertaining Companion for the Fair Sex, Appropriated solely to their Use and Amusement*, 1800. Volume 30: 41.]

૨ઢ ૨ઢ ૨ઢ

Deformity is to be considered, not as a total privation of beauty, but as a want of congruity in the parts, or rather an inability in them to answer their natural design; as when one arm or leg is longer than the other; when the back is hunched, when the eyes squint, and such similar defects: which, however, are not to be opposed as a contrast to beauty; for the unfortunate object may, in every other part of his body, be exactly well-made, and perfectly agreeable. Whereas *ugliness*, which I look upon to be the proper contrast to beauty, may exist in the human form without deformity; nor can I think the ideas necessarily connected. Ugliness always excites our aversion to the object in which it resides; deformity as generally calls up our commiseration. Ugliness seems to consist in the appearance of something malevolent to human nature. The picture of the devil always creates horror and disgust; not from the *deformity* of either his person or countenance, but from the *expression* of malice in the latter. It is from the countenance that an object is pronounced ugly, though without the least deformity, or even while an exact symmetry is preserved; for it is the expression of the soul that gives the disgust. If this opinion be well founded, it is easier to become beautiful than even to correct deformity ...

[Source: *Hebe; or the Art of Preserving Beauty, and Correcting Deformity; being a Complete Treatise on the Various Defects of the Human Body, with the most approved Methods of Prevention and Cure; and the Preservation of Health and Beauty in general. Including an extensive collection of simple yet efficacious. Cosmetic and Medical Recipes...* London, 1786, 13-14.]

ૐ ૐ ૐ

Proposals for Opening a Register-office for Beauty; or, Repository for Female Charms.

MR. EDITOR,

Through the medium of your excellent and widely-circulated Museum, I beg leave to state, that I have procured, with infinite labour and expense, the choicest collection of all the several articles requisite for mending, patching, restoring, improving, and supplying every female perfection....

I have laid in a considerable stock of unguents, cosmetics, and beautifying pastes. I have the finest tinctures to colour the hair, the brightest red salve for foul lips, and the sweetest perfumes for stinking breaths....

I have various shapes ready fitted up, of all sizes; with all sorts of cushions, plumpers, and bolsters, to hide any defects.... I have also a machine for reducing crooked backs, or flattening round shoulders.

I have artificial brilliants of all waters, whether for the bright eyes, the dead eye, the piercing eye, the sleepy eye, the bold eye, the swimming eye, &c. I have hired a French oculist to put them into any ladies' sockets, from whence he will take out, with very little pain, the squinny eye, the wall eye, the goggle eye, and all others. Hairs are plucked out of the forehead by pincers, and the smoothest mouse eyebrows, of all colours, put on by him in their room, with the nicest exactness....

I apply a particular sticking plaster to the face, which takes off the whole skin; and then I rub it over with a beautifying liquor, which adds a new gloss to it; and afterwards I paint it, as natural as the life, to any pattern of complexion. I peel off the finger-nails, and flay the entire hand in the same manner, which, in a month's time, makes them as white as hanging them in a sling, or the wearing of dog's skin gloves can render them in a twelvemonth....

I cut dimples into the grain, which never wear out. I slit the lips open on each side if too narrow, and sew them up when they are too wide, with such niceness, that the seams are imperceptible. I no less dextrously fine-draw, or darn wrinkles of any standing; and fill up all dents, chaps, or holes made by the small-pox, with a new-invented powder. I have a thin diet-drink to bring down the over-plump to a proper gentility of slimness, and a nourishing kind of jelly for the improvement of the scraggy....

Ladies are waited upon at their own houses, by their very humble servant,

ELIZABETH MENDALL.

[Source: *The Lady's Monthly Museum*, June, 1803. Volume 5: 293-95.]

૨ઢ ૨ઢ ૨ઢ

How can a pretty woman fail to be ignorant, when the first lesson she is taught is, that beauty supersedes and dispenses with every other quality; that all she needs to know is, that she is pretty; that to be intelligent is to be pedantic, and that to be more learned than one's neighbour, is to incur the reproach of absurdity and affection?

[Source: *The Lady's Monthly Museum or Polite Repository of Amusement and Instruction*, June 1, 1802. 54.]

૨ઢ ૨ઢ ૨ઢ

The power of a fine woman over the hearts of men, of men of the finest parts, is even beyond what she conceives. They are sensible of the pleasing illusion, but they cannot, nor do they wish to dissolve it. But if she is determined to dispel the charm, it certainly is in her power, she may soon reduce the angel to a very ordinary girl.

[Source: Dr. Gregory, *Legacy to My Daughters*, 1774. Quoted in John Langdon-Davies, *A Short History of Women*. New York: Viking, 1927, 332.]

૨ઢ ૨ઢ ૨ઢ

> Man to subdue, Heav'n gave the Woman charms,
> Were she well disciplin'd to use her Arms;
> To know the Force of her Artillery,
> The Pow'r of Smiles, and Light'ning of the Eye;
> The Voice persuasive, tun'd to Accents sweet,
> That can, the Victor's Victory, defeat;
> ....
> O pow'r resistless of inchanting Eyes!
> That rob the Strong of Strength, of Sense the Wise,
> Give Sense to Idiots, Softness to the Fierce,
> Refinement to the Rude, to Prosemen Verse,
> Courage to Cowards, Terror to the Brave,
> Chains to a Monarch, Freedom to a Slave;
> Make the Loquacious dumb, the Silent speak,
> And to Sobriety convert a Rake;
> Make Misers gen'rous, Youth in Age renew,
> And without Arms, the willing World subdue.
> Such is the Pow'r of Beauty, yet beware,
> Fair Nymph, lest Beauty should itself insnare;

Be cautious, whilst in Innocence you play,
Lest some perfidious Swain your Heart betray;
....
Beauty must watch its Foes with cautious Fear,
For all its Foes, like trusty Friends, appear;
To what Temptations, are the Fair expos'd?
With what illusive Snares, are they inclos'd?
Like Towns besieg'd, they can't their Danger know,
From hidden Mines, proceeds the fatal Blow;
So slipp'ry are the Paths, young Virgins tread,
Some Hand, experienc'd, should their Foot-steps lead;
If you, fair Virgin, would commence a Bride,
Be led by me, I will your Conduct guide.

[Source: Thomas Marriott. *Female Conduct: Being an Essay on the Art of Pleasing. To be practised by the Fair Sex, Before, and After Marriage. A Poem, in Two Books*. London, 1756, 20-21.]

&a. &a. &a.

Wit is the most dangerous talent you possess. It must be guarded with great discretion and good nature, otherwise it will create you many enemies.... Be even cautious in displaying your good sense. It will be thought you assume a superiority over the rest of the company. But if you happen to have any learning, keep it a profound secret, especially from the men, who generally look with a jealous and malignant eye on a woman of great parts, and a cultivated understanding ...

[Source: Dr. Gregory, *Legacy to My Daughters*, 1774. Quoted in John Langdon-Davies, *A Short History of Women*. New York: Viking, 1927, 331.]

&a. &a. &a.

Frequent and loud laughter is the characteristic of folly and ill-manners: it is the manner in which the mob express their silly joy at silly things; and they call it being merry. In my mind, there is nothing so illiberal, and so ill-bred, as audible laughter. True wit, or sense, never yet made any body laugh; they are above it; they please the mind, and give a cheerfulness to the countenance. But it is low buffoonery, or silly accidents that always excite laughter; and that is what people of sense and breeding should shew themselves above. A man's going to sit down in the supposition that he has a chair behind him, and falling down upon his breech for want of one, sets a whole company a laughing, when all the wit in the world would not do it: a plain proof in my mind, how low and unbecoming a thing laughter is. Not to mention the disagreeable noise it makes, and the shocking distortions of the face that it occasions.

[Source: *Lord Chesterfield's Advice to his Son*. London, 1795, 65.]

&a. &a. &a.

Horse-play, romping, frequent and loud fits of laughter, jokes, waggery, and indiscriminate familiarity, will sink both merit and knowledge into a degree of contempt. They compose at most a merry fellow, and a merry fellow was never yet a respectable man.

[Source: *Lord Chesterfield's Advice to his Son*. London, 1795, 99.]